THANATOS

THANATOS

FRANK HILAIRE

E. P. DUTTON & CO., INC.   NEW YORK   1971

Published simultaneously in Canada by
Clarke, Irwin & Company Limited, Toronto and Vancouver

Library of Congress Catalog Card Number: 76–148474

SBN 0–525–21550–6

A flock of fevers beleaguered the earth, and Death, who had been coming to mortals on slow, reluctant feet, now walked with winged steps. *

The day was gray with gloom and fog. Even the building he leaned against was gray. How long had he been there? He shrugged away the question. Other questions drifted through his mind, puzzling him for a moment, then, unanswered, uncared about, drifted away.

Across the filth-strewn street he watched a derelict stumble blindly from the curb and crumple into the gutter. After struggling mightily to sit up, the derelict scrabbled a bony hand to his waist and emerged with a bottle of scarlet fluid. A gummy smile wrinkled across his face, a smile of triumph and joy, even wisdom. The wizened head leaned back, the hand raised, the bottle slipped home. And when the bottle left his mouth, a smile took its place . . . that smile again. Then he collapsed sideways, lay still.

Nearby a door opened. "Louie's New and Used" read the door in script crumbling and flaky. A graceless fat man with a shiny vest and zircon-flashing fingers came through the door and locked it with a cruel twist. Turning, he stepped over the gutter-borne bundle and walked away.

And still he watched, watched but did not see. . . .

He walked, one step, then another. The gloom-tunneled street disappeared into grayness. He went toward it, attracted. But the grayness backed away, step by step it eluded him.

He stopped, looked behind. Nothing. He looked ahead again. Still nothing . . . gray-nothing. . . . He looked toward the street . . . dirty papers, other filth . . . the other side of the street. . . . He turned around, stared into a grime-crusted window, saw a fuzzy

* Gustav Schwab, *Gods and Heros*; originally: *Die Sagen des klassischen Alertums.*

5

image there. He straightened, moved a hand toward his face . . . the image grew fuzzier, then settled into a shadowy mirage. A mirage . . . ? He felt his face . . . it was there . . . but . . . but not to be found . . . a mirage. . . .

He walked again, one step, then another. He knew he walked: he watched his legs move.

He came to a corner and stopped. Which way? All roads hurried toward gray.

He watched a rag-swathed shape with scarred and twisted hands join an overalled wreck with crippled feet. They talked.

He took a step toward them, then stopped and walked the other way, faster now, faster toward the gray.

It occurred to him to wonder where he was going. He shrugged, kept going. And then he wondered where he was. He looked around, shrugged, kept going.

From a darkened doorway a specter stumbled out, banged into him.

And a sudden difference came. It rose from the street in a cloud of stench, it swarmed up from some dark place deep inside him, made his pulse pound, hazed his vision crimson. He loosed a kick. The miscreant groaned, slumped, sprawled. He kicked again, then again and again. Moaning, the tatter-bundled ruin tried to rise. Maniacally, blindly, he snatched the whining thing from the phlegm-crusted sidewalk and hurtled it toward the street.

It slammed to a stop in midair, crumpled, lay still and twisted.

He looked down.

A parking meter had cleaven the sot's skull, street dirt made mud of blood and brain.

"No," he whispered, and took a step closer. "No." It had not happened.

But it had . . . a man lay dead. . . .

PART ONE

A convict clerk approached the trio of men seated on the initial-carven bench at the end of the hall and stopped in front of them. He glanced at the paper in his hand.

"Number 17554, Whalen . . . ?" he said, his mouth puckered expectantly.

Kirk stared at the clerk, noting the starched and stiffly pressed denims, the glistening shoes.

"Which one of you is Whalen?" the clerk asked, officiously fanning himself with the paper.

Kirk stared at him for a moment longer, then stood.

The clerk propped the back of a hand on each hip and smiled— perhaps patronizingly, perhaps obsequiously. "Well, you could have said something. . . . Follow me," he directed, then turned and pranced away.

Kirk didn't move.

After walking a way, the clerk glanced over his shoulder. He stopped and wheeled around, glaring. "Well . . . ?"

Kirk strode to him and spat in his face. "I'll find my way, rat," he said, and walked down the hall until he found a door marked "CAPTAIN BRADLEY." He twisted the knob and entered.

The office was small and tidy. So was the man behind the over-sized desk. Little silver bars on each side of his collar glinted dully, reflecting the overhead light. The captain raised his round pink face and stared at the convict. "Don't you know enough to knock?" he asked impatiently.

Ignoring the question, Kirk approached the desk, gazing curiously at the haughty little man, wondering if he used cushions, or maybe a telephone directory, to prop himself high enough to work at the big desk.

The captain's face abruptly darkened with rage as he glared up at the convict. He started to speak.

But Kirk broke in. "You want me to try it again?"

Bradley stared suspiciously at the bland-faced convict as the flush slowly receded from his face. "No," he said curtly. "Just shut the door and sit down."

Kirk obeyed, and the captain spent a long moment looking at him. "I received a report," he said finally, "that you've been giving some of my officers a bad time."

"You'll have to tell me what a 'bad time' is," Kirk said mildly. "I've talked with maybe three guards in the week I've been here. None of them mentioned a 'bad time.' "

"Not guards," Bradley corrected. *"Officers."*

"I haven't talked to any of them."

The pink face darkened again, stubby fingers drummed on the desk. "Listen, smart punk," Bradley snapped, "you're twenty-two . . . with your beef, nothing says we have to turn you loose till you're thirty-two. Think about that. And remember, around this institution, it's your attitude that counts. You don't have to say a word . . . but my officers know a shitty attitude when they see one. From now on, when you get an order, you jump . . . and when you jump, you like it!" He leaned over the desk, glowering, feral as a panda bear.

As the captain talked on, Kirk let his thoughts play. He watched the plump little man become an inflatable child's toy, a clown-faced dummy. He stuck a pin between its eyes; it sagged to the floor, destroyed. He stepped on it, ground it under foot.

Sensing that the captain was awaiting his response to something, Kirk pulled himself back, and ventured, "Yeah."

"Yeah, what?"

"What you said."

"Try it again, Whalen. Yes, *what?"*

Kirk stared impassively at him. . . . *fuck you, worm* . . .

"I'm waiting, Whalen."

. . . *you'll wait a long time, runt, for me to call you "sir."* . . .

Bradley's face darkened, a vein pulsed in his temple. He snatched at the phone sitting by his elbow, but it slipped from his hand and dropped noisily to the floor. He cursed and reached for it, his chair creaking in protest. Finally, clutching at the desk with

8

one hand, he lifted the phone and dialed three numbers. "Get some men over here!" he spat into the mouthpiece. "I have a wise-mouth punk for the hole!" He slammed the phone back into its cradle and began rubbing at his temples as he glared across the desk.

Kirk rose and walked toward the desk, his eyes fixed on Bradley's. Leaning both fists on the desk, he bent over, his face close to the captain's.

Bradley pushed himself back into the chair; a tic began pulling at the corner of his mouth. "Whadda y'want?" he sputtered, his eyes darting indecisively over the convict, as if trying to decide between fear and anger.

Kirk grinned. "Let me see," he said.

The captain's eyes struggled with Kirk's. "See what?" he finally managed, pushing his chin deeper into his chest.

Kirk heard the door behind open, and leaned closer. "Let me see what you're sitting on."

A guard appeared on each side of the convict. And as they dragged him through the door and into the corridor, he laughed.

[II]

Kirk sat on the quarter-inch steel slab that served as a bunk and stared curiously at the walls of the dingy, narrow cell. He remembered the walk down the long corridor, pacing between the two guards, and he decided that worse than the foully malodorous isolation-cell block, worse than the lost feeling of being shut behind two solid steel gates and the barred cell door, worse than the now-common indignity of being forced to bend over and spread his buttocks while his asshole was peered into by a guard who gave every appearance of enjoying his job, worse than all that, he decided, was marching down the long, long corridor and being stared at by the 3,000 convicts of Alhondiga State Prison. There was an unspoken desire hanging in the dank air, an almost palpable craving for violence, for blood, the guards' blood, anybody's blood. And he had been tempted to give them what they wanted—not because they wanted, but because of his own deep need to hurt and maim. But had he exploded, had there been blood, it would have been mostly his own, for the convicts would have looked elsewhere while the

9

two guards, and more, happily "restrained" him. So he had marched obediently. Tomorrow was another day, another day in Alhondiga, the eater of days, years, lifetimes.

Alhondiga State Prison, a "modern" institution built inside century-old walls, walls of granite, tall, gray, mute. Alhondiga, penology's prize, costing millions, dedicated to rehabilitation, a prison where brutality was a dirty word. But still a prison.

It was two prisons, actually: the old and the new. Having decided to use the wall, somebody had also decided to continue use of certain of the old stone buildings, the administration building, dining halls, and a pair of five-tier cell blocks with "inside" cells— cells built in two parallel rows, back to back, down the middle of the block, like a smaller box inside a larger one. The modern blocks of the new prison had "outside" cells, built along the block walls, with windows that indeed did look "outside"—outside into the prison compound. But, old and new, Alhondiga was maintained, cleaned, and repaired by scuttling crews of convict sweepers, moppers, polishers, scrubbers, and window washers who daily plied their trades.

And for that reason he had been unprepared when the first steel gate to isolation had opened and an almost visible cloud of stink had spilled out, assaulting his nose with the smell of urine, feces, disinfectant, and something more—a nauseous ammoniacal stench—the stink of caged animals, the stink of rage and hate and fear.

The lighting in the isolation block was dim, in contrast to the artificial brightness throughout the rest of the prison. What light there was came from a row of 25-watt bulbs peering through frosted glass panes recessed into the low ceiling in front of the cells.

Kirk stared glumly at the cell walls, at the initials and names and slogans scratched deep into the sour-looking whitewash; he spent a moment wondering at the labor, the interminable hours of gouging and chipping and forming with buttons, paper clips, shards of glass smuggled (how?) into the cell, past shakedowns and body searches. He mused upon the probable blisters and broken fingernails incurred to leave behind a reminder that "Eddie hates cops," "Big Mike is a queer," "J.K. loves G.D." and on and on.

He rose from the bunk and walked to the bars and stared out. Concrete. Concrete. Nothing but concrete, cadaver-gray concrete. Everywhere.

10

He turned to face the rear of the cell, and bounced his attention from the steel toilet to the steel sink to the steel bunk to the steel bars, and felt depression dragging him to the bottom of the sea, pushing him inside himself.

He paced. Three steps, turn around, three steps, turn around . . . an exercise in anxiety.

He forced his attention to focus upon the several conversations coming from nearby cells.

To the left, two convicts were bickering from cell to cell, playing —or maybe warring—at the spelling game, "hangman." Each argued the merits of his particular spelling of most any given word, and all but the most fundamental words were not agreed upon. And they used only many-lettered, multisyllabled words. Their game proceeded slowly when it proceeded at all.

To the right, a convict—an admitted five-time loser—lisped a toothless explanation to a younger contemporary, an explanation of the law's esoteric points, ways to beat the law. He lisped out scathing denunciations of rats, queers, punks, cops, the governor and the president; and, of course, the Jews, because, he sagely explained, they ran everything, thus made each of the former possible. But what he really and truly hated, he sputteringly continued, were the dirty low-life bastards "out there" who had no tolerance for an ex-convict who had made a mistake or two or five. . . .

Kirk lay down, tried to sleep. It was futile. He tried plugging his ears, but his heart thudded loud, too loud. He sat up and smashed a fist into the mattress, the inch-thick thing he had rolled into a pillow. He hit it again, and chewed his lip, and hit it again.

Came a knock on the wall, followed by, "Hey . . . hey, next door, you awake?"

Kirk glared biliously at the wall, gave it the finger, and remained silent.

"Hey," the voice repeated, "you awake?" and the wall was again hammered on.

"Yeah, yeah, yeah," Kirk said through bared teeth. "But you keep banging that wall, you can bet a broken face you won't be awake."

After a long moment of silence, the voice came again. "Damn," it said with a happy chuckle, "now I'm scared."

Kirk thought about that for a second, then laughed, and slid to

11

the foot of the bed, and stood to the bars. He felt an unreasonable joy at the opportunity to talk.

There was a kindergarten-encounter-like exchange of names. Kirk's neighbor's name was Sam.

With the amenities over, Sam asked, "What's the beef?"

"Squabbled with Bradley."

Sam laughed. "You don't mean you beat up the fat asshole . . . ?" he asked with a hopeful note.

Kirk grinned. "No," he said, wishing otherwise. "The creep wanted me to call him 'sir.' "

Sam laughed again. "You been in long?"

"Yeah . . . a week."

Sam laughed again—he seemed to find a lot to laugh about. "You're doing fine. Three'll get you ten, you get psyched and run to segregation," he said, and added a chuckle.

"Segregation . . . ?" Kirk didn't think that was so funny. "For not calling that creep 'sir'?"

"For not falling at his feet," Sam corrected blithely. "But don't let it break you up, there's guys that've lived through it."

"Swell."

"Yeah . . . real. The psych talks to you for ten minutes and decides you hate your father and want to fuck your mother, and gives you 90 days in seg to figure how you can do it. . . ."

Kirk laughed. "What if dear old mom only comes around on Halloween?"

"Yeah . . . yeah," Sam said, laughing a little more than usual, "you're going . . . you ain't got no respect at all." He paused, and added: "Seg's in another building—you'll get a walk out of it anyway."

"Swell."

They talked on and on. Before long Kirk heard himself babbling in response to Sam's questions, trading information for query, query for information, and he wondered what had loosened his tongue, his usual reticence to divulge more than half-truths. It occurred to him that his neighbor didn't even have a face. Sam's voice droned on, something about a department-store robbery, while Kirk scolded himself for talking too much, and when Sam fell silent, he started talking again. He talked a lot.

The advance of the night guard making the head count was preceded by cries of "the screw," "*trucha,*" "asshole on the line," and more. Seconds later all that could be heard was the stealthy pad of crepe soles and an occasional snicker.

Kirk stretched out on the bunk and closed his eyes. Moments later a flashlight beam played upon his face, lingered searchingly, as if to illuminate his darkest thoughts. But it gave up after a while and went away, accompanied by the squeak-squeaky-squeak of cheap crepe.

A voice rang out, then another. "Fuck your mother, ossifer!" "How's your wife and my kids, you asshole-eatin' Gestapo?" "Gimme some head, you flatfoot queer!" And more.

The voices and sentiments of Enlightened Penology.

Dignity recovered, the voices quieted to mumbles, then to whispered mumbles, finally to snores. The isolation-cell block slept, the hush broken only by the screech of gnashing teeth, nightmare screams and whimpers, masturbators grunting, and the rustle of toilet paper wiping up embryo populations.

[III]

Morning brought a little more light—not much—and a bowl of . . . of goo, and a stiff body.

A while later a guard with squinty eyes appeared at the bars. "You Whalen?" he asked.

"Yeah."

The guard eyed him with suspicion. "What's your number?" he said slyly.

"17554."

"Say it again . . . say it slower." The guard studied the paper in his hand.

"One . . . seven . . . five . . . five . . . four."

"You're Whalen, huh?" The guard was narrow-eyed with doubt.

"Who?" Kirk asked with a timid smile.

"Whalen . . . you're Whalen, right?"

This was getting a little ridiculous, but Kirk didn't mind; what else was there to do? Besides, he could hear Sam laughing. "You must have the wrong cell," he informed the guard, wagging his head in commiseration.

The guard worked his jaw muscles. "Huh? But . . . hey! Wait a minute! What're you, some kinda smart punk?"

13

Kirk smiled. "No," he said easily. "Not unless you want to argue with the captain—he called me a 'wise-mouth punk.' "

The guard sputtered and flushed and glanced up and down the hall, then finally back to Kirk. "Look, fella," he said between his teeth, "be an asshole on your own time . . ." and looked back at the paper—now crumpled—in his hand. "Whalen, Kirk," he went on, "one, seven, five, five, four. Come on now, answer straight. Yes or no?"

Kirk studied the question and almost relented, but Sam was laughing too hard to spoil it for him. "Yes or no, what?" he asked the guard, and was rewarded by an extra loud guffaw from next door.

The guard puffed like an angry toad. "I'm only gonna say it once more," he said between clenched teeth. "Are you Whalen?"

Kirk cast the guard a pleasant smile and said that he was indeed.

Glaring, the guard thrust a blackjack-sized key into the lock and twisted. "Why didn't you say so without all the shit?"

As the cell door swung open, Kirk stepped out and looked at the guard with curiosity. "Say what?"

"What?"

"Yes, sir!" Kirk said smartly.

The guard stared and blinked and twisted his nose. Finally, with an almost imperceptible shrug, he relocked the empty cell. "Come on," he ordered, and walked toward the gate. Kirk followed, and back of him, Sam laughed.

They passed through the gate and around the corner and through a door into an office where a row of men were seated behind a long table, staring in grave silence. All were dressed alike, conservatively; all with neatly folded hands; all with identical piles of papers on the table before them. And they all wore expressions that could quickly become disapproving, if they were not already. The guard stood beside Kirk like a co-defendant or a lawyer . . . or a guard.

"Have a seat, Whalen."

Kirk sat in the chair placed before the table and looked at the man who had spoken. A plastic name plate pinned to his breast pocket identified him as "Associate Warden, Mr. Lowry." About fifty-five, myopic, plastic teeth, Kirk noted, and hoped he had ulcers.

Lowry broke the silence. "Well," he said with a jaunty note, "I

14

see by your record you're new here . . . heh, heh, heh," and added a frozen smile.

"Yeah, heh, heh, heh."

The associate warden's face slammed shut. His eyes probed Kirk's. Someone coughed. Another snuffled. Finally, Lowry shuffled the papers in front of him and fixed Kirk with what was probably a stern father-figure glare. "Well, Whalen," he said, "I have a report here charging you with insubordination and disrespect toward officials. Moreover, the captain's clerk claims you spit on him." Eyebrows raised questioningly, he stared at the convict.

Kirk stared back, his expression vacuous. What was he supposed to say, please?

"Well?" Lowry's mouth tightened impatiently.

Kirk almost said, "Well, what?" but decided against it. A different tactic was required here, he thought, something that would appeal to the righteousness and psuedo-sagacity of these goons. He looked humbly down at his hands and fidgeted. "Well," he said ruefully, "the captain and I had a misunderstanding. It seems I was expected to call him 'sir' . . . I didn't realize it at the time—"

"Oh, *bull!*"

The word exploded from Kirk's right. He jerked around, looking. He settled finally upon a lean-faced man with hollow cheeks and hot eyes, who stared at him with distaste. The inevitable name tag identified him as Dr. Trintz.

The doctor dismissed the convict's charade with a contemptuous flick of his wrist. "Whalen," he began, tapping the folder on the table in front of him, "the records indicate that you've had a little education. . . . And nobody's quite as dumb as you make out. . . . I'm not buying your tale of woe, and I'm certain that no one else in this room will."

A clearing of throats, grumbling in agreement, and the associate warden stared at Kirk, nodding his head slightly. "Have you anything further to say, Whalen?"

Kirk surveyed the row of officials, stared at each in turn. They stared back. He snorted caustically. "Are you creeps all controlled by the same string?"

The men, as one, flushed and glared.

"Okay, fella," Lowry said gratingly, "twenty days' isolation and referral to Dr. Trintz. We'll see if we can't take some of the smart away." He glared up at the guard. "Get him out of here!"

15

The guard opened the gate and told Kirk to go down and stand in front of his cell, that he'd be along in a while to let him in; in fact, he added proudly, he'd be along whenever he damn well felt like it. Then he slammed the gate.

So Kirk walked past the row of cells, peering curiously at the curiously peering faces behind the bars. He stopped in front of Sam's cell and looked in. Sam, suddenly with a face, looked nothing like Kirk had thought he might. He looked like a choirboy, a fallen angel . . . an angel that had fallen a long way to land finally on his face and smash his nose flat, maybe two or three times. A smashed-nosed angel with a grubby beard. And he was doing what might have been push-ups except that his knees were on the concrete. He looked up at Kirk and grinned lopsidedly. "You're Kirk," he said, then grunted to his feet and stepped to the bars.

He was tall, Kirk saw, only an inch or two short of his own height, with a lean and wiry twenty-seven- or twenty-eight-year-old body, and quick darting eyes, eyes made for laughing.

For some reason, seeing Sam in the flesh gave Kirk an uneasy feeling. He cursed himself for talking too much the previous night . . . it wasn't like him. . . .

"What'd our fathers say?" Sam asked after a period of mutual scrutiny.

"You wrote the script."

Sam laughed. "Maybe I ought to be broken up by it, but you know what they say about misery and company. . . . We'll be together."

"Swell," said Kirk with a wry grin, and went on: "Is there some secret to that exercise you were doing?"

Sam's eyes hooded mysteriously. "Yeah," he confided, "dig: first, you got to be bored stupid; second, you'd do anything to get unbored . . . anything but strain yourself. You saw the secret position . . . then you push up and down till you're ready to faint . . . three or four times, if you got a lot of drive. . . . Then you say, 'God, that was awful!' That's called 'exercising religiously.' Later, shadow-box, pull your hair, beat your meat—before you know it, the man with the key kicks you out the front gate . . . you're rehabilitated."

Kirk nodded wisely. "Scientific stuff."

Sam's face suddenly settled into hard lines, his eyes bored into

16

Kirk's. "The bullshit aside," he said quietly, "what kind of jolt are you doing?"

"Manslaughter."

"Voluntary?"

Kirk grinned bitterly. "Yeah . . . real, they say."

Curling his bottom lip under, Sam chewed on it and stared intently at Kirk. "I don't know why I'm cracking to you," he said slowly, thoughtfully, and fell silent for a long moment; then: "Shame on me if I'm wrong . . . you want out?"

Kirk's mind was suddenly tumbling, he forced it slower, made it repeat Sam's words. "Show me," he said at last.

Sam's face relaxed, and he smiled crookedly. "You got to trust me," he said in a rush. "The screw'll be back to lock you up in a minute or two. Don't talk about this from your cell, there's rats all over. You're going to have the shit stomped out of you, but act like you dig it, it ain't that bad anyway. And if you think you're getting into more than you can handle, just remember: if you scowl today and smile tomorrow, you're improving. That's the first law of Sam's Dynamics of Rehabilitation. Today, you're a prick; tomorrow, you're a kiss-ass—dig? Just trust my usually bad judgment and do what I do."

Kirk nodded, and heard the key grating in the gate at the end of the hall. He walked to the front of his cell.

[IV]

He stared at the ceiling from his bunk and listened to the rattle of the food cart as the second and last meal of the day was delivered to the compound. He stood and stretched, then crossed to the bars and watched a pair of guards wheel the cart past his cell, to work from the rear of the block forward.

Sam knocked on the wall, and whispered, "Get ready."

Kirk didn't give it much thought, he had been ready for a week . . . or was it longer . . . ? Peering sideways through the bars, he watched the cart roll closer, finally to Sam's cell. A guard slid a laden food tray under Sam's door, and as he turned to walk back to the cart, Sam spoke.

"Officer . . . officer, sir, excuse me, but . . ."

17

The guard turned. The tray clattered. And the guard wore a face clogged with mashed potatoes, a uniform dripping beet juice, a frankfurter lying limp across his shoe.

Laughter pealed from Sam's cell, joyous and rollicking laughter, the laughter of good clean fun.

Kirk bit his lip, it would not do for him to laugh. Not just yet. So he watched and waited.

Slinging the potatoes from his face, the guard looked as if he might cry or pound the floor with his fists. Instead, obscenities spewed from his mouth almost incoherently; he promised the convict a fiery death; inspired, he named the convict's family back three generations. After a while he got tired and clumped away, glowering, inconsolate.

But Sam kept right on laughing.

Some moments later the second guard slid a tray under Kirk's door. The convict picked it from the floor, and stood back from the bars while he called the guard, then took a step, and slammed the tray against the bars.

And the second guard, looking totally bewildered, stood adorned with potatoes and beet juice and frankfurters.

Kirk surrendered to the laughter burbling inside of him, but the sound was lost in a clamorous uproar as other convicts in the block began rattling cell doors, hooting, whistling, hollering. "Again!" "Work out!" "*Vive!*"

Squatting naked on a damp and evil-smelling concrete floor, his body moaning and whimpering in every joint, Kirk stared into the darkness of the strip cell at the rear of the isolation block, seeing nothing but a sliver of light that managed to sneak into the cell past double doors. Before the outer door of solid steel had slammed shut, leaving the cell in darkness, he had noticed the toilet hole in the corner of the floor and wondered how anything bigger than a small finger could get through the mesh of the covering grill. Judging by the stench, it seemed that very little did get through.

Feeling very alone, very inadequate, he wondered why it was necessary to be clubbed and trounced and kicked into a stinking little cell without sink or bunk or light in order to escape. It must be a sneaky scheme, he thought, but was left muddled by the complexities. Why had he been so readily amenable to Sam's plan, a plan of which he knew nothing? He, who sneered at men, at Man, and walked on them when he could, maimed them at random . . . killed . . .

He forced himself to stand, to pace, to think of something else. The beating . . . the beating he had received for flinging the tray . . . Standing to the bars he had watched a trio of guards yank Sam from his cell and haphazardly pound on him with stubby tear-gas clubs. Protecting his head with covering arms, Sam had gone limp and, in the middle of it, had peeped from between his elbows and grinned at Kirk. Then the guards had dragged the convict, feet first, toward the strip cells.

And they returned shortly for Kirk. Following Sam's lead, going limp, he had experienced the strangest desire to laugh, to point out to the guards their ineptness, to tell them how to really pulp a body. At the termination of the beating, he was in better shape than the winded trio, who could barely drag him into the strip cell. He had been hurt occasionally, and he was stiff and sore now, but mostly, he was contemptuous. But he usually was.

Maybe that is why Sam intrigued him. A convict doing life for robbery-murder who laughed the laugh of a century-old cynic. Kirk decided he liked Sam. And it was a new experience; he tried to remember if he had liked somebody before, and couldn't . . . Perhaps long ago . . .

Gray light filled the cell as a guard opened the outer door and tossed a rectangle of canvas and a pair of shorts against the barred inner door, then the door was shut and locked again.

Groping through the bars, Kirk pulled the canvas inside and spread it on the floor, making certain that it was well away from the stinking hole. Then he slipped on the oversized shorts and lay down, cold, sore, yet strangely peaceful. He let his thoughts roam the quiet darkness.

[V]

The outer door opened, and Kirk sat up and wondered how long he had been asleep. A guard stepped into the empty space between the two doors and keyed open the barred door. "Interview, Whalen," he said.

Pushing stiffly to his feet, Kirk shuffled through the two doors

19

into the hall. He felt very old and worn as he walked slowly up the hall, ahead of the guard, blinking at the brightness of lights that, yesterday, had been dim. Looking down at his body, he saw no bruises and decided that he was not so bad off as he felt.

Once through the front gate, the guard pointed to a pile of coveralls in the corner and indicated that Kirk should dress himself in a pair. And when he had complied, the guard escorted him to the door of the same room he had been in the previous day, and ordered him to enter and take a chair.

Kirk obeyed, and moments later heard someone enter behind. Dr. Trintz. He maneuvered his tall, lank frame past the convict, slid behind the table and sat down. Ignoring him, the doctor began poring over a folder of papers he had brought with him.

And finally, without inflection, Dr. Trintz said, "You're a misfit, Whalen, a real misfit."

Meeting the doctor's gaze, Kirk said nothing. What was there to say? He was terribly sorry? He wasn't; he said nothing.

"Psychopath." The word slipped quietly from Trintz's mouth and hung in the air.

Kirk was not impressed. The silence continued.

Finally the doctor sighed. "How old are you, Whalen?"

Kirk sneered. "Eleven . . . almost twelve. How old are you?"

Trintz's mouth twisted sourly, and he slapped a hand on the papers before him. "Just answer the question," he said with exaggerated calm. "Save your jokes for somebody who appreciates them." In the middle of the doctor's forehead a red splotch appeared, began spreading.

"I'll tell you what, Doc," Kirk said evenly, "you ask me questions that aren't answered in my file." Pausing, he indicated the folder on the table. "Ask me questions you don't have the answers to, and I'll answer you."

Trintz stared thoughtfully at the convict, then began drumming on the papers before him. "All right," he said finally, and shut the folder. "Make it as tough on yourself as you wish. But you might keep in mind that my report is a major determinant in your release . . . or in your continued imprisonment." He frowned. "You're in prison because you killed a man, an apparently irrational murder with no motive. I called it murder. . . . Regardless of the fact that you somehow finagled for manslaughter, murder is what I'll keep

20

calling it until you dissuade me." He looked up at the ceiling. "You see, it's my job to report on the likeliness, in my opinion, of a repeat performance. And at this point, you need all the help I can give you . . . if I elect to give you help. . . ." The doctor paused. Making a steeple of his fingers, he rested his nose on it and appeared contemplative. "Whalen," he began slowly, "I'm going to tell you something. . . . I ordinarily don't explain myself to prisoners—it tends to inhibit them more than usual. I'm not your friend, and in this position, I cannot be. Ordinarily, psychiatry isn't required to make moral judgments, but I do because it's part of the job. I'm in the position of being both guardian and scapegoat for the world beyond that wall. You'll be released—or not—as a result of my judgment. Unfortunately, I'm wrong about six or seven times out of ten. . . . The men return, and it falls on me. It's made me careful. It means that I don't recommend in borderline cases. . . . It's not to my liking, but that's the way it is, and I don't see any changes coming." He looked down at the folder. "To this point, all I can call you is a psychopath. . . . It means that I don't have any idea of what's making you go; it means that you're neither sane nor insane in the usual sense. Like a trash basket might contain waste paper, paper clips, rags, and time bombs, psychopath is a catchall label for the psychiatric wastebasket. Thousands, no, millions of people fall under the label—it's not necessarily connotative of evil —but in my capacity I have to delve for the time bomb. When I find it, or think I find it, then whoever is carrying it, they stay in prison. Nobody is altogether certain what causes psychopathic personalities, but it is known that there's a maturation process that usually burns it out during one's middle or late thirties; occasionally younger; occasionally never." He smiled faintly, very faintly. "You're in the company of arsonists, rapists, and killers of all sorts —but you're also of the stuff that's made generals, movie stars, presidents . . . even psychiatrists."

Kirk had kept his eyes on Trintz, he had listened intently, and against his will, he was impressed. Not with the imparted knowledge—he could read, too—but he was impressed with the man's apparent honesty. That would never do, it lent him a sense of obligation. He twisted his mouth distastefully. "Without the beard, you'd fool most anybody, God."

Strangely, the doctor smiled. Though remaining a stern and for-

21

bidding personality, he seemed somehow less an ogre. "Not God," he said easily, "but St. Peter? Maybe." Then his expression went flat, and he began asking questions again.

Inexplicably, as if apart from himself, the convict heard himself answering.

—Age?

—Twenty-two.

—What's the date?

Counting fingers, then,

—December fourteenth, I think . . . haven't seen a calendar for a while.

It progressed through "Who's the President?" "What's your favorite color?" "What is meant by 'A rolling stone gathers no moss'?" and on and on. Finally,

—Why'd you kill that man?

A pause, a long pause, and then,

—Every reason . . . no reason . . . I know why . . . I don't know why . . . Does that sound crazy? Yeah, it sounds crazy—even to me. But one of these days I'll figure it out so I can tell it in words. Don't ask me if I'd do it again. . . . I'm not altogether certain that I did it once. . . . I'm not crying 'bum beef' or anything like that, I remember the body . . . looking at it . . . but like I said, I'm not sure if *I* did it. . . . You believe in devils, Doc? Not the guy with the horns . . . but devils, demons that crawl around in your head, sometimes driving you to distraction, other times friendly, better company than people. . . . I think I have a case of devils, Doc. . . . Am I cutting my throat with all this babbling . . . ?

—Not at all. And I guess psychiatrists do believe in devils, but the terms are different. You think some more on it, we'll get back to it later. . . . Now, tell me about your family.

Silence. Kirk caught himself fidgeting, and fixed the doctor with a flat stare. "Try being somebody else's Big Brother. In the meantime, see if it'll reach, Doc . . . see if you can fuck yourself."

[VI]

He was three years old then, alone in the second-story apartment where he lived with his mother. The doorbell rang. He answered it, and gazed up at a man framed in the threshold.

22

"Hello, Kirk," said the man, smiling widely.

Kirk didn't think it was strange that the man should know his name; after all, his mother was always introducing him to people, more people than he could ever remember. Perhaps this smiling man was one of those people. Kirk smiled back at the man, and in a grand manner, pleased that he could help, he informed him that his mother wasn't home, she was shopping, but she'd be back in a little while.

The man took a short step and stood inside the door. "You don't know me, do you, Kirk?"

The boy shrugged regretfully. "No."

The man knelt. "I'm your father."

Kirk gaped. Was this balding, gray-eyed man the one he had so often asked his mother about? Was this is father? He became embarrassed and shuffled his feet and wrung his hands behind his back. "My father?" he asked finally. "My father?"

The man—his father—laughed, his eyes crinkling at the corners, and lifted the boy. "Yeah, son," he said happily, "this is your pop. Look here . . ." He put the boy back on the floor and reached outside the door for a large package that sat there. "Look here," he continued, "I brought you a present from Europe. . . . Come on, son, open it."

Kirk had no trouble understanding what a present was. Sitting before the paper-wrapped parcel that was as large as he was himself, he tore at the wrappings until they fell away. Then he stared. It was an intricately carved wooden chest showing eagles in furious battle with snakes. The hinges and latch were of hammered silver. Inside the blue-satin-lined interior was another chest, smaller, with identical carvings. And inside the second chest was a third; in the third, a fourth; until he finally arrived at a sixth chest, very small, and found inside a tiny silver wristwatch. He was thrilled. He had no idea what to use the chests for, even less, the watch. But they were new, and his own, a gift from his father, the father he had until then never known.

"Look here," his father said, "don't tell your mother I was here. I've got to get along now, but I'll be seeing you later." Waving, the stranger, his father, backed from the apartment, and was gone.

Kirk packed the chests to his bedroom and hid them in a closet, wondering all the while why his father had cautioned him not to tell his mother that he had been there. But he had to give it up: adult affairs were beyond him.

When his mother returned home and, as usual, began to tidy the apartment, she discovered the chests. She questioned him, first demanding angrily, then pleading solicitously, she questioned and questioned.

And soon he made a mistake in his hastily ad-libbed explanation. Then another. And another. And finally confessed everything. He became wretched; lying to his mother, disloyal to his father, weighted with things outside of himself, beyond understanding, he cried.

His mother, strangely silent, led him to the living room and sat him upon the sofa. She gazed at the boy with tormented eyes, then began talking, explaining.

And Kirk listened, hearing many things about his father, many revelations. His father was a sick man, the Germans had done something terrible to him, he had changed, doctors wanted to watch him, but maybe someday his father would live with them, not for a while though, not until the doctors said it was all right. The boy understood none of it.

She finished talking and clutched Kirk to her breast, smothering him in the scent of artificial lilacs. She cried. To and fro she rocked the boy, comforting him until he cried more.

He thought about his father occasionally, but mostly he traipsed around on urgent boy-business. So it was a surprise when he walked into the apartment one day and found his mother and father talking together.

Feeling a sudden surge of joy, Kirk crept toward his father, who was turned away from the door, thinking he would leap on him and wrestle or something.

But as the boy advanced, his mother noticed him and her eyes went wide, as if with fright, then his father swiveled and spotted Kirk. He leaped out of his chair, spun it violently across the room to crash into the wall. In a bound, he disappeared into the boy's bedroom. And rushed back to the living room, his face livid. From his fingers dangled the watch he had given Kirk. Since the boy was unable to tell time, he had fashioned a crude dais beside his bed, and there the watch had lain, much admired.

But now he watched in bewilderment as his father raised the watch above his head and slammed it to the floor, then ground it under his heel.

Turning his fevered face to the boy, he strode over and knocked him to the floor. He slapped and punched at him, slavering, raving, screaming that his boy, his only son, was a stool pigeon, a rat, an informer.

Kirk, struck dumb, paralyzed with fear, seeing through a red mist, through blood, squirmed backwards, was slammed backwards, until finally he found himself under the kitchen table. Through three rooms he had scuttled on his back.

He watched his father's legs as they walked from the table, then heard his voice screaming unknown words at his mother, then became aware of the steady drip spattering the floor under his head. Blood. He cried. Quietly.

Sometime later his mother came to him and gathered him up and bathed him and put him to bed—her bed—and caressed him until he slept, his nose full of artificial lilacs. Days passed. His body mended. But something inside of him seemed to knit poorly, misshapen.

A year later his father was back at the door, smiling. Kirk ran, his mind full of terror, and locked himself in his bedroom.

But minutes later, with his mother coaxing sweetly, promising that everything was all right, saying that his father was very sorry, and to prove it he had brought Kirk a bicycle, a two-wheeler like he wanted so much, the boy unlocked the bedroom door. Reluctantly, he allowed himself to be convinced: he did want a bicycle.

When Kirk was led to the living room, his father knelt and gathered the boy to him. He was sorry, he explained, but he had not been himself that day. It would never happen again, he promised.

Kirk spotted the tiny red bicycle and forgave his father. A dozen spills and contusions later, he learned to ride it. He liked it better than the watch.

His father came to live with them, they were a family. The boy brought his friends around to meet his dad; he was no longer confused when people asked where his father was. Bad memories faded.

And then his father bought a car, a small green coupe. Kirk was excited, he couldn't remember having ever been in one. He bounced on the living-room floor, his face pressed to the window,

25

looking down at the car parked against the curb, glistening. He could hardly wait for a ride.

"Man, what a nice car!" he told his father.

His father looked at him for a moment, suddenly snatched him up, carried him to his bedroom.

The boy was dropped onto the bed. His father ripped his shirt away. And beat him with a belt. Beat and beat. Welts crosshatched his back. The skin began to tear. His father railed and ranted and raved. "*You don't address your elders as* 'MAN'!" But after a while the boy didn't hear him any more. He passed out.

When he awoke, Kirk labored to his feet, unmindful of the bandages now covering his back, unmindful of anything but the need to flee. He limped from the apartment, down the stairs, to the storage room where his bicycle was parked. He opened the door of the little room. He found his bicycle. It had been savaged—tires impossibly twisted, frame broken in half. His father had destroyed the bicycle.

Filled with anguish, grief, helplessness, the boy sank to the ground and stared at the ruined bike. He could not cry, the pain was too great. He just knelt there, mind churning, thinking thoughtless thoughts.

He awoke in his bed, and could not remember how he had gotten there. His heart pounded in his ears. Bits and snatches of thoughts leaped and tumbled violently through his mind.

Then his father entered.

The boy cringed. Terror surged through him. He tried to make himself small, pulled the covers up to his chin, over his face. But the beat of his heart seemed to push him upward, ever upward, toward his father, toward the skin-tearing belt. Somebody sat on the bed, and he heard his father's voice.

"I'm sorry, son," his father said, softly, gently. "It won't happen again, I promise."

Kirk lay still, the covers pulled tightly over his head, hardly daring to breathe.

And his father's voice murmured on, coaxing, pleading, rueful. "I'm going to have your bike fixed. And I've got a surprise for you. . . . Wait till you see it. . . ."

His father had bought him a dog, a greyhound named Legs.

Kirk loved the dog, even more than he had cared about the unforgotten watch and bicycle (something had come up, his father had explained, and the boy wouldn't be getting his bike back; he

26

was sorry about it, but Kirk should take it like a man). The boy would have rather had Legs anyway—watches and bicycles can't be friends.

One morning some months later his father made a smiling announcement: he was taking the boy and Legs to the ocean to fish.

There, perched in the rocks high above the pounding surf, being occasionally dampened by spray, the boy felt his line suddenly begin to wiggle and jerk. He had hooked something. A whale or a shark anyway, he thought, and needed help to land the fearsome thing. An instant later his father also hooked something. He called continuously over the surf's roar for his father's assistance. But by the time his father's fish got away, the boy had managed to land his by himself. A five-inch perch.

And while his father beat him for being an *"ungrateful-son-of-a-bitch-you-made-me-lose-my-fish!"* the boy's dog growled and snapped at the flailing, skin-tearing belt. Finished with the boy, his father turned and kicked Legs in the skull, then snatched the limp gray dog from the rocks and hurled it into the surf. Legs did not come up.

Kirk never forgot, even when he wanted to, he could not; not his watch or bicycle or dog—he never forgot them. And he never cried after that; instead, he smiled: pinched, frozen, false. But he never cried. He always smiled.

He became different, withdrawn, eaten with loneliness, yet avoiding everyone. He became a shell, hollow except for a bilious and seething hate, a hate that grew to fill the shell, then grew some more, spilled over. His classmates became children, very young children. He stayed away from them. And they shied from him, sensing his difference. Their games and amusements were not brought to him. But he didn't care . . . except . . . except that he did, and did not know why he should. But when they needed a fighter, someone to champion their cause, to stomp a neighborhood bully or somebody they had merely taken a momentary dislike to, they came to Kirk. And he would fight for them—not because he wanted to help anybody, but because he wanted to fight, even needed to fight. In time he became tough; too tough and too cruel and too anxious to grind his fists, stamp his feet, use his teeth to maim, to hurt somebody, anybody. And his father beat him. And his mother was tender and smothering. And his father beat him. And Kirk did not forget.

And inside of him there grew a haunting presence. He felt it, as if someone were watching him, ever watching, ever knowing his thoughts, causing him to look repeatedly over his shoulder. And while in time he came to know that nobody was there watching, the feeling of being ever scrutinized, haunted, did not leave him. He tried to exorcise the presence, but could not—it was always there; sometimes shadowy, lurking unobtrusively, other times a screaming black thing, an all-enveloping thing; but there . . . always there.

Came the day he gave a neighborhood boy a bundle of trading stamps he had stolen from his mother and a five-dollar bill stolen from his father. In return, Kirk was given seven bullets and a rusty .32-caliber revolver.

Two days later—he was beaten approximately every third day— his father ordered him from the dinner table for eating too fast and told him to "get ready—the usual." Kirk nodded and left the table.

But he did not "get ready." He did not strip his shirt from his black-and-blue and welted back; he did not kneel before the bed and lay across the mattress. Instead, he stood beside the bedroom door and waited. He was calm, calmer than he had ever been. He gripped the revolver. It was loaded.

Soon his father stepped through the door, belt in hand. And abruptly stopped. Kirk was not lying across the bed. His face flushed. He looked around the room—and soon looked down the bore of the pistol. His mouth fell open, a frightened squawk escaped his throat, the belt dropped from limp fingers. Gasping, he sagged against the wall and fouled his pants.

Kirk smiled. A real smile. With the gun barrel shoved hard into his father's nostril, Kirk reached for the belt, then slashed the buckle across his father's bloodless face and gestured for him to assume a well-known position on the bed.

Obviously unable to speak, his father folded his hands in supplication. Kirk sneered and slashed again. His father clutched at his heart. Kirk slashed twice again, once with the belt, once with the gun sight. And his father, face bloody, slid down the wall, crumpled to the floor, whimpering.

Kirk relented. But for a price: a generous allowance—whatever he wanted, whenever—and a car. Immediately.

His father agreed, effusively. He thought a boy should have everything he wanted; and from now on, he and Kirk would be a real father and son team, wouldn't they, he asked with a quaking, blue-lipped smile.

"Shut up, punk," Kirk told him. "And remember, asshole, this is *my* room. Don't step inside it again—*ever.* Now get the fuck out of here. And act like a man." .

His father hastened from the room, beltless.

He remembered his father's favorite expression when he had winced under the lash of the belt: "Act like a man." He laughed bitterly.

He tried to savor the triumph, but was left with a sour taste. It seemed so empty of victory, anticlimactic. And strange, very strange indeed, he found himself feeling sorry for his father. But then he remembered his back, his back so welted and torn that never in his memory had he removed his shirt in front of anybody but his father. And, too, he remembered his watch, his bicycle, his dog; he remembered and remembered. And yet . . . yet, he pitied his father. It was uncanny—he put it from his mind.

He wished that he had been able to do it several weeks before, on his thirteenth birthday as he had for so long planned to do. But the five dollars had proven difficult to get: his father always carried his wallet and always seemed awake and present.

Four days later he had a car. After that he was rarely home, only occasionally to sleep. He traded the gun to another kid for a tankful of gas—not because he needed gas so badly, but because he wanted so badly to use the gun. That would never do—guns kill so fast.

A month later he rolled the car, destroyed it. His father saved him from trouble with the law and bought him another car. And another. And another.

High school passed, and with nothing better to do, he took himself to junior college.

Meantime, his mother—his hovering, lilac-scented mother—fluttered in the background, ever ready with her cipherlike personality to smother her son, the only "beautiful thing" in her life—her life, a grotesque melodrama of contradictions and indecision.

And while she prattled emotionally and flittered mindlessly into middle age, his father learned to use a cane, to live with his ulcers and palsied body . . . and son.

An ignored, harshly repressed corner of his mind commanded

29

Kirk to pity his father, to leave him at last in peace. Several times he was at the point of leaving, but each time something inside of him demanded further vengeance, a price not yet paid, and so he stayed close, incessantly reminding his father that he was near. Had his father been a horse, Kirk would have ridden him to death, feeling no more than a moment's sorrow when the animal floundered, heaved its last shuddering breath; regretting only the fact that he was afoot.

And then came the day that his father had . . . his father had—

Squirming on the canvas, the convict forced a stop to the tormenting memories, and attempted to calm the storm in his mind and body by arranging the states in alphabetical order.

[VII]

It was later, though there was no way he could be certain how much later, for the blackness was broken only by periodic beams of light when a guard cracked open the outer door's window to make certain that the convict had not gone through the wall, or maybe down the hole in the floor, when a voice came to him, a faint voice that called his name, and for a moment made him doubt his sanity. But it came again, and he placed the direction—it was issuing from the back wall of the cell. He rose from the mat, crossed to the rear of the cell, and ran a hand over the wall. In the upper right corner his fingers found a square of wire mesh; it apparently covered a ventilator shaft, for he could feel a cool current of air. Directing his voice toward the hole, he called out.

"Is that you, Sam?"

No answer.

He tried again, louder. "Sammy! Is that you, Sam?"

A moment later, when the echoes of his own voice had left his ears, he heard a response.

". . . bet you got doubts about my brainy plot, eh, Kirk?" It was Sam.

Kirk was indeed having doubts—cold, almost naked, a bed of threadbare canvas, driven by tormenting memories. No, he thought, it was not a promising beginning. "Tell me one thing," he called back, "and everything'll be all right. Have you ever thought you were Napoleon?"

Sam laughed. "We ain't got long to go," he called reassuringly. "You only got 18 more days, I got 20. It might get to you after a while, but we showed them we're intractable villains. Now, when they put us in seg, they'll stick us in an especially segregated section . . . how 'bout that: segregated in segregation. Anyway, we'll be locked way in the back of the building. There's four cells reserved for the super-hard hardcases . . . but they don't bother watching them a quarter as close as the guys up front. . . . They ain't too bright sometimes . . . most times. And another thing, when we're back there, nobody'll be able to rat on us, 'cause usually all the cells are empty. I ain't saying any more about it. . . . Sometimes the screw climbs back in the pipes behind us and listens to guys jacking off. I'll run it all down when I see you." He paused a moment. "What're you doing over there?"

"Reading," said Kirk, and laughed into the vent. "Seriously though, I can recite the states forwards and backwards. . . . Maybe I'll work out a meter to sing them to."

"Yeah . . . yeah, that's how it starts," Sam said, and laughed. "Check, I got a theory. . . . You walk round and round the cell till you get dizzy and fall, then you walk around some more, but in the opposite direction. . . . That way, you unwind . . . at least that's my theory. Why doesn't it work?"

Kirk chuckled, and then, "When the fuck do we eat? I'm hungry."

Sam laughed harder than usual. "And that's how you're going to stay," he said happily. "But you'll make it . . . at least most guys do . . ." He paused. "Hey, didn't I hear your door slam today?"

"Yeah," Kirk answered. "That creepy psych had me out, said I'm a psychopath."

"Welcome to the club," Sam said. "But it ain't a very élite club. . . . That guy calls everybody a psychopath, even the dings walking the prison yard that ain't known where they been for 20 years. Yeah, the bughouses get full up and don't want no ringy convicts, so good old Doc calls them psychopaths and pretends they're invisible." He paused. "And anyway, nowadays the word is 'sociopath,' but it ain't too strange. . . . Good old Doc is living in another century. He's got a picture of Lambrose in his office. That's the guy that said he could tell the good guys from the bad guys by measuring their heads. And he's Doc's hero. . . . So if the geek shows up with a pair of calipers and eyeballs your skull, don't be surprised. I

31

don't know," he said, and paused a moment before adding, "maybe it's me . . . but I think the guy's about as useful as a hangnail. I've seen him twice, but so far all I found out is that I'm a cave-man. . . ."

Kirk snorted. "Twice in four years?"

"Yeah . . . twice in four years. . . . And I ain't been saved yet, can you imagine a guy as fucked up as that?"

Kirk laughed caustically and made a reply. And the two convicts continued talking through the ventilator until Kirk's door was opened and a guard gave him what might have been a thick sand-wich. The guard left the cell with the front door open so Kirk held the paper-wrapped thing to the light and studied it. It was a heavy slab of something that looked like termite-eaten wood and weighed like lead; rancid-smelling and unsavory brown, it was clapped be-tween two slices of bread. Some sort of food, he was sure, but seeing it, remembering something Sam had said, he was reluctant to taste it—the smell alone was gagging.

Another guard stepped past the opened door holding a two-gal-lon pitcher and a paper cup. It was the same guard whom Kirk had flung the food on.

"Water?" the guard asked.

Kirk nodded.

And the guard emptied the pitcher on him. Loosing a happy chuckle, he danced from the cell and locked the door.

Dripping wet, the floor sloshing-deep, Kirk thought first of the sleeping mat and snatched it from the floor. But too late . . . it was thoroughly soaked. His skull tightened with hate, his heart slammed, feeling as if it were between his ears. He hammered the wall, screaming, cursing, begging the guard to open the doors for a minute, a half minute, a second; he offered to die for only a second at the guard's throat. But nobody came, the doors stayed locked.

He finally dropped to the sopping floor and began doing push-ups. After a while his arms buckled and he lay in the water, the heat gone from his body. But his mind still churned, searing itself with fiery thoughts. Finally, frustrated, he yelled to Sam, ranting and raving and blustering through an explanation of what had hap-pened.

When he was finished, Sam laughed.

"I should've warned you about that," the convict said. "I was ready for them, so it wasn't so bad. . . . It's all part of the game.

. . . But if he keeps on, just kind of grin crazylike and tell him, 'Thank you, sir,' and he'll probably leave you be."

Kirk suddenly chuckled and wagged his head. "Hey, Sam," he called, "are you sure you've never thought you were Napoleon?" and was about half-serious.

Sam laughed and fell silent.

And Kirk said, "Fuck it," and splashed in the water.

He was awake, damp and shivering, when the door opened the following morning, and a huge guard stood framed in the light, unmoving.

Kirk climbed stiffly to his feet and stood ready, snarling, adrenaline coursing.

"Oh, Christ!" the guard said caustically, and lit a cigaret, illuminating an ugly face with a misshapen, bulbous nose. "Christ save me from a tough punk." He sniffed the air. "You wanna mop out the pigpen, or are you too tough?"

The stagnant puddles of water on the floor did stink, but the convict was used to the smell; still, the puddles were annoying to roll into, and there seemed to be no way to get all the water down the toilet hole. So he nodded. "I'll mop it," he said.

The guard left, and returned shortly with a mop and extended it through the bars.

Kirk took it, mopped the cell, and returned the mop. The guard disappeared with it, then returned a moment later with a two-gallon pitcher.

"You bastard," Kirk hissed. "You big hideous bastard." He resigned himself to getting soaked again.

"Dummy up, you punk kid," the guard said tiredly, "or I'll come in there and spank you." He pulled two wrapped packages and a pint plastic container from the pitcher and put them on the floor. "Here," he said, "take this shit and if I don't get back, bust up the container and stick it down the shitter hole." He fished in a pocket, then threw several cigarets, loose matches, and a striker through the bars. He stepped back and locked the door.

Kirk gaped into the dark. But not for long.

He lay back, smoking. He belched. Two sandwiches—roast beef with lettuce and mustard; omelet with catsup—and a pint of eggnog . . . it was unbelievable, fantastic, mind-boggling. His fingers still trembled, and his throat felt stretched from cramming the food down, but he belched again, tasting a delicious blend of eggnog and mustard, and took a deep drag off the cigaret, and decided that the ugly guard had a noble face, endearing ways.

A while later the guard returned.

"Thanks . . . thanks," Kirk said. "Seriously . . ."

"Thanks for what, you punk kid?"

Kirk grinned. "All right," he said, and handed the container through the bars, "but you're not really a hideous bastard. . . . Thanks for the mop."

"It's part of the job." The guard stepped back, and the door closed.

Kirk lit another cigaret and stepped over to the vent. "Hey, Sam," he called, and when the convict answered, went on: "I want to punish you for leading me astray. . . . You know what I'm doing right now?"

"Yeah," came the disheartening reply, "that's Yancy. . . . I got fixed, too. Cool it . . . remember what I said? The vents sometimes got ears—dig?"

Kirk nodded at the vent. "Yeah. But that big creep is about half-cute . . . unless I'm getting funny."

"Check, that guy's only on two days a week, so you'd best stash a little of it. But don't get popped with anything if they bust in to shake you down. . . . That guy's compadres are laying to break it off in him. . . ."

Damn! Kirk thought, that means five days a week with nothing but that slab thing . . . whatever it is. "Hey, Sam," he called, "what's that shit they feed us?"

"Nice, ain't it?" the convict replied, and laughed. "Check, it's made out of beans, carrots, peas, spinach, turnips, parsnips, potatoes, lettuce, string beans, onions, cabbage . . . did I leave anything out? Anyway, it's made out of everything and anything they have left over . . . except meat. It's put in a pot and boiled into a gum, and then mashed into bread pans and frozen. Hell, I don't know . . . it might be all right, but I can't get it past my nose. I've done a couple 30-day jolts back here, and I still can't eat that shit. . . . But it probably ain't poison—I knew a geek that used to steal it out of the kitchen. . . . 'Course, they caught him eating his own shit, too . . . took him away in a straitjacket. But you can make it on the bread and water and whatever that other guy can slip you."

34

He paused. "By the way, if you feel like you got to shit, don't. Your body'll use it up in a couple days . . . and pushing turds down that grate ain't what I call fun."

[VIII]

By the end of the third day in the strip cells the convicts had stopped calling through the ventilators. There was nothing left to talk about. Instead, Kirk lay lethargically on the canvas and tried to think of something to think about. Sometimes he would realize that for many minutes his mind had been blank, a dark and empty void. Other times the cell became filled with brilliant colors that swirled wildly and dashed themselves against the walls, filling the cell with vibrant, multihued sparks that fell to the floor and flickered out, leaving the cell dark again. When first he saw the colored lights, he ignored them. But after a while he sat up and reached out to touch spots on the wall that the lights illuminated, and found no wall, no spots. It made him feel foolish, but he kept trying, and finally began wondering about his sanity.

Between the appearance and disappearance of the colors his mind was filled with illogical and grandiose imagery, as if he were watching a mental movie of a fourteenth-century romance, as if he were Jason, St. George, and Superman all in one. As a result, he was left irrationally anxious and irritable; but in the next instant, thinking the same thoughts, seeing the same imagery, he would laugh and become mildly euphoric.

He tried and tried to count off five minutes, but could not sustain interest that long; after counting to 50 or 60, he would wonder later if he had been counting at all. A minute might have been an hour; an hour, a minute. Days became a few hours long, hours became days long. He knew a day had passed when he was brought the slab meal that he refused to eat. He thought he should be hungry, but was not. Oft-times he would put the two slices of bread on the bars and forget them; he did not drink much water, either. It was not surprising that he didn't use the hole in the floor. He wondered what it was there for.

It might have been the tenth or twelfth day, maybe before, maybe later, when the nude, dark-haired woman moved into the cell with him. She was just suddenly there, lying on her back in the

35

corner of the cell. Kirk pushed himself to the other side of the cell and squeezed his eyes shut. She isn't there! he told himself, and opened his eyes and she was.

"Get the fuck out of here!" he screamed, and swung his head around and jammed it into the corner of the cell, his eyes shut so tightly that crimson bombs began exploding in his skull. Then he thought about it and suddenly chuckled and wondered if she could hear him. He turned from the wall and looked toward her. She was gone. He touched his eyes to be certain they were open, then scanned the darkness. Yes, she was gone. Biliousness choked him, his mind fogged with anger. *"Come back, you bitch!"* he screamed. *"Come back!"*

Sometime later he sat hunched in the corner, peeping slyly between his fingers, waiting for the woman to return. He waited and waited. Then . . . then, Jesus . . . Jesus was there . . . bloody-palmed, a cross strapped to his back with a bullet bandolier, he gazed with haunted eyes at something over the convict's shoulder.

Kirk's heart fluttered. "Oh, Christ!" he exclaimed, then snickered at himself, and repeated, "Oh, Christ," and laughed until he was exhausted.

The figure just kept staring, apparently grieved by whatever it was that he saw in the distance.

But Kirk did not look around—he knew his back was against the wall, there was nothing behind. Still, he wondered. . . .

"Hey," he said finally, "can you talk . . . ?" The figure just kept staring. "Hi," Kirk said, and waved. The figure kept staring.

He panicked. Leaping from the floor, he snatched up the canvas mat and flailed it at the apparition . . . the apparition . . . the thing he hoped was an apparition. *"Get out of here, you son of a bitch!"* he screamed, and Jesus vanished.

Some place in there the ugly guard Yancy opened the front door and left more sandwiches and eggnog, and departed without speaking. It took Kirk a while to believe it, and when he did, he decided to save some of it for later, but it was gone too fast. He cursed the ugly guard, the food, the world, and finally slept, cursing.

And when he woke, she was back. She lay in the corner of the cell, naked, peering at him through lowered eyelids.

Gazing at her, Kirk grew suddenly warm and wondered if she would stay while he climbed between her gaped legs. The thought was not at all erotic, he didn't have the energy. So he just stared and tried to remember if she looked like anybody he had known, but her face, while holding a hint of beauty, was strangely featureless. He finally smiled at her.

"Hi," he said. Unmoving, she stayed silent. "Hi, *bitch!*" he snarled. She ignored him.

And suddenly the tightly curled hair between her legs became a huge, fuzzy spider that strutted over her thigh to the floor with three small spiders following. Posturing like tin soldiers to martial music, they marched to the wall and executed a right turn, then another, and marched back across the cell. As the spider family strutted to the center of the cell, Kirk ordered: "About face!"

The fuzzy things ignored him, kept marching.

Kirk laughed . . . and the spiders disappeared, the woman vanished, then he laughed some more, until his stomach ached, his jaw muscles cramped, and tears ran from his eyes.

One day he woke from a fog and stared at a guard with his foot propped on the bars.

"Let's go," the guard said.

"Huh?"

"Let's go . . . look alive."

"Huh?"

Another guard appeared in the doorway and shone a light on the convict, causing him to blink and shut his eyes.

"Come on, fella," one of the guards said, "either snap out of it or we'll get the padded cell ready."

Kirk came to himself. "Fuck you," he said, and staggered to his feet, then bounced vertiginously against the wall, and crumpled.

"You want out, fella, or you gonna play jack-off?"

Kirk sneered, and groped for the bars to pull himself up. "Why don't you go hurt yourself or something?" he said, and wondered at the hollow, unreal sound of his voice.

One of the guards opened the barred door. "Bring the mat," he ordered.

Kirk stooped over and picked up the canvas, and walked unsteadily from the cell. Blinking his eyes against the unaccustomed light, he leaned against the wall while the guards relocked the cell, and noticed that the floor, the walls, the roof were all convex. He felt as if he were atop a mound. He closed his eyes and shook his head. And opened them again to a concave world. The floor had become a huge gutter. Despairing of trying to make sense of it, he shuffled behind the guards, pretending that the floor was as flat as it should have been, and feeling much smaller than he thought he was.

After dressing in prison blues, Kirk walked between the guards through the main prison corridor toward segregation. It was early, there were few convicts about, and he was pleased to escape the scrutiny of 6,000 hollow eyes. In his life he had learned hate and savagery and brutality; he had learned to hurt and maim and, finally, he had killed; but walking down Alhondiga's long, red concrete corridor, he felt like a piker, rank amateur, an innocent.

"All right, fella," one of the guards said, breaking into the convict's thoughts, "hold it up."

He halted and looked around, and saw the steel door with thick black letters painted on it: "SEGREGATION."

One of the guards fitted a heavy brass key into the lock and opened it. "Inside," he said with a jerk of his head.

The convict entered and found himself in a dimly lit hallway with cells on both sides. The cells were outside cells, built with doors instead of barred fronts, and in the doors were small windows that the glass had been smashed out of. As Kirk began following a guard, while the other followed him, convict faces suddenly appeared at all of the windows.

And from each convict there seemed to come the sound of many voices, yelling and cursing, ceasing only to spit at the two guards. The one in front of Kirk nimbly dodged a greenish glob of phlegm that arced across the hall from the right, and ran into another, bigger glob coming from the left. The guard halted and shook his fist and cursed and glowered and flushed and cursed; finally he jerked a handkerchief from his pocket and wiped the mess off his face. Then he wheeled to glare at Kirk, looking as if he might spit on him. Kirk grinned. And the guard spun around, and clumped on, much faster than before.

The convict was awed by the language he heard. It was not used for emphasis or in frustration, but to probe for a thin spot, to claw its way through skin, to wound, to fester. And it did, it did. But for

38

a fleeting moment Kirk saw the words, the phrases, as the mirror of the convicts' souls: lacerated, filthy, tortured, but yet . . . yet, pitiable, plaintive cries bewailing a lost and irretrievable humanness. In that moment he felt himself wilt inwardly, pulled down, crushed beneath a weight of helplessness and hopelessness and despair. But the moment was soon past; the feeling, the inner accord shriveled, withered, died.

And he cheered the convicts on, grinning at them, waving his arms for more and louder and better efforts.

The two guards with Kirk between came to the end of the hall, and turned right, past several offices, and then left, and stopped before a steel door with a small pane of wire-reinforced glass set in it at eye level.

Behind the door there were four cells fronting on a narrow hallway. Kirk was locked into the first cell, and one of the guards poked his face to the small window and glowered at him.

"What's the problem?" Kirk finally asked him.

The guard bared his teeth. "You got the problem, punk."

Kirk sneered. "Why didn't you help me with it when the door was open?"

The guard spun around in a circle and stuck his fevered face back to the window. "You punks . . . you trashy, degenerate punks . . ." he said with a quiet but fervent intensity. "God grant me the chance to kill about 500 of you scum."

Kirk grinned. "With me gone, you'd only have 499 to go. Open the door and kill me. . . . You have a pal, and I can hardly stand up. . . . Come on, open the door. . . ."

The guard hammered his fist on the door, and spun away, gnashing his teeth.

[IX]

Kirk surveyed the cell. It was large, almost twice the size of the isolation cell; the bunk had woven-wire springs; and in the rear a big window divided into small sections by thick steel panes looked into a small courtyard surrounded by an eight- or nine-foot-tall concrete wall, topped with coil after coil of rusted concertina barbed wire.

39

He found a pile of sheets, as stiff as celluloid but not so smooth, and blankets with cardboardlike spots, mementos of a slovenly masturbator, and began making up the bed. He wanted to cover the piss-smelling yellowed mattress.

Finished, he found a small broom with a four-inch handle lying under the bunk and began sweeping the cell. All around were huge rolls of dust, looking like tumbleweeds awaiting a gale. He managed finally to fight them past the draft coming under the door.

From the door came a clicking sound. Kirk pushed against it, but nothing happened, so he reluctantly turned his attention to the scummy toilet. He stared at it from a distance, hesitant to approach the malodorous thing, and wondered how long ago it had been cleaned, wondered how he was going to clean it.

"Hi," said a voice back of him.

He turned to the door and saw a blond-banged, blue-eyed convict with a girlishly bobbed nose and high-arched, plucked eyebrows. A fruit, obviously.

"You want me to go away?" asked the pretty, slinky-eyed face.

Kirk grinned uneasily and shrugged. That was something else about prison that left him addled: the fruits . . . they were everywhere. In the week he had been among the general population, dainty, mincing fairies, lecher-eyed, fat old men, unctuously patronizing fags of all sorts had made a play for him, a fondling here, a feel there. It made him uncomfortable. He could have stomped them into the concrete, but half of them acted as if that was what they most wanted, and the other half were too helpless to fight back. He had walked—hurried—away from them.

"Are you another one of those queer-haters?" the face said easily, but Kirk heard an underlying nuance, something the dispossessed had in common.

Feeling a little more comfortable, he grinned and said, "No, I'm not a queer-hater."

The face smiled. "Are you the guy that threw your tray on the bull . . . you and Sammy?"

Kirk nodded. "How did you hear about that?"

"A cop told me," said the fruit. "Your name's Kirk then, huh?" Kirk nodded again, and he went on. "I'm Leslie. . . . And if you'd shave and comb your hair, you'd be cute. . . ."

Kirk laughed. "Knock it off," he said, "I'm getting embarrassed," and he was. "What're you doing out there?" he added quickly, hoping to change the subject.

"We get to walk out here in the afternoon," Leslie said. "And on Sundays, except for holidays, we go out to that yard you see out the window. You'll be able to come out tomorrow. . . ." He leered. "It'll be just you and me. . . . There's a shower in the back . . . nobody can see us. . . ."

"Oh, no!" Kirk blurted as he backed from the door, then sat on the bunk. "Oh, no. Take it some place else. I don't fuck around. . . ."

Leslie giggled. "Relax, baby, I don't give the body away that easy. . . . You're still kind of cute, though." He paused. "I heard you've only been in a little while. . . . How'd you meet Sammy?"

Kirk sighed with relief. "In the hole . . . talking. . . ."

"How come you guys threw the food on the bulls?"

Warning bells clamored in Kirk's mind; he recalled what Sam had said about rats being all around, and fruits had notorious reputations for being stool pigeons. He opened his mouth to tell Leslie to get the fuck away from his cell and heard himself weaving a long, involved lie. He lied and lied, and wondered why, wondered why he didn't just tell the blond-banged, giggling fag to take his girlish nose elsewhere.

But he did not, and when he was finished, apparently satisfying Leslie's curiosity, he asked, "How do you know Sam? Does he mess around with . . . with—"

"Queers, fags, freaks, fruits, perverts . . . ?" Leslie smiled at him. "You won't hurt my feelings . . . if you say it sweet. But thank you, thank you anyway." He leered. "You're getting red, baby . . . you're just a little boy, huh?"

Kirk turned away, fidgeting. "Knock it off," he said finally. "And you didn't answer the question. Does Sam mess with . . . with them?"

"You're cute," said Leslie with a giggle. "Yeah, Sammy plays around—who doesn't?—but not with me. We're pretty friendly, but not sexy-friendly. . . . He doesn't turn me on."

Kirk was silent for a thoughtful moment, then: "You know he'll be over here the day after tomorrow . . . ?" Leslie nodded, and he went on. "How long before you get out of here?"

"About four months. . . . Why?"

Kirk shrugged noncommittally. But he was worried, for whatever Sam and he were going to do, this plucked-eyebrowed fag would be

41

too close. He looked up into the guileless blue eyes and said, "Why four months? I thought the usual stay was 90 days."

Leslie sighed and frowned and grimaced. "Oh, I don't want to talk about it. . . ."

Kirk shrugged indifferently. "All right."

"Oh, I'm sorry," Leslie said uneasily. "It's a long story."

Kirk stared at him. "Nice weather we're having."

"Oh, I'm sorry. . . . I'm horrid, huh?"

"You're a funny kind of . . . of fag," Kirk said with an easy smile, "and you're sorry a lot, but I don't know why—I'm really not that interested."

"That wasn't nice," Leslie said pertly. "And just for that I'm going to tell you." He stuck out his tongue and made a face. "The dirty rat-bastards wanted to cut my hair," he began with a bitingly emotional tone. "I didn't want them to, so three stinking bulls snuck in my cell and shoved a syringe full of Thorazine in my butt. They sat on me till I passed out. And when I woke up in isolation, I had a shaved skull. . . . The dirty bastards shaved all my hair off . . . the dirty bastards. . . ." Breaking off, he chewed on a slender, dagger-nailed finger, then went on: "Anyhow, they only gave me ten days in the hole, and when I got out, my hair hadn't grown very much . . . just kind of bristly all over. . . . And some guy . . . some dirty bastard punk convict thought I looked just too funny for words." He shrugged. "I stabbed him."

Kirk stared at him for a moment, then laughed. And he kept on laughing.

"Funny, huh?" Leslie said finally, pouting. "I don't think you're cute any more."

Still chuckling, Kirk asked, "Did you kill him?"

Leslie wagged his head, ruefully. "No. He's upstairs in p.c.—protective custody—and refuses to come out, so I guess I won't get to see him any more. . . ."

Kirk laughed some more. "How long was your hair—to your waist?"

Leslie stuck out his tongue again. "You're not cute even a little bit," he said with a campy pout. "It wasn't a bit longer than it is now—and yours is longer than that." After a pause he went on, explaining, serious: "See, I'm a teensy bit fruity, and I brush my hair kind of gay, but that isn't what gets them mad—it's something else. Those bastard bulls, and convicts, too—some of the rat-bastards wearing blues around this dump have more cop in them than Dick Tracy—anyway, they get uptight or something, then get together and go looking for a queer to stomp." He grimaced bitterly. "See, those queer-hating bastards are queerer than me. . . . It's true. They stand around talking about this pervert this and that queer that—and then, when they think nobody's around, they whisper sick-shit in my ear . . . the bulls, too . . . really. But the convicts are worse . . . the ones that think nobody knows about them, about the things they eat. . . . They're the worst kind of queer-haters." He smiled uneasily and nibbled a finger. "I'm sorry. . . . I didn't mean to be bitchy. Let's talk about something else. . . ."

So they did. And swift hours later a guard entered the hallway to lock Leslie back in his cell—the third cell.

And Kirk stared blankly toward the door window, trying to understand where the time had gone, and why he was not sickened and revulsed. After all, he had been talking to a man—who was not—with plucked eyebrows and long fingernails and lilting speech and an ass that probably thought it was a cunt. He thought he might even like Leslie. A staggering thought . . . to like two people in a month . . . a killer-bandit and a giggling fag. . . .

He was swirling the little broom in the scummy toilet when he heard Leslie call to him.

"Stick your arm straight out the window. I have some things for you."

Kirk thought about it, but stuck his arm out anyway. And a moment later a bar of soap tied on a line of dental floss flew over his elbow, stopped abruptly, and hung there.

"Pull it in, baby," Leslie said.

He did, and found a torn sheet wrapped around some books, magazines, and cigarets. He stared at the things while a small warm spot grew in the back of his skull. He looked toward the window and smiled. "Thanks," he said. "Thanks."

"You probably won't get your property for a few days . . . so let me know if you need anything else. . . . Oh, and we can only draw canteen on Wednesdays. . . ."

"Thanks."

"Baby, you already said that," Leslie patiently informed him. "Now tell me I'm pretty or kind of nice or something."

"Fuck you."

"Is that a promise?"

43

"I'm going to bed." And he did. And dreamed of escaping, storming the wall with Sam . . . they had submachine guns . . . the guards had huge rifles that shot Ping-Pong balls . . . somewhere behind, a fag giggled. . . .

He awoke to hammering on the cell door and a guard saying, "Here it is . . . here it is. . . ."

Food. He smelled it. He scrambled off the bed, snatched up the tray, attacked the meal. When had he eaten last? He could not remember. He gobbled, gulped, and gobbled some more. Potatoes, yams, ham, pineapple sauce, biscuits, pie, all gone in three minutes. He looked wistfully at the tray, then slid it back under the door, and stared down at it. He was still hungry, thought he might always be hungry.

He paced. He thought. Two days, less than two days, Sam would be there. . . . They could get on with it . . . leave this scummy rathole behind. . . . But what about Leslie . . . ? Whatever they were going to do, wouldn't he see them? Would he rat? They couldn't take the chance . . . have to get rid of him some way. . . . How? Break him up, send him to the hospital? Maybe kill him? Maybe . . .

But for now he wanted to talk. . . . With a homosexual, a queer . . . ? Foolishness. But he wanted to talk . . . he *needed* somebody to talk with. . . . Bullshit, he had never needed anybody. All right then, he didn't need to talk, but he wanted to. . . . With a polished-fingernailed, tee-heeing pervert, a man-eating man?

"Knock it off and lay down, Whalen," he mumbled aloud. "Yeah, yeah, lay down. . . ." He walked to the bunk, sat on it, and stared out the back window. It was raining.

Then he was at the door calling to Leslie. "Hey," he heard himself say, "I haven't seen any meals like that since I've been here. . . ." What an idiotic thing to say, he thought, and went on: "Is that usual, or do they take better care of us in here?"

"Oh, silly," Leslie said, and giggled. "This is New Year's day."

"New Year's day?" Kirk repeated, mildly shocked. He had been behind the walls for almost a month . . . an incredibly long month . . . yet it seemed only yesterday that he had first been locked in the strip cell. . . . Where had those 19 nights gone . . . ? Col-

44

ored lights, a nude broad, Jesus, spiders . . . what about the rest of it? Where was he during the rest of it?

Leslie's voice interrupted his thoughts. "You want to talk for a little while? You lonely?"

"Lonely?" Kirk repeated in a slightly caustic tone. "Lonely?" He chuckled uneasily. "Hey, has anybody ever said that you sound fruity?"

Leslie laughed. "Never ever, *dah*-ling," he said with a swish in his voice. "You want to talk?"

"Yeah . . . yeah," said Kirk, hesitantly, uncomfortably, "for a while. . . ."

They talked. And talked. And breakfast arrived.

[X]

"Hey, Whalen . . . Whalen . . . Hey, you punk kid. . . ."

Kirk shook himself awake and looked toward the door, a snarl in his mind. He saw a guard.

"Hey, you missed lunch . . . musta been feeding you pretty good in the shit-hole. . . . You wanna exercise with the queer?" The guard was grinning an ugly, lopsided grin.

It was Yancy. Kirk chuckled. "Yeah," he said as he pulled himself up, "get me out of here for a while." He grinned at the lumpy-faced guard and suddenly, unbidden, more words rushed from his mouth. "If you were a girl, I'd marry you."

While he was being amazed and dumbfounded by what he had said, the big guard peered closely at him and finally laughed, a deep and rumbling laugh. "You talk that shit, kid, and after you catch a shave, I'm liable to marry you."

Kirk laughed. "Seriously," he said, "I might not have died, but you made it a lot easier to live. . . ."

"Keep talking and we're gonna be fighting," Yancy said. "I don't know what you're saying. . . ." He paused, and went on with: "I've already unlocked your door, so in a few minutes you'll hear a click; that means I've thrown the deadlock out front. You've got to push the door open in about ten seconds or the deadlock'll be back on. You don't have to come out—but if you do, push the door shut again, or a tattletale light'll tell me you're up to something. I'm the only bull on right now, and I'll be working up front . . . so don't let

45

me catch you kissing that fruiter or you'll be back with your friend in the shit-hole." Yancy grinned, hit the door, and was gone.

Kirk stared after the massive-bodied, lumpy-faced guard, feeling puzzled, curious, uneasy. Yancy had given him tacit consent to do whatever he wanted with Leslie; Yancy had given him food when the big people decided he should be hungry; Yancy, prison guard. . . . Convicts had a basic tenet: Don't talk to the guards, don't be seen in the man's ear, don't go near a bull, a screw. Of course, being convicts, rules meant little—even their own rules. In the week he had celled among the main population, convicts were constantly holding the guards in conversation, and he had wondered at it, wondered how they got away with it, how they did it so openly. Then it came to him: convicts could talk with guards, could violate all their own quasi-edicts, and remain unharmed and secure within their cliques and "tips"; but only as long as they did not fall from grace for anything—from being suddenly disliked to informing, from being too tough to handle to too weak to fight. It was typical, he thought, typical of people everywhere. How he despised them . . . convicts . . . people everywhere. . . . But maybe he despised convicts a little more. . . . They were not content to be actors in a minor hoax. . . . No, they sneered and snarled and cursed and made binding laws and broke them . . . actors in some giant hoax . . . playing at good guys and bad guys, cowboys and Indians, cops and robbers. . . . And the bulls . . . they needed no prompting with their act . . . tobacco-chewing, lunger-spitting movie tough guys, wearing hats pulled to the bridge of their nose like Marine tough guys, talking like . . . like Yancy. . . .

He chuckled to himself, then heard a click, and pushed the door open. Stepping into the hallway, he looked toward Leslie's cell, and almost fell down.

Leslie minced and swished and pranced, jiggling all over, with a flaunted limp wrist. He was small, a head shorter than Kirk, making him about five four or five five, delicate-boned, tiny-waisted, heavy-hipped. He looked like an overly effeminate girl; a girl without tits, Kirk amended, and could not imagine Leslie stabbing anybody. He gawked, suddenly uneasy. It was as if he were confronted by some demanding criteria that he must live up to; as if Leslie, being a man, yet not, demanded that he prove his own manliness. It was idiotic, asinine. . . . But still he was left with a bewildering embarrassment, an uneasiness he had never experienced. He continued to gawk.

Leslie fixed him with a sardonic stare, a plucked eyebrow cocked, and Kirk wanted to say something flippant and casual. He opened his mouth to speak, and it stayed open. Nothing came out. He felt his face grow warm, and wondered what was wrong with him. He had been able to talk all right when he could not see Leslie's body; and he had babbled for hour upon hour last night, spilling out things that made him hurt, made him laugh, acid and honey; and now he could not talk. Maybe it was being shut away, unable to see Leslie, that loosened his tongue . . . like a goddamn confessional. . . . That's how those righteous creeps do it, that's how they get inside your skull. . . . He mentally cursed his weakness, the unnatural compulsion to divulge. . . .

And still he gawked. And he wondered if his embarrassment was because of a lingering sense of decorum, somebody else's morals, or because . . . well, because Leslie might, by reason of sordid and painful experience, be far wiser, far more observant in the ways of men . . . and because of it, find him lacking. So what if he does? he asked himself, and mentally shrugged. He didn't care . . . he didn't care . . . except that he kept gawking and feeling very young and timid, and knew he did care, but did not know why he should.

"Gawd!" Leslie exclaimed after a long silent minute. "Close your mouth! You act like you've never seen a fag." The little fruit minced closer and stared searchingly at Kirk. "Damn, baby, you smell horrid. . . . Let's go shower. Yancy always leaves some towels and clean clothes for us." He giggled. "Come on, baby," he said, and took Kirk's arm. "I promise not to molest you."

At the touch of the hand, Kirk shivered, jerked away. Leslie cast him a questioning look, shrugged, and went jiggling down the hall. He followed, finally managing to get his mouth closed, and stared at Leslie's swishing, undulating hips. "Damn!" he muttered. And before he realized that he had said anything, Leslie spun around and caught him staring. Raising his eyes, Kirk attempted nonchalantly to meet Leslie's, and felt himself reddening. He looked at the floor, then at Leslie, then back at the floor. He shuffled his feet, fidgeted. "Oh, fuck!" he spat, and snickered nervously. He was a complete damn fool, a twelve-year-old kid playing spin the bottle with high-school girls.

Leslie grinned delightedly. "Don't feel bad about looking," he said with a leer, "everybody does. I'm kind of modest, too . . . but, baby, when women lose their tempers, and when . . . how many . . . ? Anyhow, *all* those guys can't be wrong." He wrinkled his nose.

Kirk laughed, suddenly, inexplicably, at ease. "Well," he said, "you save it for them that like it. You have a hell of an ass for a boy, but I like mine without all the extra meat."

"I don't have one of those *things,*" he said, and flapped his arms in frustration. "Only a teensy one maybe . . . but around this dump, I'm a real prize . . . so treat me nice." He curtsied.

Kirk shook his head and stared. "Do that again," he said, and Leslie did, and he walked off shaking his head. It was too much all at once.

He passed the fourth cell door and noticed a fifth door, leading to the walled yard back of the cells. Across from the door, about 15 feet from the end of the block, a tiled three-nozzle shower was recessed some two yards into the wall. There was a knee-high tiled curb across the front of the shower which he sat on and began peeling off his clothes. He stank. It was three weeks since he had showered. He stank unbelievably; everywhere he turned to get some clean air he breathed stink. He stood and began stripping off his shorts, and saw Leslie scrutinizing him.

"Knock that shit off," he said, uneasy and embarrassed. "People'll thing you're queer."

Wrinkling his nose, Leslie licked his lips, and said, "Just casing the body, dear," and when Kirk's shorts dropped, added, "Well, you're all there anyway . . . not that it's anything to write home about."

He looked down at himself. "It's all I have. . . . Besides, nobody's ever complained." He cursed himself for feeling defensive, he cursed the queer son of a bitch who made him feel that way, but he cursed silently, to himself.

"Cool it, baby, you've got your issue . . . a teensy bit more maybe. And you can take it from me—bodies are my business." He giggled, and daintily began removing his clothing.

Turning, Kirk twisted the faucet and let the needles of water sting his face, then heard a second shower. He pulled his face from the spray and opened his eyes. By now, after almost a month in prison, he thought he was unshockable; but when he saw Leslie's

48

sleek-shaven body, he choked, squeezed his eyes closed again, and put his face back under the water, and thought about it.

Suddenly he turned. "Leslie," he said abruptly, "do you mind . . . er . . . uh . . . ." He felt himself reddening under Leslie's quiz-zical gaze.

Leslie grinned. "Why're you a faggot, Leslie?" he said in an ex-aggerated bass. "What's a nice boy like you . . . ? Is that it?" He looked closely at Kirk.

"Well . . . uh . . . yeah," Kirk stammered, and studied the water swirling in the drain.

"There's really not much to it," Leslie began. "I guess I'm kind of a typical psych-book case history: overbearing-slob father; lovey-dovey mother that wanted a girl, but couldn't name a boy Judy. . . . I guess I understand all that pretty well, but even so, I'm one of those weird kind of fags that digs being gay. Oh, I don't like being laughed at and beat up . . . I don't dig pain. . . . But I like men, I just like men. I don't mess with kids or sneak around in pub-lic toilets . . . or sell it. . . . I just get icky for a guy, and stick around till it's over. . . ." Breaking off, he stared blankly across the hall, then went on, sounding far away. "Sometimes I'm a drag queen . . . but mostly I'm just a boy. I used to wish I was a girl. See, when a guy suddenly finds out he's funny, a lot of them pre-tend it isn't so, and stick their heads in the sand—like an ostrich—or they run to a doctor and try to get their whammer chopped off." He smiled apologetically. "I tried both . . . but the sand wouldn't hide me, and the doctors wanted to wait till I turned twenty-one or had the money . . . whichever came first, I guess. So I lay around crying a lot, whenever I wasn't out trying to play football. . . . Then one morning I woke up and said, 'I'm a queer,' and fixed my eyebrows, squirmed into some awful tight pink pants, and prac-ticed walking around my bedroom till I was ready. Then I swished out to the living room and told my father something like, 'Daddy, *dah*-ling, look closely at your baby boy, Leslie Lemman, now a dirty pervert.' " He laughed for a moment, then, "Anyhow, dear old dad jumped up to murder me, I guess, but he had asthma pretty bad and finally fell down and turned blue. I discovered that trick when I was just a baby. . . . I used to make him turn blue an awful lot, I guess. Anyhow, while he was laying there trying to breathe, I ran around the house and stole a bunch of things, money, check-books . . . and his car keys. That's when I left. I never went back. I

49

send mom a postcard every so often, but I haven't heard from her for . . . my Gawd! it's been almost six years. . . . I left when I was fifteen . . . almost fifteen." He shrugged. "Then about three years ago I started sticking people up. . . . I fell about a year ago, a little less."

"You're a robber?" Kirk blurted in disbelief.

"And why not, baby?" Leslie said. "Even a fruit can lift a gun. And in drag it's pretty hard for them to catch me." He grinned sourly. "Don't start thinking that silly bit about the-gun-is-your-manhood. I'll admit I don't like to work, but I have. . . . And don't you just know what always happens . . . ?"

Kirk snorted. "Yeah," he said, "I guess I do. But, damn . . . I think if you came in to stick me up, I'd fall over laughing. Maybe not. . . . Like with that big hideous bull, Yancy . . . I just knew he was some kind of asshole. Then he—" Slamming his mouth shut, he cursed himself. The guard had fed him, now he was going to sell him out to a queer. He despised himself for making a stock judgment—Leslie is a queer, ergo a sleazy character—a judgment of the typical sort he held others in contempt for making. He fidgeted.

Leslie eyed him mockingly. "Don't tell a greasy-butt queer anything."

Kirk looked away. "I didn't say that."

"You were thinking it."

"Get out of my head."

"Baby . . . can I tell you something?"

"Tell. But knock off that 'baby' shit." Kirk looked up, glaring, suddenly taken with an urge to flatten Leslie's prissy little nose.

Leslie looked back at him for a moment, then his eyes filled with tears, and he turned away. "I'm sorry, bab—Kirk. I'll see you later." He started to shut off the shower.

But, unaccountably, Kirk found himself pulling the polished-fingernailed hand from the faucet. "Quit acting like a damn fool," he said hoarsely, feeling ridiculous. "Now, what were you going to say?"

Leslie looked down at his hands. "I'm only a fag," he began, "and a lot of the goons around this dump don't think they should tell fags anything. It hurts my feelings a little, I guess, but not too much. See, Yancy's a good cop, he does a lot of things for guys, but he won't mess with anybody that rats . . . and I know more about him than a thousand of the goons walking around here that like to think that fags are rats. Yancy looks out for me. . . . He's the one that told me about you. . . . Maybe it just means he's got bad judgment, but he's been working in this place since you and me were in diapers, and he hasn't been fired yet. The administration doesn't like him . . . they hear stories, I guess . . . and he knows it, so when he does something for a guy, he's pretty damn sure he isn't going to get turned in. And, bab—Kirk, there aren't many guys he does things for—but I'm one of them—so you figure out what that means. He won't take any money to run things inside or anything, but he steals food for some of the guys and tears up bum-beefs and other little things when he thinks a guy is getting messed with." He looked up. "Sometimes that big ugly bastard makes me want to cry," he said, and again his eyes filled with tears.

Kirk looked away, uncomfortable. "Do something with yourself. . . . You're acting like a fourteen-year-old broad," he said, and made himself look back at Leslie. "I don't know much. . . . All I know is that I spent a couple months in jail fighting this beef and a week here, listening to all the tough guys talking about all the stool pigeons. And you know what they say. . . ."

Leslie's mouth twisted bitterly. "Yeah, I know," he said. "But I know something else. . . . One more speech, okay? Just a little one." Kirk nodded, and he continued. "All the goons that knock queers bend me out of shape. About two percent of them are really serious—they just hate homos. About half of the other queer-haters are scared of their own secret fears. And the rest of them blither about hating queers 'cause it's something that everybody else talks about. Now let me tell you a teensy secret: since I've been here, I've gone to bed with a few guys, and all of them were queer-haters. Not only that, but I could go to bed with damn near all the queer-haters if they were sure that nobody'd find out about it. In fact, just to prove it, I used to lure them off to the side. . . . And you know what? The next thing I knew, they had my thing swallowed to the whiskers . . . and when they were finished and wiping their mouths off, they'd tell me all the different ways they'd murder me if I told anybody." He smiled. "They're about as frightening as Mighty Mouse . . . but I don't say anything 'cause I like having it on them. And really, I don't even like a guy to notice that I've got one . . . one of them." He reddened and turned away, and tucked the thing between his legs.

51

Kirk laughed. "You stupid fag, what's that hanging out the back?"

"Oh, you . . . hush!" Leslie fidgeted around, then turned and punched at him. "Anyhow," he went on, "when you get out of here, you check around. Don't listen to the goons—most of them don't know what day it is—just watch with your own eyes. And then you decide who rats more often: the fags or the supposed tough guys. End of speech." Wrinkling his nose, he stuck out his tongue, and punched Kirk's arm. With that he turned off the shower and raked a fingernail down Kirk's chest.

They dried, dressed, and began pacing the hall together. They were silent.

The hall was 18 paces long, ten or 11 paces more with shorter steps. . . . Sam, killer-bandit . . . Leslie, queer-bandit. . . . A particular type of acoustical tiling has 421 holes; the tiles are square; what is the square root of 421? . . . Thirteen bars across the front of an isolation cell; why 13? . . . Three guard shifts a day; each shift works seven hours and 45 minutes; how many hours in a day? . . . A prison toilet gulps bedsheets; why does it spit back turds? . . . Why do convicts habitually fondle themselves? . . . Why are they always in a hurry to get nowhere? . . . A killer-bandit . . . a queer-bandit . . . two killers and a queer . . . or maybe he and Sam are the queers, and Leslie the killer. . . . Little creep swallows whole cities in a single gulp . . . and that ass—genocidal. . . . Bah! what about women? . . . Just another way to go. . . . But Leslie isn't a woman—he can only kill men's seed . . . but so have I, so has Sam . . . so do women. . . . come right down to it, Leslie might be doing the right thing . . . kill the seed before others kill the minds, finally the bodies . . . support birth control, fuck a boy. . . .

"Bah!" Kirk spat, and snarled up at the ceiling. *"Fuck!"*

Leslie stopped beside him and leered. "Baby, you start throwing words like that around, and I'll get all wet and icky," he said, and added: "What's wrong?"

"Nothing," Kirk said. "Everything. It's this stinking garbage can—what a foul rathole!"

Leslie touched his arm, his eyes suddenly sad and thoughtful. "Baby . . . oh, I'm sorry," he began. "Kirk, don't mind me. . . . It's just the lady's intuition or something. . . . You think an awful lot, huh?" Kirk wagged his head, and Leslie touched his arm again.

52

"Don't shake your head to mama. . . . I can tell. Baby, don't do it . . . don't think, not around here. If you want, think about how to make better burlap bags, or a better way to sew on T-shirt sleeves, or how to turn out lots more license plates out in the industries . . . but nothing else, baby." He frowned. "Maybe you don't know it, but that's what's wrong with Sammy. . . . he clowns around a lot, but inside he's all messed up. . . . He thinks about that life sentence. . . . It's eating him up. . . . He's got four years in on it, and ten or 12 to go, and he figures he's all washed up. Maybe he is, I don't know. But if you think, and he thinks, and you two start messing around together, you're going to poison each other. . . . You'll end up slaughtering a pile of these goons that've needed slaughtering since they slid down the gash . . . but you'll have to breathe cyanide for it. It's not a fair trade." Leslie looked at him with mournful eyes.

Kirk looked back, eyes hodded, teeth bared. "Don't try to know my thoughts, fag," he said flatly. "And I told you before—get out of my head." He felt tiny, dwarfed, stunted under Leslie's pained gaze. "Yeah," he went on as Leslie's eyes filled with tears, "cry. Cry, fag."

"Why're you such a bastard?"

"Why're you a freak?"

Leslie suddenly giggled, and wiped the tears away. "We're both freaks," he said. "You scowl and I cry. . . ."

Abruptly, Kirk laughed, and grabbed a handful of Leslie's bangs and pulled, not too hard, but more than enough to hurt. "All right," he said, "don't try to crawl around in my head—or my bed —and we'll be friends. I'll stop being a creep, you stop crying."

"Nice weather we're having."

Kirk laughed. "That's my line, you goofy fruit. Let's walk."

They did, and talked a little; then Yancy came through the hall door.

The big guard twisted his knobby face into a mocking leer. "Ain't holding hands, eh?" he said. "Hey, kid, did you knock a little off in the shower?"

Leslie swished toward him, wiggling more than usual, flapping two limp wrists. "Oh, Yancy," he gushed, "you gorgeous man. Let me see that marvelous thing of yours."

Yancy, all six feet four, 240 pounds of him, blushed. He hopped away from Leslie, flopping his hands, making fists, cursing. But

mostly he flushed and sputtered. "Get . . . get away, you fag! Goddamn it . . . get away . . . get away, you queer!"

"*Dah*-ling, take off your clothes." Leslie followed him around
and around.

And Yancy kept dancing around, and cursing and flushing and
sputtering. "Whalen! You don't get this fruiter son of a bitch away
from me, you're going back to the hole!"

Kirk laughed until his sides hurt, then flapped a limp-wristed
hand, and said in a screechy falsetto "Oh, Leslie! You leave that
man be! He's mine!"

Yancy fell against the wall, slack-jawed, gawking. "Oh, no," he
mumbled. "I'm a grandfather. . . . I got kids older than you two
brats. . . . Hey, kid, you ain't really a fag, too, are you?" His eyes
were almost beseeching. "Come on, Whalen . . . be a sport, kid.
. . . Get this man-eater off me. . . . Every time I come in here, he
—*she*—damn near rapes me. What'd happen if one of the other
bulls seen that? Whew!" He looked at them both—one laughing,
the other swishing round and round—and he bolted back through
the open door.

And was back in a moment with a stubby broomstick. He glowered, snarled, scowled.

Leslie minced toward him and brushed the stick aside.

Yancy dropped the stick and leaned resignedly against the wall,
as if having accepted rape's inevitability. He might have been a
very small boy petrified by a tiny kitten. "Come on," he mumbled
pleadingly.

"You big scaredy goon," said Leslie, giggling, and walked to his
cell without a wiggle. Yancy sneaked along behind, keyed open the
door, and shoved him inside.

The big guard leaned against the wall for a moment, sighing.
Then he locked Kirk in his cell and stuck his face to the window,
looking like some mad artist's painting on a too-small canvas.
"Hey, kid," he said, "that's a good solid fag . . . but goddamn it, I
got grandkids and everything. . . . Be a sport, kid, tell him to give
me a break. I know you guys get kinda horny and fuck these fags—
but it ain't none of me. I got grandkids and everything. . . . Maybe
25, 30 years ago, I'd of buggered me one . . . to see what it was
like, maybe. But goddamn, not now. . . . Just think what they'd
say if they saw that fag messing with me like that. . . . I got grandkids and everything."

Kirk stared blankly at the big guard, feeling something writhe around inside his head. And then, as if watching from afar, he saw himself lean close to the window and whisper conspiratorially. "Listen, we both know the fag is playing with you. But if you want him to knock it off, I'll tell you all you have to do—three'll get you seven he wishes you were his father, so there's an easy remedy: grab him, and kiss him. Easy. . . ."

Yancy stared, wide-eyed. "*Kiss* him?" he said in bewilderment. "Kiss him? Are you some kinda nut? Why don't you kiss him?"

Kirk thought about it. "Yeah . . . yeah, we'll have to think of something else." But for now all he wanted was to have the big guard leave his cell; he needed to think. . . .

And Yancy did leave, finally, mumbling, wagging his head. The convict stuck his face to the window and watched the big guard disappear. He thought he knew how Yancy felt. There were a lot of things beyond him, too.

[XI]

An aged, withered guard opened his door, shoved a box inside, and had Kirk sign a receipt for it. It was his property.

After the guard had gone, Kirk stared down at the little box, and chuckled sourly. His property, his life's possessions: two paper-bound books, 12 packs of cigarets, a ratty toothbrush, a hairbrush, a cigaret lighter, and finally, a prison rule book. He chuckled some more, then slammed a foot into the box, sent it crashing into the wall, spilling. Reaching down, he snatched up the rule book, shredded it, flushed it. He grinned and began brushing his teeth.

Later Yancy brought him a razor and a beat-up stainless-steel mirror. He made faces at himself and stared for a long while into his eyes. The dark, amber-flecked orbs looked back at him, slightly glazed, slightly haunted, slightly far away. They looked a lot like convicts' eyes. . . . He tried to see behind them, but finally gave it up and started shaving.

He was still trying to scrape off the wiry growth when Sam passed the cell window. Putting his lathered, half-shaven face to the door, Kirk called, "Sam!"

"Where're you at?"

"Back here . . . first cell."

Sam came to the window and peered in. His face was drawn and haggard; his beard and hair, long and scraggly. He was grinning.

"Hey, fella," said a guard behind him, "keep moving."

"Fuck off," Sam told him; then to Kirk: "Buzz down to my cell when you exercise this afternoon . . . right next door." He paused. "We alone?"

Kirk wagged his head. "A fruit," he said, "says he knows you."

Sam's mouth tightened, his lips curled under, his eye began to tic. "*Shit!*" he hissed. "Name?"

"Leslie."

Then he was laughing. "Green light. Later." He went obediently to his cell.

A moment after the escorting guards had slammed the door and stomped from the hall, Kirk heard Leslie call out.

"That you, Sammy?"

"Don't smell much like me," Sam answered, "but I guess so. Saw a lot of super-strange things this trip . . . a Gypsy fiddler, weird fucking animals . . . going out of my head." He paused. "How you been, Les?"

"I'm shaving my legs right now—in case that means anything." He giggled. "And I like your friend, but he's kind of scared of me."

Sam laughed. "He'll get over it," he said. "But while he is, why don't you strap a little on me?"

"Marry me?"

"Up yours, sugar. Marry Kirk."

"Up both yours," Kirk interjected; two laughed, one giggled, and all fell silent.

When the door clicked unlocked after lunch, Kirk stepped into the hall and saw Leslie walking toward Sam's cell. He did, too.

Sam was standing at the window, grinning crookedly. "Fuck off for a while, Les," he said. "Me and Kirk have boy-talk."

Leslie looked first at one, then at the other, and smiled weakly. "Okay," he said softly, a little forlornly, and ambled off, looking as if he had some place to go.

Kirk glanced at Sam, who was grinning unabashedly, apparently oblivious to the sting in his words, Leslie's reaction.

"Drew something for you last night," Sam said, and fished a folded paper from his pocket. "It's the insides of a lock. Study it.

56

And when they give me my shoes and property, I'll lay some picks and a tension bar on you. Meantime, study the drawing. When you can pick a lock in ten seconds with your eyes closed, we'll move." He paused. "I can open them, but you ain't got the experience to keep a screw hung up in conversation." He frowned.

"One thing," Kirk said. "Whatever we're going to be doing . . . what about the fag?"

Sam's face tightened, his eyes probed Kirk's. "I got a pal," he said with studied nonchalance, "that'll smuggle me whatever I want in here. . . ."

Kirk stared at him curiously. "That's too mysterious," he said. "What do you mean?"

Sam grinned again, a tight and thin-lipped grin. "How would you say we should get him out of the way?"

He thought about it. "You think he might rat?"

"I know a way we wouldn't have to find out. . . ."

"How?"

"Have some dope smuggled in . . . pills . . . a capsule of cyanide. Fruits are always committing suicide around here. . . . One more won't make much difference. . . ."

Kirk pondered. "Probably be fairly simple," he said musingly, then added: "Can we use him? Do we need any help?"

Frowning, Sam chewed his lip. "Yeah," he said after a moment, "yeah . . . we could use her, she could smooth the way. . . . What do you think?"

Kirk grinned. "First, I don't think he's a her," he said, feeling vaguely relieved. "Second, I don't know enough about him . . . just that he has a peter habit. . . . You're going to have to do the thinking there; you've known him for a while."

Sam grinned easily. "I'm game if you are."

Kirk looked down the hall toward Leslie, who was leaning against the wall, facing him. "Come here, fag," Kirk called. "You get to play with us now."

Leslie pranced to Sam's cell, smiling.

They talked and schemed and conspired.

And soon Yancy entered the hall: lock-up time. Leslie swished toward the big guard, but Yancy held up a hand.

"Don't fuck around," he said. "I got something to tell you clowns." He paused. "There's a protective-custody case coming back here tomorrow . . . upstairs is filled up. Some of the cons made a try for his air. . . . He requested indefinite lock-up." He grinned. "He's a stool pigeon. . . . Sure hope you clowns keep a particular bull's name out of your mouths."

Kirk looked at the others; they looked back with troubled eyes. Then they all grinned at the guard, and Leslie chased him around while Sam cheered him on and Kirk laughed.

And finally Yancy got the two convicts into their cells. As he was walking from Kirk's door, the convict's roiling brain suddenly screeched to a stop.

"Hey, Yancy," he called to the guard's retreating back, and when he turned around, went on. "Today's Tuesday, isn't it?" Yancy nodded, and he continued. "Canteen order day?"

Yancy wagged his head and looked at his watch. "You're about an hour and a half late—supposed to be in by 2:30."

The convict pulled a long face and stared down at the floor.

"Aw, come on, come on," Yancy said gruffly. "Write down what you want and I'll drop it off at the canteen."

Kirk grinned gratefully and wrote down what he wanted, then stuck his face to the window and watched the guard walk from the hall. When he was gone, Kirk called out. "The rat's going to get a cell move." There was no answer, there was nothing to say . . . not aloud. The convict turned to the bunk and stretched out on it, grinning up at the ceiling.

The three convicts paced the hall while Kirk outlined what he had in mind for the informer who had earlier been moved into the fourth cell; when he was finished, Sam worried his lip, Leslie frowned.

"Bad deal," Sam said after a long silence.

"It is, baby," Leslie said, looking closely at Kirk. "It really is."

"Why?" Kirk asked, feeling a little crestfallen.

"You don't think the screws are going to let us get away with it, do you?" Sam asked, and cast Kirk a pained look.

"There's three of us," Kirk said. "How are they going to decide which one did it?"

"Oh, baby!" Leslie said impatiently.

Sam wagged his head. "Kirk," he said, as if to a small child, "do you think they'd have nightmares if they locked all three of us in

58

the strip cell? Do you really think they'd worry about injustice and all that other pious-shit?"

Kirk thought about it for a while. "Yeah," he said finally, "I suppose you're right. . . . It does sound a little stupid." He smiled sourly. "But I don't see any other way. . . . If the rat doesn't see us, he'll damn sure hear us. . . . So, either way, we're all in the strip cell . . . unless maybe you two want to invite the creep along," he finished on a sarcastic note.

The three convicts stood silently exchanging thoughtful glances. At length, Sam grinned widely and looked at Kirk. "We can do it your way," he said, "but it'll be a little risky. . . . Not too bad, though—if we're cool," and pausing, he went on slowly. "Check, you know what's wrong with these guys around here . . . us, too? I'll tell you. Instead of just thinking, 'Fuck you, Warden,' we say it out loud. All we do is make their jobs easier." He grinned bitterly. "Yeah, convicts ain't deceitful enough. They're notorious for ratting on themselves, not in words so much, but by refusing to cooperate. Now, me, I've learned a thing or two in four years. . . . I used to do things and snarl—now I do worse things and smile, fall all over myself being cooperative." He looked at the others. "You two want to learn how to be nice honest people?"

Kirk grinned. "Yeah, teach me," he said, and Leslie stuck out his tongue and said, "Aren't I nice like I am?"

Sam looked him over, but held class anyway; the others listened.

Later they went quietly to the fourth cell and peered in through the window. The informer was sleeping, rolled into a snoring ball at the head of the bed. The three convicts exchanged easy grins.

Shortly before lock-up Kirk unscrewed a dead light bulb that hung from the ceiling in the rear of the hall. None of the convicts thought it would be missed. It was not.

[XII]

"Canteen order, Whalen."

Kirk dropped the book he was reading and looked toward the door. A guard was peering in at him. The convict rolled off the bunk and padded to the door to accept the small paper sack that the guard pushed through; then he signed a receipt, went back to the bunk, and looked inside the bag. He laughed.

Going to the head of the bed, he reached underneath for the bulb he had stolen earlier in the day. With a pair of nail clippers, he worried the small soldered washer off the bottom of it, then chipped away the ceramic core. Finished, he inserted a pencil into the slender glass tube growing into the center of the globe, then twisted the pencil. The tube broke. He shook the bulb over the toilet. Shards of glass and filament fell out. The bulb was hollow. He grinned at it, then put it back under the bed.

A while later he fell asleep, grinning up at the ceiling.

A guard whom Kirk had never seen unlocked his door the following day for exercise. Yancy worked isolation Thursday and Friday. The convict thought about the ugly guard for a moment and was vaguely pleased that he would not have to see him again until the following Monday. He wondered why.

But then the door clicked, the deadlock was off, and the convict put his thoughts away and stepped into the hall. With Sam and Leslie, he crept quietly to the fourth cell and peered inside. The informer slept, seemingly unmoved from the previous day.

Going to the shower, the three undressed. And then Kirk filled the hollow light bulb with two cans of lighter fluid and plugged the hole with a wad of mattress cotton; finished with that, he handed Sam the bulb and struck a book of matches afire and charred the paint on the lighter-fluid cans. He layed the blistered cans on the floor, and covered them with his towel. He looked up at the others. They were staring raptly.

"Ready?" Kirk asked, and added an easy smile.

They nodded and twisted the shower faucets on. The noise was far from deafening, but it was all they had.

Kirk padded naked to the informer's cell, lit a match, and fired the cotton wadding. The little Molotov cocktail burned with a watery blue flame. Sticking his arm through the door window, he hurled the bomb at the wall above the informer's sleeping head. Then he ran to the shower.

A few moments passed before a hysterical, high-pitched scream sounded. Kirk grinned at the others. "Rare, medium, or well?" he asked, and began soaping his face. The screaming went on.

"What a punk," Sam said scornfully. "If it was gasoline, he'd have a reason to make all that noise. . . . He can't be hurting that bad." He washed his feet. The screaming continued.

"Honey," Leslie said, and leered at no one in particular, "all that bother is getting me excited." He grabbed for Kirk's crotch.

Kirk blocked his hand. "Be serious," he said, laughing. "You two ought to be feeling bad for leading me astray." The screaming went on, fading a little, taking on a whimpering tone.

"As soon as that sniveling punk decides to bust out one of the windows somebody's going to hear him," Sam said, looking at Kirk. "You'd best have those cans ready."

Kirk nodded. "The creep's not making much noise now," he said, grinning. And it was true, no more screams from the informer, just moans.

Suddenly the door at the end of the hall crashed open; three guards burst through, looked around, then ran toward the fourth cell, the cell billowing smoke, smoke smelling of sweaty cotton and burned flesh.

At the door window the three guards banged heads trying to look through; one finally made it and quickly swiveled away. "Son of a bitch!" he yelled. "Throw the deadlock! Get a stretcher!" The other two guards sprinted back through the door. The remaining guard then turned to the three convicts who now stood beside him, only one, Kirk, with anything over his nudity.

"What the hell happened here?" the guard demanded of them, then the deadlock clicked, and he turned his attention to keying open the door. He stared inside, blanched, and said, "Goddamn it! Don't just stand there! Get that guy outta there!"

Looking inside the smoky cell, Kirk choked down vomit. Back of him, Leslie gagged.

The informer, semiconscious, in shock, was sprawled on the floor, his head toward the back window. His face was blackened; except for two rolling red eyes and a purple mouth, it seemed covered with crisp scales, looking like an oversized and overtoasted marshmallow with frizzled hair. He was whimpering.

The mattress, smoldering, fogged the air with pissy-smelling smoke. And charred blankets were on the floor, soaking wet, partially covering the mess laying there. Evidently the informer had finally thought to use the water in the sink and toilet bowl.

Laying his towel carefully beside the door, Kirk stepped inside the cell and grabbed the informer's feet, then dragged him out and a little ways from the door. Dropping the feet, he stared curiously at the blackened face and noted that what appeared to be charred flesh was primarily burned blanket. He was slightly disheartened; but at the same time, he was glad. He found himself feeling something resembling pity. Looking up, he saw the guard eyeing the burned face with an expression of horrified revulsion. Then Sam and Leslie were on either side of the guard, chattering in his ears. The mess on the floor kept on moaning.

Easing backwards, out of the guard's sight, Kirk gathered up his towel, unwrapped the two blistered cans, and slipped inside the cell. He slid the cans under the bunk, then quickly gathered the largest shards of light bulb that he could find. Back outside the cell, he glanced toward the guard and saw that Sam had him in deep conversation, while Leslie stood to the side, bobbing his head in wide-eyed agreement to whatever Sam was saying. Kirk chuckled to himself as he raced to the shower, dropped the pieces of glass down the drain, and dressed.

Finished, he walked to the guard and gestured behind his shoulder. Sam and Leslie went toward the shower. "Yes, sir!" Kirk exclaimed, as if in wonderment. "It's hard to imagine, isn't it?" He stared down at the informer's glazed red eyes and wagged his head in perplexity.

The guard seemed unable to take his eyes off the burned convict. "That's what that other fellow was telling me," the guard said dazedly. "What a way to try it!" He paused and shook his head. "What the goddamn hell makes a guy want to commit suicide?"

Kirk kept wagging his head perplexedly. "It's hard to imagine," he said with a voice full of woe. "Hard to imagine."

Shortly, the prison "ambulance" came galloping through the hall door followed by the two guards. The ambulance was two green-clad convict hospital orderlies and a wire basket—ostensibly a stretcher. Setting the basket beside the informer, the two orderlies began lifting him into it.

"Hey, Hank!" Sam called suddenly, and came running from the shower.

One of the orderlies, a thin, sharp-faced convict in his late thirties, turned to look at Sam. "Hey!" he said, and added a weaselly smile. "How you been, Sam? When're you springing this dump?"

"Another 90 days . . . less, maybe," Sam said with a wink, then continued. "Hey, Hank, what do you think about a guy trying to check out by lighting himself on fire?"

Finished laying the informer in the basket, Hank looked back at Sam, his face devoid of expression. "Suicide, huh?" he said mildly. "Problems at home, maybe. . . ." He gazed compassionately upon the burned, whimpering convict.

"Yeah, Hank," Sam agreed, his eyes grieved and forlorn, "that's what he was saying before he lit the match . . . problems at home."

Hank lifted an end of the basket, and the ambulance went toward the hospital, the guards fidgeting in its wake. The hall door closed.

And the three convicts looked for a moment at one another; smirks exploded into laughter.

"Cool it, you two," Sam said finally. "This ain't finished till they question us. . . . Let's laugh then." He laughed then. "Cool it," he repeated, and straightened his face. The others fell silent, and he went on. "We lucked out; Hank'll have the whole hospital crew telling the man that the geek tried committing suicide. You can bet money that half of them will swear they heard the guy admitting it. . . . They'll probably really believe they did hear him, too." He paused. "Just hang tight and stick to the story. . . . we'll be all right."

Kirk smiled, feeling something clogging his throat, a warm spot in the back of his skull. He put an arm on each of the two convicts' shoulders. He started to speak, croaked hoarsely, and closed his mouth.

Suddenly Leslie slapped his arm away and wheeled, glaring with teary eyes. "You bastard!" he said intensely. "You dirty, dirty bastard!" He flailed at Kirk's chest with awkward fists.

"Hey!" Kirk jumped back, startled. "What's with you?"

Tears streaking his face, Leslie bared his little teeth. "You dirty bastard!" he said again. "I love you! You dirty son of a bitch!" He aimed a slap at Kirk's face, missed, and ran sobbing to the end of the hall, and collapsed against the wall.

Kirk gawked. Turning to Sam, he flapped his mouth, wordless. What had he done? How? His mind roiled, churned, but no answers . . . no answers. . . .

Sam's mouth twisted wryly, he rubbed his flattened nose. "You been fucking with the fag's hormones," he said with a happy grin.

"I'd tell you what I'd do about it, but you ain't been here long enough. And I don't feel sorry for you. . . . You should've seen it coming. . . . I did. The fag's got a case on you." He laughed briefly. "Close your mouth, you look like an asshole. And remember: you can't be friends with a fag without getting lugged. . . . I got kicked out of the fourth grade, and it didn't take a jolt to teach me that." He looked down the hall toward Leslie. "Just leave her be. . . . If everything works out all right, we'll be out of here a week from tomorrow. We can dump her somewheres. . . ."

Kirk nodded glumly, feeling as if trapped in something sticky, his thoughts a gummy mess of bubbling yellow gunk. Mumbling something to Sam, he shuffled to the end of the hall—away from Leslie—and sat, attempting to sort his thoughts, to still his inner maelstrom. And later, when a guard came to lock the convicts back in their cells, he was still trying, but more bedeviled than ever.

"Whalen . . . hey, Whalen. Put your clothes on, the A.W. wants you . . . right now."

Kirk glanced toward the door. A flashlight shone in his face. How long had he been staring into the dark? he wondered. It was late, seven or eight o'clock, he figured. They must be working overtime. He snapped on the cell light and began dressing, forcing his mind blank. Mistakes couldn't be made. . . . He would have to bear most of the questioning, for he was the newest to prison . . . inexperienced. . . . He would have to be careful . . . repeat each question slowly in his head . . . volunteer nothing . . . look ahead to questions his answers might raise . . . avoid pitfalls. . . . Otherwise he would get the three of them in more trouble than they could handle . . . the three of them. . . .

Dressed, the convict followed the impatient guard through the hall door to the small office used by the segregation guards. He was ordered to enter, and did, and recognized Associate Warden Lowry behind the desk shuffling through some papers—the inevitable papers. In the corner of the room sat a guard clad in a gray Air Force jumpsuit, glaring at him like a guilty conscience. The guard was a member of the "élite" Search and Security Squad, called, by themselves—and fittingly enough—the S.S. As the convict sat in the indicated chair, he offered the S.S. man a tremulous smile and watched disconcertion flash across the man's eyes. He was obviously not accustomed to being smiled at. Then the convict lent his attention to Lowry.

"Well, Whalen," the associate warden said quietly, but with the menacing tone underlying interrogations, "would you like to tell us about it?"

Grimacing, shaking his head with incomprehension and woe, Kirk met Lowry's probing eyes. "Well, sir," he began. "I suppose you're talking about the guy who lit himself on fire. . . ." He frowned thoughtfully. "Well, I was on my way to shower and I noticed that a new guy had come in. I stopped and said a word or two . . . you know, kind of like in greeting. Anyway, he started talking . . . raving, really, about his mother, I think it was—maybe someone else, I'm not too sure. . . . He was hard to understand." He shrugged apologetically. "Anyway, he kept yelling something like 'I'll show 'em!' Maybe I should've stayed and talked some more with him. . . . But I went on to the shower."

Lowry's nose twisted. He rubbed at it and fixed the convict with narrowed eyes. "Why didn't you try to get the officer's attention when the inmate started yelling?"

Puffing his lip and looking contemplative, Kirk answered slowly. "It's funny . . . I can't figure why, but I didn't hear anything till the guards slammed the door open. Probably because of the water running. All three showers . . ."

Lowry glanced up at the ceiling, apparently thinking about it, then back at the convict. "Where were the others . . . ?" He glanced down at the papers before him. "Robinson and Lemman?"

Kirk twisted his lip. "Umm . . . well," he began, frowning down at the desk, "let's see. . . . They were in the shower, too. No, wait . . . now I remember. . . . one of them, that Robinson guy, was doing push-ups, and the other one—that goddamn queer—was in the shower with me. Then Robinson got in, too. The queer was just getting out when the guards came running in." He shrugged regretfully. "That's about all I can remember. . . . Oh yeah, I pulled the poor guy out of the cell. . . ."

"Were either of the others standing around in front of the inmate's cell? Did you notice either of them carrying anything under their clothing?"

Knitting his brows together, Kirk gazed distractedly at the ceiling. Two questions; a right to the body, a left to the jaw; get flustered, make mistakes. He felt like grinning. "Well," he said pensively, "yeah . . . yeah. . . ."

Lowry leaned across the desk; the S.S. man straightened, moved closer. "Who?" Lowry said intensely. "What'd you see?"

Freezing a frown on his face, Kirk looked into Lowry's eyes. "What's his name . . . ? Robinson," he said hesitantly. "Robinson had a towel under his collar . . . like the damn fool thought it was a silk scarf or something." He wagged his head. "There sure are some weird characters around here. . . ."

Lowry and the S.S. man sagged like wind socks on a calm day, but kept their expressions deadpan by an obvious effort of will.

"Wait a minute, Whalen!" Lowry exclaimed suddenly, fixing the convict with eyes grown hot. He shuffled through the papers. "I remember you now," he said, all his attention focused on Kirk. "You're the one that threw your food on the isolation officer . . . you and Robinson. . . ." Pausing, his eyes took on a gloating cast. "So why are you trying to make us believe that you aren't friends with Robinson?"

Lowering his head, Kirk shuffled his feet and scrubbed his hands together. "Well, sir," he began hesitantly, "we aren't really friends. . . . You see, we were right next door to each other in isolation." He fell silent for a moment, then went on. "Anyway, some convict —I'm not saying who, I can't be a stool pigeon—called from down the way and said there was going to be a food strike . . . said everybody should throw their food at the guards . . . said anybody who didn't would get stabbed." He went on, wheedling, feeling foolish, wanting to laugh. "You see, sir, I live here. I have to go along with the cons even when I don't want to sometimes. . . . Anyway, when my tray came, I believed the son of a bitch. . . . I threw my tray . . . so did the guy next door. And you know what they did?" He glared indignantly at Lowry. "The bastards laughed. Yeah, they laughed while we had our asses stomped."

"That's not true!" Lowry interjected hastily.

"Yes, sir, it is," Kirk said woefully. "They laughed."

"I mean you weren't beaten." Lowry glared.

Kirk looked down. "It wasn't that bad, I guess."

The two men cleared their throats. "Then you didn't see anything that might indicate that one of the others threw a fire bomb into that inmate's cell?"

Eyes bulging, mouth gaped, Kirk stared. "You mean . . . ?" he said incredulously. "Oh no, sir! I mean . . . yeah, they're some pretty strange characters, but they wouldn't have done anything like *that*." It was getting out of hand, too corny; he decided to can the ham before it went bad. "Besides," he said with a thoughtful air, "how could something like that be done? How the hell could a guy make something like that? We're not allowed very much in there."

The associate warden sighed, deflated, and his eyes took on a kind fatherly cast. "I've spent more than half my life working here," he said pensively, "and if there's one thing I've learned, it's not to try to figure out how inmates do things. If it can't be done, sooner or later one of them does it anyway." He smiled slightly, almost apologetically. "Well, the inmate"—he glanced at the papers —"Stevenson's his name—isn't really burned all that bad, but he's saying he was fire-bombed." His mouth twisted wryly. "On the other hand, a couple of reliable convicts said that Stevenson told them that he did it himself. . . . Then there were the lighter-fluid cans under his bed. . . . And he's got a history of psychotic episodes, but most of the inmates do. . . . I don't know. . . ." Breaking off, he peered closely at the convict, then went on slowly. "How did you find out that the inmate was a stool pigeon?"

Win them over, soothe them, calm them; be kindly and understanding and chatty; they drop their guard; you stab them unexpectedly; guilt flashes across their eyes; you slam another question, then another; they wilt, they crumple, they confess all; they get a cup of coffee, a reassuring pat on the back, and a dark, dank cell. But Kirk had to bite his lip to keep from laughing.

"A stool pigeon?" he said indifferently, as if they were all around, which they were, then went on piously. "I didn't know anything about him . . . but stool pigeon or not . . ." he gazed into Lowry's eyes ". . . he was still a human being. . . ."

Lowry stared at him for a moment, then turned to the S.S. man. "Do you have anything to add, Sergeant?"

The sergeant fixed the convict with narrowed eyes. "If anything comes up," he said conspiratorially, "and you think we oughta know about it, you drop us a line, hear?"

Wide-eyed, ingenuous, Kirk looked at him. "You mean . . . ? You don't mean a stool pigeon . . . ?"

"Oh, no! No!" the sergeant exclaimed, sounding shocked at the very idea. "If somebody's endangering other guys' lives, it ain't being a stool pigeon to let us know. . . . That's bad thinking, real bad." He shook his head, frowning sadly. "A real man lets us know when a guy is packing a shiv or selling dope. . . . He feels safer. You can never tell with some of the hardcases we got around here." He smiled, making his eyes tighten, as if with pain. "So if you see things, you let us hear. . . . We'll keep you in cigs. . . ."

Staring at the S.S. man, Kirk wondered if he was joking, trying to set him up; if it was maybe a new wrinkle in interrogation tactics. Finally the convict glanced apprehensively around the room, as if to be certain no one else was listening. "Sure, Sarge," he said quietly. "Sure."

The S.S. man winked.

Biting his lip, Kirk turned quickly away and caught Lowry staring at the sergeant with undisguised contempt. The convict looked down at the desk, feeling like a bottle of soda pop, well shaken, about to explode. Holding a hand to his mouth, he coughed the mirth into his fist, then controlled himself and looked up.

Lowry was looking back at him, his teeth gritted, his mouth curled wryly. "All right, Whalen," he said tiredly, "you can go now. We still have to talk to the others."

Kirk gave the associate warden a grateful smile and strode from the office.

He lay in the dark, staring up at the ceiling, listening as Sam's door was unlocked. And short minutes later the convict was back, the interrogation over. Then Leslie was taken out and returned within minutes. Neither was gone long enough to indicate that the associate warden was doing anything more than going through the motions, apparently satisfied, amenable anyway, to the convicts' versions. Kirk smiled up at the ceiling, pleased with himself, content. He tried to conjure repulsive images of the man he had burned, but could not recall what he looked like. . . .

Weightless . . . bounding slow motion through tall, rippling grasses . . . flowers . . . someone with him . . . who? . . . faceless . . . a brook . . . a frog . . . more flowers . . . multihued . . . where? . . . who was with him? . . . graceful . . . someone called . . . who? . . . not behind . . . where? . . . azure sky . . . lavender orchid . . . calling again . . . far away, coming closer . . .

"Kirk! Answer me, you bastard!"

He bolted up, looked around, and moaned.

"Kirk, you bastard!" It was Leslie, sounding frustrated.

He stood to the door. "I was asleep," he said.

Subdued, apologetic, Leslie called back. "I'm sorry . . . I'm sorry. I thought you were ignoring me." He paused. "Put your arm out—I want to send you the line." Another pause, then venomously: "Sam, you bastard! If I hear you snickering, I'm going to make you my sister!"

Sam snickered. "Leslie, babe," he said, "Sam is sound asleep," and proved it with a loud snore.

Leslie made angry noises, then called out. "Kirk, is your arm ready?"

"Yeah," he lied, and made it the truth, and a moment later watched the line fall over his elbow. He pulled it in and found a folded paper attached to the soap weight. "Pull the line back," he called, then went to the bunk, flipped on the light, and read:

> Kirk baby, I'm sorry about today—really I am. But I'm not sorry about how I feel. And I don't want to be "just friends" (how I hate that phrase!). But I promise not to make any more scenes like today—one thing I can't stand is a teary fag. Maybe you'll change your mind, but if you don't I'll pretend it's all right. And you pretend you never got this stupid note.

It was signed "Love, Leslie." Kirk reread it, then folded it in half, started to tear it, hesitated, and read it again. He sat looking at it for a moment, finally shredded it and dropped the pieces in the toilet. A few words, readable, floated there. He punched the flush button. The bits of paper swirled, circling the bowl twice, then were sucked from sight. The toilet gurgled, filling itself, and he continued to stare into it, wondering where he was, where he had been, where he was going. . . .

Back of him lay maimed and broken bodies . . . a corpse . . . in front of him lay ten years . . . a ten-year sentence. . . . He might serve a year . . . or all of it. . . . No way to tell . . . nothing to hope for but hope . . . escape. . . . He would escape. . . . He would go newborn into the world with a killer and a queer . . . a queer who said he loved him . . . love . . . love . . . stupid word. . . . Who knows what love means? . . . anybody? . . . a queer, a fat-butt boy with bangs, a man-eating pervert? . . . Today a burned body . . . no remorse . . . none at all. . . . What would there be tomorrow? . . . More burned bodies? . . . Sam shoots them through the skull . . . neater, but still messy. . . . Leslie swallows them, suffocates them in fevered intestines . . . a lot neater than shooting them . . . or cleaving their skulls with parking meters . . . and sodomy can't smell worse than burning flesh. . . . But it's all dead . . . all dead. . . . The living must be beyond the wall. . . . He couldn't remember . . . but it seemed that they were dead, too . . . balls in a pinball machine . . . bouncing, glancing, rebounding, but sooner or later rolling leadenly, mindlessly, to the grave. . . . what was it all about? . . . Where was it going? . . . Was it haphazard, chance, a freak of nature? . . . Was nature a freak? . . . Was something at the reins? . . . some sinister consciousness? . . . a consciousness lusting for blood, gore, death? . . . a consciousness with a need for dank, gray prison? . . . Was there life beyond the walls? . . . life . . . how much more death before he found life? . . .

[XIII]

He looked at Leslie, Leslie looked at him, and they both looked at the floor and shuffled their feet.

"Will you look at this?" Sam said sourly. "Will you look at the two geeks? Holy-fucking-Christ!" He raised his face to the concrete heaven. "They're blushing . . . they're *blushing*," he said, almost making it a baffled question.

"Dry up, Sam," Kirk muttered.

"You're a bastard, Sam," Leslie said, and slapped at him.

"Come on, Romeo," Sam said derisively, "we got things to do." Kirk avoided looking at Leslie. "What's up?"

Sam fished in a pocket and pulled out a padlock, two long, slender pieces of steel, and an L-shaped piece of thicker steel. "Here," he said, handing everything to Kirk, "I got my property this morning," and, after a pause, added: "You been studying the drawing?"

"Yeah," Kirk said, and dropped the things into his pocket.

"Be careful of them picks," Sam said. "They're all we got. Without them, nothing goes." Then he looked from Kirk to Leslie and back again. He grinned maliciously. "Why don't you two geeks try looking at each other?"

They did, and Leslie giggled, and Kirk frowned. "Let's be just friends," Kirk said, and Leslie called him a bastard. They laughed, and could look at one another.

"Okay," Sam broke into their look, "we'll make the first move Tuesday." He faced Kirk. "That gives you the weekend and Monday to get ready . . . plenty of time. Sunday we'll give the yard a good looking over." He grinned, wide and lopsided. "A week from now, we'll either be going to the streets . . . or the hole."

Kirk didn't hear him, there was something in his mind, something clamoring for release, struggling to break from the fog in his head. Then it was there, bright, glaring. "Not Tuesday," he said abruptly.

Sam looked at him curiously. "What's the deal?"

Kirk glanced from Sam to Leslie to the ground. He squirmed, silently cursing himself, feeling as though he'd been caught stealing dimes from a wishing well. Finally, belligerently, he looked up, glaring. "All right," he said through bared teeth, "I'll tell you what the deal is. One word: Yancy." He looked down at the floor again. "He only works over here three days a week. . . . Call me whatever you want, but I don't want to move when he's on. Somebody's going to get the shaft. . . . I don't want it to be him." Looking up, he glared at them for a moment, then wheeled and stomped to the other end of the hall, and squatted down, glowering.

Moments later Leslie hurried toward him, swishing. "Baby," he said as he sat beside Kirk, "don't be like that. I don't want anything to happen to Yancy, either." He looked down the hall toward Sam and gestured. "Come here," he called, and when Sam approached, went on. "Why not over the weekend or Thursday?"

Sam shrugged. "Tuesday'd be better. Otherwise there's too much time for them to figure out what we've done." He frowned. "As it is, Tuesday's a long time before Friday, but I wanted a little air in case we miss the first time. If we move Thursday and miss . . ."

"Sammy . . . ?" Leslie looked up at him pleadingly.

Sam grinned sardonically. "Okay," he said, "we can't take the chance on trying over the weekend . . . too long to wait . . ." He grabbed a handful of Leslie's hair. "We'll make it Thursday. Damn . . ." he said, wagging his head, "what would the fellas

71

say . . . ?" He laughed. "When we spring, let's all join a choir."

Abashed, Kirk glanced at Leslie. "The creep doesn't understand the pure in heart," he said, and looked closely at Sam. "I don't have any more use for these mindless baboons in khaki than anybody else. But that ugly cop is different. . . . Not just because he gives us food . . . it's something else. . . ." He frowned. "All I know for sure is that he manages to act outside the rules without hurting anybody. You know what happens when we act outside the rules?" He grinned sourly. "It's a hell of a way to make a garden grow." He stared at the concrete, thoughtful. "Maybe Yancy has brain damage, maybe he's a mutant. . . . But he's bigger than this dump . . . maybe he's what they call human." He stood. "I'd slit his throat quicker than I'd destroy his faith. . . . Whatever the hell I mean by that." He strode to the other end of the hall, alone, thoughtful, a little afraid. . . .

He sat on the bunk, the picks, tension bar, and padlock on the blanket before him. He studied them. The picks were about four inches long, tapering from a handle a half inch wide to less than a sixteenth, and about a thirty-second of an inch thick; on the end of one were two rounded humps, on the other was a single hump.

Grasping the lock in his palm, the keyhole toward his thumb, he inserted the L-shaped tension bar in the bottom of the keyhole. Then, using his thumb to hold tension on the bar, he inserted the single-humped pick in the top of the keyhole.

An hour later he was still running the pick in and out of the keyhole. His thumb and forefinger were blistered; his face was sweating, dripping, his neck stiff, temples throbbing. But the lock did not open. He cursed, dropped it on the bunk, and glowered at it. It was impossible; Sam had him on some monstrous rib; it couldn't be done, it just could not be done.

Standing, Kirk stretched, began pacing the cell, then doused his face with cold water, and tried to massage the cramp from his fingers. He scowled at the lock, thought about throwing it out the window. But he had to learn. . . . It must be possible. . . . The trick is in the tension, Sam says. . . . Too much and the tumblers stay pushed up, don't fall into place . . . not enough, they don't stick. . . . He had to learn. . . . It was the only way they could get out. . . . The others were counting on him. . . .

Sighing, he sat and began going through the motions. Moments later the padlock popped open. . . . He gaped. How? Did he do it? He grinned smugly, felt himself glowing. He must have done it, he reasoned logically, there was no one else in the cell.

Then he sagged. To practice some more he would have to close it, start over. The thought was crushing. What if it didn't open again? But reluctantly, grimacing, he squeezed the thing locked. It clicked. Depression settled over him. He pushed it away and began trying anew. He tried and tried. Nothing. Nothing but watery blisters, cramps, aches, anxiety.

Then it popped open again. He burst into laughter, feeling mildly euphoric. The third time was easier. . . .

And two hours later, with eyes closed, he could set each of the tumblers by feel and have the lock opened within ten seconds. He gloated, wondering why they were made . . . to keep "honest" people honest . . . ?

He slept. . . . The women were beautiful . . . voluptuous . . . musky. . . . They teased, taunted, tantalized . . . chastity belts . . . locked. . . . He had a pick. . . . The belts fell away . . . giggling . . . male organs . . . granite walls. . . .

[XIV]

"I got the feeling you clowns fucked me," Yancy said, and stared closely at the three convicts. "I think I opened my yap and you guys put your feet in it." He shrugged. "Don't bother denying it, you might convince me I'm right. . . . It's messing with me enough as it is." His mouth twisted wryly. "Anyway, whether the guy lit the match himself or not, he's going to the bughouse, so he's better off than being in this shit-hole. . . ." Pausing, he fixed the three convicts with a pensive stare. "I wonder . . . I can't feature you doing it without a reason. . . . maybe you really didn't do it. . . ."

Kirk forced himself to meet Yancy's eyes. "Come on, Yancy," he said, "the A.W. says the guy even admitted doing it himself."

"I don't think that's what he said," Yancy responded. "He might have said that's the rumor on the grapevine." He smiled sourly. "Me and Lowry came to work here about the same time. He must be smarter than me. . . . I'm still a bull, he's the A.W.; but I think as much of the horseshit grapevine as you clowns probably do." He

73

shrugged. "Okay, you guys, I'll leave you exercise . . . or whatever the hell you do in that shower. . . ." He turned and walked back through the hall door.

Leslie looked at the others. "I feel horrid," he said.

Sam spun him around and pinched him. "Not too horrid," he said. "Let's go shower."

They did, quietly, thoughtfully.

It seemed centuries; interminal hours of ceiling staring, anxious hours of surging adrenaline, a too-fast heartbeat, a heartbeat demanding action, getting none, beating faster in frustration, a heartbeat promising always to beat too fast, always to keep the body at a fevered pitch, ready to explode into violence. . . .

But then it was Thursday, and he grew uncannily calm. He watched the guard pick up the lunch tray, and moved quickly, fluidly, as if he had rehearsed for endless hours. Holding his pillow under his buttocks, he repeatedly slammed himself onto the toilet. Shortly, the bowl was empty of water. Then he unraveled a roll of toilet paper, wadded it into a loose mass, dropped it into the toilet bowl, and lit it afire. The porcelain slowly became warm, then hot, finally too hot to touch. He punched the flush button. The toilet coughed, gargled, and sucked down the burning paper. Then it crackled, cracked, and fell apart. Water spread over the floor, under the door, into the hall. He used a rag of torn sheet to wipe off the most noticeable fire stains on the larger pieces of porcelain.

He was grinning down at the mess when the door unlocked. He stepped into the hall. Leslie and Sam looked down at the water seeping from under his cell door. They smirked. Sam pulled a tattered baseball magazine from his pocket and laughed. Leslie licked his lips and stripped off his clothing until he stood in a blazing pink bikini fashioned from two colored-pencil-dyed handkerchiefs— very small handkerchiefs; then with a leer, he bent over much too long and picked a blanket from the floor. He wrinkled his nose at Kirk. "Let's," he said, and stuck out his tongue.

Kirk grinned. "Leslie, I've changed my mind," he said. "I will marry you . . . as soon as you grow some tits," then he turned and walked to the hall door. He hammered on it. And about a minute later a guard framed his face in the small window. "My toilet broke, sir," the convict yelled.

The door opened, and the guard poked his head around the corner. "What?" he asked.

Kirk frowned and fatalistically wagged his head. "My toilet broke, sir," he said. "I don't know how the hell it happened. . . . It just cracked all to pieces. I guess you'll have to turn off the water and call the plumber. Sorry." He was all abashed and shrugging apologies.

The guard looked past him, toward the seeping water, and made a sucking noise. "Son of a bitch," he sighed tiredly. "I think they must be made outta plaster a Paris. . . . That's the second one already this year." He shrugged. "Well, I'll get holda the plumber."

Kirk smiled his gratitude and watched the guard back through the door, then turned and grinned at the others. "Ready?" he asked.

Sam laughed, Leslie leered; they were ready.

And a half hour later the deadlock clicked off. Kirk pulled his cell door open, then watched as the hall door was nosed open by a large cart pushed by an aged convict, who was followed by a tall guard with his hat visor pulled over his eyes. As the old man pushed the cart to the open door, Sam eased up beside the guard, jabbering, grinning, blithering, and fanning the baseball magazine in his face. The guard halted, but not for Sam. His eyes jumped to Leslie, who stood with his back turned. The little fruit looked as if he were trying to make his butt talk; it was shimmying all around, rolling and rippling; it might have had a mind of its own, an educated mind. The guard gawked, slack-jawed, his eyes mirroring horror, revulsion, fascination. And Sam kept right on jabbering, apparently oblivious that no one listened.

Meantime, the old convict pushed the cart to the cell and looked inside. Then he cursed and, turning to Kirk, glared.

Hooding his eyes as sinisterly as he knew how, Kirk stared at the old man. "Be good to your life, pops," he said, and knew there was little he could do about it if the old man was not, not with the guard right there.

The crusty old convict peered back with hooded eyes. "I'm a dumbbell, kid," he said knowledgeably, "but not so dumb as all that."

Kirk grinned and winked at him, wondering if they had been reading the same script. And then he stepped aside to let the old convict go to work.

The old man pulled a huge ring of keys from a hook on his belt and knelt before the cart. He unlocked the large sheet-metal cabinet and folded back the doors. Visible inside was a glistening new toilet, a plumber's snake, and two large tool chests with heavy padlocks.

"Gimme a hand, kid," said the old man, indicating the toilet, "and let's get it wrassled into the cell." That done, the plumber fetched one of the tool chests and set to work removing the broken toilet.

Meantime, Sam blithered on, waving the magazine, spouting batting averages, pitchers' names, win/loss records, and other esoteric jargon. And slowly he began to win the guard's attention. Leslie was not wiggling around so much any more.

Kirk chuckled and, squatting with his back against the plumber's cart, chatted idly with the laboring convict. Feeling behind, he found the second tool chest. He coughed loudly as he pulled it closer. Groping, his fingers found the lock and began to pick it. And moments later it was open. Still talking with the plumber, he signaled to Sam, who suddenly became almost violent in praising a particular ball team. . . .

". . . Now, goddamn it, you ever heard of statistics lying? How in the hell can you say that they don't have the highest r.b.i. average? Now, goddamn it, there it is in black and white!"

"But . . . I didn't say . . ."

"Didn't you just say they were bums? These figures just don't back you up! How in the hell can you argue with statistics? It's right there in black and white. . . . Here, read the goddamn things yourself. . . ."

Kirk chuckled to himself and kept his eyes on the plumber while he slipped an 18-inch Stillson wrench from the tool chest and handed it behind. He relocked the chest, and noticed Leslie swishing down the hall, swirling his blanket around his shoulders as if he thought he was a matador . . . a matadora . . . ? He minced up beside the guard and puckered his mouth, waved his tongue, then gaily continued on toward the shower. Grinning, Kirk pushed the chest back where it had been.

A while later the new toilet was installed, the old gathered up, and the guard almost sprinted out the door while the old convict followed more slowly. Kirk smiled at both of them and thanked them profusely. He reminded the guard to turn on the water again when he got to the control valve, which, for security reasons, was somewhere beyond the door. The guard nodded and closed the door. He seemed anxious to leave.

The three convicts looked at one another. A hush fell, thick and unnatural, almost reverent.

"Tomorrow," Kirk said hoarsely, adding a faint smile.

Leslie walked to him and held his arm. "You're beautiful, baby."

"You and Sam were the stars," Kirk said, then looked at Sam. "Where in hell did you learn so much about baseball?"

Sam grinned. "Shows me what you know about it," he said. "I was ten or eleven the last time I picked up a bat. . . . I used it to cave some kid's skull in." He laughed. "I hate baseball." He pulled a folded paper from his pocket and extended it to Kirk. "Study this," he said. "It's a map of the joint. You ain't been around long enough to know exactly what we're going to be doing." Kirk accepted it, and he went on. "Let's squat," he said slowly. "I got a few things to tell the both of you." They sat, and Sam chewed his lip for a moment, frowning. "This is a real idiot-plot," he began, "and I feel a little lousy sucking you two into it. But I got to take the chance. . . . I got four years in this pit. . . . I been looking for a way out since I got here, but it seems like I look a little less every day. But time don't stop. . . ." He grinned bitterly. "You two know we'll all get a five-year sentence out of this if we miss . . . ?" They nodded, and he went on. "It'll hurt you worse than it'll hurt me. . . . I already got as much as I can do. You two might be able to get out in another few years. . . ." He grinned. "Whatever you want to call me, that's okay. . . . It ain't what I'd be if I didn't try."

There was silence for a long while after he finished. Leslie finally broke the hush.

"I like it better out there," he said, looking up from the floor. "That's reason enough for me."

Kirk nodded his agreement and realized suddenly that Leslie's reason was his own; but hearing it voiced, it seemed to become almost inane. However, if it was not better, if there was nothing beyond the walls, no freedom, where was it . . . ? He had to get out . . . had to. . . . He knew he couldn't do a ten-year sentence . . . the stress . . . the mind-boggling fantasy . . . the anxiety . . . ten years without women . . . playing with himself. . . . How long before a dick gets calluses? . . . How long before fantasy becomes reality? . . . How far from a cell to a straitjacket? . . .

How do you check a runaway mind when the heart is ever racing? . . . How do you do a ten-year sentence when you can't see tomorrow? . . .

Then he saw inside his head, saw the things whose voices he had always heard. He would kill once, twice, or five times to get past the walls. He would do it for freedom's sake; he would do it for hate's sake; he would do it to assuage the dark and crawling things in his head, devils, a murderer-rapist-thief, demons. In that moment he saw what he was, and grew afraid, afraid of himself. . . .

"Baby, what's wrong?"

Kirk roused himself, focused his eyes, and looked up. "Nothing," he said with a tight smile. "Like they say in church . . . 'for better or for worse.' "

Leslie leered sourly at him. "What'd you have to say something like that for, you bastard? Now I *have* to go . . . 'Whither thou goest . . .' " He reached over and pinched Kirk's hand, smiling sweetly as his fingernails tore loose a half-moon-shaped hunk of flesh.

Wincing, Kirk glowered. They laughed. He laughed.

Back in his cell, he paced. Up and down, back and forth. He clawed at his hair, his mind clawed at him. He thought . . . thoughtless thoughts . . . agonizing thoughts . . . inarticulate thoughts that leaped and tumbled, ripped and tore through brain passages . . . thoughts larger than life, grandiose, colorful . . . a psychopath's thoughts. . . .

He had friends . . . friends . . . feeble spots of light tinging his inner gloom . . . a killer . . . a queer . . . a cop . . . a cop? . . . Yeah, a lousy flatfoot, a screw, a lumpy-faced keeper of men . . . a killer, a destroyer of men . . . a queer, tomorrow's executioner. . . . He himself, killer of an unknown man. . . . And tomorrow what? . . . Who would die tomorrow? . . . Why? . . .

He remembered the map Sam had given him. He spread it on the bunk and began poring over it, needing to concentrate on something outside himself.

[XV]

Kirk heard his breakfast tray slide along the floor under the door. Getting up, he dumped the contents of the tray into the toilet, then

78

slid the tray back under the door, and pulled on his pants. After washing, he paced. He was calm, thoughtful.

And the hours passed unnoticed until the lunch tray arrived. He flushed it down the toilet also. For if it came to it, he did not want to dodge bullets with a weight in his stomach. He wasn't hungry either.

The period between lunch hour and exercise period was usually only minutes; now the minutes dragged interminably. He waited by the door, peering out, unseeing.

Then the welcome click.

Adrenaline surged through him, waking his body. Pushing open the door, he stepped out, slammed it closed, then ran to Leslie's cell and followed Sam inside. Gripping the windowsill, he pulled the door shut. The three convicts stared blankly at one another. Then the second click sounded, the deadlock was back on. They grinned.

"Let's move," Sam said.

Leslie flung the mattress from the bunk, exposing the Stillson wrench. Sam covered two of the rear-window panes with strips of tape that he unwound from a pencil. Finished, he grabbed the wrench from Leslie's extended hand and used it to tap out one of the windows. He then pulled the tape from the shattered glass and handed it to Leslie, who threw it into the toilet. Sam plucked the remaining shards from the frame that now enclosed an empty rectangle, then tapped out the second pane and repeated the cleanup process. Working quickly, he attached the jaws of the Stillson to the vertical steel strip that had divided the two panes. He gave the handle of the wrench a hard jerk. Nothing happened.

"Son of a bitch!" he spat, and jerked again. Still nothing happened.

Kirk pulled Leslie aside and stepped in front of Sam. "I'll push," he said. "Don't jerk. Pull steady. It's only a weld joint."

Sam nodded and pulled. Kirk leaned all his weight into the wrench. He watched Sam's face flush with the effort, darken until it was almost purple.

And suddenly, with a tortured screech, the bar gave, and Kirk sprawled on top of Sam, who had fallen across Leslie's bed. Sam pushed Kirk off and got to his feet.

"Leslie first," he said.

And Leslie stuck his head out the window and pulled it back. "Looks all right." He winked at Kirk, then slid feet first through the opening into the walled yard and reached back through the window and took the wrench and two blankets that Sam handed him. Setting them down, he walked quickly to the yard wall farthest from the building and turned to look up at the tiered rows of cell windows above, any of which might hold a window-gazing informer or a too-loud well-wisher. Then he returned to the window. "It looks all right," he said quietly. "Somebody might be peeking, but there's only one sure way to find out."

Sam nodded and went out the window headfirst, with Leslie tugging at him. Outside, on his feet again, he gestured to Kirk, who extended his arms overhead and began to wriggle his way through the constricting space, which was a much tighter fit for his larger bulk. He gritted his teeth as he felt bits of glass gouge into his flesh. Sam and Leslie tugged, jerked, yanked, and suddenly he popped free and sprawled on the pavement below. Sitting up, he rubbed his sides and looked at the others. "Ouch," he said with a happy grin. "Next time I'm taking out two of those things."

Sam grimaced. "Fuck a next time," he said. "Let's go." He walked with Leslie to the rear of the right-hand wall.

Kirk stuck the wrench down the back of his pants and followed. There was no particular reason for taking the Stillson, except that without it the officials would be mystified by the broken window frame.

At the wall, Kirk stooped and snatched Leslie from the ground, and set him on his shoulders. Then he watched as Leslie reached overhead to grasp unbarbed areas of the coiled wire and slowly pulled himself up until he stood on his shoulders.

Leslie looked down. "I can't see anybody," he said, "but that doesn't mean a whole bunch. I feel kind of goofy standing here. . . . Throw me the blankets."

Sam tossed him first one blanket, then the other, and he spread them over the wire in a two-foot-wide path, then called down. "All right, I'm ready."

Kirk worked his fingers under Leslie's feet and began to lift. Straining, he pushed slowly upward until Leslie was standing on his hands, eight feet or so in the air, clinging frantically to the blanket-sheathed barbed wire, his head someplace on the other side of the wall.

"If this damages the beautiful body, I'm suing you goons for breach of contract or something. Come on." With that Leslie settled across the wire, weighting it down until there was a deep furrow across it, a living bridge. His head and arms were buried, lost somewhere in the vicious rust-red wire; his ankles hung just within Kirk's reach.

"You holding on good, Leslie?" Kirk called, giving the ankles a tentative pull. He heard a muffled reply and grinned up at Leslie's legs. "I think this is all a plot to get me to crawl on top of you." He laughed.

And Sam glowered. "Come on, funny boy," he said flatly. "You ain't going to laugh your way over the wall."

Kirk shrugged and began pulling himself up Leslie's legs, with Sam boosting from behind. Every second he didn't fall, tearing Leslie along with him, was mildly astounding, for it was difficult to believe that the frail girl-frame could hold his 185 pounds. But it did, and then he saw the grass on the other side, hoped it was soft, and let himself tumble limply toward it. It was soft and wet. He shook himself back together and looked up at Leslie's strain-flushed face, then reached up and grasped the two bloodless fists clinging to the wire.

"You're a gutty fruit," he told Leslie, then louder: "Let's go, Sam."

A minute later Sam came scrabbling over the top. And while Kirk eased his landing, Leslie began to work the blankets loose from the wire. Finally, it was done—leaving much of the blankets stuck fast—and Leslie came over headfirst, his shirt in ribbons, his arms bleeding, spots of red oozing through his T-shirt.

Feeling something stick in his throat, Kirk put a hand on Leslie's hair. "You're good," he said quietly.

Leslie wrinkled his nose and smiled.

And Sam broke in. "You two geeks keep on," he said derisively, "and you're going to make me blush." He paused. "We got past the first bad spot. . . . If the other two are this easy, it'll be fast cars and neon lights by midnight. Let's sit down for a while and go over it some more."

They backed into the outside corner of the segregation yard—an L-shaped blind spot—and squatted on the grass. Sam looked at Leslie, then at Kirk. "Our scariest move is the next one," he began. "Once we're past the laundry windows, going past the gun tower'll be fun. Kirk, you won't have much trouble. . . . Nobody around here knows you. And, Leslie, for Christ's-fucking-sake, try not to wiggle. . . . That'd be all we need . . . some damn fool to start whistling." He paused to look up at the overcast sky. "It's about 1:30. That gives us an hour and 15 minutes to make it the rest of the way. That's plenty of time—too much—so take all you need. The industries' tower guards will be gone by 3:15 . . . that'll give us 35 minutes to get over the industries' fence and go to the ground. After dark we can start hiking out of this desolate son of a bitch. By dawn tomorrow we'll be at a little hick town. . . . We'll pick up a car there. . . ." He grinned wryly. "Of course, that's all a fairy tale if the seg screw decides to be a nice guy and ask us why we ain't out exercising. He might be walking back there right now. . . ."

Kirk chuckled mirthlessly. "I'm ready to go on," he said. "Moving is better than thinking about it." He pushed to his feet and started across the lawn toward the secondary corridor, the corridor that led out toward the prison industrial area. It seemed a long, long way off, maybe 40 yards.

He stepped from the protection of the segregation-yard wall—the same one they had come over—and could feel the window-eyes of the prison laundry on his left. He had a strong compulsion to look toward the building, but dared not. Instead, he strolled along, picking an occasional weed from the lawn and wondering how anybody could possibly believe that he was in earnest. Once, unable to help himself, he glanced sidelong and felt his heart crawl up into his throat as he saw the long row of windows staring back. He didn't look again. Then, for no apparent reason, he dropped to his hands and knees, and began searching out the root of a many-tendriled weed. When finally he found it and pulled it from the earth, he stood and glanced casually toward the others. They were laughing. Maybe, too, they were wondering just what he was going to do with his tentacled prize. Repressing a grin, he dropped the weed and walked slowly on toward the corridor, angling into the corner where the laundry joined the low-roofed hallway.

At length, he made it and wondered why he had thought he would not. Now, leaning against the laundry, listening to the hissing of steam presses behind the wall, he watched Sam follow his approximate route and wondered why he looked apprehensive. Then his mind became rather addled, began telling him very unfunny jokes, which he laughed at.

Later—it seemed days later—the three of them were huddled in the corner of the laundry and secondary corridor, out of sight of all eyes, except the 50 windows of the second and third story of segregation that glowered down.

"Gawd," Leslie said as he looked over at the windows. "I feel naked. Let's get the hell out of here."

There was some wide-eyed agreement, then Kirk stooped, and Leslie climbed onto his shoulders again and onto his hands. Kirk lifted until Leslie could reach the rain gutter that ran the length of the corridor. He stepped back and watched Leslie struggle to pull himself up. Then he disappeared onto the roof.

"All right," Leslie called, sticking his head over the edge. "Throw."

Sam pulled the ragged blankets from inside his pants, rolled each into a ball, and flung them upward. Leslie disappeared again, taking the blankets with him.

Kirk and Sam filled the moment by staring at one another. Then Leslie's head reappeared, several feet to the right of where he had been.

"I'm holding onto the only pipe on this damn roof that's anywhere close to the edge," he called softly. "There's not enough blanket to tie it to, so I'll hold it and you two goons pray." He dropped the knotted blankets over the edge.

Kirk moved over beneath them and turned to look at the laundry windows. The angle was acute, but anyone close, looking out, could not help but see them. He turned to Sam and grinned. "You think they'd be mad if we went back and said we're sorry?"

Sam glowered and stepped to the hanging blankets. "You're funny as a life sentence," he said over his shoulder. "Before we die laughing, let's get on the roof. There's probably only three or four hundred rats watching us here." He tugged at the makeshift rope, then started up, Kirk boosting from below. He reached the top and disappeared. And a moment later his head popped over the edge. "Man!" he exclaimed, "you wouldn't believe what this bitch is holding on with! She's guttier than a butcher shop."

"Shut the fuck up, love," Leslie said sweetly. "Let's get Kirk up here, shall we?"

Sam snorted and ducked back from the edge. Kirk grinned. Then, hand over hand, he pulled himself up and crawled onto the graveled roof. He saw that Sam had anchored Leslie's leg while he had climbed. But something bothered him. Glancing about, he noticed a small-diameter pipe that poked four inches or so from the roof. The pipe was fully five feet from the edge and, thinking about it, he concluded that the only conceivable way that Leslie could have held onto it, while also holding the blankets, was with a single hooked heel possibly secured by the toe of the other foot. But Sam weighed at least 170, probably more. He looked at Leslie's feet. The toe of one shoe was wrinkled and crushed; the back of the other was broken and turned down, blood oozed through the sock.

"You stupid queer son of a bitch!" he exploded, snarling at Leslie. "We sent you up to tie the blanket—not to cripple your dick-eating self!"

"Can you walk all right?" Sam asked. Leslie nodded and hung his head, then Sam turned to Kirk. "Forget it. Here's where we either make it or get blown away. We got past two of the three bad spots—let's not piss it off now."

Glaring at Leslie for a moment longer, Kirk finally nodded agreement. He then turned to look in the direction of the industrial area. Part of the wall had been removed to build the corridor they stood on. Evidently someone had decided not to replace it, for the eight-foot-deep gap running the width of the corridor had been filled in with barbed wire, with a wooden bridge spanning the gap in the wall. The coiled wire lay about 25 yards from where they stood. To the right the prison chapel rose above them and the laundry was situated to their left. To the west, in the opposite direction of the industrial area, the conical roof of the armory gun tower, at the front gate, could be seen above the administration building. To the southeast, a little closer, could be seen the searchlights on the roofs of numbers eight and nine gun towers, which sat overlooking the prison yard. The three convicts were shielded from their view by the kitchen and dining hall.

Sam motioned them against the stucco-walled chapel. He then crouched and fished in his shirt pocket. Finally, holding three matches, he bit the end off one and mixed them up, then extended his hand with the small red heads peeping from between thumb and forefinger. It was part of the plan: draw lots at the last moment, for the last dangerous move, to see who would get shot first.

Leslie picked a long one. He tossed it away with a sigh. Kirk drew next. He was it. Leslie sighed again, but looked worried now.

"Baby . . ."

"Tell me about it outside," Kirk said with an easy grin, an uneasy mind. Then, crouched low, he crept to the edge of the chapel and stared at number five gun tower, to the left of the gap in the wall, only ten yards away. Sam had assured him that the tower was unmanned during the daylight hours that the industrial-area towers were manned. Had that tower not been there, they could have been doing this at night; but the tower was there, and it was not night. Moving carefully, he eased his head around the corner of the chapel. There was another gun tower, a hundred yards to the right, the gun tower that would spatter the roof with lead if the man inside saw any one of them. And he knew that he would be under the muzzle for ten yards while he crossed the open roof to get to the coiled barbed wire. Once there, the wire itself would provide cover.

Ten yards is not so far. A sprinter can cover it in less than a second—one heartbeat. But what about later, when he was burrowing beneath the coiled wire with its vicious barbs? What about the two who would follow? He thought about all Sam's assurances that the guard in the tower would be too busy thinking about getting home, paying bills, keeping out of his wife's sight, or whatever guards do during their sixth hour in a cramped tower; he wondered why he was willing to wager his life on Sam's *Applied Psychology I*—Sam, fourth-grade dropout. Then, for the second time in two days, he got a fleeting glimpse of the dark things lurking in his mind and realized his fear was not of dying. . . . It was a fear of the dark things. . . . Curiouser and curiouser, he thought, and wondered what kind of animal tends more to death than to life.

It was eerie, he decided later, but next he knew he was flying through the air, close to the roof, the barbed wire looming large. He covered his face and tumbled into the resilient wire, then he was sprawling on the graveled surface, his shirt ripped and shredded. He pulled his legs in beside the coils and looked over at the others. Sam was laughing. Leslie was chewing his fingers.

Kirk felt warmth trickling across his chest and stomach, and knew he had been torn by the wire, but there was no pain. He rolled to his back and started burrowing under the wire. The stiff coils resisted him, pushed back with cruel, sharp talons; flakes of rust chipped off, covering his face and hair, turning his hands orange. But he felt a growing elation as he realized that no whistle had yet sounded, no siren had blown, and, most important, the machine gun was silent.

At last on the other side of the wire, he paused for a thoughtful moment, toying in the gravel with his fingers, toying with the fact that he was actually outside the main prison compound, beyond the wall. And in broad daylight. It was hard to believe.

Looking to the right, over his shoulder, he could see into the side windows of tower five; to the left was the slanted corrugated-metal roof of the prison paper factory, its height shielding him from the industrial-area gun towers.

He brought his attention back to the business at hand and turned to look through the coiled wire. Lifting his hand, he waved the others forward.

Leslie backed from the corner of the chapel and set himself, then took a running start and raced forward. Suddenly, halfway across the open space, he crumpled to the roof, slid a few feet, and stopped.

Kirk felt a murderous rage well up inside. Leslie's foot had collapsed—the foot with the bloody heel. Cursing, snarling, he ripped at the skin on his arm. He cursed people in general, queers in particular. He cursed himself for having anything to do with the perverted son of a bitch; he cursed Sam for agreeing with him. Then he waited for machine-gun fire; he waited for Leslie to twitch and lay dead; he waited for bullets to rain through the barbed wire. He hoped it was over quickly.

"Damn," Leslie said abruptly, and added a nervous giggle. "It's kind of scary out here."

Kirk glared through the wire, his vision hazed with the red and gray of rage. "You stupid come-drunk son of a bitch!" he snarled. "Get the fuck over here!"

"Easy, love," Leslie said with patient sarcasm. "If that boob hasn't seen me by now, he never will." Then he was up to his knees, diving toward the wire. Squirming underneath it, he lay, minutes later, beside Kirk, and wrinkled his gravel-scraped nose.

Kirk laughed, wondering why he'd been mad. "You're probably the creepiest queer in the world," he said, believing it. Then he waved Sam forward.

And when he had squirmed under the barbed wire, rejoined with the others, they crawled together to the south edge of the roof and dropped into an asphalt-paved alley. Squatting there, behind trash cans and rubbish-filled cardboard boxes, Sam spoke.

"It's about 2:00, maybe 2:10," he said. "That means we got more than a half hour till the quitting whistle. A half hour after that, the three industry towers'll be empty. We got better than an hour. . . ." He looked around. "We'd best stash under some of this junk. . . . You two want a box to yourselves?"

Kirk grinned. "That sounds a little more like you," he said. "For a while back there I thought maybe it was something you ate." He pointed toward where the granite wall of the main prison compound joined with the barbed-wire-topped cyclone fence that enclosed the industrial area on three sides. "That where we're going over?"

Sam grinned sardonically. "Told you before that the plan wasn't real brainy."

Kirk stared at him, then back to the spot where they were going over the fence. It was directly below number six gun tower. They would be eight feet from the top of the 20-foot wall, about 12 feet below the machine-gun muzzle. Of course, they would be behind the tower, while the guard would be looking into the prison proper . . . or would he . . . ?

"Come on," Sam broke into Kirk's second thoughts, "let's get under cover."

The words had scarcely left his mouth when a door into the alley banged open and a trash cart appeared. They dove behind the nearest cover, a pile of cardboard boxes, and stared blankly at one another, listening. The trash cart creaked closer, closer, then clanged against something. Then nothing. Silence.

Finally Kirk could no longer stand the suspense. Carefully he raised up and peered over the box before him, then gawked. He dropped back down, staring blindly at the asphalt, and thought about it. He decided it was not happening, then raised his head again and saw that it was.

A convict, standing sideways to them, was bent over with his hands braced on the side of the trash cart. His pants were dropped around his ankles, and a tall black man, similarly attired, was in the act of mounting him from behind.

Leslie tugged at his arm, looking puzzled, mouthing "What?"

Kirk put his mouth against Leslie's ear. "Coffee break," he whispered, then went back to staring over the box, disgusted with himself.

And a moment later Leslie's mouth was against his ear. "Baby, for five cents an hour, did you think they worked?" he murmured, and followed it with a wet tongue.

Kirk pushed him away and kept watching. Snuffling and snorting, the black convict finished up, sighed while he pulled up his pants and patted the flaccid, pale buttocks of the other. Then he stepped back through the alley door. And another convict, dark and swarthy, carrying a small rubber bladder, stepped out unbuckling his pants. As the pants fell to his ankles, the swarthy convict lifted the bladder to his mouth and drank from it, then belched. *"Chingao,"* he said almost reverently, and climbed on the other's back. A bare moment later another convict came through the door, dropped his pants, and hopped onto the trash cart. He then grabbed a handful of the convict's hair—the one getting dug in behind—and pulled his face toward his crotch. *"Chingao,"* said the behind digger, then guzzled from the bladder, and kept digging. "But . . . but . . ." stammered the one in the middle. And the newcomer smiled nicely, pulled the head a little closer, and said, "It's not butt I want," and proceeded to get what he wanted.

Kirk slumped back down with a skull full of heat. . . . He had to get out . . . had to. . . .

Suddenly, a crash. Then another. Then the sound of running feet. A scream. "Grab him!" yelled a gloating voice. "All right, you fucking animals, put your goddamn clothes on! Get that wine from Gomez! Liza, you filthy cocksucker, pull your goddamn pants up!"

Leslie gripped Kirk's arm. "The cops!" he hissed. "Three of the bastards!"

Kirk knew. Somehow, he had known from the first harsh syllable that their plan was dead. He stared blindly at the asphalt, inwardly wilting, sinking farther and farther down. Then something made him look up. He saw a guard looking down, his mouth smirking. Rage, a brilliant red fury, slammed through him, shot him upward. His head smashed into the guard's face, ruined it. The guard went back, down; and Kirk was over him, kicking, stomping his ribs, his face. He remembered the Stillson stuck down the back of his pants, the wrench he had carried all this way for nothing . . . but not for nothing. . . .

Whipping it out, he charged the other two guards, a scream in his ears, his own scream. His vision was fogged, a red-flecked gray. But he saw the guards standing there, apparently rooted in place, saw their terror-frozen faces. And swung the wrench at them. But it missed, slammed to a stop against his own thigh, numbing it, tumbling him to the ground. Then he was up, still moving toward the guards. One had disappeared through the door. But one was left.

He hefted the wrench with both hands, bounded closer, and swung it like a baseball bat. It crunched into the guard's arm and ribs, lifting him, knocking him across the alley. He raised the wrench overhead and stalked the guard, who lay on his back, knees drawn up, one arm extended toward the wrath above him. His other arm was limp, twisted at an odd angle. As he stood over the guard, watching his contorted face, watching the spittle dribble from his mouth, Kirk grew suddenly calm, dispassionate. He chuckled down at the guard, thought he looked ridiculous, wondered if he could cleave his skull in two with a single blow. He would try. He gripped the wrench, hefted it.

And somehow he found himself sprawled face down, asphalt scraping his face. A panicked moment passed as he felt himself being crushed, ground into the earth. Then came the realization that Sam was sitting astride his back.

He heard words—cursing, beguiling, cruel, tender—and felt the wrench being pulled from his cramped-tight fingers. Leslie, he thought dully; Leslie pulling the wrench away, and Sam holding him. He promised himself that he'd kill each of them slowly, torturously, savagely, listening to their screams, their pleas for mercy. And he would try, try, try to keep them alive past the point of death that he might kill them again and again. Knowing it was over for the time, he sought to let himself go limp. But his body would not obey, his fingers would not loose the wrench. And he wanted to cry, to howl the moon from the sky, but tears would not come. Then Sam's voice sounded in his ears, a faraway gray-colored voice.

". . . It'll be all right, pal," he was saying. "Listen to me. Listen. This is big trouble if you play your hand wrong. Be nice, smile, give them everything they want. Tell them you blacked out, you can't remember a thing. Talk to that psych, but don't talk too much. Tomorrow's another day. . . . Keep that in mind. Play it right and we'll all be out of seg in six months. Hard-ass them, and you're in trouble. . . . You'll finish up your ten in there."

The voice droned on and on, calming him. His temples were being rubbed; Leslie, he thought. Crying shame to put a dick on him . . . poor perverted little creep . . . maybe not. . . . He knows where he's at. . . . His mind isn't perverted . . . not really. . . . Just thinks a little funny . . . for a boy, anyway. . . .

Then Sam's voice became louder, sounding as if it were wearing a huge angelic smile.

". . . Yes, sir. He just went kind of crazy-like. You know how the time gets to some of these guys. . . . They don't know what they're doing. . . . Yes, sir. Yes, sir, I'd advise sedating him. . . ."

His eyes are wide with brotherly love and compassion and altruism, Kirk thought vaguely. A mashed-nosed killer-bandit with a line of shit that'd charm the scales off a snake . . . his pal. . . . What would dear old mother think? . . . Bring her killers and queers. . . . Maybe she'd have a heart attack. . . . Maybe he could give the world a heart attack. . . . All he could do was hope. . . .

Later—Leslie still rubbing, rubbing; Sam still talking, talking—he felt a sudden prick in his thigh. And a little later—though it was difficult to know how much later, for time seemed frozen—he wondered if they had run the needle through his pants. What about germs . . . ? He chuckled to himself, then looked toward the welling blackness; it promised warmth, shelter. . . . He smiled and went toward it . . . a womb . . . a tomb. . . .

PART TWO

[XVI]

"Wake up, Whalen! Wake the fuck up!"

No dream, that. Head rattling around . . . images fading, going gray, wispy. . . . Where was he? He tried to remember. Bright light . . . somewhere, everywhere . . . eyelids translucent. . . . He fought to open them, fought for memory. Neither would come. Rest; rest, he advised himself; rest and try again, harder. Willing himself to relax, he lay for a moment forcing his reluctant lungs to expand, suck in oxygen, life. And then, thinking to trick himself, he decided to sneak up on his eyelid muscles and have them open without his knowing it. Somehow, that seemed ridiculous and he laughed to himself. And next he knew his eyes were open, staring into the naked brilliance of a 200-watt light bulb. A panicked instant followed as he squeezed them shut again and wondered if the pain in them was caused by burning lighter fluid. He could not imagine where such an idea came from.

"Whalen! you hear me? Open your eyes again; I'll shield them."

He did and in a moment was trying to decipher the mystery of the many-lined palm hanging a short distance off his face.

"Sit up," ordered a voice behind the palm.

Trying, his muscles would not obey. No pain; but, he thought dully, no feeling, either. Except that his throat felt as he imagined a dried herring might feel. And his head seemed filled with lead; it was much too heavy to move. He sensed himself being lifted, lifted; and finally he was sitting up, his head reeling, vertiginous; and he was not at all surprised to find that he wore only his skin. And, he noted curiously, a football-sized yellow-blue bruise on his left thigh, plus crusty little scabs all over. He wondered what had happened.

"Whalen!"

He shook his head around, trying to make the parts fall into place, then slowly, laboriously turned toward the irksome, demanding voice. His eyes rolled sluggishly in his head, like marbles in gritty butter. But finally, after traveling tortuously along the tawny-colored floor, his eyes found a black shoe toe and, climbing upward, the cuff of a pair of pants—a grass-green cuff. Green clothing, what does green clothing mean? Something told him that he knew, but he could not recall.

"You remember me?"

He raised his eyes to the green-clad man's sharp, weasel-like face, attempting to summon memory, failing, trying anew. Suddenly, without knowing how it happened, his mouth opened and he heard himself say, "Hank."

Sighing, Hank bared his teeth and said, "You've been out for more than two days."

Kirk wondered what he was talking about, but more than anything, he wanted water. Everything would be all right if only he had some water; of that much he was certain. "Water," he heard himself croak. After the water, he decided that he'd learn to control his mouth; hearing himself speak unbidden was disconcerting. He watched apathetically as Hank lifted a paper cup to his mouth. Clay! It was clay; tepid, insipid clay! He spat the filthy mud from his mouth and then decided that it had indeed been water. Lifting his hands, he grabbed the cup from Hank, sloshing its contents as he brought it tremulously to his face, then poured it over his mouth, nose, chin. Some little trickled down his throat. Not enough. Swallowing, his throat expanded, stretched until he was certain that it would tear open. He thought he could hear life rushing into sluggish capillaries.

"Listen to me, Whalen; it's important," Hank insisted, shaking him roughly.

The empty cup fell from his fingers, and he wondered what could possibly be more important than water. For a fleeting instant he decided that the thought was extremely profound, even astounding, and he wanted to develop it, but the tugging at his shoulder would not let him think. He brought his eyes to focus on the thin-faced convict. Hank looks remarkably like a ferret . . . or is it a weasel? He wanted to ask which, but instead, he said, "I'm rummy," and snorted in an attempt to laugh.

"Listen, Whalen," said Hank, still shaking him, "you're in

92

trouble. You're going to be hypnotized today. They want to find out if you were sane when you went after those bulls. You've got only one hope, kid, and that's insanity. Trintz'll be questioning you, and he ain't a dummy. If you've got any brains at all, you'll need them to beat him. He's injecting you with sodium pentothal."

Kirk mulled it over for a while, then decided that Hank was talking about someone else, someone distant from him. It also occurred to him that he was in a padded cell and the opened door was impossibly thick. It held his attention—it was three-quarters of a foot deep if it was an inch, he concluded, and the window sunk deeply in the upper half was a foot wide by only two inches high. Even the floor was padded, he noted, and felt an urge to bounce on it.

But Hank shook him again. "Look, you asshole," he said, his voice grating with suppressed anger, "cut your throat if that's the way you want it. I don't give a goddamn, personally, but Sam told me to look out for you if I could. You going to listen or not?"

Sam, he thought; the name's familiar . . . but the face . . . ? And then he remembered, remembered everything, and was shocked instantly and totally alert. He was also totally terrified; his sluggish heart leaped into his throat, stifling him. "I'm with you now," he said, his voice sounding unreal. "Go ahead."

Hank eyed him dubiously. "Sam and the fruit are in isolation," he began. "They'll be going to outside court for attempted escape. The word I get is that you'll be arraigned for the escape along with an attempted murder or two. I don't guess you need to be told that you've got a cinch ten or 15 years looking at you. And the only way you can beat it is to convince Trintz that you were nuts when you went to work on the bulls. You crippled one of them pretty good, and there ain't many on that side of the fence that want to see you go on living. But if you can convince Trintz that you were out of your head, the prison people won't take you outside for court. They'll figure you can beat the rap and maybe get committed to the bughouse. And a character like you, they don't want to take their claws out of." He paused.

And Kirk broke in, his mind still a little fuzzy. "How'd you see Sam?"

"They had to come over here for treatment," Hank said. "They were both cut all to hell from the barbed wire. That ain't important, you want to listen to what is or what?" Hank stared at him in disgust.

93

Kirk wagged his head and tried to grin. "Go ahead," he said. "My head's a little bad."

Hank grinned. "You been out damn near three days. I guess it ought to be," he said, sounding less harsh. "Look," he went on, "this is the deal: Trintz called early this morning and said to have you ready for a sodium-pentothal session. That means you'll be taken out of here and put in the Quiet Room and fixed with truth drug. And, unless you're a pretty weird character, you'll blab. But in this case, you'll only get enough jabber-juice to get you high. I've tapped about two-thirds of the ampule and filled it with salt water. I dig the shit for my own purposes . . . and it ain't making people talk. Anyway, while you're supposedly under the spell, you better do what drug-hypnotized people do, or you'll fuck us both out of a bunch of years." He paused and looked closely at Kirk. "You ever been hypnotized?"

Kirk shook his head negatively. Hank stood and reached in his pocket, then squatted back down, and offered Kirk two white pills. "Take these," he said. "A couple of bennies. They'll offset the pentothal a little." Kirk took the pills and swallowed them with a cup of water that Hank poured for him. "Now listen carefully," Hank went on. "I can't repeat myself. I'm supposed to be cleaning the cells along here, and you're supposed to be unconscious. If the M.T.A. comes along, you fake it. You listening? All right, then . . . when they come for you, act like you're still under and then . . ."

Hank talked on while Kirk lay on the warm vinyl-covered floor and listened, attempting to imprint each word in his drug-sludged mind.

After Hank was gone, with the cell door closed but unlocked, Kirk lay on the crinkly floor, going over all that the convict had told him. Occasionally he looked toward the glaring naked bulb hanging from the ceiling, wondering if the warmth in the cell was because of it. It was so bright that even with his eyes closed its brilliance seemed to light the blood vessels in his eyelids. He decided that he'd break it out if he had to remain in the cell for any length of time. The ceiling was high, maybe 15 feet; the bulb would be hard to get to. Water. He would throw water on it. Grinning to himself, knowing how to be rid of the blazing thing, its brilliance seemed to dim slightly, was not so bothersome. He turned his attention to what lay ahead.

And a while later he felt the benzedrine waking his body. But the hangover from three days of knockout drug—thorazine, probably —was not easily shaken. However, his head was clearing. He remembered attacking the guards. But no matter how he tried, he could not put a face on the guard he had hit with the wrench. In fact, the guards—all of them—as with the attack itself, seemed removed from him, as if he had been a bystander; as if he were watching a thrice-seen farcical television serial. And although he acknowledged that it had indeed been him wielding the wrench, and with an intent to kill, it was difficult to believe. Somehow, while he could remember swinging the wrench, it did not seem that it was truly he. Maybe it had not been he; he felt no guilt. It was all quite confusing. "Tell it to the judge," he said aloud, and laughed, then spent an addled moment trying to figure out what was funny.

Wrenching his attention back to the problem at hand, he began anew to go over what lay ahead. He repeated psuedo facts over and over, pushing them deeper and deeper into his head.

Sometime later as he lay against the wall, out of sight of the door window, pondering the patternless crinkles of the vinyl that upholstered the cell, the door suddenly opened. He slammed his eyes shut, cursing his hammering heart, and attempted to make his body limp. A harsh Southern-accented voice ordered somebody to "pick the son of a bitch up an' get 'im on the son of a bitchin' gurney." He was lifted to a half-seated position, and a second person began lifting his legs. A moment later soft coldness touched his spine, buttocks, thighs. It was refreshing, cooling the fever in his body. With a jerk, the gurney began moving. He let his head roll limply to the side until his ear rested against the cool pad. Very faintly he could hear the wheel below turning on its axle.

The gurney banged into something, halting abruptly, then went a little farther and stopped. Footfalls receded from his hearing, and voices began droning in the distance. As he strained to make the voices intelligible, he heard more footfalls approaching now. Leather soles, he decided, and knew it was not a convict—they wore only rubber and Neolite. The footsteps stopped nearby, and he could feel somebody watching him. Suddenly, unaccountably, he was taken with an urge to laugh. But he controlled it, and a moment later there came the sounds of shuffling feet and tinkling glass—almost like Chinese wind chimes, but not so resonant. Sudden coldness touched his inside elbow, and his palms began sweating. He solemnly cursed them, for if they were noticed, the ruse was over. He concentrated on thinking about his toes in the event whoever was there was telepathic. Then a needle pricked his arm, and he relaxed. When the needle was removed, his heart thumped violently, then came a swelling in his head. It grew bigger and bigger, and finally burst, shooting fiery white light across his brain. His heart slowed. He could no longer feel it beating. It was no longer an effort to keep his eyes shut. Euphoria spread, radiating from his scalp, numbing his face, letting his body go limp, calm, peaceful. He thought of a woman, a sensuous woman made not for sex, but rather to touch him, to massage, to tingle, to rub his every muscle, to linger long, first here, then there. His thoughts stretched, tumbling lazily, impossibly slow. A voice came, scrambled, incoherent. But soft, so soft, a compliment to the sensuousness he felt, and he cared little whether he could understand it or not.

The voice faded . . . came again . . . closer, closer. Droning, yet melodious . . . a voice to dream by . . . a lullaby. . . .

"Whalen, I want you to relax and trust me. Trust me entirely, because I'm here to help you. I want very much to help you, but you must also help me. I'm going to ask you some questions, very easy questions, and you should answer me. That way, I'll be able to help you. Trust me, Whalen, I'm here to help you. Do you understand?" The voice belonged to Dr. Trintz.

Kirk's mind murmured a warning, chipping the gloss off the voice's soothing quality. With great reluctance he heeded the warning. He thought to tell Dr. Trintz that he did indeed understand, he understood everything. He decided to tell him exactly how much he was aware of. But upon attempting to speak, he found that his lips were as muscleless as two slabs of liver, his tongue a thick, uncontrollable deformity. He was warned by it. He fought for control of his voice, his mind. And finally he found the muscles that worked his mouth, and with his tongue willed thick again, he drunkenly slurred, "Unnerthhan," and almost chuckled.

"Good," said Trintz soothingly. "Very good. Now, trust me. I want you to remember back to your cell Friday afternoon. It's important that you remember. It's the only way I can help you. Now remember, it's Friday, you're in your cell. Do you remember?"

"Membaa. Yeth, 'member Fridaa."

"Good. That's real fine. Now, I want you to tell me everything you can remember. Just take your time and don't leave anything

96

out. You must do this or I'll not be able to help you. Now, trust me, tell me everything."

Doc, Kirk thought, along with every other scummy thing you are, you've sold them your soul. I wish I could tell you a few things, Doc; like if they—whoever the fuck *they* are—could make you the crawling thing you are, maybe they made me what I am. And, Doc, making beasts like us is going to be the finish of them. But maybe that's what they want; it *must* be what they want—why else would they call you an honorable man, Doc?

It's too bad you can't fit me in a category, Doc. But my head is normally human, so is my body. So your wish theories of "bad-blood," "mutants," and "throwbacks" don't hold up. What's left, Doc? If I was actually human once, what happened to me? Think about it. And while you're thinking, think about Frankenstein's pet, think about what it was made from, what it did. Think about it. And when you've thought it out, think about me, Doc. And, Doc, don't forget yourself; don't forget the millions more like us. But, Doc, do you have any idea what a piker I feel like beside you and your kind? If I'm one man's cyanide, you're germ warfare; I'm a killer, Doc, but you're genocide.

Well, it's time to get on with this farce, Doc—we both know about things farcical, don't we, Doc?

Using slurred and garbled speech, Kirk began relating the events of the previous Friday. He worried little about facts; but such facts as the authorities were certain to be in possession of, he not only admitted, but also took the blame for. He told the doctor that the plan was his own; that he, and he alone, had stolen the wrench; that he had coerced the others into going with him. He hoped that all the "confessing" would lend a greater credibility to the tacky part of his confession.

Unlike a true hypnotic trance, sodium pentothal does not probe beyond the conscious mind. If one is consciously obsessed with guilt, one might as easily confess to crimes committed during the French Revolution as to crimes committed by oneself. Also unlike a hypnotic trance—wherein lying is rarely encountered—sodium pentothal promises to elicit about as much "truth" as a well-soused drunk will volunteer, for the drug, as with alcohol or the anonymity of the confessional, serves merely to lessen inhibitions.

And Kirk was neither guilt-stricken nor did he have a sufficient

97

quantity of the drug in his system to lessen greatly his acuity or inhibitions—no more so than a partygoer feeling lighter by a half dozen highballs. Actually, when everything was considered, he was having a fine time. And it promised to get better.

Finished relating everything up to the moment of the assault, he screwed a puzzled expression on his face, ceased talking, and squirmed.

"Go on, Whalen," Trintz prompted. "Go on. What happened next?"

Contorting his face more, Kirk was silent for a long moment before he slurred that past the point he could recollect nothing.

Silence. The hush grew, became so complete that Kirk thought he could hear air molecules bouncing against his eardrums. He had an urge to peep open an eye and tell the doctor that he was a dunce.

"Whalen," Trintz said abruptly, "I want you to tell me about your past medical history. Head injuries and that sort of thing."

Kirk squirmed around on the pad and frowned perplexedly, then answered that he had had no head injuries, not that he could remember.

"Have you had any spells in which you've blacked out?" Trintz asked, his tone insistent.

Grimacing, wriggling about, Kirk reluctantly answered that he had indeed had two such spells, but that he'd been much younger, a boy. In questioning him further, Trintz asked if he could recall the doctor who had treated him and what had been diagnosed. Kirk replied that he had no idea what had caused the spells, and he wasn't entirely certain, but he believed that the doctor's name had been Smyth or Smith or Schmitt or something. He went further, volunteering that he had called the doctor "Benny," and he gave the name of the city in which Benny had practiced. Benny was a nice doctor, Kirk added offhandedly, he used to give him peanuts; in fact, he told Kirk to eat a lot of peanuts and to drink lots of milk, too. Something about he didn't have enough sugar in his blood. When he finished talking, Trintz was silent, and Kirk wanted to chuckle. Should the Doctor check on his story, he would find that a Dr. Schmitt had practiced in the city Kirk mentioned. But, alas, the nice Dr. Benjamin Schmitt had since died in a fire that had also destroyed his records. Kirk wondered that Hank should store such apparently useless information.

Suddenly footsteps receded from the gurney, and a moment later Trintz called out. "Doctor! Dr. Russell, would you have the orderlies return this man to the cell? And then step in here a moment, Doctor."

Seconds later two persons approached the gurney, and Trintz spoke. "Doctor," he said, "this man is to remain in the same cell until I order him removed. Also, draw a blood sample and have the sugar level read."

There was a moment's silence, then Kirk felt gentle fingers touch the crook of his elbow, and the second man spoke. "What does it look like?"

"Hypoglycemia," Trintz said. "From what I gather, he may have been afflicted with it when he was younger. The stress of the attempted escape may have caused a recurrence." Footsteps retreated from the gurney, then stopped. "And, Doctor," Trintz went on, "leave him on the diet I prescribed."

"But—" began the other man.

"But, what?" Trintz broke in. "He's to be on the diet I prescribed until orders to the contrary. Is that clear?"

A pause, then, "He could die . . ." The voice sounded reluctantly resigned.

"Doctor," said Trintz in a vaguely conciliatory tone, "we don't know at this point whether hypoglycemia is the proper diagnosis. I'll have to investigate further. Meantime, run a lab check on his blood."

"Doctor," said the other quietly, "from what I know about it, it won't show in his blood . . . not at this late date. But if he has it and doesn't have a proper diet, he'll—"

"He'll get what I prescribed, Doctor," Trintz interrupted, and walked from the room.

Kirk felt the hand leave his elbow, and next he knew his eyelid was being peeled back. Panicked, he rolled his eye toward the back of his head. But too late. He knew he was too late, for he had caught a fleeting glimpse of a wizened face, gray-brown hair. He was caught. He felt a rage growing inside.

Then his eyelid was released as the man loosed a snort. A moment later he walked from the room.

Kirk opened his eyes and watched the white-smocked retreating back. His pulse had betrayed him, he concluded; his benzedrine-stimulated pulse. The second doctor had probably noticed it the moment his fingers had touched his arm. He wondered that the man had not immediately blown the whistle on him.

Suddenly two convict orderlies entered the room and Kirk shut his eyes. He was on the way back to the padded cell.

[XVII]

He was laying on the warm, resilient floor staring at nothing when a tap sounded on the window. He ignored it and lay still, thinking that somebody wanted to see if he was awake yet. But the tapping was repeated past the point of idle curiosity. So he sat up and looked toward the narrow window. It was Hank. Kirk went to the window.

Hank held a circled thumb and forefinger to the glass, then opened his mouth in laughter, although nothing could be heard through the door. He held a strip of paper to the window with printing on it: "T. taped report saying you were blacked out. Recommends you don't go to trial. Have made copy of tape in case you need it. Left orders that you stay locked high-security till further notice. Might be day or who knows? Convicts not allowed to talk with you. Can't help the food, but will drop smokes in bowl. Hang on, you've got a mean ride coming."

After reading the message, Kirk nodded his head, then remembered the blinding light, and after repeated gestures, Hank understood; he signaled that he'd leave it turned off on his shift, but that the orderlies on the night shift would probably rat on him if he asked them. Hank waved then and disappeared. A moment later the cell light went out.

Kirk lay down, staring toward the shaft of light coming through the window. He was afraid. The thought of staying in the padded cell for any length of time terrified him. He did not know why it should, but it did. He considered pleading with Dr. Trintz, begging to be released. He knew he'd hate himself, but the idea of being locked in the cell he hated more. Somehow, the padded cell was vastly more demoralizing than the cold, smelly concrete of the strip cell. In cowardice, he decided to leave the bulb in the ceiling alone; he decided to obey all orders. He felt as if he were falling apart, but was less worried about that than about staying in the cell.

Later—it seemed much later—he was lying on the floor, his body savoring the last vestiges of drug glow, and the door opened. Closing his eyes, he lay still, then felt something nudging his ribs. "Come on, boy," said a high-pitched voice. "Wake up. Now, wake up, boy, it's time to eat."

Kirk let himself be nudged a while longer, then rolled over and looked up. An old man in civilian clothes stared down at him. Behind, a convict orderly held a large metal bowl. Kirk stretched. "Where am I?" he asked dazedly, thinking it might be expected of him.

"You're in the hospital, boy," said the old man. "Seems you raised more hell than a young fella ought."

"The hospital?" Kirk stammered in show of bewilderment. "What happened? Who're you?"

"I'm the M.T.A., boy," the man said, beginning to sound impatient. "Now, take your food. You haven't eaten for a while, and you only get fed once a day. Isn't my idea . . . don't look at me like that. . . . Sorry, boy, but I've a job and do it well's I can."

Kirk's expression had not changed; the M.T.A., it seemed, was a man with a guilt. The convict wondered what was in the bowl to make him feel guilty. He watched the orderly set the quart-sized bowl on the floor and leave the cell. Then the M.T.A. handed him a capsule.

"A vitamin pill, boy," he said. "Take it about two hours after you eat."

"Water?"

"No water, boy," he said, and walked from the cell.

Kirk sat for a long minute staring toward the bowl, almost afraid to go near it, afraid of what he would find. But after a while he could take it no longer. He was hungry, famished. Crawling on all fours, he sneaked up on the bowl and sniffed at it. Eggnog. What's wrong with eggnog? he wondered, and gulped it down. A small plastic-wrapped square caught in his teeth. He threw the bowl at the door, belched, and unwrapped the packet, and rolled a smoke.

He sat there smoking a while before he noticed the strange taste in his mouth. An aftertaste the eggnog had left. After puzzling on it for a time, he decided it was salad oil. It seemed an odd ingredient for an eggnog.

But a half hour later he understood. As he squatted over the grill-covered hole in the floor, spraying his feet and the surrounding area with shit, he understood, and laughed. He was being purged of evil

101

spirits. Once upon a time it was done with the rack, thumbscrews, the stake, and other ways. But now they were humane: for purgation of heresy, they used a purgative. Kirk kept laughing while he tried to clean the spattered shit off the grill and floor with a wad of toilet paper he'd found. Maybe he had been purged of an evil spirit or two, the odor was foul enough.

A while later he rolled and lit a second cigaret, smelling the stink of his fingers, and cursed. He cursed the fright he had felt, he cursed the people who had built the cell that made him frightened. He cursed everybody. Then he leaned against the wall and relaxed. He would shit out his heart before he folded up.

[XVIII]

He was conscious when they came for him; crusty with stink, 48 pounds underweight, but conscious. And he was clear-headed as a mystic, lucid as de Sade. He was smiling.

Two convict orderlies wrestled his body onto a gurney while the old M.T.A. stood by, watching. All three had their noses pinched with distaste. He was pushed to the end of the hospital corridor, and into a large windowed room where dull beams of light shone through dancing dust, then the gurney stopped before the door to a green and white tiled bathroom. The orderlies, still grimacing in silence, lifted him from the gurney and carried him into the bathroom, and sat him on the floor of a single-stall shower. They turned the water on and departed. He closed his eyes and sat there.

A long time later he opened his eyes, and saw Hank standing over him, staring, his thin face set into rigid lines. He grinned up at him. "Hank," he croaked, his voice still and hollow.

"Goddamn, kid, goddamn," Hank muttered, his teeth bared. "That dirty motherfucker . . . that dirty motherfucker . . ."

Kirk looked down at his washboard-ribs, knobby hipbones. "Yeah," he said, and smiled at Hank.

The sharp-faced convict wagged his head, then fished in his pocket and brought out two eggs. He spent a moment peeling off the shells, and finally handed them to Kirk.

Accepting them, Kirk held them in shaking palms, letting the water beat on them. He chuckled. From eggnog to eggs. He swallowed them whole.

102

Hank reached in and shut off the shower, then produced a pitcher of orange juice, and poured Kirk cup after cup. He doubted that he would ever get enough. He drank until his stomach distended.

Then Hank took the cup away. "That's all for now," he said. "Can you stand?"

Kirk reached for the shower nozzle and slowly pulled himself to his feet. It seemed a long time before the blood reached his head. "Goddamn legs feel like Jello," he mumbled.

Hank frowned and chewed a thumb. "How do you feel besides that?"

"Wasted."

Hank left, and returned shortly with a razor and soap. He handed them to Kirk. "Do what you can with yourself," he said. "And take your time. Trintz left orders to keep you hidden till you come up a few pounds."

Kirk grinned. "Good of him." He turned on the shower again.

Hank nodded and said sourly, "Yeah, you disappointed him. . . . The bastard wanted you dead."

Kirk leaned heavily against the shower wall and tried scraping at his face with the razor. He gave it up after a moment. "Hank," he said with an easy grin, "I wish you wouldn't talk about the good doctor that way. . . . I'm reformed."

Hank laughed. "You and me," he said. "I've been reformed for years. About seven of them. It happened in a blinding flash of light —the kind you read about. In fact, it happened the day they shut me up in this hole."

"Took me longer than a day," said Kirk. "But I've seen the same light. Look, I'm smiling," and showed his teeth—and bleeding, pulpy gums.

Hank smiled uneasily, then eyed him narrowly. "Kid," he said slowly, "you ain't asked how long you were in there. . . ."

Touching his beard, Kirk said, "Three months . . . ?" but was being facetious. He had no idea how long he'd been in the cell, but three weeks or a month seemed reasonable, or unreasonable—depending upon how you looked at it.

"Fifty-nine days, kid," Hank said with a note of awe. "Fifty-nine days . . . and you're grinning. . . ." He looked closely at Kirk. "I've been working this hospital for seven years . . . and the only guys I've seen last more than a month in there were carted away in

103

straitjackets." He paused. "I started counting on the eleventh day . . . the first time I watched you running your head into the wall. . . ."

Rubbing his hairy chin, Kirk thought about it. Two months. Where had they gone? More than three months in prison. He could recall about 30 days of it. Hallucinations, shitting on himself . . . what else had he done? Where else had he been? He wagged his head, and continued showering, scraping weakly at his whiskers. A moment later he gave it up again. It would have to wait, his arms were too shaky. He looked up and saw Hank's eyes still on him. "By the way," he said, "there isn't any way I can tell you thanks. I have an idea of the hassle you went through . . . but it's not a one-way street. Anything, any time . . . all right?"

Hank looked down at the floor. "Kid," he said quietly, "I was sticking up hot-dog stands when you were wearing diapers. I used to think I was about the meanest bastard alive." He looked up, grinning wryly. "But I've got a hunch that if it was me in that cell, I'd have sold out for a bed and a meal."

"Sold out?"

"You know what they'd have done to me if they'd found out about the pentothal?"

Kirk grinned. "Funny thing," he said pensively, "I didn't think about it. But right at first, if it had occurred to me . . . yeah, I might have." He thought for a moment. "After the first little bit, though, I can't remember too much." He turned off the shower, and braced against the wall, stepped out.

Hank threw him a towel. "Anyway," he said, "I've been chewing my guts out waiting for the ax to fall." He grinned. "I wouldn't have been real mad if it did, you took the worst they could throw at you . . . the worst I've seen, anyway. These kind of things used to be common when I first started doing time three jolts ago—but nowadays they usually keep the primitive shit hidden in the backs of their heads. You know what the baby rapers and killers and the rest of the 'scum' are saying? 'Nobody'd do anything like that.'" He laughed. "Yeah, none of the animals can believe what the good guys have been doing to you."

Kirk wanted to laugh, but it stuck in his throat; the hot water had drained the last of his strength; so he snorted and kept rubbing the towel over his body, watching curiously as roll after roll of dead gray skin peeled away.

Finished drying, Hank threw a robe around him and took his arm. "Come on," he said. "You'll be locked up, but the M.T.A. will let me in and out, so anything you want, just bang on the door. Tell the orderly or whoever answers that you want to see me. I'll probably be upstairs in surgery." They came to a room with a single high bed, and Hank helped him climb onto it, then went on. "Me and some of the guys have been doing a little stealing since we heard you were getting out. We've bagged enough food to make you a fat man in a week. Even short-stopped a lobster that Lowry ordered. And here"—he handed Kirk a bottle of vitamin capsules—"take a couple a day."

Taking the bottle, Kirk stared at it for a moment. "You're being too good to me, Hank," he said, smiling. "And if I ever said you look like a weasel, I was lying."

Hank laughed. "Okay, kid," he said, and turned to leave the room, then stopped by the door to add: "Look, the guys around here think you're some kind of minor hero. They'll be offering to do favors. . . . Some of them'll even be trying to eat the crotch out of your pants. But watch out . . . this place is plagued with rats. . . . They'll be reporting your every frown. . . . You've got some people scared of you. . . . Some of them don't even believe you were blacked out. . . ." He waved, stepped through the door, and poked his head back in. "By the way," he finished, "keep smiling. It looks like the real thing."

[XIX]

He lay on the hospital bed and read book after book, discussing each aloud with himself. He exercised, forcing himself to do squats, push-ups, sit-ups, and more. But mostly, he ate. Sometimes five meals a day, sometimes one meal lasting all day. Hank would not stop bringing food. He could not stop eating it. There was a cold, hollow spot that he tried to fill, but it remained cold and hollow. He began to think it had nothing to do with hunger.

He lay awake through long hours of the night and stared toward the ceiling, his eyes unseeing, his mind blank, emotionless. Waiting. He knew it was waiting, but not what for. So he kept waiting.

On the eleventh afternoon Hank got the M.T.A. to unlock the door to his hospital cell, and entered, without food this time.

"How's it?" he asked.

"That's what you asked an hour ago, Hank," said Kirk with a grin.

The sharp-faced convict fished something out of his pocket. "Here," he said, and pitched Kirk a roll of slender, pinched-end cigarets. "You'll be leaving pretty quick from the word I get. Take those back to seg with you. Tell Sam and the queer I said hello."

Kirk stared quizzically at the bundle, then flipped open the end of one of the cigarets and shook it over his palm. Marijuana. He could not believe it. "Damn," he muttered as he looked up at Hank with a wide grin. "This is an awful lot of precious vegetable to be giving away around here."

"I grow it," Hank said easily. "This is part of my first crop this year."

Kirk stared at him for a moment. "You grow it?" It was difficult to credit.

"Yeah, that's right." Hank was laughing. "I've got nine window boxes with flowers and this stuff growing in them. Don't ask me how I get away with it. . . . I don't have the foggiest. I keep the plants clipped small. . . . I don't know. . . ." He looked toward the door, then at his watch, then went on. "I've got a few minutes, so let me tell you a quicky. About four years ago, when I first got the idea, I talked the doctors into letting me order some planter boxes from the carpenter shop. I fed them a line of shit about the patients' enjoyment. Then I had some seeds kited in and started planting them. And you can believe this, weed grows like weeds. So pretty quick I was running around half-frantic trying to keep the plants small enough to pass for ferns or whatever. Anyway, I was making my rounds one morning when a group of doctors, chemists, and pharmacologists came through on a busman's holiday. I didn't think anything about them—groups are constantly coming in— they find the joint mysterious or something—anyway, I kept on with my usual daily harvest. But after awhile I noticed this one guy that was following me around. I didn't want to act paranoid, so I kept on with my business and tried to pretend the guy was invisible. Finally, when I was about 30 feet from the main group, the guy came up and looked over my shoulder. I was plucking some leaves. He nudged me and said, 'Rather unusual manner of cultivating *Cannabis,* isn't it?' Well, I snapped. That's the Latin name for the stuff." He grimaced and wagged his head. "I still remember . . . I turned cold as an igloo in December. I thought the guy was the law. Anyway, I told him that I didn't know what he was talking about, that all I do is keep the planters clean. He just ignored me and reached over and pulled a leaf off and held it up. 'You know the difference between a male and female plant, I presume?' he said. Then he looked at me and shook his head. He said he was surprised that I hadn't been caught out. He talked like a butler in an English movie. Anyway, I asked him what he was talking about, and he pulled out a business card and put it in my hand. Then he said, 'I work in the urinalysis department of the university where you people send suspected drug users' urine. When you desire a negative reading, tear a small ragged piece from the laboratory slip—make it the lower left corner. Good day.' Just like that, he was gone." He paused, then went on slowly. "I thought maybe the guy was a nut or something. Things just don't happen like that. But the next time the bulls bring in a guy they think's been playing with heroin, I tore the corner off the lab slip. It was like I had myself on a rib. Then the report came back negative—and I knew the convict; his piss was full of junk." He grinned wryly. "Four years that's been going on. . . . Whoever the hell he is, he keeps coming through. Sometimes it puts me in a bad spot, 'cause the bulls have started thinking that I have a way of keeping the traces out of these guy's piss. I guess they're right, actually. And I suppose they think it's a little strange that the only reports that come back positive are the rats'. But if I get them a clean bill, they're liable to rat on themselves and get me and the chemist flushed down the shitter. Another thing that shows you how stupid some people are: some of the guys that've come back negative two or three times get the feeling that they have some kind of God-given immunity. And I can't tell them otherwise, or sooner or later somebody'll use the story for a parole. And what happens is that some of the guys that've gotten a couple negatives start using right away when they get out. Their parole officer has them piss in a bottle, and a couple days later they're on their way back to the joint just knowing they were framed. If it wasn't so sad, it'd be funny." He laughed. "By the way," he added, "Sam don't know about that guy. . . . You're the only one I've told about him. Do what you want with it."

"What guy?" Kirk said, grinning.

"That's best." Hank pointed to the roll of marijuana. "Why don't we?"

"Yeah . . ."

They fired a couple and inhaled, filling their lungs with pungent smoke. A while later they left the prison, went some place without walls.

The following afternoon Dr. Trintz stepped inside the hospital cell and stood there, gaunt and severe, burning the convict with hot eyes.

Kirk smiled at him.

After a long moment the doctor strode to his bedside and stared impassively down.

"I'm feeling better, Doc," said Kirk, not wanting to play the doctor's war-of-nerves game. He considered himself already the winner; he was certain that Trintz had no idea what lay on the bed smiling up at him.

Still staring, the doctor said, "You'll be returning to segregation later this afternoon." Kirk nodded, and Trintz went on. "Whalen," he said, looking closely at the convict, "I've submitted a recommendation that you not be paroled for at least five more years. Considering everything, you're lucky at that. . . . A Space Age society cannot tolerate Stone Age people . . . and you are a primitive."

Kirk heard and understood and was mildly surprised that he felt no particular anger; in fact, he felt nothing. But, he decided, it's hard to put anything in a pot that's running over. He did, however, want to tell Trintz a few things about primitives, but he thought the doctor—with his great and good social militancy or orthodoxy or whatever he called it—might not understand. He wanted to tell him that his revered Space Age was indeed ushering in a new phase of evolution: retrogression; and that he was himself merely an example of things to come, as was the good and righteous doctor. But his tongue was still, he said nothing, only smiled.

Then Trintz was watching him closely again. "It took me a long time," he said slowly, "but I finally talked with your mother."

Kirk's heart bounded to his throat and stuck there. A thousand fragmented thoughts tore through his mind. He knows! He knows I've never had a blackout! The slimy, skeleton-faced son of a bitch has been toying with me! A fog of mottled gray rose before his eyes, he forced his gaze to wander to the ceiling.

"She refuses to discuss you, Whalen. She said you were dead as far as she was concerned." The doctor sounded smug.

And Kirk felt himself soaring, euphoric, wanting to laugh and laugh. He could not believe his good fortune. For a moment he almost remembered his mother with fondness. He fought his mouth, trying to keep it straight, trying to keep it from guffawing in the doctor's smug, skeletal face. And when at last he could control himself, he screwed on a pained expression and met the doctor's eyes. "We had a falling, Doc," he said ruefully. "I haven't seen her for nearly two years."

"Tell me about it, Whalen." Trintz looked about the room, then walked to the single wooden chair and pulled it to the head of the bed, out of Kirk's sight. "I've got all the time I need, so don't skip anything."

In a short second, Kirk made a decision: he would give the doctor what he wanted. Rather than be caught weaving a complicated lie, he would offer the truth. Besides, sincerity was important to the face he wore, and he could not be properly sincere with a hastily contrived story. And at this point, he was unconcerned if the life he had previously led was exhumed or not; he felt entirely removed from it. So he talked, taking the doctor through his early years, adolescence, and further. His voice had an almost hypnotic effect on him; it was as if the droning in his ears came from afar, as if he were hearing his own words without knowing what next his mouth would say. He went on and on.

I hadn't been living at home since my last year of high school, but I was never very far away. I couldn't bring myself to leave. When I finally quit school and went to work, I passed within a block of my parent's house every day, and found myself dropping in on them quite a bit. Usually the old lady invited me for dinner. She probably considered it the proper thing to do. There were a hundred places I'd have rather gone, but there were 200 places my father would have preferred that I go. So I always showed up. He never said anything, he'd just sit there with his face almost in his plate, not looking at me. Every now and again I'd bring along one of those Dr. Spock books and read to him through the meal. All the while the old lady would be making gestures and flapping her arms, telling me to stop. She was easy to ignore. And every time I'd ease up on him, he'd look at me funny, like he couldn't believe it . . . like he was addicted to the pain I caused him and couldn't stand the withdrawal symptoms. So I kept the screws in him. It wasn't hard to do.

Then one morning on my way to work, I stopped by and the old lady told me it was my father's birthday; she invited me over that evening. I'd never even considered that he might have birthdays— it was hard to believe that he'd actually been born. Anyway, I told her that I'd come by. And she asked me to bring him a gift of some kind, and to "be nice for a change, dear." I promised.

During lunch I looked through a few stores but couldn't decide what to get him. It was like shopping for a stranger. Then it occurred to me what to do, so I made a few phone calls and went on back to work.

Later, at their house, we ate. I smiled a lot and toasted his health, and every so often he'd look at me like he thought I was sick. Meantime, the old lady was sitting there, grinning stupid as a jack-o'-lantern and making gushing noises. Finally she excused herself and was back a minute later with a birthday cake full of candles. She put it on the table in front of him. He stared at it a moment, then looked at me and smiled. He'd never done that before.

That's when the doorbell rang. I started to answer it, but the old man waved me back, said he'd get it, then picked up his cane and went to the door. He usually shuffled along all hunched over, but right then he was walking tall, acting almost snappy, like he felt years younger. Then he opened the door, and it was like his spine turned to sand and ran down his leg. He fell apart.

He turned and stared at me, then stepped back from the door, closed it, and sagged to the floor. In his hand was a leash; at the end of the leash was a dog; a greyhound identical to the one he'd given me years back. There was a huge tag hanging from the dog's neck; it read "LEGS."

I don't know how long we stared at one another, but it seemed hours. He just sat there, an arm around the dog's neck, staring. That's when I decided it was finished. I didn't feel victorious or smug. I felt empty, tired, finished with him, with both of them. Always, when I was younger, I wanted to lean on him till he died. But I knew then that he was already dead . . . a long time dead.

Finally I couldn't look at him any longer, so I got up to leave. And the next thing I knew I had my hand on his shoulder, touching

110

him. It was eerie. A son touching his father. It occurred to me that it was the first time in my life I'd touched him. Twenty years old, almost twenty-one, and I'd never touched my father unless I was hitting him. That's when I first realized he was human; a broken-down, beaten old man, but human. Maybe it's the first time I realized that I might myself be human.

Without a word I left and drove back to my apartment. There was some broad living there; I kicked her out, told her to come back the next day. Then I packed, I was leaving in the morning. I didn't know where, didn't care . . . anywhere would do as long as it was far away. That decision brought me a strange peace, like something corrosive inside of me had eaten itself out; like there was a large hollow spot inside me that I could build things in. Everything seemed to take on a different coloring, a brightness, like all I'd ever seen were shades of gray, and suddenly I could see in color.

A while later I went to an all-night grocery and cashed a check to clean out my account. Back at the apartment, I started writing the landlord a note telling him to keep the deposit or flush it or shove it or do whatever he wanted with it. It was a ridiculous note but I kept on writing and writing, spilling out nonsense, saying nothing. Maybe I just wanted to be heard. I think I was happy—or learning what happiness meant.

Then the phone rang. Only a few people had the number and none of them would be calling me for a midnight chat. It rang and rang. I stared at it and broke out in a sweat. Something was wrong. . . . I felt it crawling up my spine. . . . I picked up the phone and held it, didn't say anything.

"Kirk?" it asked. It was the old lady, she sounded odd, almost friendly. I was certain then that something was wrong. "Kirk," she said finally, "your father is dead. You killed your father." She hung up.

I don't know how long I sat there or what I thought about. I just sat and stared, numb, my brain feeling dried up. It was getting light outside when something made me look up . . . and there she was, pale, ghostly, looking as if she'd coated her face with rice powder. We looked at each other a while, then she pulled a chair close and sat down.

"He waited till you left," she said, sounding distant, echolike, "then he put the dog in the bedroom and said he was going for a drive. He always went for long, lonely drives, but you wouldn't know that." She stared blankly, then went on, saying how a call came a couple hours later from the highway patrol. They'd found his car and body in the ocean. It was impossible to say whether or not it was suicide, because he'd crashed through a guardrail on a newly constructed S-turn that he couldn't have been familiar with. He hadn't been going fast, they said, just straight; did he leave a note? He did not.

"But," she finished, "it was nothing else but suicide." Of that much she was certain. It might have been the first time in her wishywashy life that she was certain of anything. In fact, I'm sure of it. The bitch had become flesh and blood to spite me. She and my bastard father actually liked each other. She said she wanted to tell me about him so it'd eat my guts out. That's the word she used —"guts." Another time it would have been funny.

She told me about my father being captured during the war. I'd listened to that sad story till I was sick of it when I was younger. . . . It was about the only thing I identified him with, the measure of his life in my eyes. Anyway, she went on, telling me how they'd tortured him, driven him mad. She didn't have to tell me that. . . . But, then, with the war over, she told me how he'd come home obsessed with the notion that his son should grow up devoid of weakness, of emotion. He had an idea that the only way I'd never suffer or be hurt was to be insensitive to pain, a special breed of tough. It seems as if he had brought home his captors' superman complex.

At any rate, when I finally shoved the gun in his face, he realized that he'd made a monster; all his cowardice came back . . . everything he'd known during the war came back to haunt him. . . . He turned to dust . . . yellow dust. . . . He'd built me of his fears, and his fears had come home. . . .

She found him in the car that night, unconscious, a hose from the exhaust to the window, the motor on. She never told me. . . . It wouldn't have mattered if she had.

Twice more she found him like that. Each time it was after I'd slapped him around. . . . Actually you'd think he'd have found something more effective if he really wanted to go. . . .

Anyway, some place in there, something happened to him. He wasn't afraid any more. He just didn't care. It was as if he'd become disinterestedly interested in what more I'd do to him, what

I'd become, how long it would be before I just out and out killed him. I guess he wanted me to. Not merely to put him out of his misery but, in a way, to put me out of my own, to kill the things he'd made inside me. But by the time I had the gun, I no longer wanted to kill him. . . . I wanted him to live a long, long time. . . . I needed to torture him a long, long time. . . . And once started, I couldn't quit, it was addicting . . . even when it caused me discomfort, attacks of conscience, and was more trouble than pleasure, I couldn't quit. It was like eating—I had to torment him to live.

Maybe he finally realized that when I had the dog delivered. Maybe he thought he could clean the poison in me by killing himself. Or maybe he knew that the poison had dried up that night. . . . Maybe he knew it and killed himself because his life had long been over and he knew mine had only begun that night. . . . Maybe it was his revenge for all the years I spent getting my revenge. . . . Then, too, it may have been an accident. . . . I'll never know. . . .

The old lady demanded that I go with her to the funeral. I refused. But she kept nagging and nagging . . . a damned Harpy, trying to eat my soul while there was a little life left in me. . . . I don't know why I didn't knock her down and walk out. . . . I should have. But she finally said that after the funeral she never wanted to see me again. That was the nicest thing she'd ever told me. So I agreed to go.

But even when we got there, she wouldn't let me rest. She kept nagging, poking, pestering, telling me to go look in the casket, to see him one more time before the worms ate his face off. She was so changed from her usual witless self that I was shocked. I told her to shove it. It didn't faze her. Then I told her to get fucked, and she just smiled maliciously and kept on poking. I didn't want to go forward. . . . I was afraid . . . no reason, not a rational one, anyway. But there was some nameless dread . . . like if I saw him dead, it would mean that he'd once been alive and real, that he had some value. . . . I couldn't accept that. . . . But she kept on in my ear all through the service, and there were other people I didn't even know who were crying for him. . . . I didn't know anybody knew him . . . funny. . . . Anyway, I couldn't think. . . . My head was fuzzy. . . . The bitch started pulling me . . . pulling me . . . then she'd push . . . push. . . .

And there he was . . . smiling. . . . The bastard was smiling at me . . . just laying there smiling, looking smug, showing me that he'd won after all . . . smiling. . . .

Something happened in my head. Maybe I screamed or just thought about it. But next I knew I was in my car, headed nowhere.

What I did, where I went, I don't know. I just drifted. I wasn't alive, but I wasn't dead, either. If I'd ever had a self, I lost it somewhere. . . . I was just a thing . . . or maybe a non-thing. . . . There was no significance . . . not to me, not to anybody else. All biological, no humanness, no identity . . . not even a face in a faceless crowd . . . nothing but a shadow without substance. . . . At first, I knew it . . . later, I didn't care. . . . Nothing mattered. . . .

The car burned up. . . . A junkie paid a few bucks for it. . . . I thumbed to another city, going nowhere. . . .

Well, the rest of it is no easier to understand . . . but here I am. . . .

When he finished, the room was hushed. He lay still, eyes shut, feeling drained, light-headed, almost disembodied. He'd talked too much, but didn't care.

"Whalen," said Trintz, his voice a clarion call shattering the quiet, "how do you feel about having been in that cell . . . ?" Breaking off, he was suddenly standing over Kirk, looking down, his expression as unreadable as ever. "Never mind . . . never mind," he muttered absently, then strode toward the door. There, he turned slowly around and stared at the convict, frowning, pulling at the bottom of his jacket. "Whalen," he said hesitantly, "there are 3,000 prisoners here. I have to speak with at least 300 of them a year. I can't—" He stopped abruptly, then stared across the room, clenching his fists, making jerky movements. "If you want to talk with me, send a note," he finished with a rush and spun around and hammered on the door until it was opened.

Watching him leave, Kirk shrugged and laughed aloud. "Don't get soft, you scum-sucking creep."

[XX]

Two guards escorted him from the hospital to segregation and past all the screaming and cursing convicts. Kirk laughed, waved to them, urged them on.

114

When they came to the rear of the building, the guards ordered him to enter the office where he had been interrogated by the associate warden. Behind the desk, bent over a green-paged logbook, writing, was Yancy, his iron-gray hair throwing off dull glints.

The big guard looked up and, as he recognized Kirk, smiled. He nodded to the pair of escort guards. "I'll take him from here," he told them.

Back of him, Kirk heard one say hesitantly, "You . . . uh . . . sure? He's a bad one."

Yancy's face went wide-eyed with exaggerated interest. "Is that right?" he said in amazement. "Did he give you any trouble?"

"Uh . . . not really . . . but . . ."

"But?" Yancy prompted.

Kirk glanced over his shoulder at the two guards; he had not bothered to notice them before—a guard is a guard. Clad in the anonymity of khaki, it was difficult to distinguish one from another, particularly when most of them pulled their hat visors over their eyes, low to the bridge of their noses, so that they had to walk with their chins in the air to see where they were going. Chins have a way of looking alike.

One guard leaned negligently against the door frame, his lined, haggard face wearing an expression of bored unconcern. The other, the speaker, stood rigid, sweaty, big in the stomach. He looked as fit for a tussle as an aged cocker spaniel. His eyes were fixed intently on Yancy, almost beseeching. "Well . . . uh," he muttered, "they say he's a . . . a bad actor, this one."

Yancy twisted his mouth in a sour, lop-sided grin. "And what would you do if he started acting bad?" he said, then gestured impatiently. "Forget it, forget it. I'll take him from here."

The guard leaning against the door winked at Yancy, then touched his hat and shrugged resignedly. He walked from sight. The second guard spent a moment darting his eyes from the convict to Yancy, then he, too, shrugged resignedly and walked out.

"Whew!" sighed Yancy, waving both hands disgustedly toward the door, then looked at Kirk and said, "Sit down, kid."

Kirk dropped into a chair before the desk. "You're working a different schedule, huh?"

"Yeah, over here for the full five days now. It's better." Yancy

115

stared down at his hands, opening and closing them. "You look like they've been feeding you grasshoppers," he said distantly.

"Yeah," Kirk said, watching the guard shift uneasily in his chair, wondering why. There was a long silence.

And finally Yancy looked up, frowning, chewing his lip, eyes narrowed. "What the fuck's wrong with you?"

Kirk was instantly infuriated. "What's wrong with me?" he repeated, teeth bared, seething. "There's something wrong with me because I hate this fucking garbage can? I'm demented because I made a play for the wall?" He took a breath. "Tell me about it, Yancy. Tell me something's wrong with me because this place crawls inside me and starts eating, tell me those walls aren't really there."

Yancy wagged his head and looked down at his hands. "Kid," he said slowly, "I'm not talking about the try. Far as that goes, I don't think anybody's real mad about that. There's some red faces, there always is, but that's because some people take themselves too important. I'm talking about the rest of it. . . . I'm talking about the fire bomb you didn't have anything to do with, the assault you weren't responsible for, the two months you spent in the ding-a-ling cell. . . ." Looking up, he gazed for a moment at Kirk, then went on. "Kid, you know how short life is? This ain't a sermon, but a guy hasn't got enough time to piss it away in these places. And keep this in mind: the joint ruins most guys. . . . They're never good for a goddamn thing after four or five years inside. That goes for the guards, too—like that asshole that just brought you back—I haven't seen two of them worth the brass in their badges after working five years behind the walls. I ain't excluding myself. Maybe it's the people places like these attract; or maybe it's the rottenness of the place that turns people rotten. I came here after the war because my feet were tired of mud and filth. And thinking about peddling brushes kept me awake at night, and I'm bright enough to know I couldn't sell nothing but maybe Halloween masks. . . ." He grinned wryly. "But the mug don't come off. And as far as skills go, I have trouble with my shoelaces. So I ended up here . . . and between you and me and the fencepost, I haven't been too proud of myself. But just like a lot of convicts, I found a home in prison." He fidgeted, then glared at the convict. "But goddamn it, kid, you're young; you can do a couple more years and pick up the pieces and fuck looking back." He broke off and

116

offered Kirk a cigaret, lit it, then continued. "I ain't one for advice, but I got an idea that the best thing you can do for yourself is keep on hating this cesspool with all your heart. . . . Advice like that could cost me my meal ticket. . . . Right now, I'd tell them to shove it . . . but, tomorrow?" He snorted. "Tomorrow's a hell of a time when you start piling up the years. It's when the bills come. . . . It's when you're reminded that you're finishing up and you want a little ease. So you keep making the bucks and hope retirement comes before you rot like everything around you. . . . Oh, fuck! I ought to get me a pulpit." He looked closely at Kirk, his eyes pinched. "Kid," he said with painful intensity, "don't hurt yourself no more," and went on briskly, "Get out of here. Go tell the bull at the door I said let you in. You're in the same cell and your property's still there. Them two guys you made go with you are probably hanging on the door. That goddamn fag'll probably come on himself." Abruptly dropping his head, Yancy lent his attention to the logbook, ignoring Kirk.

The convict stood, his mind full of words, his mouth squeezed shut. Looking down at the top of the guard's head, he rapped his knuckles hard against the desktop, then walked quickly from the office. Damn that ugly son of a bitch, he thought; damn him for a decent bastard.

Leslie was in front of the shower drying off when Kirk walked through the hall door. He spotted him and, wrapping the towel around his waist, ran toward him, his knees together, legs swinging outward in a manner that was at once awkward and graceful, hair stuck wetly to his forehead, making squeaky, breathless noises. Smiling, feeling warm, Kirk watched him near. Then Leslie was up in the air, grabbing him, squeezing, screeching, blubbering, burying his face in Kirk's neck. "Baby, baby," he sobbed.

Kirk spun him around once, then pushed him away and let him down. "Hi," he said quietly, smiling.

Leslie held his arm, searching his face with teary eyes. "Hi," he said finally, then flapped his mouth and choked.

Kirk tousled Leslie's hair. "Give me back my arm, you goofy queer."

Leslie leaped on him again, his mouth still flapping wordlessly. But Kirk pinned his arms. "None of that sexy shit," he said, laughing. He ran his fingers gently through Leslie's hair, and when the little fruit blinked and smiled questioningly, as if he found it difficult to believe, he smiled lovingly and yanked. Then he ran.

At the rear of the hall, he turned, hands held defensively before him. "I was only kidding, Leslie," he said, and added a puppy-dog face.

But Leslie leaped on him anyway. Kirk pinned his arms again and carried him to the front of the shower. He grinned in at Sam. Sam grinned back. They grinned for a long time.

Then Leslie was tugging at his arm again. "Yancy's been telling us what they've been doing to you," he said in a rush. "Gawd! it was horrid. I haven't been able to sleep without crying. . . . Okay, okay, you don't want to hear it. But it's delicious to see you again . . . and you don't look any battier than before . . . just skinnier. . . . But all the stories . . . wow! They had you out of your head. Sam and me got nailed with another five-year sentence but they ran it concurrent. . . . They think Sam saved that bull's life . . . and he probably did. My dear, you were positively in a thing—"

"Shh!" Kirk interrupted, and clapped a hand over Leslie's mouth, then turned to Sam, who had shut off the shower and was drying.

Sam laughed quietly as he worked the towel over his body. "You made it," he said. "You did it, you beautiful bastard. We been walking the wall, but you made it. I can't say nothing now. . . . You got my head bad. Go away and gain some weight." He was having trouble talking.

Kirk's mouth was curled in a grin that was almost painful. "I didn't do anything," he said finally. "Not really. Hank's the one. . . . The guy's unbelievable. He sent some joints with me, too. Let's wait till they cut us loose to the yard."

"Yeah," Sam said, waving him off. "Now blow away and let me get dressed before I start acting like that dizzy broad. Look . . . the fucking nut-nuzzler's crying. . . ." Sam lent his attention to the towel.

And Kirk saw that Leslie was indeed crying, not just the previous sprinkling of tears. "Come on," he said, clutching at Leslie's elbow and walking from the shower, "quit acting like a little old lady."

Leslie leered through the tears and stuck out his tongue, then gave Kirk the finger. "I'm not an *old* lady," he said, stamping his foot. "Besides, what kind of fag would I be if I didn't make

118

scenes?" Then he smiled and wiped his eyes, and continued. "Let's sit down, I have a million things to tell you. . . ."

They did, and Kirk learned that the guard at the hallway door was a new security measure; that gun tower five was now manned around the clock; that the three of them were tentatively—depending upon good behavior—scheduled to be released from segregation in June or July.

And he continued, talking exuberantly and gesticulating. He leered a lot, too.

Later, in his cell, Kirk lay atop the bunk and wondered at the quietness in his body and mind. He felt like a machine. There were feeble spots of warmth inside him when he thought of Sam, Leslie, Hank . . . and Yancy, but it seemed a warmth generated by his mind rather than emotions. But for others . . . who? . . . Was there anybody else? . . . Beyond what he could see there was a void, an emptiness . . . or perhaps the emptiness was inside of him? . . . An emptiness bigger than boredom, bigger even than apathy? He thought about it for a moment, but without interest; and soon the thought was gone. Then he wondered why he thought so little of late, why he mentally skirted abstractions that would necessarily lead to thought. He shrugged. It didn't matter, nothing mattered. He slept.

[XXI]

During exercise period the following day, the three convicts huddled together at the end of the hall and Kirk related his stay in the padded cell and concluded the recital by mentioning the visit from Dr. Trintz.

Frowning, Sam worried his lower lip, then grinned. "I think you got that punk Trintz fucked up," he said. "I think you can do a little twisting and make that punk squirm. He had an attack of conscience and was simple enough to let it show. Next thing he'll be showing you his kids' pictures and telling you what a messy housekeeper his wife is." He stared hard at Kirk. "If you don't stick it off in that bastard, and keep twisting till he begs, you're a damn fool. You could have him eating your shit if you sneak up on him right."

Kirk nodded. "I've already thought about it," he said slowly. "But I'm going to let a little time pass . . . see what comes up. If nothing else happens, then I'll start working on him to tear up that five-year-denial recommendation. But there's time. . . . I don't go before the parole board for . . . what? Seven, eight months, I guess." He looked closely at each of them. "But I don't want to have to grease that motherfucker. I don't want to do another seven or eight days in this stinking son of a bitch."

Sam glanced at Leslie, who looked at the floor, then turned back to Kirk, shaking his head. "You're going to have to," he said. "We're dead and stinking in here. They have a bull glued to the hall door, keeping an eye on us. So, short of taking a hostage, I can't figure any way out of the building, let alone past the wall. And as far as a hostage goes . . . well, it doesn't. It's a dead-end street; the armory bull's got orders to open up even if he sees the warden's throat about to be sliced. Look," he paused, and went on, "we took a long chance and got further than we should've. For right now the best thing we got going are big smiles." He showed his teeth in something that might have been a smile but was not. "And when they spring us . . . well, that's another thing. I been playing with a few ideas. But the thing now is to lay dead and wait."

Kirk nodded, reluctant to accept it, but knowing he must. "Yeah," he said with an easy grin, "wait."

"Hey," Leslie said suddenly, tugging at Sam's arm, "tell him about the new warden."

Sam's lips curled sardonically. "Yeah," he said, sounding at once scornful and hopeful, "that's right. You probably ain't heard, but Yancy brought us a newspaper article about this dump. Hell of a story, but nothing we don't know. About every ten years the geeks in the legislature stumble over some twenty-year-old statistics and figure out their penal system ain't working too swell. They throw it on the table and kick it around for awhile, then the incumbent warden starts sweating and promises point five percent rehabilitation if only he's given a little more time and a lot more money. The government people have hot pants for a secretary or valet or something, so they usually give the guy more money than he wants with the understanding that he'll go away and quit embarrassing them for another ten years." He paused for a thoughtful moment. "Well," he continued, "this time one of the senators wasn't going for the worn-out routine. He got to somebody; somebody got to somebody else. . . . Now we're getting a new warden . . . end of the month. A guy by the name of Benson. Nobody's ever heard of him. . . . They say he ain't been inside a prison before, doesn't have anything but—and I'm quoting—'ideas.' Whatever the hell hat they pulled his name out of, nobody seems to know. Wardens are supposed to be promoted screws, not some guy off the street. And this guy, Benson . . . he's a psychiatrist. . . . Weird. . . ." He wagged his head perplexedly. "Anyway, when he went before the legislature to have his appointment confirmed, they threw the usual questions at him—the ones that can't be answered wrong. But he started *offering* information. . . . For instance, he told them that the death penalty was, in his own words, 'antediluvian and in many cases has the same deterrent effect as threatening a child with an ice-cream cone.' And while they were gagging on that, he said he's planning to phase out ex-guards holding counselor positions if they can't pass the proper tests and that he'll replace them with sociology majors. By that time the government people were chewing paper clips. But Benson didn't lighten up. He stuck them with one that had nails in it. He said he's going to increase the psychiatric staff to three the first year and seven the year following, plus the same number of psychologists. Then one of the senators jumped up and said he'd refuse to approve a budget increase for 'such frivolity.' Benson said he didn't need more money—he'd do with less cops. He said that any time a staff of almost 600 is necessary to keep 3,000 walled men from getting away, there's something wrong somewhere." Sam laughed a moment. "So one old bastard jumped out of his chair and said Benson is trying to set penology back a quarter century. After that, the only way they could stop the laughing in the gallery was to confirm Benson's appointment." He paused to frown. "I ain't too bright, I suppose, and I don't see things like other people see them. . . . For instance, all the 'humane' ex-wardens and their pea-brained wives that write books blowing their horns a lot and taking credit of other peoples' ideas . . . well, they make me puke. Same thing with these greasy ex-convicts that spend a couple years in prison then write a book 20 years later talking about all the swell fellas they met and how much they were inspired by the light in the warden's eyes. They don't bother mentioning that the whole system is rotten from the core out . . . no, they're concerned with the indignity of shitting on a toilet without a wooden seat. . . . They don't say anything about having your asshole peered in every second time you wipe it; they don't men-

121

tion tear-gassing guys in their cells, but they talk about having beans too often. . . . Aw, fuck it." He broke off and looked at the other two. "One last thing," he added, "Benson's news because he makes noise. But anybody can make noise with a plastic whistle. If he acts like he talks, swell; if he doesn't . . . well, I get almost sexually excited watching a guy that thinks he's full of principles choke himself on them."

Kirk shrugged his indifference. "Either way, I'm not too enthused. He might be the nicest guy in the world, but I'll bet my life he doesn't tear down the walls. As far as I'm concerned, a guy needs hanging when all he hopes for is that the new warden will serve eggs on Sunday." He stared at them for a moment, then, suddenly curious, asked, "By the way, who's the warden now? What does he look like? What does he do?"

Sam burst out laughing, and finally, still chuckling, said, "Kirk, you're quick. It took me almost three years before I found out there *was* a warden. I'd always thought he was maybe something like the boogeyman, something to scare people with. But one day I looked up and saw some geek with a cowboy hat and high-heeled boots leading around a bunch of representatives for the state appropriations committee. He didn't look like he knew where he was going himself. And he was the warden." He chuckled again. "Anyway, come to find out, he was wanting more money for the coming year. So he took all the brass around to see a 'cross section' of the prisoners. . . . Somehow they all turned out to be shitty-nosed stool pigeons. Then," he added, "I saw him one other time—when I was in here, up front. That was when a handful of half-assed liberal congressmen decided to redraft some of their more insane laws. The warden brought them into seg and stood them in the hall. The congressmen went away wiping the spit out of their eyes, dreaming of sweet Auschwitz. So you see," he said wryly, "there really is a warden . . . whatever his name is. . . ."

Kirk laughed for a moment, then Leslie leaped on him, all over him, slobbering, making hungry, almost famished noises. "Get off of me!" Kirk yelled—not too loud, the guard might hear. "Get off me, you fucking barracuda. . . . Quit biting! Hey, Sam, get this—ouch!—get this man-eating son of a bitch off me. *Sam!*"

But Sam had gone to shower.

Spring came, with warmer nights, one blanket. It meant something else, too, something for all seasons.

They were pacing the hall together when Yancy opened the door and stepped inside.

"Come here, you clowns," the guard said and, when they did, went on: "Listen, there's a guy coming in right now that got ripped off by about 20 guys. He's going to testify against them." He paused and fixed the three convicts with a flat expression. "It'd be kind of hard to explain if he decided to light himself on fire. He ain't going to be coming out of the cell, and I can't see any way he'll be bugging you guys . . . but if he does, for crissakes let me know and I'll figure out another place to put him. All right?"

They agreed, and Leslie, wide-eyed, said, "Twenty guys! All at once, that sounds like enough to make a boy pregnant."

Yancy made a face and jumped back through the door.

The three convicts looked at one another and shrugged, then walked to the fourth cell and stood idly awaiting a glimpse of the convict who had been raped—raped times 20, according to Yancy —and who was going to say so on the stand.

"Damn," said Sam. "Testifying against 20 guys means a total of ten centuries if they all get made. Now, that really sounds like rape."

Kirk laughed. "Yeah, but it's a cinch they wouldn't do it again. Fifty years is enough to teach anybody the evil of having a stiff dick."

Leslie punched him. "What do you know about a stiff dick, you eunuch?"

Kirk laughed some more. "A hell of a lot less than you."

Then the hall door opened and Yancy stepped inside. The three convicts looked at the prisoner with the big guard, then at one another, incredulously. The newcomer looked as if he had come a long way . . . all the way from the prehistoric past. Set atop an emaciated body was a brown-haired, pointed skull with a prognathous jaw, and a forehead that sloped steeply to the crown, then dropped straight to the shoulders. The convict's haystack-like hair grew from a point about an inch and a half off the bridge of his nose.

"Gawd!" Leslie whispered hoarsely. "Whoever raped that guy had a thing about monkeys."

"Phew! Tell the truth," Sam agreed.

As the convict neared, his face lit up with a wide, simianlike smile. "Hi," he gurgled.

Sam grinned. "Hi, Sad Sack."

The convict smiled even wider and made some happy noises, then stepped through the cell door that Yancy held open.

The guard locked the door and approached the trio. "Come on, you guys," he pleaded. Circling a forefinger at his temple, he lowered his voice. "The guy's only got half his marbles."

"Half?" Sam said wryly. "That guy ain't ever had any . . . just an empty hole."

"Come on, you clowns," Yancy said earnestly, "take it easy on him." He walked from the hall.

Kirk approached the newcomer's window and looked inside. The convict was sitting on the edge of the bed, smiling at the walls. Kirk banged the door and he turned.

"You're the guy had a little trouble, huh?" Kirk asked, curious, not fully believing what he saw.

The convict grinned vacuously. "Yeah," he said. "Dey even had me inna hosp'tal." Judging by his chortle, he found that very funny.

"Tell me about it," Kirk prompted, then went on quickly. "You care if we call you Sad Sack?"

The convict rocked his head, bouncing his ears off his bony shoulders. "Sad Sack wotsa piple call me," he said happily.

Watching Sad Sack bounce his head around was giving Kirk a headache; he wished he would stop. "Tell me about what happened to you, Sad Sack," he said.

The convict burped out a couple giggles, then said, "Dey stick dare tings in mouf and here." He patted his buttocks.

Kirk learned, by degrees, that Sad Sack—a name Sam had tagged him with, only to find that he was not the first; a name earned by virtue of his looks, not his moods; he had only one, it seemed: idiot happiness—had been invited into some convict's cell, and there had had his clothing removed and had been gangbanged. It was difficult, from what Sad Sack related, to see where the rape element entered, for the convict seemed to feel that it had been a very fine adventure. He was not at all grieved by relating

124

one after the other all the different ways he'd been mounted and the large variety of sizes, shapes, and colors of "tings" he'd had in his "mouf." However, as a result of his adventure, he had begun to bleed; it ran down his leg, would not stop. Subsequently, he was taken to the hospital, and after he'd related his adventure to some "mens," he had been asked to look through piles of "pitchers"— mug shot—and to point out the "frens" who had joined in his adventure.

Kirk questioned him further, asking him why he was in prison, and Sad Sack giggled and chortled and stammered through an explanation that he'd "pwayed wit 'ittle girl a wong time ago." He made it known, though, that he "wiked it here" because he had more fun than he'd ever had when he was living at a big house with a lot of other children who poked him with sticks and pulled his hair; in fact, he added in his inimitable manner, he "wiked" the "mens" for helping to send him to such a nice "pwace."

When Sad Sack was finished, Kirk tried to rub the tightness out of his head. He turned from the cell, gnashing his teeth.

Sam snorted, and said, "Why don't you two go stand by the hall door so the screw can't see down here?" He grinned at Kirk's look of curiosity, and added: "If I stand on the hinge of his door, my joint'll go through the window. I've played with myself so long I got permanent hooked fingers—"

"Shut up!" Kirk spat, glaring at Sam with bared teeth. "You make that guy eat your dick—count on getting it kicked between your ears!" He spun away, seething, rabid. At the hall door, he leaped up and smashed both feet into it, then leaned against it, tearing at his hair, at the fire inside his skull.

Seconds later the door flew open, slammed him to his knees. Without thought, he was up, spinning, charging toward the door, toward the guard standing there.

The guard went wide-eyed, quickly disappeared. Kirk wrenched the door wide and dashed through, an animal snarl loud in his ears. He raced after the guard, watched him skid into the office, slam shut the door. The convict threw his weight at the door. It held. Unthinking, mindless, he smashed a fist through the wire-reinforced glass. Reaching through, he twisted the handle, then leaped inside. The guard was behind the desk, cowering, his face ashen, oily, his eyes wide with terror. The convict moved toward him.

And suddenly a khaki-colored arm swung under his chin, bow-

125

ing him back. He threw his arms up and behind, then leaped upward, letting his body drop heavily, legs parallel to the ground. His hands locked together behind his captor's neck at the same moment the arm holding his own neck was wrenched loose. He attempted to flip the guard overhead into the desk. But the body didn't flip, didn't budge, not with all his weight hanging from the man's neck.

Yancy, he thought, and without knowing how it happened, he crumpled to the floor, then climbed slowly to his knees and deliberately crashed one fist after the other through the front of the wooden desk. He knelt there, eyes shut, teeth gritted, head hanging limp, both hands captured to the wrists as if in stocks.

Numb, unthinking, Kirk heard movement and noises, then only a hollow roar inside his head, the sound of a forest fire.

"Kirk, baby . . ."

Leslie's voice, faraway, mournful. Then fingers were in his hair, stroking, rubbing.

"Kirk, baby . . . are you okay now?" Leslie asked softly. "Yancy's got the bull up front telling him about knocking guys down with the door. That's your story, baby."

Kirk raised his head, shaking the fog from it, and looked up at Leslie with a smile. "I like you bunches, fag. Why aren't you a girl?"

Leslie's mouth curled in a quavering smile, and suddenly his eyes were swimming, teary. "I'm sorry," he sobbed, and hurried from the office.

Kirk shrugged, wondering what he'd said but not really caring. He pulled his hands from the splintered desk. They were lacerated across the knuckles, in addition to a number of scratches; more blood than damage, though, he concluded.

"Let me see." Sam stepped into the office and squatted to look at Kirk's hands. "Bust back to the shower and wash yourself off. I got to rearrange the furniture and get rid of the glass." Pulling Kirk's head back, he gazed into his eyes. "I ain't running for no elections," he said, "but I was just kidding about Sad Sack."

"I know it, Sammy," Kirk said. "My head got bad, that's all . . . forget I said anything."

"You'd best start freezing on that shit," Sam said. "You got Yancy liking you. . . . He might be able to pull you out of this one. You been lucky so far . . . but don't count on luck to last forever.

. . . It doesn't, it can't. So give it up, buddy. Like I told you before, I ain't too bright, but I'm enough older than you to know that a guy can't make this scurvy world any better than it is." He helped Kirk to his feet. "Hurry up. I got to get this place rearranged before Yancy brings that other screw back here." He pushed Kirk out the door.

Kirk turned on one of the showers and washed the blood from his hands. Leslie materialized with a towel and a half dozen Band-Aids. Setting Kirk on the tile step in front of the shower, he dried his hands and covered the worst of the cuts. The silence between them grew heavy.

When he had finished tending the cuts, Leslie turned Kirk's palms up and buried his face in them. "Baby," he cried, "don't do this to me any more. They'll kill you, baby, they'll kill you. Be good . . . *please* be good."

Kirk pulled one hand away and dug his fingers in Leslie's hair. "Hush," he said gently, pulling his head back. He wiped the tear-stained face with the bloody towel. "Hey, blue eyes, are you the same creep who sticks up stores and stabs people? I'd tell you to act like a man, but you'd probably hit me . . . and all I'm trying to say is that I wish you'd stop crying. It upsets me. Really."

"Oh Christ! Scaring bulls to death and holding hands with a man!" Yancy hovered over them, amazement sketched deep in his lumpy face. "Oh, for the love of Jesus-fucking-Christ!"

"Dirty old man!" Leslie exclaimed, suddenly grinning up at Yancy. "Look, baby," he added to Kirk, "the goon's got crepe soles so he can sneak around and spy on people."

Kirk stood up, looking closely at the big guard. Yancy held his gaze, straight-faced, his eyes mirroring bewilderment and grief and something more . . . something the convict couldn't read . . . perhaps bitter impatience, perhaps compassion. "I don't know why you're troubling yourself, Yancy," he said slowly. "But I appreciate . . . fuck that . . . there aren't words. But I can't do anything for you if they come after your badge."

"I'll worry about my badge, kid. You worry about that temper or whatever the hell it is, because I'm real worried about it. If you'd have pulled something like that on the yard, they'd be getting ready to embalm you by now." He stared intently at Kirk. "The way I get it, the bull accidentally knocked you down with the door, but you must've thought he did it on purpose. He's young—younger than

127

you—and he's still on probation. He don't want no off-colored marks on his record, like maybe a hint of brutality. Since I'm the guy that makes out his report, he asked me to forget it." Pausing, he frowned. "I wouldn't forget it if I thought 30 more days in the strip cell would make it right. I'm getting the carpenter and glazier over here tomorrow to square the place away. . . . But no more, kid, break the habit." He started to turn away, then stopped. "I'm moving that guy up front tomorrow, so you can forget him. I'll make room for him somewhere."

"No!" Kirk blurted. "He's all right here," he added slowly. "They're liable to fuck over him up front. In fact, you can let him exercise with us if you want. He'll be safe."

Yancy stared searchingly at him. "All right," he said abruptly. "That's the way it'll be then."

And that is the way it was.

[XXIII]

Five weeks later, with spring weighing damp and sticky, the three convicts were under the showers, lethargic, and Kirk was boring them further with his thoughts about the duality of Mephistopheles. In the middle of it, they were rescued, for the hall door banged open and Yancy stepped inside.

"Hey," he yelled to them. "You clowns better not be doing nothing funny in that shower, 'cause here comes the new warden."

They turned to stare questioningly at one another, then, as one, looked around the edge of the shower. A man was ambling toward them, stopping to peer into each of the cells. He was a strange figure, of medium height, wearing a baggy yellow sweater, voluminous shiny pants, a small paunch, and unkempt gray-black hair. They stared at him, then at each other.

Sam shrugged and said, "Fuck it."

That meant they would stay in the shower and let the warden handle it the best way he could. And Kirk was anxious to see what that way would be. He had not previously seen a warden, let alone met one in the flesh. Not an experience to be voluntarily foregone.

His rambling tour completed, the Warden stood before the shower and looked in at the three convicts. He was perhaps forty-five, but his face was deeply wrinkle-furrowed. It was only a moment, however, before it became apparent that the wrinkles lacing his face were caused by smiling, for as he did, all the wrinkles fell into place. Perhaps he knew how his eyes glistened and how much he looked like a little boy.

"Hi," said the little-boy Warden.

What in the fuck is this? Kirk asked himself, bemused. Glancing to the side, he noted the others' bewildered expressions. He turned back to the warden. The man was still smiling.

Deciding he needed something to snap him back into form, Kirk reached for the soap and lathered his crotch with a good deal of unnecessary fondling, then smiled mechanically. "Hi," he said with exaggerated verve.

The warden, an adept dissembler or hopelessly naïve, merely widened his smile. "What're you fellows in here for?" he asked.

The others seemed unable to find their voices—or didn't look— so Kirk answered. "We dared to try to escape this garbage can. Can you imagine that?" His voice was leaden with amateurish sarcasm.

The warden bobbed his head. "Yeah," he said, sounding as if he were going on a picnic, "yeah, I can imagine that. I don't even like it here, and they pay me to show up now and again. By the way, my name's Benson." He turned and peered curiously toward the end of the hall. "Who's that fellow?" he asked, pointing.

"Oh, yeah," Kirk said, his mind suddenly racing. "You have to meet Sad Sack, Warden." He raised his voice. "Sad Sack," he called. "Come here . . . and bring your toys."

The warden's smile faded until his face was slack-jawed. Then Sad Sack wobbled jerkily to his side and peered into the shower at his "frens." His clothing and hair were in a state of wild disarray, and in his hands he held a paper airplane and a tin can . . . the hangar.

"Show the man how nice your airplane flies, Sad Sack," Kirk said.

Sad Sack chortled and giggled, drooling a little, then held the paper plane at arm's length. Suddenly he spun around with maladroit movements. "Zzzoom!" he exclaimed.

The warden stared incredulously at Sad Sack's simian grin, then turned to the others, his chin trembling. "You're kidding!" he said hoarsely. "You have to be kidding. . . ."

Kirk laughed bitterly. "Yeah, Warden, it's a joke. Ain't it funny?

Ha ha. Ain't it a scream?" He turned to Sad Sack. "Hey, fren, show the man who thinks you're a joke how well you know the alphabet."

Sad Sack made some noises and furrowed his single eyebrow.

"Come on," Kirk prompted, "show the man what we spent a month teaching you. Say the alphabet."

Sad Sack looked around and bit his tongue a while. "Albabet," he muttered finally, frowning. ". . . um . . . a . . . b . . . c . . . uh . . . d . . . uh . . . um . . . G!" He nodded triumphantly and giggled, then ran off, his voice floating in the air. "Zzzoom!"

"What's he doing in here?" the warden demanded with no trace of a smile.

"You're the warden, mister," Kirk said through bared teeth. Leslie tugged at his arm, and he pushed him away. "They tell me you're a doctor, too. . . . Maybe you can give the guy a pill and make him disappear. . . ."

"What's he doing here?" repeated the warden demandingly.

Kirk told him what Sad Sack was doing there. "Get him out of here," he finished, his voice flat and harsh. "Get him to a bughouse or a place for the retarded. Just get him out of here." He did not attempt to gentle his voice as he stared intently at the warden, almost snarling, knowing he was foolish to trust to the caprice of a man whom he didn't know, didn't want to know. But what was he risking . . . ? So he kept staring, wanting to smash the man's wrinkle-scarred face.

The warden stared back, but with unseeing eyes. He finally focused his gaze on Kirk. "I can't," he said slowly, even reluctantly. "It takes a court order."

"Bullshit!" Kirk spat, snarling now, muscles taut, ready to explode. And all the while he wanted to be quiet, but could not. "Yeah, Warden Dr. Benson, that's what I said: bullshit. You have a warden's prerogative to transfer anybody any time you like. You declare an emergency and say they're dangerous villains. If it works when you want to punish somebody, when you want revenge, then it'll work if you want to pick up some pieces . . . if you ever wanted to do anything like that. . . ."

Benson gazed down the hall toward Sad Sack. A long moment later, he looked back at Kirk. "What about the trial?" he asked hesitantly. "What about his testimony? He has to be in the area when he starts taking the stand."

"Does he *have* to? You think the world will be any safer if the creeps that fucked him stay in the pen 50 years? You think Sad Sack'll sleep any easier? You think he'll even know what he's doing on the stand?" Breathless, he rested for a moment, then, too filled with bile to stop, went on: "Tell me about your ideals, Doc; tell me about the fine and noble things in men's hearts. Tell me about justice. Then maybe you can tell me why kids poked Sad Sack with sticks; or why an altruistic lawyer stood beside him while he was railroaded; or why a selfless district attorney and an honorable judge collaborated to make society safer by sending an idiot child molester to prison . . . an idiot who thinks his dick is something to piss with. When you get finished telling me about all that, then maybe I'll know the answer to the question about the chicken and the egg." He stared at the warden, feeling like a collapsed balloon, no longer angry, just disgusted, contemptuous.

Benson turned slowly and looked down the hall. "The chicken and the egg," he said quietly, a little wryly, then looked back at Kirk, smiling again. "You're not supposed to talk to the warden like that. . . . That stung. . . . You start talking about original sin, and you get everybody feeling guilty. . . ." He laughed briefly. "I'll have him flown out of here tomorrow."

Sam choked. Leslie giggled. Kirk brayed. "You have a sky-hook connection, Doc?" he asked scathingly.

The warden continued smiling, apparently taking no offense; he seemed to expect their disbelief. "You have my word," he said simply. "I came by to ask if there were any complaints. . . . I don't think I'll bother, though." He glanced at his watch. "If you fellows want out of here, have your things packed in the morning. . . . It's too late to make the move today. . . ."

"Make the move to where?" Sam asked with a barely repressed sneer.

"Out to the general population," said Benson, still smiling. He rested a foot atop the tile step in front of the shower and leaned forward. "Once the building is empty, I might be able to get a better idea why we have a prison inside a prison, and why fellows get sent here. . . . It seems ridiculous that we can't come up with a more effective means of control than a warehouse. . . ."

Kirk found himself suddenly mystified, almost entranced. The warden is either a well-polished hypocrite or a hopelessly addicted "good fellow," he thought. Probably not the former, he decided, or

131

Benson would have been president or something; and if it was the latter, Kirk was certain that the warden had disillusionment ahead. He wanted to tell Benson to dry up and go away; instead, he smiled, trying to be wry but managing only condescension. "Doc," he said, "I think you might've taken a wrong turn somewhere. You're in a place of cages . . . things in cages swing on the bars. . . . As head turnkey your job is to keep us swinging on the bars. . . ." He broke off as he stared down at the warden's water-spattered shoe, a shoe incredibly dilapidated, a thread or two from total ruin. For some reason it bothered him; he found himself hoping that Benson was not a miser.

"Doc," he said abruptly, without thought, "your shoe's getting wet."

Benson glanced down, then rubbed away the water drops with the frayed cuff of his frayed sweater, left his foot there.

"Anyway," Kirk continued, "if you walk around this place with a glass slipper, you'll end up eating it in little pieces. And if you expect anything more, your feelings are going to be hurt."

"Maybe they will, maybe they won't," said Benson with a shrug. "What will worrying about it do?" He leaned farther forward and slipped. Kirk and Leslie caught him before he fell headfirst into the shower. He was soaked in the process. He grinned at them and put his foot back on the tile step. "But," he went on, as if nothing had happened, "while what you said about these fellows swinging on the bars might be almost true, it doesn't have to be. Now, wait a minute"—he held up a hand to the noises coming from the three convicts—"let me tell you what I think. I think the fellows in here are psychologically scarred. . . . But so are millions of other people who never come to prison. The only difference between you and them is that you did something wrong enough to get stuck in this place. But once that happens, the difference becomes a big one because you're further scarred in places like this. But that's done and there's nothing anybody can do to change it. However, it doesn't have to go on happening. I know that what we have isn't conducive to it, but some place—with our help or without it—you have to find the motivation to bury yesterday and look to tomorrow. . . . Now, for some of you fellows, that's a hell of an order. . . . You're so hung up being a born loser or hating father that it taints the air you breathe." He fixed Kirk with an odd look as the convict chuckled, then went on: "I'm not going to run around here giving these fel-

132

lows excuses—but I'm not going to condemn them, either. . . .
They've undoubtedly been condemned a little too often. But what I
am going to do is try to find out why convicts are about the most
nonpersevering, nonmotivated group of people in the world. Then
maybe we can start doing something. . . ."

Kirk stared at the man's smiling face, at his too-young, too-starry
eyes. He heard him talk on, heard but was not listening. He was
wondering. . . .

[XXIV]

He sat at the foot of his stripped bunk, leaning against a cardboard
box that contained his personal belongings, still wondering.

When the warden had left the previous afternoon, Sam attempted to laugh, but it caught in his throat; Leslie giggled but
sounded as if in pain; and he himself merely frowned, trying to sort
his muddled thoughts. Of all of them, Sad Sack alone had been ar-
ticulate; he had waved and said, "Bye-bye." Kirk wanted to laugh
the man out of his head, and was left bemused because he could
not.

Yancy appeared at the door window. "Ready?" he asked.

Kirk grinned. "I've been ready to leave this dump all my life."

The guard unlocked the door and pulled it open. "Drop your
stuff outside the office and wait a second while I spring your pals. I
want to kiss you clowns good-bye."

Kirk gathered up his property box and walked from the cell
without looking back.

A moment later Leslie and Sam joined him at the office and de-
posited their property beside the door. They traded smiles, then
Yancy appeared and told them to go inside and sit down. He
stepped in behind and closed the door. Sam and Leslie took the
chairs so Kirk and Yancy sat on the desk.

"I think this might be hush-hush information," Yancy began,
"but nobody told me to keep my lip zipped, so the hell with it." He
grinned. "I guess a guy's getting old when he starts gossiping and
liking it. Anyway, from the word I get in the squad room out front,
it seems that after Benson left here yesterday, he decided to take a
quick spin through the hospital. Just by fluke he caught Trintz giving a con shock treatments. After a minute, he walks away shaking

his head. Then one of the orderlies—a guy by the name of du Bois, Hank du Bois—well, he sidles up to the warden and lays a medical folder on him. It's the folder of the guy in the shock box. Benson don't know what's happening, but he starts flipping through it and all of a sudden blows his top. He walks to the shock box and starts ripping out the wires, then starts hollering at Trintz—right in front of everybody—telling him to either hand in his resignation on the spot or he'll get a cell ready for him. Trintz is surprised, but he finally tells the warden to go to hell, that he's civil service and can't be fired. Then he backs off and asks what all the steam is about, anyway. Benson shoves the guy's medical folder in Trintz's face and says that he's an epileptic and schizophrenic on top of it. So Trintz starts wilting and has to sit down. Then Benson slows down a little and puts a few more questions to him, and finally Trintz admits he hasn't read the guy's medical history. So Benson asks him what the hell the guy's doing in the shock box if Trintz doesn't know his history. Trintz says the guy's an incorrigible. After that, they had to almost hold Benson in a chair, he was out of his head. And Trintz tries to clean it up by saying it's an accepted method of punishment . . . said he's been using it for years. Goddamn . . . they tell me the warden turned blue. . . . But he finally tells Trintz that if he shows up for work tomorrow—today—he'll have him arrested." The guard grinned briefly at Kirk. "You want the capper?" he asked. "Well, Trintz goes back to his office and types out a letter of resignation. Then . . . get this, he writes a directive, ordering that from now on, no inmate can be held in the padded cell for more than 14 days and, without exception, they're to be fed two hot meals a day. . . ." He paused and stared questioningly at Kirk.

The convict thought about it for a moment, then shrugged. "Don't ask me," he said. "If you'd have asked a long time ago, I'd have told you that I thought the creep was demented."

"Anyway, let me finish," Yancy said. "After Benson leaves Trintz, he calls this du Bois and a few of the other orderlies into an office and holds a gripe session. The outcome is he decides to take over disciplinary cases. That means that Capt. Bradley and A. W. Lowry have been turned into glorified office boys. Benson says he'll run the prison and leave the paper work to his subordinates, says that's the way it should be . . . never mind how it's been." He grinned. "All the bulls are shook up. Two say they're resigning and

50 more are talking about it. It's like when they took the clubs away a while back. . . . All the bulls thought they'd be killed. It'll blow over, but right now the climate in the general population is treacherous. With Benson turning the whole seg block loose and just generally sticking chewing gum in the machine, the cons are thinking they got somebody on their side, and the bulls think they're being dehorned. So what's happening is that some of the cons are getting way out of line, and the bulls're coming back even stronger. They've been shaking the joint down and coming up with some pretty funny 'evidence' to show Benson what dangerous dogs you guys are. So you clowns better watch your moves and keep clean. . . . They'll be watching you . . . especially you, Kirk." He leered at Leslie. "And you," he warned, "better keep off your stomach."

Leslie feinted a hand toward the guard's crotch, and when Yancy scooted back on the desk, almost going off the side, said, "A lot you know about it, you big goon. You do it to a boy on his stomach. . . . I'm a lady."

"Oh, dummy up," Yancy said, and lifted a big paw as if to backhand him. The fruit puckered his lips and stuck his jaw forward, and the guard put his hand in his lap and scooted farther away. "I got something else that might tickle you guys . . . you too, Lady Leslie," he said, laughing. "You're a bunch of half-assed heroes . . . though there're some that'd argue about it. There's a car coming after lunch to pick Sad Sack up. Benson's having him driven to the airport. . . . He chartered a plane at state expense to take the poor bastard to a training center for the retarded. He's a cock fucker, that warden. . . . He'll probably last another month or two. . . ." He stood, then eyed the trio with irritation. "Why don't you clowns get the hell out of my office? Go bug somebody that likes you." He made shooing gestures toward the door, looking like an ugly, featherless bird with stunted wings.

"Okay, Batman," Sam said, "we're going. We probably won't see much of you any more, so take it slow. You been a sweetheart, Yancy." He walked from the office.

Leslie, almost blubbering, extended a hand and waved it frantically. "Shake my hand, you big goon."

Yancy leered and stuck out a paw. Leslie shook it briefly, then pulled away and hurried from the room. Kirk rather anticipated

135

the inevitable tears, and as Leslie rushed past him, he looked and was not disappointed . . . except that he did not like seeing the fruit cry.

Kirk gazed for a moment at the lumpy-faced guard. "You've been decent to me," he said slowly, "more than decent. I don't know what it's worth, but elephants have been known to be jealous of my memory. Hold yourself together, Yancy." He turned to leave.

But the guard stopped him. "Listen, kid," he said, "I'm a know-nothing cop. . . . But I'm getting to be an old man, and sometimes when a guy starts getting old, he starts seeing a lot. . . . Don't get blown off the wall, kid. There's always a way around that. . . . Don't give this cesspool your air. Now get out of here."

Sam and Leslie were waiting for him. They smiled at one another, picked up their property, and walked through the main hall of segregation toward the corridor door. And once again the cell windows mysteriously burgeoned with convict faces, but instead of cursing and spitting, each of the faces was now cheering and whistling, all in gratitude for Leslie's wantonly gyrating hips.

"Hey, hey, sugar!" an appreciative voice called, then others joined in: "UMM mmm! Baby, shake that thing!" "Hey, Sammy, tell the girlie to save me some of them cupcakes!" "Goddamn, honey! my pants is smoking!" "Help! God, help me, girl! My dick's so hard it's pulled the skin over my eyes. Help!"

Kirk grinned at the convicts, unable to decide whether he was embarrassed or glad to be with the siren. He wondered that the men in the cells could be so altered from the previous times he had walked past them. Of course, he'd been with guards then, not Leslie. An obvious difference.

They reached the end of the hall and Sam pounded on the door to get the attention of a corridor guard. Kirk helped him, kicking it. Meantime, Leslie shimmied provocatively—in a manner forbidden to boys—and was resoundingly cheered by an audience either joyous or sick or joyously sick.

The door was finally opened by a short, bland-faced guard with a clipboard in his hands. He peered into the cardboard boxes, examining a few items, then asked their names and numbers, and checked them off the clipboard. After carefully replacing his pen in his shirt pocket, he handed each of the convicts a slip of paper with their cell block and cell number written on it.

They left the guard and walked north through the corridor, in the direction of the cell blocks.

"Let me see your cell-assignment slips," Sam said to the others, and when they handed him the papers, he looked at them for a moment. "We're all going to E block," he told them with a grin. "That's the one furthest down the corridor . . . part of the old prison. They call it Skid Row . . . and that ain't no joke. E and F blocks are about the two lousiest ratholes in the world. You both been celled there . . . but neither of you has probably been around long enough to know that all the jailhouse hardcases love those filthy, noisy sons of bitches. Yeah . . . real tough guys." He laughed wryly. "They're too tough for me. . . . If they dig the pain, I guess it's their trip. . . . But far as I'm concerned, they can travel without me." He glanced from Leslie to Kirk. "How about if we wait a day or two and I'll piece off the housing clerk to get us moved out to an honor block?"

Kirk and Leslie agree. For the honor blocks had outside cells with hot water while the old cell blocks had inside cells and no hot water, except for the showers.

"Okay," Sam said. "We ought to bust down there and dump our stuff before they start the lunch line. Then we can go eat and get some sun." He looked again at the slips of paper. "If I remember right, according to the numbers, you two'll be on the fourth tier . . . the wall side. I'm on the fifth, same side. And, Leslie babe," he said with a grin, "according to the red mark on your slip, they won't let you have a cell partner . . . or at least not till you pay somebody off. I wonder why? Usually they only do that to queers. . . ."

As they hurried through the nearly deserted corridor, Leslie seemed to find it difficult simultaneously to wriggle and to walk fast, so he kept apace, walking fast.

Striding down the brightly lighted, seemingly endless red concrete corridor, Kirk swiveled his head right and left to look through the occasional windows along the wall, and was rewarded by fleeting glimpses of narrow grass strips between the blocks. It was as if he were in a slow train, moving past the programmed sameness of

137

slum-replacing apartment buildings, and equally depressing. Or even more so, for here there was not even the impression of being unchained.

The lawns between the cell blocks were green and meticulously manicured, beautiful lawns. And easy to maintain since no prisoners were allowed near them—except for maintenance. They stretched into the distance; sterile, untouchable bits of nature that somehow managed to be as unnatural as the gray granite wall against the horizon.

Each time they passed the open doors of the cell blocks to the right and left, their progress was followed by groups of stiffly starched convicts who apparently considered themselves resplendently arrayed, for they incessantly hitched their knife-edged pants a little higher and tugged at unyielding collars, posturing grandly all the while. Other than that, they did not seem to have much else to do but lean against the wall and practice icy stares. They stood in racially segregated groups, and when not attempting to chill occasional passersby, one group would stare icily at another, with their members frequently breaking off to light a cigaret in the most sinister manner conceivable or to squirt a stream of spit between their teeth. That the spit spattered to the ground, as spit almost always does, seemed to amaze them, for they would stare at it and try time after time to hit the same spot. The floor bore silent witness to their poor aim.

At length, the trio arrived unchilled at the far end of the corridor and turned right under a large sign proclaiming the doorway to be "E BLOCK."

Inside, they were greeted by a large, hollow silence. Light spilled through the rows of towering narrow windows along each wall—windows reminiscent of a cathedral, the stained glass replaced by steel bars. The slanting rays of sunlight seemed, somehow, unnatural, almost obscene—as if the light had battled through the bars only to dash itself to death against the cold grayness and lay there unmourned.

A half dozen yards into the block were two sets of metal stairways, coming almost together in a flat-bottomed V. Both stairways ended on the steel-railed second-tier landing and there the double stairways leading to the third tier were repeated. And so it went until five tiers high. From directly below, it was a monotonous geometric pattern that might have been a rain of blunt-tipped arrowheads about to shower on those below.

To the right, a tiled row of open, sterile-looking showers was set against the wall, extending a third of the 65-yard length of the block.

To the left was a cubicle flimsily constructed of plywood paneling and wire-reinforced glass. It was painted an odd shade of yellow-orange and, considering the gray gloom of the block, was decidedly incongruous, even unsettling. It was the guards' post.

The trio walked to the cubicle and found a pair of guards sitting with their chairs tilted languidly against the wall. Both were drinking coffee. One wore the metal chevrons of a sergeant pinned to his collar. He had his feet propped on the desk, the only furniture, other than the chairs, in the office.

Sam approached the door. "We're just out of seg," he said. "I guess we're supposed to check in here." He extended the three slips.

Swinging his feet from the desk, the sergeant groaned and reached for the slips, then, without rising from his chair, wheeled himself behind the desk, where he thumbed through a metal file box. After a moment he handed each of them a plastic-coated identification card with their respective picture and number sealed inside.

The sergeant tilted the chair against the wall again and pushed his hat to the back of his head, revealing an unlined, mild-mannered face with a thin, gray mustache. "My name's Carol," he said, "and no cracks. This is Witonski." He gestured to the other guard. "There's another bull running round the block somewhere. His name's Sherman. Obey the rules, keep your cells clean . . . that goes for your noses, too . . . and stand to the bar when the count whistle goes off at four. And, you"—he pointed at Leslie—"don't let me catch you eating anything that ain't cooked." He laughed in delight at his wit, and leaned back against the wall. "Hey, you guys hear what Joe Lewis died of?" He paused a moment, then: "The blackleg!" and almost laughed himself out of his chair. Witonski joined in, holding in his stomach, which needed holding in anyway.

The three convicts looked blankly at one another.

And Carol controlled himself, staring flatly at them. He glanced down at the cell-assignment slips still held in his hand and looked back up with hard eyes. "Which one of you is Whalen?" he wanted to know.

Kirk stepped forward.

Sgt. Carol pulled his hat low, staring down his nose at the convict. "You be careful," he warned. "You're on real thin ice. There's them that take you serious . . . real serious. And I'll always back my men; remember that. If you fuck with the bull, you get the horn. And don't count on that pantywaist warden to mother you. He might think he's got tits . . . probably does . . . but he ain't going to be round long enough to turn this place into a nursery school." He dismissed Kirk with a hard look and a wrist flick.

Outside the office, the three looked at one another and shrugged away the sergeant's warning. Sam led the way to the stairs and up to the fourth tier, where they found the inclusive cell numbers painted on the end of the block which included the numbers of the cells that Kirk and Leslie had been assigned to.

Sam stopped. "You two go ahead and dump your stuff, and I'll see you downstairs." He climbed on toward the fifth tier.

Following Leslie along the narrow walkway in front of the cells, Kirk glanced warily over the guardrail, until he could see the concrete floor four stories below. He edged closer to the cells and did not look again. It was a long way down. Considering its availability, it seemed an infrequently used method of murder . . . or suicide. He shuddered and turned his eyes to Leslie's rear end. He became dizzy and looked toward the cells.

Each cell had a number above the barred door, and Kirk lowered his cardboard box to the floor before the cell with the number written on his cell-assignment slip, then watched Leslie continue a half dozen cells farther and stop before his cell.

Kirk looked into the cell that was to be his. The floor of the four-and-a-half-foot-wide cell was carpeted with torn newspapers and magazines and dirty socks. The double bunks were unmade. The toilet, in the light of two fluorescent bulbs, shone white where it was not streaked with filth. It didn't shine much. Home.

A guard appeared at the far end of the tier and pulled the handle of the deadlock bar, releasing the steel tongues that hung before each of the cell doors. Kirk pushed his property box inside the cell and, stepping back out, closed the door.

Back in the corridor, the trio walked toward the dining halls. At the junction of the main corridor and the corridor leading to the vocational shops and administration building, they fell in beside a sparse but steady flow of pompous-acting prisoners who all had a weighty multitude of varicolored pens and pencils clipped to their breast pockets and hanging from belt loops were key rings containing a vast assortment of keys—so many keys that a corresponding number of locks seemed doubtful, even in a lock-conscious prison. These were the prison clerks and "personal" secretaries. If prisons have brains, then these prisoners were the nervous system, the backbone, without whom everything would fall apart. And at least half were known stool pigeons; the other half . . . well, a convict learned to walk warily and talk quietly in their midst. They were not difficult to spot, even aside from their overloaded shirt pockets and key rings. For some reason it seemed that most of them, including those who attempted to swish daintily, smoked pipes, were overweight, and held their heads in a manner that might have been kingly . . . or queenly, as the case might be. And also, because they were the victims of unfortunate circumstances and weak genes, they had become—against their will, of course—alcoholic check forgers and sex offenders. They despised criminals.

The three convicts remained silent as they filed to the side-by-side dining halls and were directed into the second one by a faceless guard with lazy arms.

Passing through the open door, they fell into a single file that wound before the long steam table, behind which convict servers, dressed in white, ladled food onto the extended trays. Sam led the way up the middle aisle of the dining hall until a guard with hat pulled too low pointed them to a table. The dining hall was filled with small four-place tables, so Sam quickly flipped a spoonful of beans on one of the seats to discourage unwanted company. Then the three of them sat down.

After eating in silence for awhile, Sam pushed his tray back, and said, "We got a little problem that ain't happened yet, but needs some thinking about." He fixed Leslie with a meaningful look. "You know what it is, blue eyes."

"Oh, brother," Leslie said indifferently. "I'm as frantic as I ever was." He fanned the table with a nonfrantic limp wrist.

Kirk looked from Leslie to Sam. "What's happening?" he asked.

"Maybe nothing, maybe a whole lot," said Sam. "Either way, Leslie's got trouble coming till he hooks an old man. Trouble I ain't worried about, but I like to make my own." He looked at Leslie.

"As long as you ain't in my bed, I don't give a goddamn who or what you play with. But stabbing some sorry punk because he wants some asshole is a drag."

"Slow it down, Sam," Kirk said. He was lost. "You mean Leslie's going to be lugged by some creeps wanting his keister?"

Leslie looked at Kirk and sighed with mock despair. "If I haven't got anybody steady," he said with exaggerated patience, "little funny gangs of spooks, Mexicans, and white guys make tough faces at one another and whisper sick shit in my ear. It's a bore, but I really wouldn't care except that all the neo-Nazi-type punks get all uptight if somebody without a white skin talks to me. They want to start race riots and all that nonsense if I don't make it with them. But, baby," he added, wrinkling his nose at Kirk, "they won't mess too bad with the lady. She's got claws." He scratched Kirk's hand.

"Why don't you just tell anybody with a big nose that it's you and me? That way you could have time to convince some poor bastard you're really a girl." How had they overlooked something so elementary?

Leslie made a face and said, "Blah," and Sam grinned in a faintly patronizing manner. "Kirk," he said slowly, as if talking to a child, "most of the characters in this pit are real clods . . . besides being gutless. But you can't fuck with their pride. Yeah, it's mostly a what'll-they-think-of-me pride, but that don't matter. If you spread the story you're Leslie's old man, and somebody finds out you're not climbing in her back pocket, you'll find out that ten times worse than being the greasiest stoolie in the world is being a jailhouse cock-blocker. When these geeks get eyes for a fag—and Leslie's about the best catch in this town—they'll sit down for somebody else having her, but they won't sit down for a baby sitter. You're bright. . . . You figure what their problem is. . . . I'm a dumbbell and I figured it out." He paused and looked closely at Kirk. "You're tough . . . or mean anyway—I'll give you that. But if you get found out telling a tale like that, they'll be paroling you in pine."

"You mean . . ." Kirk caught himself before he said, "you're afraid." "You mean that Leslie has to drop a pipe on two or three of these phoney punks before they leave him alone; he's supposed to keep from getting nailed by the bull; and he has to protect himself from possible revenge; all without help from anybody, and all because he has a cute ass?"

142

Leslie giggled. "Baby," he said, "fag chasing in this place is as usual as being bored." His eyes went wide with surprise and he giggled again. "That was a cute remark," he said proudly, then looked at Kirk. "Let me tell you something, my naïve sweetheart: there're a half dozen guys that come to the joint every week of every year that have never messed with a fag and think they'd die before they'd consider it. Two weeks later, or maybe a month, you see them again and they're swishing just as gay as you please. Why? Because they didn't have any friends or couldn't fight very well or because they didn't have a sharp knife handy when the jackals came to fuck. After that, they're too afraid to say anything; or they like it . . . really like it." He leered. "All I'm trying to say is that their only problem was having what you call 'a cute ass.'" He gazed intently at Kirk for a moment, then shrugged and averted his eyes. "I can handle my own problems," he said quietly. "I always have."

"Shit!" Kirk spat in disgust. "If you can handle them, I can handle them better. You just might be a terror in the Y.W.C.A., but I'd have to see it to believe it. Far as I'm concerned, if you have to stab or pipe somebody because you don't want them poking in your prize, then I'm going to be there letting a little blood myself. And no static." He glared at both of them. "Fuck their 'rules' and their mothers and their little baby sisters. I'm not in here for obeying rules and when I finally get to the point where I let these sawdust-brained zombies tell me what to do, I hope they do parole me in a box." He rose from the table and strode from the dining hall.

He retraced the route through the corridor to the yard door, and paused there to stare toward the distant wall. The sun was out, beckoning, warm, something natural, unspoilable. They can't pervert that, he thought, and took a step toward the light. Then he envisioned smokestacks and chimneys belching and farting, layering the sky with stink. "Shit!" he hissed.

Suddenly Sam and Leslie were beside him, tugging at his arms, pulling him through the yard door, to the pebbled path leading to the prison yard.

"Cool it, madman," Sam said impatiently. "Let's get out of the corridor. . . . There's a hundred bulls prowling."

Kirk allowed himself to be led off the path that bordered the yard. They wandered to about the middle of the thin and balding lawn, a noted contrast to the ones that convicts were not allowed

143

upon. And as they were about to sit down, Leslie pointed to a group of convicts some 30 yards distant. "Look, baby," he said to Kirk, "that's what I meant."

Kirk saw that each of the convicts was wearing a bright-colored bikini. They were paired off and preoccupied with applying what appeared to be suntan lotion to one another's bodies. They did a lot of rubbing.

"They're all fags," Leslie explained, "and they were all raped or tricked out of their bodies since they came to the joint. Each one of them swears up and down, 'I've been like this since I was nine years old.' " His falsely falsetto voice became a parody of the falsetto it usually was.

The spectacle left Kirk indifferent; he didn't want to care about it. He did wonder, however, how the bikinied convicts managed to get in so much rubbing so openly. Turning back to Leslie, he shrugged and said, "I'm not going to fondle your body, but I'm not going to stand around and watch while these punks bother you. When you find somebody you want to play house with"—he slapped Leslie's hand away from his leg—"besides me, I'll be real happy to back away. But till then, tell anybody who wants to know that I'm dad."

Sam wagged his head and chewed his lip and, sighing fatalistically, turned his face to the sun. Leslie smiled with a sort of happy sadness, then tears filled his eyes and he gave Kirk the finger. "You're a dirty bastard," he said, and turned his face to the sun. Kirk turned his face to the sun, too.

Some time later, Kirk was almost asleep when he heard a noise and looked up. Hank was standing there. Kirk grinned up at him.

"Heard the terrible trio sprung today," Hank said, grinning back.

Kirk told him, "Squat," and sat up.

Hank did, gazing wistfully at Leslie, who was stripped to the waist and stretched out face down on the grass. "That's a lot of candy that broad carries around." He stared a moment longer, chewing a thumb.

Leslie opened his eyes and smiled at Hank over the crook of a pillowing elbow. "Tell him!" He indicated Kirk. "He's a hard one to convince."

Hank winked and grinned lasciviously. "He'll learn what's good.

He's still a baby." With his voice lowered, he said to Kirk, "Can I talk around the fruit? Is he with you guys in all of it?"

Kirk nodded before he thought about it, then felt a stir of anger that Hank should assume otherwise.

Hank raised his voice to include all of them. "There's a guy in G block that's a real miserable bastard . . . but he's a bastard with an idea. He says he busted out of Walla Walla and that he wants out of here. About the only difference between him and all the rest of the escape artists is that he's willing to do a little work, and like I said, he's got an idea. Around this place, ideas are like walking on water. I've been talking to the guy—he's called Hippo—on and off for a year and just today he cracked about wanting out. He knows I know you, and he read the newspaper story about your miss. Now he's wondering if he can count on help from you guys." He hesitated, then went on slowly. "Before you nod, let me tell you this: the guy ain't any part of a stoolie; but from what I know of him, he's a self-important asshole and about six times shittier in the attitude department than any cop in the world. But all that don't mean he can't have a way out." Pausing again, he frowned. "And another thing: if you decide to work with him, I'll do anything I can to help, but keep me hidden. I don't want any active involvement in the plan's preliminaries. I should've been paroled three or four years ago, and I'll be seeing the parole board in about six months. . . . I don't want to blow a kick-out over a plot that might blow up. On the other hand, if you have room for me when the time comes, invite me and I'll go." He looked at the three of them. "Hippo didn't give me much information, but it sounds like a tunnel. He says that's the way he left Walla Walla. If you guys want in, you're supposed to get a cell move to G block as quick as possible. He says he's tired of waiting . . . wants to move right away."

Kirk looked at Sam. "What do you think?"

Sam shrugged and spent a moment looking around the yard. "I know the guy he's talking about," he said indifferently. "Not to talk to, but I've seen him around. The guy looks like a geek."

Kirk grinned. "What's a geek look like?" he said, then went on quickly, "You have anything else?"

Sam fixed him with narrowed eyes. "No," he said finally, "nothing right off hand."

Kirk turned to Hank. "Tell him we'll help," he said.

145

Hank pushed to his feet, his eyes darting to Leslie. "I'll tell him," he said absently. "Well . . . duty calls and all that sort of shit. I'll see you guys later. . . . And, Kirk, don't let that beautiful thing get away. . . . If she was mine, I'd chew my initials on her butt." He threw a kiss to Leslie, waved to Kirk and Sam, then turned to walk away. Stopping abruptly, he slapped his shirt pocket. "Damn near forgot!" he exclaimed. "Here's a few joints." He squatted in front of Leslie and bounced the roll of marijuana on his nose, grinning mischievously. "For a kiss?"

"*Dah*-ling," Leslie crooned, wrinkling his nose, "for those, you can have some body." He raised up and kissed Hank's mouth. Then he turned to Kirk and stuck out his tongue.

Moaning piteously, Hank stood and pushed down the bulge in his pants. "Son of a bitch . . ." he muttered, then, wistfully, walked toward the yard door.

Leslie slipped off the rubber band that bound the stick-thin cigarets and handed them around. Lighting up, they let the confining corridors, stone wall and ominous gun towers become unreal; they went some place without captives, without wretchedness.

[XXV]

He made up the bunk and, after a fight, managed to sweep the debris on the floor through the cell bars onto the tier. From there somebody else could worry about it. While he was cleaning the filthy toilet, the count whistle sounded and he stood at the bars until a pair of guards passed by, clicking automatic counters with hypnotic regularity. Then he washed up and lay down, awaiting the all-clear whistle to signal the opening of the doors for the evening meal.

Sounds filled the block. Close by, a flute wailed plaintively, while farther away a trombone stumbled over a piece of Dixie Land. Commingled with that was the pandemonium of a typewriter, low-keyed mumbling, humming, and whistling. But worst of all were the vocalists. The convict songsters seemed to exert themselves to share their voices with their neighbors. Now, measured by the calendar, he had not been in prison long, but it was long enough to have classified at least three species of convicts. There were the Autobiographers, who modestly expressed that they, among all others, had led the most dashing and romantic lives and would "someday" write of themselves an all-time-record best seller that would thrill generations to come; there were the Conversationalists, who seemed certain that they had something of interest to tell everybody and were blindly oblivious to the fact that they were consistently mistaken; then there were the Vocalists, the warbling falsettos and basso profundos, who sang and sang, ignoring the bad taste of others, who asked them to shut up, until the inevitable day they could sing no more, not with punctured lungs.

When finally the bar was thrown, simultaneously opening all the cells on one side of the tier, Kirk stepped onto the walkway and was immediately caught in a crush of bodies as the convicts held their evening race on the four-foot-wide path to see who would be first to the dining halls. With no other choice, he let himself be carried to the landing at the end of the tier, then stepped to one side and watched the convicts rush past and down the metal stairs, filling the block with a resounding clang that went on and on.

Moments later, Leslie appeared. He was caught in a tight-packed mob of convicts, all of whom were flapping their mouths in his ears. Leslie, eyes straight ahead, looked bored. But at the sight of Kirk, he wrinkled his nose and smiled. The convicts around him, realizing that they were not the cause of Leslie's pleasure, looked impatiently about until they saw Kirk, the interloper, staring contemptuously back at them. They faded abruptly and the two were left alone.

Leslie smiled softly and shrugged. "It's hard to believe most of those guys have wives and kids and swear they hate fags, isn't it?" he said with a rueful tone.

"Save the compassion, Godiva," Kirk said with a grimace. "These creeps wouldn't know what to do with it." He turned to go down the stairs.

Leslie stopped him, pulling at his arm, looking up into his face. "Baby, you're wrong." Pain was registered in his eyes. "Sometimes I think you try to be wrong. . . ."

Kirk broke in. "Knock it off, Leslie. As a den mother, I don't need you." He pushed Leslie's hand off his arm, then turned him around, facing the stairs. "Let's wait for Sam at the bottom. These creeps make me think of a haunted house."

At ground level they again stepped from the mainstream of rushing convicts. Kirk watched them with a certain amount of interest.

147

It seemed impossible for them to create such a thought-killing hub-bub and yet appear so utterly lifeless. Somehow, most of them looked as if rigor mortis had set in and were angry or befuddled because life would not leave them. Though they snarled and grinned, laughed and scowled, their expressions might have been molded with undertaker's putty.

Sam joined them finally. With Leslie between them, they began the journey through the corridor to the dining halls. They had not gone far when Sam glanced over his shoulder and laughed quietly. "If you get the feeling we're being stared at," he said, "don't think for a minute that you're imagining it."

Kirk grimaced. "My imagination isn't that good," he said, uncomfortably aware of the stares they were attracting. "The creeps must think Leslie's queer because his ass moves a little funny." His laugh was devoid of humor.

"What can you do?" Sam shrugged resignedly. "After we eat, I'll track down the housing clerk. It'll cost about three cartons of 45 packs to move us to an honor block. And as long as we're moving out of that ratty son of a bitch we're in, I'll get it fixed so we go to G block. . . . It's about the best one. It's the only one in the joint with floors instead of open tiers. So even if this Hippo character turns out to be a dud, we'll be in half-decent cells . . . and have our own key during the day." He looked at the others. "You two game?"

"Yeah," chorused Kirk and Leslie.

Sam's eyes hooded slyly. "All the cells are single," he said, "except on the third floor. For an extra five packs, I can get you two fixed with a nest there. . . ."

Leslie yelped, "Yes!" and threw a hand over Kirk's mouth. There was a good deal of sniggering back of them.

Kirk pushed Leslie away. "A single cell, Cupid," he said to Sam. "Thanks, anyway. And if this man-eater keeps attacking, move me into the bull's office."

"Well, if you—" Sam began.

"*Sammy!*" The interruption was screeched in a high-pitched voice.

Kirk turned and saw a tall, dark-complexioned young convict whose mannerisms might have been copied from Leslie. His eyebrows were plucked to a fine line and, like his eyelids, heavily mascaraed. His wide mouth, colored crimson, contrasted richly with blue-black ringlets of hair curled over his forehead and small golden loops hanging from his pierced ears. All this framed a heavy nose and a shadow-black beard which, at one time or another, must have proved an irritant to somebody.

"Gypsy!" Sam exclaimed happily, and reaching out, affectionately grasped the nape of his neck and pulled him close. "Come eat with us," he said. "You know Leslie, but Kirk's a stranger. Say hello."

Gypsy winked at Kirk. "Hi," he gushed, making the word a lewd, four-syllable song. "I've been hearing tales about you three." His black eyes glistened . . . except for a fleeting instant when he looked at Leslie. Then he latched onto Sam's arm with a proprietary air. "Are you going to work?" he babbled. "Why don't you come out to industries with me? Do you want to—"

"Whoa, babe, slow up!" Sam interrupted. "First things first. Are you making it with anybody?"

Gypsy's smile faded and his dyed lips pursed sourly. "With Dave," he admitted.

"Which Dave?" Sam asked. "The Greek?"

Nodding, Gypsy pulled closer to Sam, peering expectantly up at him.

"Cut him loose," said Sam. "Start an argument if you want to be nice about it . . . or just tell him that it's you and me. If that fucks him up, tell him to sharpen his knife. He ain't tough enough to get real mad about it. We're all moving to G block and you'll be my cellie. You like?"

Gypsy melted up against him, looking as if he would kiss him at any moment. "Daddy, I *like*," he oozed.

Arriving at the first dining hall, the four convicts were waved inside. And after being served, they made their way to a table and sat down.

Sam leaned close to Kirk. "How many joints we got left?"

Kirk slapped his shirt pocket. He had completely forgotten the rolled marijuana laying loose in there. "Damn," he muttered, his hands suddenly sweating, thinking about carrying another ten-year sentence—a manslaughter sentence. He shuddered, then held open his pocket and counted the sticklike things. "Nine," he said.

"Give me two," Sam said. "We don't have enough cigarets to pay the clerk, so I'll sell the joints for three cartons. That'll cover it with what we got."

Kirk palmed two of the joints from his pocket and handed them to Sam.

Putting them away, Sam turned to Gypsy. "Hurry up," he said. "I want to get the hell out of here and take care of my business . . . and then, babe, I been playing with myself for a million years. And this bitch"—he waved toward Leslie—"has been acting like a goddamn nun since Kirk showed up. You got a spot we can go get naked?"

Gypsy arched his eyebrows and leered. "I've still got the key to the priest's room."

Sam laughed heartily. "That's where it'll be. This is like coming home." He turned to look at Kirk. "You know the best fuck-spot in the joint? The priest's bedroom." He laughed again. "They built a room behind the altar for him to sleep in during emergencies. So far, there ain't been many emergencies . . . and he don't show when there are. Anyway, the room's fitted with a sink, stove, and john, besides a super-springy bed with uptown sheets. Usually the priest's clerk rents it out to gamblers and whoever else wants it, but I made a couple keys a long time ago to get around paying the geek." He grinned. "If that holy-water-sprinkling bastard had any idea how many guys get laid in his sacred bed, in the same room with all the rest of his hocus-pocus, he'd probably crank up a new inquisition."

Kirk thought about it for a moment. Sterile sex on the sterile bed of a sterile order. It seemed an ideal and appropriate compliment.

Gypsy and Sam made faces at one another until Sam stood, gestured to Gypsy, and, laughing, walked from the dining hall with his tray partially supported by the bulge in his pants.

Kirk and Leslie decided to shower and climbed the block stairs to get their towels. They had just reached the third-tier landing when a voice behind called out, an accented, high-pitched voice that somehow managed to carry a distinct menace.

"Hey, mahn. You, broad; you, *bato.*"

Feeling something grip at his spine, Kirk turned, ready to fight. The speaker was a baby-faced, sloe-eyed Mexican, who seemed as innocuous as the three look-alikes standing with him. Kirk scorned his uneasiness but could not shake it. There was a feral aura about the four expressionless Mexicans, an aura boding less a threat than a promise . . . of what, Kirk could not say. But deep inside, something primitive warned him, bid him be wary.

He stepped in front of Leslie, keeping his face carefully expressionless. Each of the four had their hands plunged deep into their pants pockets; and under their pants, down to their knees, was an identical ridge. Knives or pipes, he decided, and slowly moved an arm behind his back, as if to scratch himself, and crossed his fingers, hoping Leslie knew what they were faced with. He casually pulled open the snaps on his shirt, his only defense against whatever they had in their pockets. He pictured himself with pierced palms and almost chuckled. He would use the shirt, he decided, or run like hell and get a knife of his own . . . pierced palms he didn't need.

He approached the group, smiling lazily and slipping off his shirt. Coming to a stop just out of arm's reach, he directed himself to one of the convicts standing beside the apparent leader, and asked, "What's happening?"

The Mexican stared back at him silently. An ominous hush grew. Then he blinked and shifted his gaze. And before he could look back, Kirk turned quickly to the next man. "What's happening?" he repeated blandly. The same scene ensued.

Counting two away, but not down, he turned to the leader. "What's happening?" he said for the third time, and suppressed an urge to chuckle at the thought of how like a broken record he sounded. But he would laugh later—now there was nothing funny.

The darkly handsome leader bobbed his head as though his neck was a well-worn spring. "Ees zat your broad, mahn?"

Kirk smiled pleasantly. "Yeah, he's mine."

The Mexican shifted his eyes to Leslie. "You making eet weeth thees *bato?*"

Before Leslie could answer, Kirk spoke again. "I told you he's mine," he said softly. "I speak for the kid."

The Mexican looked back at Kirk. There was a long, heavy silence. Kirk felt every muscle in his body screaming for movement, but he stood fast and gazed impassively at the Mexican.

"Mahn," the convict said at last, "I want to buy the broad. I give you *quince cartones.*"

Kirk grinned and meant it. If there had ever been anything to win, he had won it. "Fifteen cartons!" he exclaimed with feigned amazement. "Listen, the broad eats 50 dollars' worth of canteen a

151

month . . . bad breath . . . bum fuck. . . ." He looked down at the floor. "But he's got my nose opened. . . ."

The Mexicans all grinned at once, revealing four sets of brilliant white teeth that looked too perfect. "She is a fine broad," the leader said, sounding faintly mournful. "I see her before and want her. . . . Always I am too late, she has a *bato*." He shrugged dejectedly.

Leslie came up behind Kirk and hung possessively on his arm. Kirk smiled lovingly down at his upturned face and felt like a thorough idiot.

A moment later he turned back to the Mexicans, curious, thoughtful. He wondered at the quiet ferocity they emanated while appearing so childlike, so unspoiled. He did not think he could ever find them likeable—not more than superficially—but nevertheless they were intriguing. He reached in his shirt pocket and fumbled out three of the marijuana cigarets, then showed their pinched tops between his thumb and forefinger. "Why don't you guys walk up to the fourth tier with us while we get our towels?" he asked.

"Ai!" exclaimed the leader. "*Sí*, we meet you. . . . First we go now to see somebody." The four of them hurried around the corner of the tier.

Kirk and Leslie looked at one another and exchanged sighs of relief, and started up the stairs again.

"That could have been positively horrible," Leslie said with a shudder. "When those guys go prowling, there's most always a corpse or two left behind. They're part of some semisecret organization that sprang up a few years ago. They call themselves the Mexican Mafia. Nobody knows for sure how many belong, but they sure have custody scared to death . . . not to mention half the convicts. They're supposed to be one of those racist-type groups. '*Viva la Raza*' sort of thing. But mostly all they kill are Mexicans . . . funny, huh?" He shook his head. "No," he added, "not so funny, I guess."

Swinging his shirt over his shoulder, Kirk said, "Whatever they are, they make me feel like a choirboy. I wonder if they know how sinister they seem . . . ?"

"They know, baby," Leslie assured him. "You can bet your life they know. . . . But don't. . . . I like you too much. . . . You're my hero." He grasped Kirk's arm and bit it.

Kirk pushed him away, so he bit another spot, then another. "Get away, you dumb fag," he said, holding Leslie at arm's length.

152

"You don't bite heroes. And if you keep on, I'm going to take those 15 cartons of cigarets. You're not worth a pack of it."

They stopped before Kirk's cell, and he reached between the bars for the towel lying on the bunk. As he turned around, he saw the four Mexicans coming around the back end of the tier. It was a relief to note that their weapons had been stashed.

Kirk handed the leader two of the joints and joined them in sitting on the tier, their legs dangling off the edge of the walkway. He lit the joint he held and passed it to Leslie.

After several rounds the leader of the Mexicans introduced himself. "Me," he said, "I am Rudy." He indicated the others in turn. "Thees is Manuel, Sleepy, Jesus."

Each of them nodded in response to their names, but Kirk was left with the feeling that he'd never be able to distinguish one from another. They were almost identical in appearance and their actions were virtually indistinguishable.

Kirk introduced himself and Leslie. Then, their legs dangling in space, they sat there inhaling pungent-scented smoke and began sniggering and giggling about the oddest things.

And when they parted later, Kirk was calling each of the look-alikes by name. He wondered that he'd ever been confused, for they now seemed as much alike as apples and walnuts.

[XXVI]

They decided to play chess, so they took themselves to the rear of the block and Kirk checked out a chess set from the "recreation room," which was actually a cell without a door, then they sat on one of the six "game tables," which were actually a series of long benches upon which green paint adhered along the sides and appeared in occasional flecks on the tops, and upon which it was impossible to sit without taking on innumerable splinters.

They faced each other, straddling the bench with the board between.

Kirk was bored. He moved the chessmen boldly and surely. Pawns were bishops, bishops were castles. Leslie didn't like the way he played, said it wasn't fair. He didn't care. He wanted to escape. You can't escape playing chess. He explained that to Leslie four or five times, but the little fruit still didn't like the way he played chess. Kirk considered taking the set to the fifth tier and dropping it on somebody, but it was too far to walk. Instead, he leaped a pawn across the board and captured Leslie's king. The game was over whether Leslie thought he played fair or not. Leslie wanted to play again, wouldn't take no for an answer. They set up the board.

"I win," said Leslie as he captured Kirk's king with a castle on the opening move.

"Yep," said Kirk. "Good move." He started putting the pieces back in the box.

"Oh, no!" Leslie exclaimed. "Best two out of three is champion."

Kirk shrugged and crushed both kings' plastic heads. But Leslie made him set up the board, anyway. Whoever heard of playing chess with a headless king? But he obeyed, there was little else to do, except maybe stand around and look tough.

Before the third game could be decided, Sam and Gypsy showed up. Gypsy sat behind Kirk, Sam behind Leslie, straddling him.

Sam grinned wearily. "You don't know what you're missing," he said to Kirk, and held Leslie's waist while he ground his body against him, nuzzling in the fruit's lank, blond hair.

Kirk chuckled to himself as he watched Leslie continue to set up the chessboard. He had made Sam invisible.

"Maybe you're right," Kirk said, his mouth twisted wryly, "but if this goofy fag lays like he plays chess, I'd just as soon keep on playing with myself. Besides, Sam," he added earnestly, "how in the hell can you convince yourself that queers are girls and really don't have five pounds of meat—"

Gypsy gasped loudly, interrupting Kirk. Looking up, he saw the dark-eyed, mascaraed fruit glaring indignantly at him. He watched curiously while Gypsy snorted and huffed in a decidedly unfeminine way, then spun around and stomped heavily toward the front of the block. Kirk gazed after him, indifferent to his evident anger —whatever had caused it, he neither knew nor cared—but he did find cause to grin as he noticed how easily Gypsy's mincing gait had altered to the powerful stride of a mountain climber.

"Oh, bother," said Leslie lackadaisically, then made the first and last move of the third and final chess game.

Sam jumped up and cast Kirk a look of anger and grief, almost misery. Then he hurried after Gypsy.

Kirk watched him go, thinking he looked ridiculous, suddenly infuriated with him. Turning back, he asked Leslie, "What's with the fag?"

"Oh, *please!*" Leslie said with disgust. "That's a two-bit pressure punk, not a fag. We came to the joint about the same time, and for the first two or three days, that punk was telling anybody that'd listen what a triple-tough multimurderer he was. Then some guy got tired of it and jacked him up, and made him drop his drawers. . . . Ever since, he's been acting like he was a gear job since his diapers came off. He's done all that to himself since he got here—the pierced ears, the lipstick—all of it. And when you said 'fag' right now, he must've remembered what a phoney punk he is, and it shattered his belle-of-the-ball complex." He glared blindly, little teeth bared. "Just because I feel bitchy, let me tell you something: about every three months he lets his eyebrows grow back. Know why? 'Cause that's how often his wife and three kids come to visit. He probably tells his kids what a mean hombre their daddy is, kisses his wife good-bye, and goes to his cell and gets forced to suck a dick and acts like he likes it. And as long as I'm running my fat mouth, I'll tell you why he's falling all over Sam. He wants somebody to protect him and keep him smoking. He's a canteen punk . . . and I think he's a rat, or wants to be . . . kind of like to get revenge for losing his manhood." He jumped up and glared at Kirk, snarling. "That dirty, gutless cocksucker makes me feel filthy. I can live with being a queer, a dick-eater, a scummy pervert, and all the rest of it . . . but then I see a punk like Gypsy and I know everybody thinks we're the same. . . . Bah! Leave me alone!" He slapped at Kirk from five feet away, then hurried off, his neck glowing like a taillight.

Watching him leave, Kirk felt vaguely satisfied that Leslie, unlike Gypsy, walked prissy even under obvious—but nonetheless unfathomable—distress. Other than thinking all the emotional byplays ludicrous, he was bored with the whole episode, everything.

He stared blankly at the chessboard, skipping his thoughts from square to square. Sam had chased after the emotionally wounded Gypsy like a dog after a bone . . . or a beggar after a dime. . . . That made him wince. And, Leslie . . . what was he mad about . . . ? Maybe they were both nuts, stir crazy. . . . But they'd been all right yesterday, even this morning. . . . Or had they been . . . ? Did he know them as well as he thought? Probably not

. . . who knew anybody? Hell, sometimes he almost forgot his own name. . . . But those two . . . he had found himself relying upon their predictability. Maybe he'd even laid guidelines for their behavior. Yes, he had . . . he knew it now, now that they'd stepped outside the lines. . . . But who was he to lay guidelines for anybody? Presumptuous at best, immoral at worst. . . . Now, immorality didn't bother him, but laying out others' lives did. . . . Maybe he ought to run for God or president or something. . . .

"Let's talk, Kirk."

His thoughts shattered into miniscule shards by the interruption, he looked up and saw Sam, who was glaring down, a tic pulling at his mouth.

"All right," Kirk said suddenly, irrationally furious, with an urge to mash Sam's face flat. "Spit it out."

Sam glared for a moment more, his usually playful eyes glinting like two steel rivets. Then he snorted and glanced away. "Look, Kirk," he said, shuffling his feet, "we been all right. Let's not piss it off over a queer." He snorted again, reeking of prison-made wine.

Kirk choked down a vicious contempt. "Who's pissing what off over what?" he demanded. "All I can remember doing is calling a queer, who's my friend, a fag. Then some other queer, who definitely isn't my friend, acts like I'm a Marine who got caught shitting on the flag. Personally—and I hope this doesn't break you up—I don't like the creep, and if he's offended . . . well, tell him to slap me with a chewed-off foreskin or something. But as far as you being his protection or his daddy or whatever he calls it, I don't give a goddamn if you ride him till he can tie his shoes with his hemorrhoids. But don't even consider telling me that I should watch what I say. . . . It'll never happen, particularly around some clown-faced punk who acts like his ass is a grease trap." He looked closely at Sam. "If anything I've said shakes you up, Sammy boy, then my feelings are hurt a little, but I'm not taking a word of it back."

He turned his face away from Sam, away from the weakness he saw pulling at his eyes and mouth. But he was too late. . . . For it was there, naked and glaring, a magenta billboard on a desert road: defeat. The quick-thinking, glib-tongued Sam Robinson defeated? No, no, it couldn't be. . . . He would not accept it. . . . But . . . but, yet, the eye movements, the sag . . . yes, Sam had cracked, the stuffing had run out; he'd given up, been beaten. Defeat weighed on him like ballast on a ruptured balloon.

Kirk grew nauseous, something inside him wept, writhed, convulsed, would not lay still. He glared into space, seeing nothing, steeped with bile, wanting to crush humanity with granite boulders as Sam had been crushed with granite walls. From afar, between heartbeats hammering tympani-like in his ears, he heard a crippled, spiritless voice.

"It's funny," Sam was saying, "I didn't even know it till right now. . . . I'm tired, bone tired." He paused and chuckled weakly. "I brought the fag back here to tell you we won't be moving to G block till Monday—four days. The clerk can't swing it any sooner. But I got him to move Gypsy in with me till then. . . ." His voice trailed off, then went on slowly. "You hurt the fag's feelings and I got mad. . . . I even thought about killing you. I went chasing after him to soothe the pain away . . . me and Don Quixote . . . but nobody ever said his milkmaid had a dick. . . . What's happened to me . . . ? I don't know . . . yeah, I do, too. It was the escape . . . the escape that wasn't. When we got sprung today, all I could think about was catching me a fag tonight. You know what? I fucked Gypsy six times and wouldn't have stopped then if time hadn't run out. Maybe something else ran out, too. . . . What a way to go. . . ." He chuckled mirthlessly. "Yeah, they took my soul away and gave it back looking like a Chinese puzzle with most of the pieces missing. But—and it's weird—I feel almost good about. . . . I'm tired of fighting them. When I get hold of another gun, when I have something to fight back with . . . well, it'll be different then. Meantime, pretend I'm invisible. Now that I think about it, maybe I really am. . . . I feel like it. . . . Anyway, I'm staying drunk from now till Monday, maybe forever. Yeah, drunk and shoved off in the fag's ass. Only I won't call him a fag. . . . He'll be a girl. . . . But you're right, Kirk, he's a miserable son of a bitch and as real as a plastic pearl. But—you want a laugh?—I dig that punk." He hesitated. "Am I boring you, Kirk? That's all right. . . . How many times does a guy get to die inside? You can't walk out on a teammate's obituary. Hey, you probably thought I was a dumbbell. . . . I ain't too dumb, somebody even wrote a poem about me. Let me say it:

> Each narrow cell in which we dwell
> Is a foul and dark latrine,
> And the fetid breath of living Death

157

Chokes up each grated screen,
And all, but Lust, is turned to dust
In Humanity's machine . . .*

"Cute ain't it? So I'm off, friend, I'm off to reproduce my kind, to procreate in my own image: a dab of grease, a few dribbles of come, a daub or two of shit; mixed well; called love in some moods, lust in others, and death in truth."

Kirk sat unmoving, unseeing, his thoughts switched off. Much later he became aware of the bustling, mindless noises in the block. He stared down at the bench, at the spot where Sam had been. He searched the splintery grain . . . searched and searched . . . but nothing of Sam remained.

There was a tickling sensation under his eye. He reached up to scratch at it, then froze, his thoughts suddenly tumultuous. A tear! All those years . . . a decade and a half . . . no pain had been enough. . . . And now . . . now a tear. . . . Leaning over, his mind an opaque fog of gray, he let the tear drip from his chin onto the bench where Sam had been. He watched it spatter off a fleck of paint, then seep into the dry, grainy wood. A dark trace of moisture remained . . . a grave marker . . . the bench, like an ancient lachrymatory, holding for a while a memento of a life that was. . . .

* From *Ballad of Reading Gaol,* by Oscar Wilde.

158

PART THREE

[XXVII]

"Y'all be named Kirk?"

Focusing his eyes, Kirk traveled his gaze from the wall to the bars, beyond. Standing there was a short, black convict with oddly Semitic features, peering in at him with eyes curious and yellowed. In his hand was a large broom, which he rhythmically bounced in a pile of dirt. The man's hair was graying, he weighed 50 pounds less than Kirk, and was probably a quarter century older.

"Yeah," he admitted gruffly, "my name's Kirk."

"Der's a dude downstairs that be askin' for y'all. He be named Hippo." Squinting, the little convict peered closely at Kirk. "Y'all be new here," he said slyly. "Do Hippo be a friend of y'all?"

"No," he said with a grin, "Hippo isn't my friend. . . . I've never even seen him. And I thought convicts minded their own business."

"Ain't no business get by Shorty," he said with an air of grave mystery. "I knows ever'thin' happenin' in this ole block. I be heah 17 yeahs come Septembah." He bounced the broom in the pile of dirt for a moment, then went on slowly, "I knows y'all an' that sugar-bottom gal is tight as the cheeks a my ass. An' a darlin' lil whoe she be, too." With his eyes squinted again, he glanced furtively up and down the tier, then pressed his mouth between the bars and whispered. "Any chance a me bonin' that gal? I gotta lotta zu-zus. I go high as a box . . . only take me a tick."

Wagging his head negatively, Kirk hoped the convict would not press the issue. "I guess I'd better go see Hippo," he said, trying to change the subject. "What time is the next unlock?"

Grinning weakly, Shorty shrugged, as if to say he'd known all along that he would never get to bed the one person who really mattered. "Y'all got about 20 minutes," he said dispiritedly. "Ever change your mind, y'all let Shorty heah, heah?"

159

"Will do, Shorty."

The black man gazed distractedly at the broom in his hand, then patted the handle. He cast Kirk a guilty grin and ambled off, pushing away the pile of dirt, humming something full of hopelessness.

Kirk watched him go and felt his face tighten, his skull begin to ache. Shorty was dead, living only to grow cold and cease moving. Perhaps an hour in bed with Leslie would cause him to live again. . . . But, no. Do ashes burn? For how many of his 17 years behind the walls had he been dead? Seventeen years! For genocide you get 20 but usually less. Had Shorty killed? Probably. But obviously not often enough. For quantity the cost is less. But he was no doubt indigent and ignorant; criminal to the monied and crafty. So Shorty dribbled his life away, finally died, pushing a broom and prowling the tiers in search of a fruit to bed. Surely an unnatural man, Shorty. Perhaps the fact that he was a garrulous and degenerate and ignorant old man, fit for nothing but floor sweeping, was proof positive of a nature intractable, ignominious, malevolent, villainous; proof positive of bad blood, a demonic taint, an innate criminality. For 17 years he had been solicitously coddled that he might dwell upon the sacredness of life and upon his evil . . . and thereby become an honorable and upstanding citizen . . . a good man . . . a man like his keepers. . . .

Waiting for the unlock, he sat at the foot of the bunk and gazed through the bars of his cell, then through the bars of the window until he could see the patternless rectangles of granite piled one on another to form the bleak gray wall some 50 yards distant. He thought of Sam, though he didn't want to. He had not seen him since Thursday evening. In fact, he had not ventured from his cell since then. After all the time in the segregation cell, he wondered that he was not on the prison yard playing baseball or something. He was just not interested, not in anything except getting out. Leslie had stopped by often during the last couple of days, bringing donuts and cheese sandwiches and not asking questions. He stood outside the bars, offering to run errands, to talk, to just stand there. Mostly he offered to sneak inside the cell and . . . well, whatever. But he had not talked about Sam or in any way mentioned that Kirk was acting odd. So that had hung between them, making the silences loud and uncomfortable, for Kirk was certain Leslie in his uncanny way knew what had happened.

When the bar was thrown, Kirk left the cell and walked down the tier, feeling as though he were departing a cloister, seeking rebirth. Looking around, it seemed that the dreary grays were less gray, less oppressive. He could not understand it. The grays were softer, the emptiness of the block was not so depressing. Was he so empty there was nothing left to chill? Is hate hot or cold? dismal or bright?

At the bottom of the stairs he glanced around. Suddenly it occurred to him that he had no idea what Hippo looked like. Probably heavy, he decided, where else would he get a moniker like "Hippo"? But look as he might, he could not find a convict fat enough to be called Hippo and young enough to dig a tunnel. He was about to give up, wait until the following day when he would move to G block, when footsteps approached behind and stopped close to him, making his spine crawl, telegraphing the knowledge that he was being watched. He didn't turn around, though he was certain it was Hippo. Hank had said the convict was "a miserable bastard." Kirk decided to be a little miserable himself, not that it was hard to do. He felt childish but didn't turn around, anyway.

"Are you Whalen?" demanded an offensive, heavy voice from directly beside his ear.

Kirk supposed he should jump out of his skin or maybe faint. This creep ought to be piles of fun, he thought, then turned slowly and scanned the convict with bored deliberation. Hippo—and he was certain that it was Hippo standing there—stood six four and looked as thin and fragile as a dry twig. With skin darker than a mulatto's, his nose flared as wide at the bridge as at the nostrils, he had an almost nonexistent upper lip while his lower lip drooped red and pendulous. He looked upon the world through eyes huge and lackluster, black eyes belonging in something dead, a taxidermist's creation. They were chilling things. And all this was capped by a flowing mane of ash-blond hair. Seeing that face day after day in the mirror would make anyone's attitude testy, Kirk concluded, shuddering inwardly.

Who in the hell, he wondered in amazement, could have ever been friendly enough with this zombie to stick a misnomer like "Hippo" on him? Maybe he was wrong.

"You're Hippo?" asked Kirk, trying to keep the wonder from his voice.

Expressionless, the dead-eyed convict dropped his head in a barely perceptible nod and continued to stand in silence, boring his eyes into Kirk.

Looking back, reluctant to give an inch, Kirk bored his eyes into Hippo.

After a long minute the convict jerked a thumb over his shoulder. "Let's walk to the yard," he said.

Kirk felt a wave of relief wash over him, for he did not think he could have continued looking into those inanimate eyes much longer. He nodded and fell in beside Hippo, heading toward the yard. He decided that the convict was all Hank said and more. He didn't like him at all.

After walking silently for 50 yards, Hippo, his eyes straight ahead, said, "You wanna try again?"

Kirk glanced at him, wondering if he was trying out for a role of some kind. But he decided that Hippo was not the type for charades: whatever he was, he was, which is not always a bad thing to be, but in Hippo's case probably was.

"What do you have?" Kirk asked.

"An idea."

Kirk almost said, "Spill it," but decided not to. "I've learned a few things about other people's ideas," he said instead. "I'll listen to what you have, but I'm not moving a foot till it sounds right. And," he added, "it might not sound right till I've made a few changes." He walked on in silence, hoping Hippo choked on it.

"All right," said the dead-eyed convict after they had gone another 50 yards. "But it's all my show. I made it outta Walla Walla, you ain't made it outta nowhere." He paused for a moment, then continued solemnly, "Besides, I'm ten, fifteen years older than you."

Kirk glanced over at him, wondering if the last remark was a joke. Hippo was not smiling, but probably couldn't. Until then, Kirk had felt slightly disadvantaged in the company of the unusual-looking and seemingly inscrutable convict. But Hippo had talked too much, shown himself to be just another clod who happened to be ugly, and now Kirk could be contemptuous again, and was glad of it.

"Tell me what you have," he said, interested in spite of himself.

Hippo was silent for a moment. "There's an almost identical joint underneath us," he said slowly, appearing to find words difficult. "I got the plans to it. It's almost all concrete, but directly under the blocks—all except E and F—there's little doors with security locks that lead to dirt-floored rooms. At the end of the blocks is big doors with heavy-duty locks like the screws carry the big brass keys for. In the main corridor—right underneath us— there's grill grates. Look." He stopped and glanced around, then backed against the wall of the corridor and pointed to a six-inch-wide gap running vertically up the side of the wall. "There's riot gates in there," he explained. "Something happens in the hall, and the control screw sees it, he punches a button and seals off the hall about every 20 yards." He walked back beside Kirk and they kept on toward the yard. "In the basement the gates are permanent. But you can still get through them if you can handle the heavy-duty locks. Some parts of the basement is full up with civil-defense supplies—it's supposed to be a bomb shelter—and there's shovels and all the other tools we'll need."

Hippo fell silent and Kirk grew thoughtful. "You left a lot out," he said slowly. "Like how do we get down there? And if you're talking about a tunnel, where do we start digging from and where're we headed to? And what about shoring? Digging a tunnel without shoring means you don't like yourself."

"Don't need shoring," Hippo said tersely. "Didn't use none in Walla Walla, don't need none here. I can start from two places: under the chapel, digging down under the corridor and following it out to industries; or from under the block and take a liner straight for the wall."

"Wait a minute," Kirk said, coming to a halt. Slowly he formulated what was in his head. "You said it's the same underneath as up above. Why can't we get into the corridor, follow it out to industries, and go over the fence at night, when the towers aren't manned?"

"That part of the joint ain't duplicated. The basement ends under the chapel."

"Something else bothers me," Kirk said, feeling a little crestfallen. "Why aren't you down there digging? Why do you need help?"

"I get in trouble with them locks," Hippo said. "I can handle the security locks, but I take too long. The others, the big ones, I don't fuck with them." He looked at Kirk and added, "Can you get them?"

"No," Kirk said. "The security locks, yeah. . . . They're almost like any other kind; but the heavy-duty ones I don't know anything about."

Hippo gazed impassively at the ceiling. "I'll have to start under the block then," he said. "There's no way to get past all them grill gates." He paused for a moment, then, "You in or what?"

"You still haven't said how we're going to get down there. This place wasn't built to make tunnel digging easy."

"There's a way down," Hippo said, "but it ain't easy. It's a tight squeeze but you can make it if you move good. One guy by hisself can't take enough water down to last an hour. . . . That's another reason I can't work alone. You need water down there. It's almost a hundred, maybe hotter, all the time because of the generators and steam pipes. We're going to be needing a shovel—a trowel'd be better. That civil-defense stuff ain't under G block. . . . It's under the hospital."

"Okay," Kirk began, "this is what I see: you have a way to the basement. We go down there with water and tools. Then we dig an unshored tunnel. . . ." Breaking off, he stared at Hippo. "You know how far it is from the end of the block to the wall?"

Hippo moved an eyebrow fractionally. "Fifty yards."

"Yeah," Kirk said with a snort. "Fifty yards, plus the road around the outside of the joint. Call it 60 yards . . . 180 feet. What about air?"

Hippo stared blankly at him. "You want in or what?"

Bad as it sounded, Kirk had already decided that he was "in," but still . . . "I want to look at it before I nod."

"You talking for your friends, too?"

Kirk thought about it. What friends? Who? "Yeah," he said finally, "I'm talking for them, too."

Hippo was silent as they approached the yard door. There he halted and turned to Kirk. "I'll take you down tomorrow night," he said. "You'll be working the locks, your friends'll have the point—they won't go down at all till the tunnel's dug. I got picks in case you don't." He gazed at the wall back of Kirk. "I'm going back to the block. If I don't see you when you get there tomorrow, meet me on the third floor after supper." He turned and retraced his head-bobbing, loose-jointed steps.

Kirk stared after him until other convicts stopped and stared, too, then he turned to the yard door and walked outside.

On the graveled path circling the lawn he stopped and looked at the many convicts scattered over the grass, their bodies bared to the midspring sun. He decided to walk around once and stare. It was either that or sit in his cell and be stared at.

Walking slow, in a counterclockwise direction, he passed two convicts who were on the grass, both naked except for loincloths. One, his face turned up to the sun, sat in the lotus position; the other, in a similar position, but upside down, stood on his head. Kirk kept on, an inch at a time now, looking over his shoulder, waiting for the man to topple over. Then he stumbled into another convict and started looking ahead.

He came to a cyclone fence that kept him from walking to the front gate. The outside was right there . . . past about a thousand coils of concertina barbed wire atop the fence, the wide steel slates of the gate itself, and a squat black silhouette sitting high over the wall in the armory gun tower, menacing the yard with its lead-spitting 30-caliber muzzle. He stared toward the gate until his head began to hurt.

Turning away, he walked a little farther and stopped beside the tennis court. Two of the "girls" were having a gay time prancing to and fro, swatting at the ball with limp-wristed swings of their rackets. They swatted a lot and missed almost as often. But that seemed the best part of the game, for when the ball arced past, they took out after it with a sort of practiced franticness and a lot of wriggling, being pinched and caressed and fondled along the way. When finally they captured the ball and were back on the court, it was not for long. Within three swats, one of them would manage a deft miss, and off they would go again. Of tennis they played little.

Kirk walked on, thinking about it. He had not gone far when he heard a voice behind. He turned to look.

Coming toward him, walking very slowly, was a wrinkled old man holding a red leash. On the end of the leash a large gray squirrel toddled. The old convict was cooing a constant flow of encouragement to the obviously reluctant animal. "Come on, honey," he was saying in baby talk. "Come on, daddy's 'ittle boopsy. That's a good girl. Come on, Nancy. . . . Oh, you're such a pretty 'ittle baby. . . . Come on now, daddy's gonna feed you pretty soon. . . ."

Kirk felt his skull catch on fire, burn. He watched the old man putter by and wanted to smash his face; he looked down at the squirrel and wanted to crunch it underfoot. He stood there a long time, unmoving, staring at the granite wall, trying to understand how moss and clumps of grass grew on its sterile face, trying to decide where he was and why, trying to convince himself that he had not seen a large gray squirrel on a red leash being cooed to, trying to think of a crime so heinous that a man could be taken from himself and given in return a squirrel. A while later, his mind forced blank, he walked on.

And a little ways farther he noticed two men on their hands and knees, skittering around in the grass, looking down. Stepping closer, he saw what they were after. Lizards, tame lizards . . . wearing collars. . . . Eyes closed, he rattled his head around, then looked again and saw the men stroking the lizards. . . . He walked on, quickly now.

At the base of the wall beneath number eight gun tower was a plywood shack used by the lawn-maintenance crew to store tools and other equipment; and around the shack a chicken-wire fence had been flimsily erected. A short convict with a bald head and tattoo-covered arms sat cross-legged inside the wire fence. Before him sat a wooden box full of kittens. He was evidently quite fond of each, for his kisses and imitation meows were indiscriminately given.

Kirk stared for a moment and was about to walk on when a tall, distinguished-looking convict with luxuriant steel-gray hair approached the fence and caught the attention of the tattooed man. "Mr. Catman," he said with a smooth and dignified voice, "might I see Patricia?"

The tattooed man—Mr. Catman, apparently—left off cuddling a blue-collared kitten, and said testily, "Oh, all right! But only for a minute. . . . They have to eat soon," then reached into the box, picking gingerly through it until his hand emerged with a kitten wearing a collar of yellow leather. "Here's Tricia," he said, and reluctantly handed the little cat to the gray-haired convict.

Accepting the kitten, the man said, "Thank you, Mr. Catman," and rubbed noses with the animal and purred.

The kitten cast him a cross-eyed stare and pawed toward his face.

Suddenly holding the little cat at arm's length, the gray-haired man glared at it. "Tricia, you are an ungrateful kitty," he said sternly and petulantly. "After all the money I've spent buying you milk. . . ."

Patricia squirmed, meowed.

The man's face paled as his eyes widened with anguish and injury. "Oh . . . oh . . ." he sputtered. "You . . . you *bitch!* All the money I've spent . . . no affection . . . no *affection!*" He thrust the cat toward Catman and clumped away, head down, shoulders shaking.

Kirk backed up, one step, then another, feeling a quivering in his legs, an acidic taste in his throat. He turned, strode toward the yard door, toward a tunnel he would dig with his teeth if he must.

[XXVIII]

At supper unlock that evening Kirk told Leslie that he wasn't waiting for Sam to be released; so they walked together in silence to the dining hall and stood in the line of convicts waiting turns at the steam table.

"Baby," Leslie said, breaking into the surrounding babel with a voice subdued and faintly apologetic. "I don't want to drag you into my problems, but I've got an idea there's trouble coming."

Kirk grinned, starting to feel better. "Around this place, trouble's like air. . . . You need it to live."

"Kirk!" Leslie exclaimed in exasperation, stamping his foot. "I'm serious!"

Grinning wider, Kirk stamped a foot, too. "So am I."

Leslie glared at him for a moment, then flapped his mouth and a limp wrist. "Damn you," he said finally, and went on quickly before Kirk could say anything else. "It's gotten around that you're my old man. Now there're a few boobs thinking they'd like to bounce your head around." He looked at the floor. "I'm sorry."

"Will you quit being sorry for everything?" said Kirk impatiently. "Now, give it to me slow and from the start. With only the punch line, there's no joke."

"Oh, I'm sor—" Breaking off, Leslie glared and slapped at him and stamped his foot and almost fell.

And Kirk, along with others around them, laughed.

Then Leslie smiled sweetly, put a fist in his stomach, and went on, talking softly. "You're an absolute bastard," he began, "and I'm all upset, but here it is from the start. There's a clique of guys— white guys in this case—that're vultures. You've probably heard them called 'low-riders.' Anyhow, three of them drove on me yesterday and said I had to be their kid. I told them to get lost. They left me alone. They'd heard about you, I guess, and wanted to test me, see if I'd get scared and go willingly. So today they came around smiling and asked me to turn out another kid for them." He looked up, catching the question in Kirk's eyes. "I'm supposed to take the kid to bed," he explained, "but instead of him laying me, I'm supposed to stick him. Now that's a hell of a thing to ask a lady. . . . Anyhow, after I do it—if I did—the goons step in and sell the kid to somebody else. It's considered a sophisticated hustle. . . . Besides, if the kid decides to rat, there's really not too much he can tell." He paused for a breath, then continued. "So I told them to shove it. They put all their brilliance together and decided it's all your fault. Don't ask me how. Probably because it's an insult to take 'no' from a fag. See, with you being my old man, they think you'll get revenge if they do something to me. So they've decided you're their enemy and they have to get you before you get them. They're wonderfully clever, don't you think?"

Kirk shrugged, then they passed in silence before the steam table, their trays held out to the convict servers. When they were seated, Kirk looked at Leslie. "Damn," he said with an air of graveness, "I don't think I'll be able to eat. My knees just won't stop shaking."

Leslie leaned over the table, his eyes fixed intently on Kirk's. "Laugh, funny boy," he said, "but I don't want to be the one to pull the knife out of you."

Grinning, Kirk leaned his face close to Leslie's. "Listen, fag," he said, "you do the worrying for both of us. But don't lose sleep over it. . . . Those punks would be doing the world a favor by killing me, but to do that, they have to stop scaring 120-pound queers. . . ."

"Okay, Kirk," Leslie said distantly and poked at the food on his tray.

Kirk ate a forkful, then sat and gazed at Leslie. "You're afraid, aren't you?" he said quietly.

"For you," Leslie said simply.

That caught in Kirk's throat. He spent a moment choking it down, wanting to pet the little fruit, to tell him everything was all right. "Leslie," he said softly, "tell me about these guys. . . . I'll go see them after we eat."

Looking up, Leslie smiled weakly. "There's not much to tell, really," he began, "just that they're vicious and yellow. They get sent to the joint for snatching purses and robbing newspaper boys, and when they get here, they sniff around till they find others that smell like them. When there's enough of them, they loiter around the canteen waiting for young kids that ought to be in high school or old men that ought to be in a hospital, then five or six of them—using shivs—drive on whoever happens to have a box full of cigarets and other stuff. When they're not doing something like that, they're agitating race trouble or raping youngsters that can't hold their hands up." He paused for a moment and picked at a crumb of bread. "Baby," he went on, "these punks are nothing to be afraid of, but you should be careful. All of them have been in on prison killings. . . . Sure, it takes a half a dozen of them to put somebody away, but dead is dead. And I don't ever want to hear one of those punks bragging about killing you. . . ." He smiled and started to leer, but shuddered instead. "You know, baby," he added, "I'm not a very good hater, but if I could run a gas chamber for a month, I think I could get rid of a lot of ugliness."

Kirk smiled. "I have the picture," he said. "When we get finished here, you show them to me." Looking down at his tray, he spent a moment in thought. "I think I can understand how these guys fall in bed with fruits as easy as they do. But, damn!" he wagged his head, "there's enough of them walking around this place to sink the Greek navy. Oh, hell," he added disgustedly, "let's talk about something besides jailhouse rapos."

Leslie nodded and ate in silence for several minutes before he looked over at Kirk. "Tell me to dry up if you want," he said hesitantly, "but I wish you'd tell me what happened with you and Sam." His eyes mirrored grief, as if he could not bear the thought of a falling out between friends.

Kirk saw the hurt and hoped he was not so readable. "Not much happened," he said, and bit his tongue before he went on lying. "He has a mild case on that big-nosed fag and I imagine he got pushed out of shape when I hurt the poor little guy's feelings." That was enough, he would not explain further, for what he felt was private, unsharable. And, too, he found himself with a profound embarrassment. . . . He was embarrassed for Sam.

"That isn't all of it, baby," Leslie said in a tone mildly chiding. "You haven't been out of your cell until today, but I have. And I've been watching Sam. Whenever he isn't hidden away with Gypsy, he's drinking, gambling, and filling his arms with dope. He's already in debt a yard and a half. . . . That's all I know for sure, it might be more. The good guys are starting to stay away from him. . . . He's showing his ass too much. . . . Gypsy's making a fool of him. . . ." His voice trailed off as he stared searchingly at Kirk. He leaned across the table, so close Kirk could count his pale eyelashes. "Let's get out of here," he said with fervent intensity. "Let's get out of this filthy place. It's crushing my skull. . . . I can't even think about going to bed with any of these punks without wanting to puke. I walk down the corridor and watch their idiot grab-ass games . . . hear them calling each other names. . . . It's eating me alive. Baby, get us out of here. Whatever happened to Sam . . . don't let it happen to us. I can't crack this cesspool, but you can. . . . I know you can. I'll do anything to help . . . anything. Baby, don't let me scare you away. . . . I'm a fag, but I'm your friend first. . . . I don't want to haunt your life, you can leave me outside the walls. . . . But get us out. I can't keep living in this coffin. . . ." He rubbed at the red splotches that had blossomed on his cheeks.

Kirk gazed a moment into his heated face, then patted his hand. "Fag," he said kindly, "I'm starting to like you. We'll get out . . . just as long as that's what we keep wanting. When we move tomorrow, we'll get something started. Just hang on, funny thing, we'll make it."

When they got back to the block, Leslie directed Kirk to the game tables and pointed out the convicts who had been pressing him. Sitting side by side were six men with shaved heads, their function seemingly to hold down the heavy green benches and stare in silence at the blank wall in the rear of the block.

Kirk had not taken many steps in their direction before he realized that Leslie was no longer beside him. Puzzled, he halted and looked about, and finally saw him bounding up the back stairs. The ground opened and swallowed him. He was a foot tall, all fury and pain. Leslie was running away. It couldn't be . . . but there he was . . . running frantically up the stairs two at a time, sometimes four. A needle-studded fog of blackness rose around him, his head ached, he quivered, unable to stop. Afraid he would topple over, he inched to the wall and leaned against it. "He's only a queer," he muttered aloud. "He's only a queer. He's only a queer." Maybe he was, but saying so did not take the pain away, a pain so intense, so blinding that it was beyond pain, almost luxuriant.

He stood there a long minute before he looked again toward the six skin-headed convicts. Hate slammed through him, tightening his muscles, curling his lips back, making him snarl. He stalked toward them.

"I think you guys are looking for me," he said flatly from directly behind them. "I'm Leslie's old man."

As one, the convicts swiveled and stared up at him. One of them, a convict five inches shorter than Kirk, but heavier, stood. He wore a T-shirt bulging with muscles and across his forehead and shaven skull was tattooed a huge tricolored eagle. His eyes scanned Kirk. "Yeah?" he said after a moment, with a voice deeper than life. "Who says we're looking for you?" His expression was carefully bland.

Keeping his features equally expressionless, Kirk put a fist in his pocket, hoping the others would assume he had a knife. "Heard it," he said tersely, boring his eyes into the tattooed man's.

For a fleeting instant the convict's eyes looked to Kirk's pocketed hand, and he tensed visibly. "Why'd we be looking for you for?" he asked, sounding like something slippery sliding under a rock.

"Couldn't say," Kirk said flatly. "That's all I heard."

Keeping his eyes on Kirk, the convict turned his head to the side. "Any of you dudes looking for this stud?" he asked.

They all shook their heads in denial and one, a short, dark, heavy-featured man, probably an Indian, said, "Ain't never seen him before, Zeke. Who's he?" There was an inch-square swastika tattooed in the dark skin over his cheekbone, another on his chin.

"Dunno, Moon," said the first convict, Zeke. "Maybe he's paranoid." The others chuckled their appreciation for his wit.

Easing forward, Kirk worked his eyes to a fever, glaring hard at Zeke. The tattooed convict looked back for a moment, then his eyes darted about, became hesitant. "Yeah," Kirk said quickly, his voice hoarse and menacing, "I'm paranoid. Somebody's been messing with Leslie and they have my name in their mouths." He stared intensely at each in turn. And all the while, he felt like laughing. These creeps, he thought contemptuously, look like a bunch of grammar-school bullies planning to heist a Coke machine. Taken

171

altogether, they would probably frighten crippled old women and take sinister mug shots, but unless the odds were six to one and one laid down, they were about as feral as a flock of penguins.

"Pra'ly the niggas, ma-yan," drawled one of them in a Southern accent that would have wilted a Texas cottonwood. He was a tall and gangling convict with a face shot full of ripe pimples and bulging eyes the color of window glass. On both earlobes were tattooed swastikas.

"Yeah," Zeke said, his mouth twisting in a serious grimace, "yeah, it must be the niggers. Why don't y'go see the burr-heads and tell 'em—"

Suddenly Leslie was beside Kirk, causing him to start. "What's happening, baby?" he asked coyly, interrupting Zeke.

A quick glance, and Kirk noted Leslie's right hand plunged deep in his pants pocket—pants already stretched to the bursting point. The knife running down the front of his leg was as apparent as everything else his pants revealed. It was a big knife, more like a small sword, extending from pocket to knee and as wide as a wristbone. At first glimpse it seemed more likely to be a bar, but the point had cut through at his knee. Protruding was a shining triangle of double-edged steel. Pleasure dropped over Kirk, wreathed him in a soft cloud. He gazed upon Leslie's face for a long minute.

And then he took his hand from his own pocket and wrapped his arm around Leslie's waist, squeezing his fingers into Leslie's pocket, grasping the knife haft. He stared at Zeke, feeling 12 feet tall and armor-plated.

The others missed none of this nor were they meant to, but they studiously avoided looking at Leslie's bulging pocket, his shiny knee. Though they did not back away or visibly cringe, the air was heavy with their wariness. Zeke finally spoke, his voice cracking a little.

"This is your old man, eh, Leslie?"

In silence Leslie nodded.

Fishing a cigaret case from his pocket, Zeke offered them around. "Well," he said amicably, and added the kind of smile that dentists get from patients, "he looks like a all-right dude, Leslie."

Leslie smiled sweetly. "I'm real glad you like him."

Zeke bobbed his head, his shiny skull glinting dully, then looked furtively about. "You two wanna buy some smack?" he said conspiratorially. "We got a coupla papers left."

From heroics to heroin, Kirk thought, and almost burst out laughing. "No, thanks," he said, grinning. "We're broke. . . . Besides, I still want to find out who has my name in their mouth." Leslie was tickling his hand as he loosened his grip on the knife.

"Ah, y'know how dudes talk," said Zeke with a vague gesture. "Don't mean nothing. Know what I mean? Probably just interested in who y'are. Y'got the finest broad in the joint—makes dudes talk. Know what I mean?"

"Yeah," said Kirk, nodding his head gravely, "I didn't think about that. You're probably right." Pausing for a moment, he smiled widely. "Well," he added, "we have to go upstairs and pack. . . . We're leaving in the morning." He pulled his hand from Leslie's pocket—it was difficult to be comfortable with his hand in another man's pocket, necessary or no.

"Moving?" Zeke said incredulously, his eyebrows climbing upward, ruffling the eagle's feathers. "What're y'moving for? This here's the block where it's at. . . . This here's where everything's happening. Know what I mean?"

"Happening?" Kirk was curious. "Like what?"

"Man, y'know," said Zeke informatively, with a vaguely patronizing air, as though Kirk should have possessed such knowledge long ago. "This here's where all the good dudes is at. We got things sewed up 'round here. Know what I mean?"

Kirk did not, but acted like he did. "Well," he said, shrugging deprecatingly, "we'll probably move back; but for right now, I want to move around a little . . . kind of check out the scene." With his eyes hooded mysteriously, he bobbed his head, wondering if he should snap his fingers or spit between his teeth.

Zeke's eyes filled with tacit understanding of Kirk's esoteric designs. "I can dig it, man," he said solemnly. "Hold it down, and y'have any trouble with the niggers, lemme know. Know what I mean?"

"Right," Kirk said. "Later, guys." Grasping Leslie's elbow, he turned and walked toward the rear stairs.

On the second tier landing, he paused and looked toward Zeke and his clique. "Leslie," he said sincerely, "tell me those creeps are a nightmare."

"They're a nightmare, baby," Leslie said. "But we're living it."

Kirk tried to shake the ache out of his head but could not. "Those rockheads are unbelievable. Give them an unlimited supply of gangster movies, a chain to twirl, and nickel cigars to talk around and they'd stay here forever trying to look cool." He glanced curiously at Leslie. "What'd that eagle-faced creep mean when he said they had everything sewed up?"

Leslie's face became a mask of disgust. "They've got masochism sewed up," he began contemptuously. "With the canteen they steal, they go around to the dope dealers and score—sometimes for real dope, sometimes crushed aspirin. The dealers like to see them coming because they know that anything that'll go through a spike will get those goons bombed. The dealers call them 'hope fiends.' When there's nothing else around, they sniff shoe glue and drink watered-down pruno—home brew—with the kick of a small frog and a four-day hangover. Oh, yeah, the little darlings aren't living right unless they spend their time geezing hot water or stomach pills . . . and it's absolutely essential that they spend four or five months a year in the hole. They stay tough that way. Know what else?" he asked as they started toward the third tier. "Most of those guys with Zeke have five years or more inside. Zeke's done 12 so far. . . . He stole a bumper jack from a locked car. He should've done maybe 18 months or two years, but he just keeps parlaying it and fancies himself being too slick for words. It's hard to believe those idiots were born human." Bobbing his head, expressionless, he deepened his voice. "Know what I mean, dude?" he mimicked.

Laughing, Kirk grabbed a handful of Leslie's hair and shook his head around, gently. "Where'd you get the guillotine?" he asked, pointing to the knife bulging through Leslie's too-tight pants.

"Rudy lent it to me," he said as they stepped on to the third-tier landing. "It's not too funny, I guess, but it's kind of ironic. . . . It's the same one he had the other night."

Kirk looked again at the outline of the weapon. "Damn," he said almost reverently. "I'm glad I didn't get a good look at it. . . . I might've peed on myself. What do you use, one hand or two?"

Leslie smiled, wrinkling his nose, and told Kirk to wait a second, then disappeared around the end of the block.

It took more than a second but he came back with Rudy. "Here," he said, winking, "you can thank him yourself."

Kirk grinned at the expressionless Mexican. "Yeah, Rudy," he said, "thanks for the loan. . . . I'm about half-sorry I didn't use it."

Rudy spent a moment gazing at him. "Eet's funny you have trouble with the *gabachos*," he said finally, inscrutably.

174

"Funny? No, I don't think so," Kirk said slowly. "What would be funny is if I didn't have trouble with them."

Rudy frowned. "Eef the *gabachos* are not friends with you, who will be?"

"You're supposing friends are necessary. . . . But even if they were, being white doesn't automatically make them swell fellas. If that's the picture you have of me, you ought to take another one."

"Maybe yes, maybe no," Rudy said with an indifferent shrug. "But I think everybody need *compadres*. Without friends, you are alone, when you are alone . . ." He raised his eyebrows and shrugged. "Everybody, they want you Leslie. . . . *Quién sabe?* You are alone, maybe one day they get her."

Kirk stared at him, wondering what he'd just been told, but the Mexican's face told him nothing. "Rudy," he said quietly, "I'm not too tough . . . or maybe I am. Tough isn't mean faces and muscles, it's something that makes you go a little farther than the other guy. And past where I'm willing to go, there isn't any room. So if somebody wants to kill me for Leslie, they better want him a lot . . . a whole lot."

Rudy smiled faintly and nodded. Returning the nod, Kirk resumed climbing the stairs, Leslie beside him. He stopped again on the fourth-tier landing, staring thoughtfully at the little fruit. "Did I hear what I think I heard?" he asked.

Leslie pulled at his lip, frowning. "I don't know," he said pensively. "But here's something you don't know: after he gave me the knife, him and Jesus filled up two buckets with water—those five-gallon mop buckets—and stood on the fifth tier over the top of those guys. I had the idea they were covering us in case we got in trouble. Now . . . I'm not so sure . . . maybe not. . . . He's a funny little guy."

"Yeah, about as funny as that sword," Kirk said wryly. "He gives me a giant lopper then stands over me with a 50-pound bomb. . . ." Shrugging, he rubbed his nose. "I'll be glad to leave this creepy block. The characters around here are too weird for me."

Leslie nodded in agreement, then walked quickly to the corner of the tier and peered down its length; a moment later he hopped and jiggled across the landing and looked down the other side.

"What the hell are you doing?" Kirk asked.

"Shhh!" Leslie hissed. He put a finger to his lips and walked toward Kirk. When he was close, he whispered, "You thought I was running away, huh?"

Kirk shrugged, feeling guilty. "What're you whispering for?"

"Shhh!" Leslie repeated, looking around, making Kirk look around. There was nobody near, but Leslie, whispering anyway, said, "Do you like me?"

Kirk mulled it over. "About this much," he said begrudgingly and measured between thumb and forefinger a minute distance.

"Come here, then," Leslie said, still whispering, and put his mouth close to Kirk's ear . . . and suddenly threw his arms around his neck and held tight. Then he was kissing, licking, slobbering, and nibbling, trying to eat Kirk's face, his ear, his eyes, his nose, the corner of his mouth.

Kirk spent a moment being startled, another being disgusted, then threw up his hands and tried to push Leslie away. But by then Leslie was straddling his waist, legs hooked together. "Stop it!" he yelled, hoping the guard wouldn't hear, but better he did than this. "Get off me, you fucking queer! Get away!" Leslie licked his eye.

He finally managed to pry him off and push him to arm's length. Glaring, he wiped the slobber from his face feeling faintly revulsed, greatly enraged.

Meantime, Leslie stuck out his tongue, his thumbs poked in his ears, fingers wagging mockingly. He looked about twelve and a half.

"You fucking queer!" Kirk exploded. And then, unable to stop himself, he laughed. "You're a come-drunk, man-eating fairy!" he said finally. "And if you do anything like that again, you're getting muzzled and sold to the first bidder. You're a total fucking degenerate . . . you're a man-kissing, nut-nuzzling pervert." Then he, too, stuck out his tongue and made faces.

"And you're the dirtiest bastard in the world," Leslie retorted between facial contortions. "You're a miserable, sexless, impotent, nutless . . . you're a *monk!* You molest little boys, steal panties off clotheslines and jack off at stag movies. You're a miserable, good-for-not-a-goddamn-thing jack-off junky, and if you don't go to bed with me, I'm going to lay 15 guys tonight."

"Oh, Leslie," Kirk moaned with an expression full of grief and anguish. "What if you get pregnant?"

With that he sprinted down the tier, headed for the guard's office, escaping Leslie's talons by only the barest of margins.

Kirk and Leslie climbed to the fifth tier and went to Sam's cell. They found him sprawled naked on the lower bunk. And Gypsy, similarly attired, but half under a sheet, lay on the top bunk. They were deeply asleep.

After Kirk rattled the cell door for a few seconds, Sam squirmed, and finally worried his eyes open. "Wha . . . whaddaya want?" he groaned.

"Get up," Kirk said coldly, "it's Monday. . . . Let's get out of this block. . . . Pack your stuff, we'll see you over there." He was filled with a desire to spit at Sam but glared contemptuously instead.

Sam required a long time and much cursing to sit up. But he finally made it and, sitting cross-legged, looked at Kirk with bleary eyes. "Oh, yeah," he mumbled, "today's the day, ain't it?" Then, ignoring both Kirk and Leslie, he reached overhead and bounced Gypsy's bed. "Get up," he said tiredly. "My dick's getting hard."

That was not quite the truth, but neither Kirk nor Leslie wanted to stay until it was. They departed. And after asking a guard to throw the bar, they gathered their belongings from their respective cells and headed toward G block.

G block had been intended as a kind of psychiatric observatory. It was planned that representative cross sections of prisoners would be housed in control groups under 18-hour-a-day clinical observation by psychiatrists, psychologists, and sociologists.

The block had been constructed with three separate floors and only 48 cells to a floor, rather than the usual 60-cell tiers, in an apparent attempt to dispel the convict's feeling of anonymity. Toward the front of each floor four capacious offices had been constructed for the batteries of observers. And across from the offices were large television rooms. However, soon after construction of the block, it was found that, while the television sets would be forthcoming, the observers would not. The cause for the latter was due —allegedly—to political intrigue on the parts of various right-minded legislators who felt—allegedly, again—that criminality should never be pandered to. . . . Besides, they had better ideas about what to do with such characters . . . except, of course, that they were civilized. . . . And furthermore, the militia needed the money for gas masks. Where's your sense of priorities, anyway?

And so the prison administration was left with the problem of doing something with the 144 cells and 12 offices that had been built. Eventually, after many high-level meetings, it was decided to turn the entire block into an "honor unit," with the offices becoming card rooms—cards, of course, though available through channels, were contraband. The decision was hardly of earth-shaking moment since all the cell blocks of the new prison had been termed "honor blocks." Thus it required little administrative paper work and no effort on the part of the prisoners to incorporate a new concept in either their thoughts or their vocabularies, for it is well known by prisoners and prison staff alike that an honor block is one in which a convict is given a key to his cell but nevertheless cannot open it until the deadlock bar is first actuated by a guard; it is also well known that to be eligible for such a status, a convict must have either 90 days clean conduct or an in with the convict clerk in charge—albeit with unofficial sanction—of cell movements. And "in" means cigarets. Or in some cases, particularly if the clerk has had a bad month with the horses or poker or whatever, it is necessary for a convict wanting a move to qualify with both the cigarets and the 90 days clean—the latter, of course, being cigaret-purchasable from another clerk who does amazing things with ink eradicator. Now, ordinarily clerks have a way of being informers. But while they might tell on everyone about them, it is rare that they tell on themselves. And for a carton or two of cigarets, they are the most reliable sort of people, enduring even bread and water. Besides, if they told on themselves, how would they ever get an early parole date?

As soon as Kirk stepped with Leslie through the door of G block, he saw Hippo slouched against the wall, staring.

"Second floor, Leslie," Kirk said absently. "Take your property up. . . . I'll be there in a minute." He walked to Hippo and lowered his property box to the floor.

"What's that you were with?" Hippo said, his tone conjuring pictures of something floating through a sewer.

Kirk straightened, feeling rage lashing at him, and looked into the man's dead black eyes. "What's on your mind, mister?" he said through grated teeth. "You smell something maybe?"

Though Hippo's eyes held fast to Kirk's, his expression took on a look of vague puzzlement. Finally he asked, "You mess with queers?" and somehow, his voice vomited maggots.

178

Kirk, snarling now, glared at Hippo, wanted to smash bones in his face. But he stood fast. Getting out was more important. "Let me tell you something," he finally managed to say quietly. "That queer is *mine*. He was with me before when I tried and he's with me now. When you handed around the invitations, he was automatically in. . . . If there's something about that that you don't like, you better spit it out now. I don't give a rat's ass if you think you're Dillinger . . . but if you flap your mouth about that fag, and I hear about it, you better be real close to the hospital when I catch you, because—"

"Wait a minute," Hippo cut in. "You said enough. I don't like queers and I don't like queer lovers—"

Lunging, Kirk snatched Hippo's collar. But the convict quickly caught his fists in his own hands, clamping them. "Cool it," he said hoarsely, gesturing with his head. "The screw's in the office. We can make this noise later if you want. Let me finish first."

Reluctantly, Kirk looked toward the open door of the guard's office a short distance away, then relaxed his grip. His chest heaving, he took a short step back. "Talk. Quick . . . and make me like what you say."

If Hippo was impressed, it did not show, but the scornful cast left his expression and his voice was not so harsh as he spoke.

"I don't like queers. . . . I don't trust them. And I didn't know you was with a queer on that thing or you'd never got invited by me. I suppose the queer already knows all about what I told you, so I don't guess it'll hurt anything having him along." Spinning around, he walked several paces and stopped. "I don't like you any better than you like me," he said without turning. "But I'm smart enough to get out of here. . . . maybe you're smart enough to help me." He went toward the rear of the block, did not look back.

And Kirk watched him go, envisioning one tall, ugly convict buried alive in an as yet undug tunnel. Why, he didn't know or even care to know, but second only to the wall around him, he hated the dead-eyed convict.

"Kirk!"

He recognized Sam's voice and turned around, driving his hate into a dark corner. Sam and Gypsy, both laden with property boxes, approached him. Sam carried something more, something heavy enough to bow his shoulders—not much, but noticeably. Noticeable, too, were the puffy pouches under his eyes, and the stink of carrion about him—not a scent picked up by the nose, rather a sort of mind stink. Looking at him, Kirk felt a profound sadness, a sadness so huge that it would slay Sam and call it mercy. Perhaps he's not what I see, he thought. Perhaps he needs only a rest, a week stuck off in Gypsy, a letup of the mind-crushing boredom, the will-sapping routine. Perhaps . . .

When they stood before him, he turned his eyes to Gypsy and stared openly at him. Gypsy found something of interest to study on the floor. But after a while, ignoring Kirk, he turned to Sam. "Honey," he said, "I'm going to run upstairs and dump my things. Then I'll pick up our key. Bye." Turning, he went mincing to the stairwell, sexy as a stork.

"Still the guardian angel, eh, Kirk?" Sam said bitterly.

"Still? I can't remember having ever been." He stared curiously at Sam, noting his answering shrug. "Listen," he went on, "everything's ready with this creep, Hippo. Are you going to keep on with the lost-soul routine, or do you want to do something with yourself?"

"Hold your tongue, pal," said Sam between his teeth. "I need a savior like I need leprosy. Yeah, I want out—but I don't want to listen to no pious platitudes. Tell you what, Kirky babe," he added, "you think and I'll do . . . just as long as it ain't too hard. My brain's paralyzed with assholitis."

Biting his tongue, Kirk was able to keep his face straight, to mask his disgust. "Well," he said, attempting to sound indifferent, "it's a start. I've already gone around and around with Hippo about Leslie—fags he doesn't like. So don't tell Gypsy anything about this. Don't ask me where it came from, but I've heard it said that he's weak as water under the wiggles."

"Let's not go to war, Kirk." Sam's mouth disappeared, a tic pulled at his eye, his fists balled tight, bloodless. "I don't tell him anything that can hurt anybody but me. But don't call him a rat till you got something solid to back it with. And then don't bother telling me. . . . Just kill him." Wheeling, he strode quickly to the stairs.

From a distance Kirk followed, entering the small stairwell alcove. He climbed two levels of stairs, and on the second-floor landing, spoke to Sam's back. "Be around tonight after chow." He walked into the second-floor hallway and looked inside the guard's office. Empty.

180

Having nothing better to do and unable to get in his cell until he received the door key from the block guard and not wanting to get in bad enough to go looking for him, Kirk walked down the hall, peering into the cells until he found Leslie's. The little fruit had evidently found the guard, for he was inside making up his bed.

Backing out of sight before Leslie saw him, Kirk put his mouth to the crack of the door and called in a squeaky, crackling voice: "Hey, yur new here, ain'tchya, kid? Wanna jelly bean? Pant, pant, lust, lust . . ." and put his face to the window and leered.

Leslie left off making his bed and came to the window, where he gave Kirk the finger. "Up yours, eunuch. I wouldn't go to bed with you for mink. But if you keep talking—"

The cell door flew suddenly open, pushed Kirk back. Leaping into the hall, Leslie grabbed his arm, yanked him inside the cell, and threw him to the bed in one fluid motion too fast to defend against. Falling on him, Leslie put his face against Kirk's, and as Kirk turned to the side, trying to get away, wondering what had happened, the little fruit lunged forward and caught his nose in those sharp little teeth. He held tight, real tight. Tears came to Kirk's eyes.

"Maybe you thought the deadlock was on, huh, bastard?" Leslie mumbled, and tickled his tongue against the clamped nose.

The pain was terrible, excruciating. He thought of pushing Leslie away, but he saw the teeth holding fast, himself without a nose, and rapidly concluded that the pain had not made him so crazy as all that. Instead, he decided to plead. . . . It was not much of a decision, really. . . . What else could he do?

"Ah, Leslie, come on. That hurts. I'll never do it again, honest! OUCH! GET THE FUCK OFF THE NOSE, YOU PERVERT!" Tears flowed from his eyes. How had he allowed himself to fall into such a strait? How could he ever explain that a 120-pound queer bit off his nose?

"Temper, love," Leslie mumbled sweetly around his nose, never for a moment letting it go. Saliva trickling from his mouth ran into Kirk's. "I learned this from a Marine. . . . Terribly clever, don't you think? You big, brave, sniveling boob . . . how does my spit taste? Yummy, huh, you scurvy, puritanical louse?" With that, he reached down and grabbed a handful of Kirk's crotch. And abruptly releasing his teeth, he jumped from the bed, keeping a handful of Kirk twisted tightly in his fist.

"The nose!" Kirk yelled, writhing. He thought about pulling the hand away, but didn't dare. No nose . . . well, he could at least picture that . . . but losing what Leslie had a hold of . . . ? Oh, no. . . . "The nose! Bite the nose . . . please, bite the nose. . . . Leave that thing alone!" His temper flared, and Leslie smiled sourly, twisted even more, and he decided he was not so mad after all. "Come on . . . I'll be nice," he pleaded. That he was whimpering more than a little bothered him not at all. . . . Better to whimper than to squat to pee. In a cell there was really little else he could do with it, but still . . . "Please, Leslie . . . ? I'll tell you what: I have a few bucks in canteen ducats. . . . Let loose the wick and I'll go buy you a box of popsicles to suc—OOW! I WAS JUST KIDDING!"

"*Dah*-ling, how very peculiar," Leslie crooned, sugary and soft. "You don't sound at all tough. In fact, you sound like a little girl. Maybe *that's* why you run from me!" His eyes widened with mock astonishment as he twisted and squeezed a fraction more.

"YEAH!" Kirk yelled. "I'M A GIRL! I'M A GIRL! OUCH! YOU DIRTY COCKSUC—OUCH! I WAS ONLY KIDDING! HONEST, LESLIE! HONEST!" Oh, you fairy bastard! he added to himself, wait'll I get loose . . . if . . .

Then suddenly he was released. But before the realization came, Leslie jumped away and through the door. Groaning, Kirk touched himself gently to see if he was all there. He was. Leaping from the bunk, he slammed through the door into the hallway and looked around. Leslie was standing at the end, the stairwell at his side.

"Leslie," Kirk called with his nicest voice, "why are you standing way down there? Come here, I want to tell you a secret," and added a disarming smile.

"Fuck you, eunuch," Leslie said, giving him the finger. "Find another dumb blonde—"

A guard stepped from the stairwell, stood beside Leslie, looking down the hall toward Kirk. "What're you two doing on the floor?" he demanded in a voice sounding like a snore.

Raising his voice, Kirk answered: "Just moved into the block; I guess I need a key or something."

With Leslie beside him, almost on top of him, the guard walked toward Kirk. He was a veritable giant, standing at least six seven and monstrously built. But for all his great size, he walked hunched over, shuffling tiredly, as though finding it a great task to lift his

182

feet. And no wonder, for his feet were the length of a normal person's forearm, the width of a thigh and the toes of his shoes looked a lot like doorknobs. His hair, uncombed, tawny-colored, fell limp across his forehead, almost to the freckles liberally speckling his nose. His eyes were of a nondescript color, some sleepy shade.

The guard halted within a few feet of Kirk and looked him over. "Just moving in, huh?" he said amicably, then smiled, exposing big gapped teeth. More than vaguely, he resembled a jack-o'-lantern.

Kirk smiled at him and nodded, trying to ignore Leslie, who stood just back of the guard's shoulder, making faces, daring him to do something about it.

After feeling around in his pockets, the guard dug out a key and handed it to Kirk. "Deadlock goes off at 6:45 in the morning; back on from 3:55 to 4:10 for count; evening deadlock at 10:00 o'clock; no loitering in the halls during the day; you wanna visit somebody in their cell, you leave the door blocked open a little; you wanna watch T.V. during the day—and you ain't supposed to be working —then you watch it on the first floor or keep it turned so I can't hear it. . . . Ain't supposed to be no one on the second and third floor during my shift"—he looked around, then back at Kirk and winked—"but what I can't hear, I don't know . . . follow?" He looked up at the ceiling. "Hmmm . . . I forget anything . . . ? Nope." He showed a bunch of teeth and winked again, sly as a hippopotamus.

Kirk bit his tongue and winked back. "Thanks," he said with a happy, carefree, and phoney grin. "My name's Whalen and this is Lemman. . . ." he indicated Leslie. "What's yours?"

For a moment it seemed the guard would shake his hand or say, "Aw shucks," and shuffle his feet or something, for such friendliness he had obviously seldom encountered. "Dunn," he finally answered, smiling hugely, then patted his shirt pocket and shrugged. "Got a smoke by the way? Musta left mine somewheres."

Kirk gave him a cigaret and picked his property box from the floor beside Leslie's cell. With Dunn beside him, shuffling languidly, he went toward his own cell, watching the door numbers. Finding it, he slipped the key in the lock, twisted and pull d open the door. Dunn held it back while he entered the cell—a cell identical to those in segregation with the addition of a metal locker under the window and a towel rack on the wall—and dropped the property box on the mattress. As he turned to leave, Dunn stopped him with a mysterious look. "Didn't bring no coffee today," he said out of the side of his mouth. "Old lady forgets to pack it sometimes. Got any?" He winked.

"Sure," said Kirk, adding a wink, feeling ridiculous. He stepped to the property box and rummaged through it until he found a small jar of instant coffee. He handed it to the guard, saying, "Keep it, I have plenty."

"You sure?" Dunn's pocket swallowed the jar as fast as a toad gulps a fly.

"Sure, I'm sure." What would happen if he wasn't?

Smiling, Dunn glanced around at Leslie, who stood in the doorway, and turned back to Kirk. "Uh . . . listen . . . uh," he began, "listen, you two, I don't care about nothing you do if I don't know you're doing nothing. But you get outta line too far and the other cons'll start talking. . . . Won't be long before it'll get to custody. So . . . so kinda look out for my interests, will you?" He winked again.

And Kirk answered him with a wink and, "You bet, Dunn. There's nothing to worry about." He wanted to take a solemn oath on it, but did not think he could stand another of the guard's winks.

Dunn turned, started to walk, then hesitated. "Give me a coupla more smokes, will you? Think my pack's low." When he got the cigarets, he left, shuffling slowly.

Kirk and Leslie spent a moment looking at one another, wagging their heads. "Wow," was all Kirk could say.

"You've just met Big Stupe," Leslie said. "I'd heard about him before. . . . He's harmless, I guess, but when I got my key . . . Yeah, 'Wow' is the word for him." He stepped all the way into the cell. The door closed automatically behind. He leered. "Fuck all that, you boob. What'd you want to tell me before Dunn came along to save you? I'm all alone with you now. Maybe you'd like to spank the lady's bottom, huh, you big scaredy?" He turned, bent over, and wiggled and jiggled.

Kirk thought seriously about it for a moment and finally decided that, though Leslie had coming some diabolical punishment, he would not be the one to mete it out. All he wanted was to get some distance between those hot hands and his own body. He had been man-handled enough, too much. If only he could get past Leslie and out the door before it happened again. . . . "Come on, Leslie,"

184

he said gravely, trying to be dignified and lofty, above all such childishness, or whatever. "Quit acting like that." He very slowly eased toward the door. "Be serious."

His leer turning sour, Leslie said, "You bastard, I am *serious!*" and leaped at Kirk, fingernails to the fore.

Throwing himself against the wall, Kirk ducked under Leslie's claws, caught his belt and shoulder and threw him atop the bunk, tumbling into the property box, knocking it to the floor. He bounded out the door and ran. At the stairwell he paused a fractional second to glance over his shoulder. As he feared, Leslie was coming, and fast. Down the stairs three at a time he went, and ran out into the middle of the corridor and looked frantically about. There was a guard leaning against the wall some 40 feet distant. He felt safer but not safe enough. He eased toward the guard.

Leslie darted from the block door, looked, saw him.

"Aw, Leslie," Kirk wheedled, "is this the only place I'm safe from those hungry little hands?"

Leslie looked at him for a moment, then the look turned to a glare; he propped a hand on each hip as red splotches blossomed on his cheeks. "Bastard, bastard, bastard . . . nutless eunuch bastard!" He flounced off, headed toward the yard.

[XXX]

After the evening meal, Kirk gathered Sam and Leslie and climbed with them to the third floor to look for Hippo. They spotted him at the back window, looking out.

When he neared the dead-eyed convict, Kirk also looked out. The wall was there, gray and bleak, nothing more. He stared at Hippo, wondering for a fleeting moment why he hated him, then the moment was gone.

"We're ready," he said.

Hippo turned and looked at him closely, then at Sam, not at Leslie. "Let's go, then."

"Let's." He hoped the plan was better than the dialogue.

Hippo gazed blankly, looking thoughtful. "One of them keeps point in the stairwell," he said, gesturing in the direction of Sam and Leslie. "The other works the lock on the door we go through."

He handed Kirk a lock pick and tension bar. "Come on." He walked toward the other end of the hall, passing the others as if they did not exist.

At the far end of the hall, past the stairwell, Hippo stopped before a handleless green door. "This is it," he said to Kirk, pointing at the door. "Put one of them"—he gestured again—"in the stairwell to watch for the screw and anybody else happening along. The other one walks the hall and knocks on the door every five minutes or so. When he hears a knock back, he lets us out. The lock is only turned enough to hold the door closed—not to lock it." He paused. "The most important thing ain't worrying about the screw. . . . It's watching out for convicts coming from the television and game rooms. A lot of them go to their cells every hour or so to make coffee. If anybody sees us, we can forget it. . . . It'll be just a mattera time before somebody rats." For the first time, he let those dead black eyes look at Leslie. "Get the door opened."

Clenching his fists, Kirk forced himself to stand fast, breathe deep. Tomorrow was for Hippo, now was for getting out. "Leslie," he said, "you take the stairs and, Sam, you know how to work the door," and he turned his attention to picking the lock. Then the lock twisted, and using the heavy end of the pick, he began prying open the door.

But Hippo held his foot against it. "Wait a minute," he said. "When we get inside, you listen close and do everything I say. You won't be able to see nothing and if you move around, you're likely to get stuck. You get stuck, I'm stuck, too . . . so don't move around unless I say so." He took his foot from in front of the door.

Kirk pried it open, revealing a dark and gloomy plumbing chase crisscrossed by a maze of pipes. The walls, very narrow, and floor were unfinished concrete, coated with white dust.

Hippo slipped inside, leaving just enough room for Kirk to squeeze in behind.

Kirk looked at Sam. "You have something to turn the lock with?"

Sam nodded and pulled a nail file from his pocket, then pushed the door closed, forcing Kirk tight against Hippo.

When the door clicked, indicating that the tongue of the lock was securing the door from swinging open, the two convicts were left in a sweltering darkness that droned with the sound of distant machinery.

186

Hippo lit a match, held it overhead. "Look," he said, pointing to a pipe overhead that ran parallel to the chase. "Grab holda that. No more light till we get down." The match flickered out, made the blackness seem even blacker than before.

Kirk felt Hippo brush against him, pulling himself upwards. Then he waved his hands where the convict had been, feeling nothing but thick black space. It was vaguely unnerving.

Moments later Hippo's panting voice sounded from somewhere above. "Pull yourself up now. . . . Stand on the pipe."

Gripping the pipe, he started up, squeezing between wall and pipe, his back scraping, tearing against the rough wall, lungs beginning to burn. A long minute later he was finally standing upon the pipe, panting, starved for air, sweat leaking from every pore. He felt as if he'd run a desert marathon, unable fully to believe that only shortly before he had breathed cool air, seen light.

"Up?" Hippo asked.

"Up." He thought he now understood why Hippo was sparing words.

"Okay . . . lean against the wall . . . walk toward me . . . hands in front of your face. . . . There's too many pipes to warn you about all of them . . . but there's enough room to go under them. Let's go."

One hand a feeler, the other across his face, elbow to the fore, Kirk inched toward the rear of the chase. He remembered watching something long ago . . . a birthday party . . . pin the tail on the donkey . . . Hippo, the donkey. . . .

He ran into a pipe, went under it; another pipe, under it; another; yet another. And long, steaming minutes later, after stooping under the many large and small pipes he banged into, his sweat-wet hair muddied with the dust of plaster and asbestos, his extended fingers poked into Hippo's chest. He was sorry he did not hold the pinned tail.

"Okay," Hippo said, "we're at the back of the chase. I'm going down first. I'll stop now and then and tell you what to do. Don't do nothing I don't tell you or you're likely to get us both plugged in here. Memorize what I say—I don't want to lead no more tours."

Then he was scrabbling in the pipes, the sound diminishing so slowly as to be stationary. It seemed a long time before his voice, panting and rasping, rose from the inky depths.

"Now, sit on the pipe facing the door. Then slide down the right-hand side, but keep your knees hard against the left-hand wall. You'll have some trouble 'cause there's a one-inch pipe about eight inches from the wall. But when you get that pipe across the small of your back, bend your knees till your feet're against the same wall as your back. You'll be bent in an S. After that . . ."

Following instructions, Kirk contorted his body in S's, L's, almost Z's, and other configurations defying the alphabet. Skin tore from his hands, his head repeatedly banged into the wall, sweat drenched him, his lungs were fire-gulping bellows, claustrophobia stuck its fingers down his throat. And then he remembered that this trip was to practice. . . . He considered just letting go. . . . Too bad the pipes below would stop him. . . .

A century later, his body a wet dead thing, he heard Hippo's voice. "You're in the basement."

The occasion was worth more than that laconic announcement; if not a short applause, at least a cheer. Never had he experienced such total enervation. But what was amazing, had kept him from collapsing for half the tortuous journey down, when will had died, was Hippo's seemingly boundless stamina. The frail-bodied, dead-eyed convict, like Kirk, gasping stertorously, did not hesitate or stop for a breather, had gone on and on. Kirk hated him more than ever.

A round trip each day, along with digging in the sweltering and claustrophobic atmosphere? With sweat running in his mouth at every labored breath, feeling as if he were drowning in an inkwell? Better, he thought, to take a chance with the machine guns or even wait for a parole. After all, ten years isn't twenty. . . . He had an idea that he was caught up in the kind of child's game that promises a great and good time for all but turns out to be exhausting exercises in futility.

He was pleased when Hippo finally spoke again. It made him mad, gave him cause to forget his considerable weariness.

"You rested enough to go on?" he asked. "It took us about 20 minutes to get down. . . . It'll take the same to get up. . . . Don't forget we got to go back." He seemed to be reminding himself.

"I'm ready." What else could he say? Besides, though it was painful even to think of moving, a vague hope flitted through his mind: maybe Hippo will give up, collapse.

A match flared in Hippo's hand, showed that they were atop a

188

pipe several inches from a spider-webbed wall, and all around were insulated pipes and bare pipes and little pipes and big pipes. And looking overhead, Kirk mentally blanched, his head began aching. How had they snaked through that labyrinth of pipes? He wished he had not looked. . . . Returning appeared improbable, out of the question, impossible. And if one of them became wedged, the one leading the way . . . what? They would both remain one with the pipes, the heat would mummify them, centuries would pass while the building slowly crumbled, them with it. It never occurred to him that anybody had ever worked on and among those things. And had it occurred to him, he would not have believed it.

"Let's get on with it," he heard himself say, knowing he had to stop looking at the overhead maze.

Hippo, too, had trouble pulling his eyes from the pipes, but finally the match burned out. "Feel your way like at first," he said. "It gets easier from here on."

Blinking away the lingering image of the pipes, Kirk inched slowly from the back of the chase, following the shuffling noises ahead. Inch by inch by inch, then . . . nothing! He plunged downwards, choked back a scream, knowing the earth had opened up before him. Arms flailing, seeking purchase, finding none, down he went, down toward the bottomless blackness. Down. And then he hit bottom, the floor of the abyss. He felt very foolish, for his foot was still on the pipe, the other at the bottom of the abyss . . . an abyss six inches deep . . . the floor of the basement. If only he was certain that he knew the route through the overhead pipes. . . . If he did, Hippo would draw very few more breaths. Never had he felt so thoroughly foolish.

But it passed as he suddenly realized that what had been impenetrable blackness was now a faint luminosity. It was coming from just ahead.

With vigor renewed—slightly refreshed, anyway—he felt his way forward and finally stepped out of the plumbing chase into the basement hallway. Directly to the right, where the main corridor would have been had he been upstairs, was the corresponding basement corridor. A feeble light shone through a wire-screened door.

Lured toward the light, Kirk went to the door and peered through its heavy mesh. Straight ahead was nothing but the dead gray of unfinished concrete, and to the side, visible by pressing his face hard against the screen, was a barred gate across the corridor basking in the radiance of a 25-watt bulb. He looked the other way, saw a similar gate.

Almost unnoticeable until now was a relentless, thought-killing hum, a low-pitched whine that seemed to come from everywhere, seemed to keep the entire building slightly tremulous, throbbing.

Hippo came up beside him, tugged at his arm. "We ain't getting nothing done here. Let's go in the back," and a moment later begrudgingly added, "Watch out for pipes again." Then he faded into the black.

Silently Kirk cursed him for a mechanical man. But he followed Hippo's scuffling noises, moved deeper, ever deeper into the gloom.

After walking stooped over for what seemed an interminable distance, the noises ahead ceased, left only the all-pervasive drone of machinery, and then, for the second time, his fingers poked into Hippo's chest. They were at the end of the block.

Hippo struck another match, lending their situation a ghostly cast. Immediately before them was the end of the block, a wall pitted and gray that served as a backdrop for what might have been a quarter of all the spider webs in the world. To each side were walls of the same spider-webbed concrete. Also noticeable, set into the wall on the right, was a two-foot-square green door.

"Yeah," said Hippo, answering the question Kirk was thinking, "that's the door." Firing another match, he held it close, illuminating the brass barrel of the lock. "Get it opened."

Kirk fumbled in his pocket and found the pick and tension bar, and put them in the keyhole. The match went out as he began setting the tumblers. A while later the plug clicked, twisted. "Light."

A match flared, showed the keyhole to be slightly off center. Kirk removed the pick and turned the tension bar until the keyhole traveled through a 180-degree arc, and stopped. He ran the pick in the bottom of the keyhole—which was now turned up—and pushed up the single "security" pin. That single pin, he had learned, was what set the lock apart from any other pin-tumbler, lock, lending the misnomer "security lock." Twisting the tension bar, he turned the plug an additional 45 degrees and released the lock's tongue. On its own, the door swung outwards, creaking.

A shaft of dusty light and cooler air flowed over the two convicts. Without comment, Hippo climbed through the door. Kirk followed.

Inside, immediately noticeable, were two screened vents on the easternmost wall five feet above the dirt floor. The area was roughly 12 feet north-south by 20 feet east-west. Set into the west wall was a door similar to the one they had come through.

"What's on the other side of that one?" Kirk asked, pointing.

"Same as this. After you go through a half dozen of them, you get to the main corridor. You saw what's down there."

Kirk walked to one of the vents and peered through, then leaped back, wheeling toward Hippo. "Son of a bitch!" he spat, shuddering. "You know what kind of spiders make these webs?"

"Black widows," Hippo said mildly, his face almost cracking, as if trying to smile. "Maybe a million of them. But they're the best friends we could have. . . . The screws won't go near them."

"Then they're not so stupid after all," Kirk said, staring at Hippo, wondering. . . . "Friends? Did you say 'friends'?" He could not believe it. Turning back to the vent, he poked the lock pick at something wrapped in webs directly below a grape-sized black body. "A mouse!" he yelped, choking on the very idea. "These goddamn spiders eat mice!" He stared at Hippo again and shuddered. "You have any idea how many of these things we had in our hair getting down here?" He had no idea himself, but when he ran the pick through his hair, collecting sticky strands of web, he made a rough estimate and got a headache.

Something happened to Hippo's face. Kirk stepped closer for a better look. Hippo was smiling. Kirk was stupefied, dazed. He would have bet that the dead-eyed convict was congenitally unable to smile, but there he was. . . . His headache got worse.

"Black widows," said Hippo with an air of solemn seriousness, "will live their whole lives in one spot if they're not bothered. The males are the only ones that do any moving around, but they're small, brown and harmless. The females will usually run if they're bothered, but if something tries to get her eggs, she'll fight. If you leave those white sacks alone, you won't have any trouble. If you don't . . ." He shrugged. "Well, some Indian tribes used to use their poison to hunt with. . . ."

Kirk tried not to gawk but did, anyway. The big creep loves spiders, he thought; hating queers is great, but loving spiders is greater. He needed to think about that, so he knelt and began feeling the earth. "Damn stuff's like all the rest of it," he muttered. "Concrete."

"Yeah," said Hippo, sounding like himself again, "but that's just on top. Down a few feet it softens . . . least, that's the way it was in Walla Walla."

Holding some clods to the dim light, Kirk examined them. "You really think this will hold together without shoring?"

"It has to. Maybe I forgot to mention it, but ain't no way we can get wood enough down here. . . . Ain't that much wood in the joint, either."

Kirk gazed at him curiously, then rose, shaking his head, and went back to the vent. Using the pick, he pushed aside the friendly spiders and peered through the screen. His eyes were only a foot above the grass behind the block; the view of the wall, however, was unimpaired. "It's 50 yards if it's a foot," he said slowly. "Call it 60 to allow for the road on the other side. . . . Then add a depth of 10 or 12 feet—190 feet, maybe more. In this heat, and without air . . . At least the chances of them stumbling onto it are small. And," he added, eyeing Hippo contemplatively, "with spiders for friends, how can we miss?"

[XXXI]

Breakfast over, the four convicts met on the nearly deserted yard to begin mapping their moves, and somehow, it seemed to fall upon Kirk to do most of the mapmaking, for it was obvious that Hippo, though aloof and stony as a statue, was uncomfortable around Leslie, and Sam was primarily interested in keeping his face turned to the sun.

With talk finally finished, and agreeing to meet back in the block after lunch, Sam and Hippo went separately back to the corridor, each with a mission to accomplish.

"What do you think?" Kirk asked Leslie when they were alone.

"I think maybe that big funny-faced scarecrow doesn't like me."

"Will you be able to sleep?"

"Do you like me?"

"Not when you ask. And the way you're talking about, never." Kirk spent a moment looking at Leslie. "In all seriousness, why don't you find yourself somebody to get you out of heat?"

Leslie bounded up and kicked his shin. "Why're you so cruel to me?"

He rubbed his shin. "Cruel?" he asked in bewilderment, further bewildered by Leslie's wet eyes. "It's cruel because I'm not geared to get in bed with men? It's cruel because I sometimes think we're friends, but I don't believe you're a girl?"

Leslie sat back down and wiped his eyes. "I'm not a man," he said simply, quietly.

Kirk gazed at him for a long time. "Leslie . . ." he mumbled and didn't know what else to say. Inside him there was something bleeding for the little fruit, something he could not touch, could not staunch. "Leslie . . ."

He turned grieved and haunted eyes on Kirk. "Baby . . ." he said softly, so softly. "Baby, I didn't mean anything. . . . I'm sorry. But sometimes I get so loneseome. . . ."

"Leslie . . . I'm not trying to be funny, but you know how many of the guys around here want you?"

Leslie gazed upon him, his expression thoughtful and remote. "Sometimes you seem to know so much. . . . Other times you're so young and dense . . . callous, even. Sure, you're a little different than most people . . . nuttier, anyway. . . . But if you really didn't want to, you wouldn't have to live inside yourself. . . . You could go where you want, be what you want. Baby, can you picture me with a wife and kids? Or even a mustache? Just a little bit, baby, that's my loneliness."

In silence Kirk stood, then stooped and lifted Leslie to his feet. They stood there looking at one another. What happened next, Kirk was never to be certain of, but he felt his lips curl back, heard himself snarl as an icy sweat popped out on forehead and spine. With bone-crushing fingers, he squeezed Leslie's arm until the little fruit paled, almost fainted.

Next he knew, Leslie was wiping his forehead, crooning ". . . baby . . . baby . . . are you okay? Let's go inside now, there're things to do."

Kirk spun around and closed his eyes, quivering. A long minute later he looked back at Leslie, at the buttons on his shirt, not his face. "You all right?"

"Yes." A pause. Then, "Baby . . . ?"

"Save it. Let's go."

With two of them below the building and the other two above, it was necessary to syncronize their movements. For that they needed a pair of watches. And Kirk had assigned himself the task of coming up with them. No great task actually, for the prison canteen sold watches that usually lasted a month or two when handled gently. But between them they did not have available in canteen script the necessary 22 dollars. Thus it was that Kirk, with Leslie leading the way, got introduced to Doc Gillis.

They sneaked past the B block guard and climbed to the second tier, where Kirk followed Leslie to a cell.

"That's him," Leslie said with a smile, pointing toward the door window.

Kirk looked inside and muttered, "Damn," and looked closer.

Sitting cross-legged on the bunk, facing the door, reading a book, was an enormously fat old man with an unruly thatch of snow-white hair, who at first glimpse appeared naked but was actually wearing a jockstrap buried deep in his flesh, clothing him in a girding wrinkle. Toothless, he was worrying a piece of chewy candy.

Leslie put his face to the window and knocked on the door. The old man looked up, fixed him with a guileless gaze from soft gray eyes, whites the color of porcelain, bright and unblemished. His face, round and nut-colored, was without a wrinkle. After a moment he laboriously straightened his legs and, visibly puffing, rose to his feet and trundled to the door.

"Hello, Lethlie," lisped Doc Gillis, adding a gummy smile. "Come in, both of you, come in." They did, and Kirk pulled the door closed. "Lethlie, Lethlie," Doc sighed. "Where have you been?"

"In seg a little while," Leslie said, then pointed to Kirk and went on. "Doc, would you take care of my friend here? I have some real important business to take care of."

"Important business?" Doc said wryly, spraying the esses all over the cell. "What, little friend, can possibly be important around here?"

"Not being around here," Leslie said cryptically.

Kirk stared at the back of the little fruit's head and seriously considered driving a fist into it, but picked up the blue-bound book the old man had been reading. Why had Leslie answered like that? he wondered. What if the fat creep was a rat? He thumbed back the cover of the book, read the stiff and yellowed title page: a century-old English edition of Schopenhauer's *The World as Will and Idea*, passages underlined in red, pencil scribblings in the margin,

194

chewed crumbly in spots by hungry creatures. Scanning the pages, he heard Leslie and the old man talk for a moment, then felt sharp fingernails gently raking his cheek, neck. Looking up, he saw Leslie with a pertly wrinkled nose, lips puckered in a kiss.

"Bye, baby," he said, and swished from the cell.

Kirk and Doc spent a moment gazing at one another, then the old man reached for the book and pulled it with gentle resolve from Kirk's hands, and closed the cover. "You want wa-theth, I think," he said mildly, with a searing and impatient contempt not far under the surface.

Kirk stared at him with equivocal feelings, revulsed by the oozing obesity of his body, by his outward friendliness, yet attracted to some underlying thing, something that might have been a huge, all-embracing loathing of everything, everybody. "Not want," he told the old man finally. "I need them. . . . There's a difference."

Guilelessly the fat man stared back at him. And finally, "Under the bed . . . pull the box out," he said, and went back to the bunk and plopped on it, almost crushing it while the woven-wire springs squawked in protest.

Kirk stooped and, from under the foot of the bunk, pulled a large cardboard box bulging with wallets, rings, bracelets, hairbrushes, hats of denim and straw, a black satin yarmulka, a felt hat festooned with a band of brilliant-colored fish flies, alarm clocks, and watches—or wa-theth, maybe.

"Find two you want, cigarets on the line," Doc said, reading again.

Kirk snorted. "Need, Doc, need. Not like that candy you're gumming to death. . . . I need; you want."

Doc Gillis cast him a curious look and closed the book, setting it in his lap.

Kirk fumbled around until he came up with two abused timepieces, then stared at the old man, expression deadpan. "Two watheth."

"A hundred dollarth a pieth."

Kirk rose. "Thove 'em up your fat athh." He stepped to the door and pushed it open.

Sudden laughter sounded back of him. "Come back, thon."

He turned and saw the old man's belly jiggling, bouncing all over, his gummy mouth gaped wide, gurgling laughter, chortling.

Kirk laughed, too, he couldn't help it. And he laughed harder when Doc reached for a cup sitting on his locker and fished out a set of teeth and shoved them into his mouth.

"Thove 'em up your own athh." Doc laughed some more. And a while later grew still, fixing Kirk with a look of puzzlement. "You need, you need," he said finally and shrugged gigantically. "Take them. When you don't need them any more, bring them back."

"Free?"

"Free."

"What if I decide I need them for always?"

"Then I'm a fool for always, which is nothing new."

Kirk thought about it, then, "Thanks," pocketed the watches and turned to go.

Doc stopped him again. "Wait a minute, son," he said, and when Kirk turned back, went on, "Do you know this book?" He waved it in the air, his eyes probing, avid.

Suddenly uncomfortable, Kirk gazed absently about the cell. "Know it?" he said distantly. "Once, about a thousand years ago, I thought I knew it. . . . I was eighteen. . . . I knew so much then. . . ."

"It's given to the young to know," the old man said from far away, then went on, fervent and eager. "Schopenhauer was but twenty-six when he began that book. How very young he must have been when it first began crystalizing in his mind." He sighed. "What he began as a young man, he developed and perfected until his death. . . . Somehow, he had the courage to remain loyal to his youth. Most men leave youth behind and think themselves well shut of it. Perhaps that is why something—God, if you believe; evolution or whatever, if you don't—decided we must die." He stared at Kirk for a moment, then looked at the elongated piece of candy and gnawed it some more, made it longer.

Kirk was uneasy but did not know why. He wanted to leave. "Uh . . . I'll see you later, Doc," he muttered and began backing through the door, leaving for the third time in fewer minutes.

"What are you here for?" the old man asked hurriedly, as if reluctant to let him go.

Kirk thought to tell him he had a big nose, but it was not the truth, so he said instead, "Manslaughter."

Clucking, the old man wagged his head. "For the right reason or the wrong reason?" he asked, a wry twist to his mouth.

"No reason." Kirk was angry. "You have a license, Doc?"

"Killing is the act of a child," the old man said, ingenuously ignoring Kirk's impatience. "It might be said that in many cases it is an act of honesty, a child's honesty, unequivocal."

"Lectures I didn't come for, Doc. But as long as you're talking about children, tell me about that tire around your gut and that gunk you keep cramming down your throat."

Doc chuckled, bounced all around. "Thoughtless of me," he said happily. "Would you like a candy bar?" Kirk shook his head negatively, and the old man ripped open another candy bar, taking it from a bountiful pile at the head of his bed. Munching, he peeled the cellophane off a huge cigar, gulped down what was in his mouth, sighed ecstatically, and lit the phalluslike thing. His first puff made an ash a half inch long.

Kirk was disgusted. "Why do they call you 'Doc'?"

"I was . . . once."

"A veterinarian? You worked around pigs a lot maybe?"

That made the fat man laugh until he began choking and wheezing, and his face became red and wet. When finally he could not go on, he looked at Kirk with twinkling eyes. "It's been so long since I found somebody to talk to," he said slowly, with a tone suggestive of a self-caress. "Sit down." He pointed to the end of the burdened bunk. "Sit down."

"Pass, Doc," said Kirk, feeling something squirming inside him. "I have things to take care of." The sudden look of anguish pulling at Doc's face made him add hastily: "How about later, maybe?"

"Yes," the old man said with a voice remote and forlorn. "Yes, later, maybe."

Kirk sat down. "Okay, I have a question: you're a doctor, you claim; with my own eyes I see you reading a book that I think frightens me; and with the same eyes I see you looking like a giant Buddha, eating and smoking yourself to death; all the evidence is against it—including being the neighborhood junk man; so, why?"

When he finished with the speech, the old man sagged, looked down at his lardaceous lap, then poked himself with stumpy fingers. And Kirk went on, unrelenting.

"And talking about children—if I've put all the pieces together right—what's more childish than killing yourself?" He paused. "And if you really know how to read, tell me something more antithetical to what it says in that book." Kirk wondered at the anger burning inside of him, irrational but undeniable.

Doc was smiling when at last he looked back at Kirk. "Son," he said quietly, "suicide—since that's what you think I'm committing —is only childish when it's used as a push toward life's realization or as an atonement of sins. If a person wants to die knowing there is no redemption for either himself or anyone else, why is it childish?"

Kirk stared thoughtfully at him. "Are you nuts or what?"

"That kind of talk I can get from anybody."

"Doc," said Kirk, "from the creeps around here you can get anything: syphilis, TB, clap . . . even a razor blade—that'd be a lot quicker." He rose, determined to leave.

"Son!" the old man called. "Listen!" Kirk turned back, his tongue clamped hard between his teeth, and he continued. "You speak with contempt of those around you," he said haughtily.

"You don't, I suppose?" Again he turned to leave.

And again Doc stopped him. "Look closer, son, look closer. When you look close, what do you see? Convicts? The dregs of civilization? Better you don't. Better that you see the world microcosmically. Better that you see caged Cassandras shut from the sight and hearing of the willfully blind and deaf. And in the far distant background, better that you remember the wisdom of the ancients. Zeus, not satisfied merely to bind Prometheus and have him disemboweled by eagles for giving men fire, promised: 'I shall give men an evil as the price of that fire. They will clasp destruction with the laughter of desire!' " The old man stared at Kirk, his eyes flaming, almost rabid.

"Nihilism's soothsayer reading Schopenhauer . . . that makes a lot of sense." Kirk snorted.

"Schopenhauer's world—the world of the will is dead! Better for men to be fertilizer. . . . At least they would nourish life. Once men were human, with the capacity to suffer, to grow godlike. But it has been allayed, has become jealousy, hatred, avarice. . . . Man, battling will against will, has destroyed life, made of it an infernal thing. In the end, and we are living through it, men who profess knowledge but who are stupid beyond belief, men professing education but who are merely superficially informed—these are the ones who must prevail." Flushed, gasping for breath, the old man

198

slammed the aged book to the bunk. It bounced, bounced again, then lay still. Doc stared at it.

Kirk stared at him, feeling uncomfortable.

Doc Gillis raised his ponderous head, his eyes guileless again. "Don't let me scare you away, son," he said quietly, smiling. "There are so few people to talk to . . . so few . . ." He loosed a long, wheezing sigh. "Have you any idea of the loneliness of living one's life in the fishbowl as a whale in the fishbowl?"

"Life?"

"All of it."

"How many years so far?"

"Twenty-four."

That staggered Kirk. He stared. "Twenty-four years . . . ? Murder . . . ?"

The old man grinned wryly, and a moment later the grin became a grimace. " 'Murder' is a word presupposing a value. Something without value cannot be murdered."

"How about *someone?* I've heard it said that people aren't things, that there's value in the basest."

Doc shrugged. "It's relative."

"I'm confused," Kirk muttered, telling the truth, then rubbed his temples, trying to chase away the murk in his head. "A doctor," he began, mumbling to himself, "dedicated to the preservation of life, reading Schopenhauer, murdering people . . . himself . . . preaching nihilism. . . . And loneliness . . . he says he's lonely." He looked narrowly at the old man. "What the hell are you trying to say?"

Doc shrugged and chortled. "How the hell do I know?"

Uneasy, wanting to laugh, Kirk laughed uneasily. "Hey, Doc," he said, almost serious, "has anyone ever sniped at you with silver bullets?"

The old man smiled, eyes twinkling, looking like the fellow Kirk had in mind. " 'Let nobody ask me on my oath/Whether I shame me for my kind;/But you, when you speak the words "the devil"—/You've something big in mind.' Know that?"

Kirk nodded and started to smile but shivered instead.

Seconds later he was in the main corridor, hurrying, wanting to look over his shoulder, not daring to. He hurried.

* * *

199

He awoke trembling and sweaty and lay for a while staring at the ceiling. Stretching, he felt the watches in his pocket and pulled one out: 20 till 1:00, time to find the others.

Leslie was in his cell and opened the door to Kirk's knock. "I got a funny little shovel from a gardener," he said with coy proudness, as though wanting a pat on the head. "But it cost five packs. *Five packs!* Just for a dirty little shovel . . . can you imagine? It upset me so bad that I stole a rope from him." He giggled. "When the bulls come around to lock his rope up tonight, I bet he moans a lot. Anyhow, that's what he gets for being a five-pack mercenary."

"We have it," said Kirk, hoping to shut off Leslie's motor, "that's what counts. Having a rope around means he's probably a stoolie anyway." He pointed Leslie toward the stairs and walked with him to the third floor, to Sam's cell.

When Sam emerged, Kirk handed him one of the watches. "It's set," he said. "Did you get the things . . . or have you been too *busy?*" He heard the sneer in his voice and wondered where it came from.

But Sam did not question the sneer, for he seemed to know where it came from. "Yeah," he said with a tone of quiet menace, "too '*busy.*'" Staring flatly at Kirk, he continued. "You want to be somebody's conscience, little boy, dry behind your ears first. In the meantime, if cute remarks are what it takes to excite you, go ahead on. But you'd best get yourself another whipping boy. . . . My skin's real tender."

Without thinking, Kirk threw a hand to his mouth, eyes wide with mock amazement. "You poor boy!" he said scathingly. "I wouldn't be able to sleep nights if I thought I wounded your tender—"

"Turn it off!" Leslie jumped in front of him, glaring. "I don't know what your story is, tough guy, but a whole lot lately, you've been acting like a real punk—"

Kirk lifted a hand to shove Leslie aside. The fruit slapped the hand away. Kirk knotted a fist.

"What're you going to do?" Leslie asked him, his jaw stuck forward pugnaciously. "Hit me? Gawd! You're an absolute terror! I'm petrified, you big, tough bastard!" Breaking off, he sneered at Kirk, then in an undertone, almost as if to himself, he added: "I'm beginning not to like you a whole bunch."

Sam pulled Leslie back. "Okay," he said easily, "the pleasantries

200

have been handed around. Now let me show you what I got hold of." He turned and walked toward the television room.

Kirk stood frozen, staring at Leslie. There was a choking sensation inside his head; he felt betrayed, forsaken. He wanted an explanation—needed one. He found himself reaching for Leslie's shoulder. But his hand was dodged, eyed distastefully. Then Leslie wheeled and hurried after Sam. Kirk raised his hand to look at it, first the palm, then the back, then the palm again. He was a leper without blemish, a leper to a mashed-nose man-kisser and a mincing man-eater.

"Dirty cocksucker," he muttered biliously, then followed the others to the rear of the television room and waited, staring at the ceiling with a great display of unconcern while Sam picked open the lock on a door recessed into the back wall.

With the door finally open, Sam stepped through into the dark interior and gestured for the others to follow. Kirk walked in after Leslie, and as he pulled the door shut behind, Sam tugged at a string hanging from the ceiling. An overhead light blinked on. The room was about eight feet deep, six feet wide, and bordered on three sides with ceiling-high shelves crammed full of blankets and pillows.

Sam dug in a stack of blankets, throwing ragged work clothes, a big plastic bag, candles, and other things on the floor. Then he turned and fixed Kirk with an odd look. "Guess what I use this room for?" he said blandly, and slowly pulled his hand from beneath some blankets. Held in his fist was a two-foot-long double-edged knife. Straight-faced, he went on. "I hope it don't upset you, Mr. Calvin, but this is where I fuck Gypsy . . . usually three times a day. Sniff the air. . . ." He sniffed. "That's what fag-fucking smells like. Nice, ain't it? And, of course," he added informatively, "that doesn't count the times I saddle him in the cell at night." Smiling sardonically, his eyes on Kirk, he rummaged with his free hand in another pile of blankets and emerged with a plastic bottle. "To diddle a man, you got to use slip-ins. In case you're ever interested, a little dab'll do you." He pushed the bottle back where it came from, then staring expressionlessly at Kirk, ran the point of the knife under a thumbnail. Silence filled the little room.

"What's with you two?" Leslie suddenly exploded. He shoved Kirk back into the door, kicked Sam in the shin, and snatching at the knife, yanked it away. Grasping the haft with his other hand, he menaced both Kirk and Sam with the now blood-smeared blade. "Either of you bastards wants to play," he said with a snarl not entirely convincing, "think about this: I'm going to run this in the first one of you that raises a hand. Now, just act like you think I'm lying." He glared first at one, then the other, fearsome as a china doll.

Kirk laughed. "Mata Hari," he said with an unforced smile, "you win the day." He looked at Sam. "No threat," he said mildly, "but if you do that again, use it." He walked from the room.

Hippo was in the first-floor television room sitting against the rear wall. Kirk gestured and got his attention, then stepped back into the hallway. Hearing voices behind, he turned and saw Sam and Leslie approaching, talking together. He ignored them. They ignored him.

When finally Hippo came stilt-legged from the television room, Kirk eyed him questioningly.

"Bad deal," said the dead-eyed convict. "I got all the stuff I went after, but I could only get two of you assigned as block workers." He looked at Kirk and Sam. "I got you two over. There was only one block job open and I bought another guy's job for eight packs. I hit on another one. . . . He wanted 15 packs. I told him okay. . . . Then he changed his mind, got suspicious. He told me if I wanted his job bad enough, I'd pay his price. . . . The price is upped to five cartons."

Kirk mulled it over. "He'll have an accident," he decided.

Sam snorted disgustedly. "Too many people have accidents around you. You'd best start saving your luck for when you might need it." He looked at Hippo. "Is this five-carton geek the only one we can be sure won't holler cop?"

"Yeah."

Sam chewed his lip for a moment. "We need block jobs to move around inside without getting rousted," he mused. "We need *his* job." He broke off and stared at Hippo. "Who is he?" he asked.

"I think he's called Jake," Hippo replied. "Tall, glasses . . . thinks he's a pretty-boy."

Sam grinned. "Yeah, that's Jake the fake." He puffed his lower lip in thought. "Get a carton ready," he said finally. "When he comes around asking if you still want the job, offer him five packs. . . . Go to a carton when he starts whining." He strode quickly from the block and disappeared into the main corridor.

Kirk watched him leave, then turned to Leslie and started to say something . . . anything. But his mouth opened and closed, said nothing. He shrugged and went to his cell.

[XXXII]

In silence Kirk and Leslie ate the evening meal. Poked at it, actually. After a while Kirk looked up and found himself pinned under Leslie's eyes, eyes that searched his every pore, looking for a way into his head. Or maybe they were inside already. It felt like it.

They stared at one another for a long minute, the silence loud; even louder were the nameless emotions winging between them.

"Ready to leave?" Kirk asked finally. The blue eyes had won, gotten to him. Inside he was squirming, ready to explode. He picked up his tray and started to rise.

"No," said Leslie from a remote distance. "Sit down for a second." Kirk did and they stared for a while longer. "Kirk," he intoned, "I don't know what you've got going with Sam, but you're driving him against the wall. You're also eating my heart out. Don't say it!" Eyes squeezed shut, he plugged his ears and frantically shook his head.

Kirk noticed the bandage across his palm and was reminded of how Leslie had earlier snatched the knife. Something inside choked. He started to speak.

But Leslie, glaring, went on. "I'm so sick of your sarcasm and your petty little sadisms, I could spit! And I know you don't give a goddamn. . . . That's the trouble with you. You sneer at everyone. . . . You don't care about anything . . . not even yourself. . . ."

Kirk curled his lip contemptuously.

And suddenly Leslie's face tightened into hard lines, his eyes gone icy. "Make faces, son of a bitch . . . but make them at somebody else." He picked up his tray, started to stand.

But Kirk leaned across the table and grabbed his wrist, cruelly twisted until it bent almost double. "Listen to me," he hissed. "Listen good! I don't give a fuck what Sam or Hippo or the priest or you or your mother thinks about me! If any one or all of you don't like the way I am, change me! I'd really like that. I'm laying for some creepy punks to try to dent my head." He put his face close to Leslie's, snarling now. "And you . . . you, my fair little fag, you better not think for a minute that you have a privileged status. You ever raise a hand to me, and you have no more break coming than any other motherfucker with a dick. So go gum a ball-bag or something, but keep your mouth off me or I'll destroy it!"

White-faced, Leslie rose slowly from the table and pulled his wrist free. "Is that right, asshole?" he whispered hoarsely. "Is that right?" He leaned close to Kirk's heated face and viciously backhanded his mouth. "Kill me then, you low-life punk!" Almost running, he departed the dining hall.

Numbed, he sat touching his mouth, tasting blood, wondering what had happened. It's not true, he thought. Leslie was his friend. It couldn't be true. Leslie wouldn't do it; not Leslie; he couldn't; he didn't! But the sting across his mouth would not go away, could not be denied. He'd been *slapped*. In the middle of a crowded prison dining hall, a swishing, mincing 120-pound queer had slapped his mouth. It could not be denied.

But he might have denied it, anyway, if the fog clouding his mind had not been penetrated by sniggering from nearby. Swiveling, he traced it to a table two rows away. Four convicts in their late thirties were sitting there, two openly amused, the other two hiding their mirth behind their hands.

Kirk rose and stalked toward them. And as he neared, their humor strangled, died. Standing over them, staring coldly at each in turn, he felt titanic, all muscle and fury. "Tell me the joke," he said between his teeth.

As one the men studied their trays and fidgeted. Two toyed nervously with their eating utensils, one broke his plastic knife. No one spoke.

Kirk leaned a fist on their table. "Let's hear it."

"Kid," one of them said anxiously, "there's two cops in the mess hall. . . . 'Sides, you got ever'body looking at us."

It was true. "All right," Kirk said amicably, "I'll wait for you assholes outside." He took a step back toward his own table.

"Wait a minute, kid," said the same convict hastily, stopping him. "You got the best hand. . . . None of us want no trouble. . . . It's just that . . ." His lips kept moving but his voice disappeared. He worked at a smile until his mouth began trembling. "Well . . . you know . . ."

"I know this," Kirk snarled. "I want to break pieces of your heads and—" Of its own volition his mouth slammed shut. He

204

looked closer at the four men, seeing them for the first time. He was menacing men who would die of fright before they could ball a fist in anger. Besides, what had happened probably was amusing . . . maybe just a little. If it had happened to somebody else . . . He chuckled self-mockingly, almost abashedly. "Later, guys," he muttered, and went back to his table and picked up his tray. Heading toward the exit, he felt the stares of many eyes probing his back. The eyes he could ignore, the rejection he felt . . . that was something else again. Stupid, he thought; childish. But it did not go away.

Back at the block he went quickly to the third floor and sought out the others. Leslie was missing. Probably sulking, Kirk thought, and began to feel a little better. "Did Leslie get a block job?" he asked Sam.

Grinning sardonically, Sam nodded. "I told Jake the fake that I had some dope coming in—some yellows—and that I'd give him a deal. Three packs each instead of the usual five, but I need the cigarets out front. Jake's an ordinary geek, maybe a little stupider. . . . He got an idea from somewheres that a guy ain't 'in' till he pumps his veins full of anything and everything. That's where he gets the moniker from. He tells everybody he's been a hype since he was twelve. And he don't know heroin from bath salts. Anyway, he got the cigarets from Hippo, gave me back nine packs, and the job is Leslie's. Jake'll bug me for six months for the dope before he snaps he's been had."

The recital bored Kirk. They had the job; they could move—or loiter—freely during the day; that was all that mattered. He turned to Hippo. "Is everything ready to take down?"

"Yeah." The dead-eyed convict moved his head in a slow arc. "Where's the queer?"

Without thought, Kirk's hand went to his mouth, poked at the still heated spot. He caught Sam gazing at him with a secret smile hidden some place behind his eyes. "Why don't you find Leslie," he told Sam, trying to be casual, "and get him positioned? Hippo and I have to get the stuff ready to take down."

Sam cast him a knowing look. "She may not want to," he said, sounding almost smug, his eyes twinkling. "In case you don't know it," he added offhandedly, "it's all over the joint." He turned away and walked to the stairwell.

Kirk glanced at Hippo and received a questioning look, which he ignored. He walked to the shower and pulled open the half-glassed door. "Keep everybody out," he said over his shoulder. "Tell them the shower's broken. I'll get everything ready." He stepped inside the red and green tiled shower room and let the door close automatically behind. Hippo stood with his back to the door, blocking the view through the glass.

Against the wall was a bench, its green—the inevitable green—paint bubbled and peeling. Kirk fished a pile of dirty sheets from beneath the bench and found the cache of supplies. Holding open a pillow slip, he dropped into it the hand trowel, the knife, a box of matches and several candles. He rolled them into a small bundle and bound it tightly with rubber bands, then laid it aside. Opening a second pillow slip, he lined it with the capacious plastic bag and filled it with water from the shower, letting the floor support it as it grew heavy. When it was filled to within inches of the top, he drew it closed and wrapped it with heavy twine. The loose ends of the twine he tied to the first bundle. Then to the formless water bag he joined the Manila rope that Leslie had stolen and tugged at the knot until certain it would hold. Pushing everything back under the bench and once again covering it with the dirty sheets, he went to the door and told Hippo that they were ready.

Unsnapping his shirt, Hippo entered the shower. "By the way," he commented, "Sam says your girl friend wants to see you before we go down. . . . He's on the landing."

Kirk mulled it over for a moment and decided not to see him. Let the queer son of a bitch suffer, he thought. "Go ahead and change clothes." Then he found himself in the hall, on his way to see Leslie. He passed Sam, who stood across from the television-room door, staring absently at the ceiling and whistling innocently. Somehow, "Whatever Lola Wants Lola Gets," coming from him at a time like this, did not sound right. But Kirk went past without mentioning it.

And at the stair landing, he found Leslie bent over the rail, his stretched-too-tight pants seemingly about to burst. He was watching below for convict and guard alike who might wander from television programs or checker games, a rare occurrence.

"What do you want?" Kirk asked tersely, touching his mouth, remembering the slap, remembering his threats. He spent a moment thinking about putting his foot in the fruit's unnatural keister, booting him over the rail, blond bangs first. But he didn't; he wanted to hear him snivel a little.

"Whalen," said Leslie without looking around, his voice a distant monotone, "I don't want you in my life. If you have anything to say, keep it business. And the only business we have is this tunnel. As of tonight, I've got somebody . . . somebody to get me out of heat. . . . Pain from you I don't need. . . . I have enough scars. So don't bug me any more."

Blindfolded with gloom, hands and feet bound with chains, Kirk was prodded to the end of the plank and into the water. He sank. Down and down, and down some more. He leaned against the wall but almost fell, anyway. Leslie's back raced away, raced close, then away again. From far away, booming through the murk, came a voice.

"Leslie . . . all right, Leslie," then continued petulantly: "Me bugging you? I always had the idea it was the other way around."

The next he was aware of, he was donning the ragged work clothes, preparing to go to the basement. When had he been so totally abandoned, so wretchedly abject? "Filthy pervert!"

"Huh?"

"Let's go," Kirk said, feeling himself redden, then hefted the unwieldy water bag and coiled the rope around his shoulder.

Hippo eyed him curiously, shrugged slightly, and pushed open the shower door. "All right?" he called down the hall to Sam, and a moment later stepped from the tiled room, signaling Kirk to follow.

Sam had the door to the plumbing chase held open. Hippo and Kirk stepped inside and as Sam was pushing the door shut, Hippo said, "Eight o'clock?"

"Yeah," Sam agreed, then closed the door, leaving the two convicts in darkness.

Kirk listened as Hippo pulled himself atop the overhead pipe.

"Okay," said Hippo finally, indicating he was up and secured.

Kirk stepped under the voice and raised the bags and rope. When they were pulled from his hands, he, too, pulled himself atop the pipe. There he groped in the dark until he was once again holding the cumbersome bag, and followed Hippo's scuttling noises to the rear of the chase.

At the proper point, Hippo began the tortuous descent as Kirk lowered the bag, attempting to play out just enough rope to keep the bag directly over his head as he weaved around and through and under the maze, guiding the sack as he went. Occasionally at first, then incessantly, Hippo cursed, gasped, wheezed, gave up, decided to try anew, and cursed. He cursed a lot.

Listening, Kirk began feeling almost gleeful. He uncoiled the line inch by reluctant inch and wished the dead-eyed convict had a mile or two to descend or that the bag was lead and full of sharp spikes or that there was a corpse inside it . . . a blond-banged, blue-eyed . . .

"I'm . . . down!" The voice crawled up through the labyrinth until it reached Kirk, strained to its last whimpers.

He dropped the rope and began snaking down through the pipes, pleased that he had little trouble remembering the Chinese-puzzle-like route; pleased, too, that he had so little difficulty whereas Hippo had had so much.

On the bottom he rested for a moment, then began duck-walking toward the rear of the ink-black basement. Ahead, a match flared, illumining Hippo's dripping face.

When Kirk came close, he could hear the convict's labored breathing and felt smug, for he was himself sweating very little and not panting at all hard.

Getting to business, he had Hippo hold a light over the lock in the door. Noticeable immediately was the fact that the keyhole was canted three or four degrees off center. He had left it that way, for all that was necessary to open it was gently to insert a flat piece of metal in the keyhole and turn it. If it was done clumsily, however, the lock plug would be jarred the fraction necessary to let the tumblers fall into place, requiring that it be picked open again. Should a guard happen to make a security check of the area, the lock would close itself the moment the plug was touched and allow the key to enter. Hence, if the lock was found secured, it would serve as warning that somebody had been there.

Kirk twisted the lock and waited for the door to blow open. It did not, so he pried it open and climbed through. Hippo then heaved the unwieldy bag through, climbed through himself, and, puffing, watched Kirk drag the sack to the wall and set it more or less upright beneath the nearest vent.

Using a razor blade, Kirk cut loose the small bundle, then sliced off the rubber bands and dumped out the tools. He pulled a watch from his pocket and held it to the light straining through the vent. It was 6:30.

"We have at least an hour," he said, feeling the first hint of excitement. "Why don't we play around a little and see what it's going to be like?"

Hippo, still blowing hard, was on his knees, intently observing all his many friends. "We, shit," he said dully. "You."

Kirk chuckled. For being so thoroughly exhausted, he almost liked the skinny convict. If only he'd lay down and quit breathing altogether . . .

Squatting, he picked up the knife. "I guess about three feet square ought to do it," he mused. "Yeah," he agreed, "three feet is about right," and used the knife point to scribe a rough square in the hard-packed earth. He rose and circled the square, studying it. Then he shook his head and erased the lines with his feet. It was too close to the wall of the building. Backing up, he inscribed a second square, which satisfied him. Then he began forcing the knife into the earth, hammering at it with a shoe, the blade held at a slight angle so that all the sides of the square would eventually come together to form a tetrahedral hollow if the center was removed. The ground was dense, hard-crusted. But he hammered and hammered, and finally drove the knife ten inches deep all around the perimeter of the square. He began to pry upwards, gently, a little here, a little there. He pried and pried. And a half hour later the knife gave abruptly, the entire square of earth shifted minutely.

"Goddamn," he muttered, then proudly: "I'll be damned!"

Previously he had given it some thought and decided that a "door," which would serve as a lid for the tunnel entrance, could be removed in one solid chunk of earth, or maybe two. He had been certain it could be done, had in fact, known it could be done. But finding that he was right filled him with headiness and a thousand compliments for his glowing brilliance.

"Come on," he told Hippo with a tone which he would himself have spat upon another for using, "help me lift the door." "Door" had eight syllables the way he pronounced it.

Hippo mumbled something and reluctantly pulled his attention from the shiny black and red things infesting the wall. Standing over the square, he gazed at it with indifference. "A lot of shit for nothing," he muttered peevishly. "The screws never come down here."

Kirk was too full of self-complacency to let Hippo's tone bother him. Secretly, he was a little let down but tried not to show it. "Well," he said casually, "it's done. Give me a hand."

With their fingers stuck into the gap, they alternated with the knife, prying, until they were able to slide both hands deep enough to lift the square. It was heavy and awkward. But together they finally managed to heave it from the hole and flip it over. The bottom side of the chunk of earth was jagged and crumbly. Using the knife, Kirk smoothed it, then handed the blade to Hippo and told him to cut several five-foot lengths off the Manila rope. He studied the thick slab of crusty earth for a moment, then turned his attention to the bottom of the hole. The dirt was dry and without the compact cohesiveness of the top layer.

When Hippo returned with the knife and lengths of rope, Kirk lay on his stomach and, using the knife, hacked at the bottom of the hole. And a while later, using the trowel, he scooped out the loose dirt and scattered it over the surrounding area. The fresh earth was somewhat darker but not too noticeable.

When the hole was finally cleaned out, he placed into it the water bag, tools, and remaining rope. Then he lay the five-foot lengths that Hippo had cut across the top of the hole and, with Hippo's assistance, flipped the heavy slab of earth back into place. And finally, after covering the ends of the rope with loose dirt, he stepped back and admired his handiwork. Even objectively, he decided it was well done. The earthen lid was only slightly below floor level and when he stepped on it, it sank only an additional half inch. It would easily pass a cursory inspection, about the worst that could be expected.

"Not bad," said Hippo, sounding pained.

Kirk looked over at the stilt-legged convict and for a moment almost liked him. "Yeah," he said, trying to sound bored, "it'll do," then added briskly: "Let's get upstairs. Starting tomorrow we'll go at it heavy."

[XXXIII]

A multitude of thoughts clambered one atop the other, scrambling higher, each begging for notice, until one toppled and the rest followed, sinking back into the gloom from which they came; then from the gloom came nameless apprehensions and uncertainties, and these formless things trundled through his coal-colored mind, leaving it ripped and muddled.

And then amid the low-keyed buzzing of a hundred conversations and the rattle of countless eating utensils, he heard a familiar note, the musical lilt of Leslie's laughter. He closed his eyes but could still see the emptiness of the table where he sat alone; opening his eyes, he glanced around the mess hall and saw the smiling faces, the sour faces, the scowling faces; other eyes met his and moments later looked away, leaving him with the feeling that he had not been seen. An alien among aliens.

Next he knew he was turned half-around, looking. His eyes found Leslie's, and for a long moment their glances held. The moment passed, as moments must, and Leslie turned away to look adoringly at the convict who sat beside him, talking. Shortly, Leslie laughed again, the too-happy sound rippling across the room finally to smash Kirk's eardrums.

He attempted to study casually the convict at Leslie's side, assumedly the fruit's old man or daddy or jocker or whatever the word in vogue happened to be. He looked to be twenty-four or -five, not short, but not tall either; with neutral coloring and bland good looks that added together to make him faceless. Kirk watched him make some comment that caused Leslie to tinkle with laughter, and decided that he did not like him, even thought about breaking his nose . . . and Leslie's while he was at it. . . .

Of a sudden he realized that he was causing a number of convicts to search out whatever he was staring at. Flustered, he turned back to his breakfast tray and mechanically poked his fork into something. He lifted it toward his mouth, but gagged on the knot in his throat.

Back in the block, headed toward the stairs, he glanced into the guard's office and saw Dunn leaned back in his chair, feet propped on the desk, asleep. Wake him? he wondered; or let him be caught and replaced by somebody duty-bound? No choice at all. He stepped into the office and banged a knee against the desk.

"Let me have some cleanser, Dunn," he said loudly.

Came a grunt, then: "Huh? Huh?"

Kirk repeated himself and the guard responded.

"Cleanser? Oh, yeah . . . yeah . . . cleanser," he mumbled, and unfolded from the chair. Pushing back his hat so he could see, he shuffled to a cabinet in the rear of the office and pulled out a can of cleanser. Yawning, he handed it to Kirk. "Got a cigaret?" he asked, patting his pockets. "Musta left mine somewheres."

Kirk gave him a cigaret, then told him that he was now assigned as a block worker, that he would be sweeping and mopping the second floor, maybe he'd even wash the walls, he added with a sycophantic smile.

Maybe Dunn heard and maybe not, but when Kirk was through, he nodded and told the convict that he could not find his cigarets, they were just gone; and goddamn, he hated to ask, but could he have a couple more to last him, maybe four or five?

Kirk threw a half pack on the desk and gave the guard a mysterious wink. The wink he got back.

Chopping. Stabbing. Hacking. Then removing the chopped and stabbed and hacked black dirt. Trowelful by trowelful by endless trowelful.

By the second day of digging the hole was seven feet deep, straight down, too deep to work in from the rim. So they had to squat froglike on the bottom and chop with the knife at the patch of earth between their feet. When the dirt was loosened, it was scooped into the pillow slip, which was handed overhead to be dumped. Then one foot was put in the newly created depression and the area where the foot had previously been was chopped loose, scooped up, and passed overhead. Repeat the operation with the other foot. Finished with that, turn 180 degrees and hack out the other side. Ah, there! An inch deeper. And so it went; the pit dark and cramped, the air hot and stifling, and an inch deeper into the gritty, unyielding earth.

And another inch, and another pint of sweat, and another tortured breath, and still another inch deeper; ever deeper, but so slow, so very slow. It went on forever, an eternity of black dirt.

But an hour past midday, Hippo pulled himself up the rope which had been attached to the screen of the nearest vent, and flopped beside the hole, breathing stertorously, spraying sweat, and gasped, "Deep . . . enough. . . . Widen bottom. . . ."

Kirk could not believe it. He struck a match, then lit the entire book afire and dropped it into the hole. The bottom seemed incalculably far away . . . 11 feet anyway.

"Yeah," he said, trying to keep the satisfaction from his voice, "it's starting to look like something."

Hippo left off guzzling from the water bag and staggered to the lip of the hole and looked into it. "Ain't getting nothing done up here," he muttered.

Kirk silently cursed him for a skinny, ugly, officious, taciturn son of a bitch, cursed him some more for being right, and slid down the rope.

Crouched on the bottom, he groped around until finding the trowel and knife, and began hacking at the side of the hole. They wanted a bell-shaped chamber at the bottom of the shaft, with space enough to maneuver into a prone position to begin digging the small-diameter tunnel that was planned. Besides serving as an area in which to cache the water and other equipment, the chamber would be used by the second convict as something of a relay station. That is, while one of them worked in the tunnel, filling the pillow slip with dirt, the other would remain in the chamber to pull out the filled sack by means of an attached rope. He would then climb to the top of the shaft, pull out the filled sack, and spread the dirt. Meantime, the one who had been digging would back out (there would be no room to turn around) to the chamber and rest. Then the other man would lower himself and drag the empty sack into the tunnel and dig until he had filled the bag again with dirt. Thus, it was planned, they would go forward.

But all that was ahead. Now was for working.

Kirk continued hacking at the earth and continued scooping the loosened stuff into the pillow slip and continued to sweat and continued to gasp the superheated air and continued to curse inch by miserable inch of the dry, choking, cohesive and crumbling, steel-hard and limestone-soft earth as it begrudgingly yielded to his puny, antlike scratchings on its vastness. It resisted the knife, devoured the tool steel before his eyes; it spilled with willful malice from the trowel, causing the same scoopful to be repeatedly scooped. And always, it was still there, taunting, mocking, daring anybody to scar its boundless black mass.

And then somehow, ages later, the sack would be filled and hoisted overhead, bumping the sides of the shaft as it went, as though reluctant to leave. And more dirt—surely more than the sack itself held—would shower down . . . always more dirt. . . .

But finally there was a five-foot, almost round chamber. It

213

seemed fantastic, too much to hope for. He felt about in the sweltering gloom. It was so. He marveled at it. Checking the watch, he was astounded to find that it had not taken the century which his body had aged. It had taken only an hour.

Dropping the tools, he leaned against the earthen wall, the wall he had created, and stretched out. He was glad no one could see him right then, for he was certain the smile on his face was idiotic. But there was no help for it. Wasn't the chamber finished? "Yep," he gloated, "it's dug," and started chuckling.

"What's happening down there?" Hippo called out. He probably thought that people who dig holes should not talk to themselves.

Looking up, Kirk saw his silhouette hanging specterlike over the rim of the hole. "It's finished," he said, attempting to sound businesslike but succeeding merely in sounding childlike. "We have a chamber."

"It's getting late," Hippo responded, apparently unrejoicing of the monumental accomplishment. "Let's get the hell outta here."

Kirk ignored him, too self-satisfied to let the dead-eyed convict's phelgmatic attitude reach him. He thought ahead, of the weeks, maybe months of grueling, body-torturing toil. Somehow, it seemed easier to face now that the chamber was completed.

"What time you got?" Hippo called out.

This time Hippo got through. He glared up at his silhouette and gave it the finger. That Hippo could not see it didn't matter. "Yeah," he muttered with disgust and petulance, "I got the message. Haul up the dirt."

The bag bumped its way to the lip of the hole and disappeared. Shortly it dropped back inside, empty. Kirk pulled himself up the rope and went to the water bag. "We better take this up with us and fill it tomorrow," he said, then gulped the remainder of the tepid water. With the bag empty, he folded it, along with its pillow-slip covering, and stuck it under his belt.

Together, they replaced the earthen lid, then left the area, hurrying. Waiting above was cool air, water cold enough to make teeth ache, showers with water impossibly cool, cold sheets to rest between. If only they hurried.

And, too, there was tomorrow . . . tomorrow for burrowing through blackness, under walls of deathly gray . . . life-gnawing walls . . . soul-devouring walls. . . . Perhaps beyond them was a world of color . . . maybe life. . . .

214

Breakfast over, they descended to the basement, taking with them an additional length of line made of twisted bed sheets and the refilled water bag. That damn water bag! Even allowing for evaporation and the fact that much of it was spilled and used for cooling their bodies, it was still incredible that they had used 40 pounds of water in two days. Even to imagine making another dozen or more trips with the cumbersome weight of the willfully malicious thing was nightmarish. Several times Kirk was on the verge of asking Hippo if he wouldn't try to make do with less; or better, none at all.

When the watch decreed they quit for the day, it seemed to Kirk that they should have quit days before. They had progressed a pain-wracked, torturous, lung-searing, hand-blistering ten feet . . . the longest and blackest ten feet in the universe. But they had progressed. And to the point that it was necessary to keep an oxygen-drinking candle burning in the main chamber to insure that the tunnel shaft veered neither left nor right, up nor down. They had progressed. And far enough to experience the enervating fearsomeness of knowing that the tons of unsupported earth above might or might not—depending upon fate's caprice—stay there; far enough to know a mind-boggling and strength-sapping claustrophobia that would cause a miner to blanch, a mole to become insane, a fetus to miscarry. But progress is progress, and ten feet—however measured—is ten feet. Only 170 to go. . . .

Saturday they did not go to the basement, for too many convicts were about on the weekends. So Kirk lay on the bunk gazing toward the door, waiting.

By afternoon he was seething, for it occurred to him that whatever he awaited would not be along.

Sunday morning he found himself walking past Sam's cell, peripheral vision picking up the blacked-out door window. Guiltily, looking around first, he listened. No sound. Or wait . . . squeak, creak, squeak. . . . Bed springs . . . ? No, footsteps approaching behind.

"Son of a bitch," he muttered, red-faced.

And back on the second floor he saw Leslie's anonymous-faced friend walk into his cell with what seemed overbearing smugness. The door stayed open. But still . . .

For a fleeting moment he wondered what Hippo was doing, then gnawed a knuckle until it bled.

The rest of the day he held open a book and tried to read. Tried and tried. Mostly, though, he cursed.

And years later it was the next day.

When the two convicts went to the basement, Hippo began digging while Kirk sat idly in the base chamber and watched the line as it was pulled inch by hesitant inch into the tunnel. It moved slowly—impossibly slowly. How many times must it twitch forward and stop? How many inches in 180 feet? *How many?* The rope was mesmeric. There was nothing to do but watch it . . . watch it . . . watch it. . . . He would almost rather work . . . almost. . . .

Then he saw the line twitch and twitch, become a living thing. It took a while, but he finally translated the twitchings into the signal they were meant as. He glanced at the luminous watch hands and was mildly astounded to find that Hippo had taken only 20 minutes to fill the bag . . . 20 minutes to go forward perhaps six inches. He pulled the line, felt the bag resist as it squeezed past Hippo's body, then become a dead weight as it ground its way toward him. When it was close enough to see, he maneuvered it around the candle and sat it in the center of the hole. Securing the end of the bag rope in a belt loop, he forced stiff muscles to pull him arm over arm up the ladder rope to ground level. And then he hoisted the laden pillow slip to the surface and spread its contents thinly over the ground.

At this point the entire floor was lightly covered with fresh earth, which made successive levels of new dirt entirely unnoticeable. But all the dirt dug, all the sweat sweated, had yet to raise the level of the floor a centimeter.

Finished spreading the dirt, Kirk dropped the bag and rope back inside the hole, then lowered himself.

On the bottom he found Hippo flopped against the wall, puffing like a Diesel earth mover, limp as an earthworm.

Looking at him, Kirk felt sorry for himself—it was his turn. "Bad?" he asked.

"Bad," gasped Hippo, spraying sweat.

Handing him the watch, Kirk peered into the dark, forbidding shaft and tried not to feel puny and overwhelmed. He had no success, but finally worked up a certain amount of resolution. With the pillow slip poked through a belt loop, he maneuvered over the top of the candle, letting it pass between his hands and shins while Hippo kept the rope from dragging over it, and crawled into the tunnel.

Actually the hole should have been easier to move in, for it was supposed to have been about three feet square. But somehow in the digging, it had become only slightly wider than two feet and about 30 inches high.

You crawl on your elbows with your butt riding your heels. Put your hands as far forward as possible and pull. Push with your knees in short jerky movements. With luck you go forward six inches before the roof of the tunnel scrapes that bloody raw spot on your tailbone. You'd like to curse but you're already winded, and there is still most of the way to go. You crawl.

Kirk's only solace as he worried and panted himself deeper into the blackness was in knowing that Hippo, being taller than himself, must have more trouble. As solace it was not much, but hungry people have eaten grass.

When finally his fingers found the end of the tunnel, he lay flat on his stomach and contorted an arm to pull the dirt sack from his waist, then past his face to the end of the hole. After a moment of groping he found the tools. Twisting around he looked back over his prone body and saw the candle beacon more or less straight behind. He thought about it for a few seconds, but found no reason not to start.

And so he did, chopping with the knife at the crushing blackness, his blows weak and feeble, frustrating and full of pain. With fiery lungs, body wet and cramped, his trembling muscles strengthless and soggy, he chopped and hacked and stabbed. He thought of moles and gophers and badgers and other burrowing things and continued to scratch and prick at the earth, continued to stab into the choking black, wanting to slay it but knowing he never would. It was before him, always before him, always unrelenting.

And finally there would be a scoopful of loosened dirt to fumble into the bag. Ages later, another scoopful. And yet another. He progressed. At a speed of 28 one-hundred-thousandths of a mile an hour. . . . But that thick, palpable blackness was still there . . . always would be.

Then there was loosened another precious few ounces of dirt and he raised up to scoop it into the bag and the tunnel caved in.

It was a long moment before realization came. Then he gulped a panicked breath, inhaled dirt, bowed his head, and slammed upward. Still the earth fell. It clogged his lungs, stopped the workings of his brain. Rushing down, it hissed past his ears, covered his hands and legs and back.

No! No! was his only thought, *not like this! Anything but this!*

Then, as suddenly as it started, as if acknowledging his screaming thought, the avalanche was over. He could not believe it. Not yet. He must first accept the fact that there had been a cave-in. So he lay still, breath held, fighting the urge to move. His eyes were squeezed shut, and certain that the slightest movement would bring down tons of earth, he kept them that way.

After what seemed many minutes, with only the company of his madly pounding heart, he knew he must breathe. He dared expel his breath and gulp in new air. Air hot as rocket exhaust. But it would do. It had to.

He flexed a finger. Then another. He gulped another breath and ventured to move an entire hand. With painful slowness he pulled it from its burial place. It came free. He breathed again. The air was hotter. Inch by inch he brought his freed hand to his face. The heat of his skin was incredible, it dripped sweat like water from a squeezed sponge. But he was alive. In itself, that was the most incredible of all.

Carefully he reached overhead, above his bowed, dirt-covered neck. His fingers found the tunnel roof an arm's length away. Moving them gingerly, he traced the earth above and found a domelike ceiling. It felt solid. He moved his head, twisting slowly, slowly. Loose dirt cascaded from his hair and neck and shoulders. Then he turned and looked toward the candle, the entrance. No candle. No entrance.

Then he could no longer ignore what he'd known all along; the weight on his legs was dirt; he was trapped.

Panic wrapped around him like a straitjacket. He fought it off, breathed again, trying to feed his oxygen-starved brain, trying to think. How to get out? What to do? If there were answers, he could not find them, for there was only one thought alive in his strangled mind: get out, get out now!

He took no heed of his slamming heart or rasping and bellowing

218

lungs, but wrenched his other hand from the covering earth. And straining, he fought to lift his legs from under the crush of earth. They would not budge. Without thinking, he put both hands against the end of the tunnel and pushed with every fiber of muscle. He went backwards. An inch. With raking fingers he moved loose dirt from the floor to the rear of the tunnel and straining, pushed backwards again. Another inch.

An inch at a time he struggled backwards; feet first, he fought to leave the grave; feet first, he sought life.

With heart-stopping suddenness a foot moved freely. He refused to think of it. Feet do not breathe, lungs do, his were not. But knowing the tunnel had not collapsed along its entire length and that air was only as far away as his foot, he was heartened. But that was no help for his exhaustion or his lungs of leather bellowing fire and dirt or his heart of rusty chain clanking in his chest, now a little, now a lot. So he scooped more dirt from beside him, from under his chest and face, bulldozed it to the end of the shaft, and strained against it, pushed backwards with an uncanny strength, a strength he did not possess. His elbows crackled, his shoulders popped. And suddenly he was able to move both legs in the luxurious capaciousness of the tunnel behind. But he did not stop. More loose earth was moved. Another push. Another inch won. Yet another push. Until he could not push again. It was futile. Better to rest. He pushed again.

Then his chest was buried, then his head. Eyes shut tight, breath held, mouth closed, he strained, pushing and squirming, with a last quivering effort.

And slid from his tomb, newborn, a creature squirted from the bowels of the earth. It took a moment before the realization slammed into his skull with a mailed fist: he was clear.

He was clear!

He knew he should rejoice, but it seemed to mean so little compared to the air he sucked into his greedy lungs. It was cool, soothing. He became heady with it, giddy, almost rapturous. He lay still, drowned in pleasure.

A while later he pulled both arms free and turned to look toward the tunnel entrance. Nothing. Blackness. Where was the candle? Hippo? Buried? But, no, only the end of the tunnel had caved in. Or had it?

Struggling, he rose to his elbows and knees, fingers brushing the

219

rope attached to the dirt bag, the bag buried where he had himself been buried. It suddenly occurred to him that Hippo must be hurt, maybe buried. Otherwise, why hadn't he attempted to pull Kirk from the tunnel with the rope? How easy it would have been. He wondered that he had not previously thought of it.

"Hippo!" he yelled, his voice croaking and cracking.

No answer.

With painful slowness, he scooted back and finally came to the chamber. It was clear of dirt. He realized then that no light—however dim—came from the opening. Lying flat on the ground, gasping still, he mused upon where the light had gone. The chamber hadn't caved in; there was no loose dirt to indicate . . . Hippo . . . where?

And then with blinding clarity, he understood. Hippo had abandoned him, left him for dead. When the roof of the tunnel had fallen, dust had probably puffed through the shaft, possibly dousing the candle. After that, with either panic or calculation, Hippo had climbed from the hole and wrestled the cover into place. If he'd been panicked, would the cover be in place?

Rising to his knees, Kirk looked again toward the top of the shaft and muttered, "Son of a—" and sank back down, panting. He was without the strength for passion. Resting, he lay there with a blank mind.

A while later he drifted out of the fog, no longer breathing so hard but still with a steaming body, strengthless muscles. He had to get out. He had to climb from the hole and push aside the gravestone. The thought of moving was painful, destroyed his blissful state. He lay still another moment, wondering if he shouldn't wait for Hippo to return with help . . . with Sam. . . .

That made him chuckle. "Yeah," he mumbled, "return with help . . ." and once again rose to his knees and groped in the darkness for the rope. What agony it would be to pull himself up! But he must, for he had no idea how much time had passed. It seemed ages. Longer. It might be count time, maybe later. In fact, he may have been missed already. There might be a search under way. . . . He must hurry. He groped. "Where's the rope?" He groped. "Where in the fuck is the rope?"

Wherever it was, it was not where it should have been.

He sank to his haunches and banged his head against the ground. "Son" bang "of" bonk "a" bang "bitch!" But his head already hurt too much, nothing could add to it. "You lousy, skinny punk bastard," he swore toward the lid sealing him in the earth. "You track-covering, rope-stealing punk." And again he sank to the ground and lay still. For what else was there to do?

Sometime later he chuckled, then laughed. Laughed and laughed until salty tears ran from his eyes, mingling with the salty sweat running from his face. He clawed at his hair, bit at his fingers, and continued to laugh, wondering what was funny.

Until finally, exhausted, he pushed to his feet and resigned, stared into the darkness above. Why would Hippo leave the rope hanging when he'd covered the hole? It would merely serve to point out his whereabouts when he was missed—had he been already?— and the guards searched the basement—were they up there now?— as they did whenever a prisoner disappeared. A lingering sense of irony touched him and he chuckled tiredly.

But somehow, he must still get out. Reaching up, he felt the sides of the hole. He could reach only eight feet high. Simple arithmetic said that ground level was at least a yard higher. Reaching would never do. He tried jumping. But before his knees could straighten, they slammed into the side of the hole. It was frustrating but not a big disappointment, for he had not really believed he would jump out, anyway. That would have been too easy. Another way. . . . How?

Steps . . . he could carve steps. If only he had the knife or trowel . . . if. The tools were buried, though. He did not consider going back in the shaft after them. What else . . . ?

Could he push his knees and back hard against the opposite sides of the hole and inch upward . . . ? If he jammed himself tightly? If . . .

He would try. He must, for the air in the shaft was running out, getting thicker, too heavy to breathe. So lifting both arms overhead, elbows pushed tight against the sides of the hole, he raised a leg and wedged his knee and shin against the wall, forcing his spine against the opposite wall. Supported like that, his entire body flexed, pushing against itself, he raised the other leg and jammed it against the wall slightly higher than the first. He climbed six inches and fell.

He melted into the earth, ground his face, beat it with both fists. Apprehension throttled him with black fingers, fingers blacker than the black he was being drowned in. Once again his lungs were fiery, his body running rivers of water. He admitted defeat, prepared to die.

Then picked himself from the floor of the pit and tried anew.

His chest a tortured and thumping bellows, fingers and toes scrabbling and clutching talons, he climbed. He flatly refused to fall again. He gained an inch. Another.

His brain and lungs needed oxygen and fought toward it. He had not the will to argue. Neither did his impossibly strained body. His mind had decided to fight for life, and he had not the strength to deny it. So he climbed. Another inch.

Then his fingers brushed the earthen cover, the tombstone. So great was his astonishment that he leaned back to peer upward and began sliding downward. A feeble squirt of adrenalin saved him. He jammed his body tight, tighter. And, again, fighting down the urge to rush, fighting down panic, he fought upward. Upward. His hands finally touched the cover again. But still he continued to ascend torturously. An inch. Another. Then suddenly, miraculously, he raised his head and felt his hair brush the lid.

With legs and spine locked, he lifted both hands and put his palms against the cover. Pushing, straining, he raised the cover. Light came, shooting pain through his temples. Air followed, rushing in, bathing him in luxury. A convulsive heave and the cover was off, then he swung his arms wide, clinging to the sides of the hole. He struggled over the edge and crumpled there, floundered.

Never would he get enough air. Never would his limbs cease quivering. Ah, but it mattered so little. He'd been buried, yet he lived. Delivered from the grave. . . . That had a nice ring. He savored it, thought of Biblical miracles, Hindu mystics, Ripley's "Believe It or Not," . . .

A while later he realized that his parched throat, feeling as if seared with a blow torch, demanded water. Would he never be satisfied? He chuckled self-mockingly, then staggered to his feet. After waiting until the blood found its way to his head, he stumbled toward the water bag. He found a splotch of muddy adobe, no water bag.

He flopped to the ground, dazed. Twisting around, he scanned the area and, except for the open hole, found nothing but bare dirt. Hippo had hidden or taken with him anything which would indicate somebody's presence.

"The skinny bastard," he muttered, then looked toward the green door and yelled. "You skinny punk bastard!"

He stared at the door. It was closed. Had Hippo locked it? He'd removed the rope, covered the hole, dumped the water bag. . . . Had the dead-eyed son of a bitch locked the door, too?

Had he crawled from a hole in the earth only to be locked in another, a worse hole? When they missed him—if they hadn't already—he would be found. Of course, he could crawl back into the ground . . . never come up. . . .

But wait . . . he had yet to try the door. Maybe . . . but, no. . . . It was too much to hope for. Despite himself, he advanced on the square green door, almost sneaked up on it. Close, he paused and stared at it, fearful to touch it, afraid he would find it locked. After a long moment he took a deep breath and blew on it. Nothing happened. Then suddenly, without knowing how it happened, a hand streaked toward it. His palm crashed into the door. It flew open, banged against the outside wall, and slammed shut again.

Chuckling, he melted to the earth and almost wept. Death was back of him, a hole in the earth; before him, a square green door. . . .

Coming to his hands and knees, he crawled to the chunk of earth and wrestled it back over the hole. The tunnel as a plan was dead, but perhaps at another time the basement would figure in other plans; or maybe one day somebody else would try to dig out, using shoring and air bellows and all the other equipment they should have had—probably could have had, had it not been for impetuosity and impatience.

When finally the area looked as it had before they began digging, he crawled to the door and through, then closed it. In the darkness, he groped for the lock and with a thumb pressed hard against the plug, twisted it to full unlock. He did not have the tools to turn it past the 180-degree security pin to relock it. If, on a routine inspection, a guard found the door unlocked, he would probably curse the last guard through. And if he brought it up, there would be a firm denial which nobody would believe, and the matter would be closed. It was doubtful that the guard who found the door unlocked would even mention it.

As quickly as his rubbery legs would allow, Kirk went to the plumbing chase and started the tortuous climb up through the pipes. Twice he admitted defeat. He could not go higher. Not an inch. But he did. Somehow.

And an eon later he was at the top, trying to catch his breath, trying to pierce the darkness, trying to hear himself think amid the thumping in his skull. He stood on the pipe, peering blindly down toward the door.

And then with brain-smashing abruptness, he realized that Sam would not open the door until the prearranged time. Three o'clock . . . an hour before count. How did Hippo get out? Was it past three o'clock? Had he come this far to be ignominiously caught in the plumbing chase? To be caged for years in segregation . . . in segregation where days were years long.

He became frantic . . . to come this far . . . to fail now. . . . What time? . . . Where's Hippo? . . . He dropped off the pipe and pressed his ear against the door's coldness. There was no sound, no voices, nothing but a loud, hollow silence, a seashell's roar.

He tried to think but could not. He could only hope, but for what he was not sure.

A long time passed before he heard an indecipherable mumble of voices directly outside. One of the voices sounded familiar, almost like Leslie's. He raised his hand to knock. . . . But, no! It might be anybody . . . Dunn . . . a stool pigeon . . . a search party of guards looking for him. . . . But hope—a damnable thing—surged, would not be denied. He wanted it to be Leslie out there. . . . He willed it to be him. . . .

Then he hammered both fists on the door.

The voices fell silent. He cursed himself, his impatience, his choking fear. Of course, it wasn't Leslie! He was caught, and by his own frantic, hammering hands. Depression rose and sank its teeth in his throat. From the earth he'd arisen, then ceded to some irresistible, juggernautlike force.

The door clicked, and he grew uncannily calm. Crouching, he prepared to fight. They would get him, but a guard would die. If there was no other way, he would chew out a guard's jugular vein. Perhaps they would kill him on the spot. . . . He hoped, it was all he could do. . . . Death was preferable to languishing for years in the carrion house, in segregation.

The door cracked open. Kirk crashed into it, flew across the hall, slammed into the hall, and wheeled to face the guards.

Where . . . ?

What . . . ?

Sam and Leslie . . . dismayed . . . frightened. . . .

Kirk collapsed to the cold concrete floor, his skull exploding in red and black. He lay there, cradling his heated face, feeling his body tremble and quiver and shake. It all happened again, running slow-motion through his mind. And he continued to tremble and quiver and shake with fatigue, relief. Then from far away, droning, he heard Sam's voice.

". . . knew something was wrong. I knew it," he was intoning. "Leslie, we got to get him out of the hall. He looks like something crawled out of a sewer. Pull him to the shower while I get the lock closed."

And then Kirk felt his arm being tugged, and tried to jerk it away. "Just help me up," he muttered, and cursed his terrible weakness.

Slowly he was pulled upright, and smelled the talcum-powdered, perfumed scent of Leslie's body. He smiled to himself and shook his head, trying to clear the haze and dancing spots from his vision. He finally saw Leslie's face pinched with concern and deep puzzlement, his eyebrows arched high. In a squeaking, mimicking falsetto, he said, "Don't bug me any more."

And Leslie, as might be expected by now, wept.

Sam came up from somewhere back of him and said, "Save the pleasantries. Let's go to the shower and get those clothes off so I can get rid of them. Anybody sees you like this, you're a sure bust," and pausing, added, "Besides, I got a lot of questions."

"Me, too," Kirk mumbled, and shuffled toward the shower, supported on either side by Sam and Leslie. "First question," he said hollowly. "What time is it?"

"Uh . . . 12:30."

That was a surprise. He shuffled on, thinking about it.

At the shower door, Leslie pulled it open and Kirk shook their hands off and stumbled inside, then collapsed wearily onto the bench. Leslie began tugging at his shoes while Sam ripped off his tattered shirt. "How in the hell did that punk get out of the chase?" Kirk asked finally.

"About an hour and a half ago—"

"Fuck *when!*" Kirk exploded. I want to know *how!*" Why it was so important, he had no idea. Neither could he understand the rage inside him.

225

"Take it easy," Sam said. "I was walking from my cell to the T.V. room when I heard knocking on the door. Figured something was wrong, so I opened it. It was Hippo. He said you sent him to find another water bag. . . . Said yours busted. . . ."

"Water!" Kirk croaked hoarsely, remembering his parched throat. He rose from the bench and staggered to the showers. Spinning one of the faucets, he gulped lukewarm water from the nozzle. It filled his mouth, spurted out, and began spraying over him, soaking his heated body, his destroyed pants, making all the dozens of abrasions he hadn't been aware of sting wonderfully. Ah, water . . . ambrosial stuff. . . .

He coughed and choked and gagged and drank gluttonously, more and more. His stomach distended. And finally he vomited.

So he stopped and stepped out of his pants and threw them to Sam. Then he let the water run in his face, his hair. When had a shower been so good? He thought of lying down on the tiles, all the showers running, staying there forever. But forever would not be long enough.

"Well," Sam said impatiently, "are you going to tell us what happened?"

Kirk rubbed the water from his eyes and turned to face the others. "Yeah," he said, "I'll tell you what happened. It's easy. The sky fell in and the skinny punk left me. He covered the hole too," he paused and added. "I guess I have the same privilege coming."

They both stood silently, exchanging looks of shocked disbelief, and finally Sam cast Kirk a searching look. "You want a blade?" he asked quietly.

Kirk thought about it for a moment, then shook his head. "No," he said slowly, "I might accidentally kill him." He let the water spray his face, then continued. "Wait till I feel alive and go find that guy. Think of some way to trick him up here without telling him that I'm out. Then you two take the point while I talk to him."

"Okay, talk," Sam said with a mocking chuckle. "You'll be all right in what? An hour? Hour and a half?"

"Give me a half hour," said Kirk, forgetting his tiredness. "And get me a pipe . . . about seven inches long. Can you do that?"

Sam nodded, then turned to Leslie. "You go get him some clothes. After that, we got some things to take care of."

Leslie nodded once and wiped his eyes. He followed Sam from the shower.

He stayed under the water until Leslie returned with a bundle of clothing and a towel. Setting the bundle on the bench, he turned to leave, but stopped to gaze at Kirk.

Wanting to say "Thanks" or "Hello" or anything, Kirk looked back at him. But when Leslie finally hurried from the shower room, it was too late.

Sometime later he dried and dressed, finding rolled in the clothes a half dozen candy bars, which were gone in a trice. Squatting beside the door, out of sight of anybody passing the shower-room window, he used his damp towel to clean the dirt from his shoes. And he rested, waiting patiently for Hippo. Gone was the memory of the cave-in, hate had burned to ashes, leaving nothing but an empty spot. The empty spot he would fill. He waited.

It was closer to an hour than 30 minutes when suddenly the door was wrenched open and Hippo came sailing in, propelled by Sam's foot. Stepping inside, Sam looked at Kirk, his eyes twinkling. "Catch," he said playfully, and threw Kirk a stubby length of pipe. "I found the punk hiding in the library," he added, shaking a knife from his sleeve. "He didn't want to come with me, but changed his mind. You sure you don't want to kill him?" he finished with a hopeful note.

Kirk shook his head, so Sam shrugged and left the shower. Looking at Hippo, Kirk gripped the pipe snuggly in his right fist, the ends protruding on either side. He smiled. "Anything to say?"

The dead-eyed convict leaned, half-seated, against the back wall, and stared at him indifferently, silently. If he was afraid, it did not show.

"Get to your feet," Kirk said quietly, advancing toward him.

Hippo uncoiled slowly, keeping his eyes unwaveringly on Kirk's, his hands by his sides.

When Hippo was fully up, Kirk stood directly in front of him and stared into the dead black eyes. "You don't know how long I've been waiting for this," he said solemnly, then with every ounce of strength, every pound in his body, he swung his pipe-wielding fist toward Hippo's mouth. And missed. He would never know if Hippo had moved or his aim had been off or if he was just too drained or whatever. But he had missed. And as his fist flew past Hippo's face, a chill touched his spine, for he was defenseless and too sapped for a protracted fight. With what seemed slow motion, he managed to brake the wild fist. Then, almost in panic, he some-

227

how pivoted and drove his left hand upward, under his extended right arm, toward Hippo's mouth.

He connected this time. Came a satisfying crunch and the tinkling sound of teeth falling on tiles. Hippo was down, lying on his back, staring up. His mouth was a mess.

"Up, punk," Kirk said, calm again, briefly wondering why Hippo had yet to speak or even raise his hands in self-defense. Then he drove a foot into his ribs.

And still, Hippo lay supine. When Kirk kicked him again, he didn't even grunt, just winced slightly and lay there, staring up, impassive. It was eerie, unsettling.

Kirk straddled his waist, mystified. Then he jumped with all his weight coming down in the soft of Hippo's stomach. The air whooshed from his lungs, his face darkened.

Kirk chuckled. "That's a little of what it feels like, you Walla Walla-tunnel-digging punk." He slowly and deliberately raised a foot high over the middle of Hippo's face and let the convict stare at it for a while, then slammed it down with all his 185 pounds behind it.

Hippo's head crunched, bounced once, and lay still. His nose was crushed flat, his front teeth gone, lost someplace amid purple-pulped lips, and his dead black eyes—now glazed—stared sightlessly in different directions.

Dispassionately Kirk began to kick the convict's ribs in. Only a short while later the blood dribbling from Hippo's mouth took on a deeper crimson tint, maybe indicating a punctured lung. He then stooped and carefully placed both Hippo's hands on the tile floor. Noticing the borrowed watch on the man's wrist, he chuckled and pulled it off. Twice he lifted a foot. Twice he slammed it down. Both Hippo's hands lay pulped and formless. He spent a thoughtful moment gazing down on the destroyed body, then stooped and pulled the remainder of Hippo's mouth apart. Looking inside, he found the four upper front teeth missing. But the lowers were still there. He used the pipe to bash them out. Then he sat tiredly beside the wall-eyed, staring mess and studied it, thinking. He decided finally to break Hippo's knees and started arranging the limp legs so he could do it with two jumps.

Sam came through the door and gazed indifferently at the wasted body. "Is he dead?" he asked laconically.

"Hope not," Kirk replied sincerely. "Otherwise, what'd be the sense . . . ?" He prepared to jump on Hippo's knees.

But Sam tugged at his arm. "Give it a pass. The geek's finished. Even if he lives, he won't be good for anything. Let's clean up and dump the pipe. Anybody sees you over this guy, you're in trouble." He bundled Kirk's ragged clothing. "Use that towel to wipe the blood off your feet," he said briskly.

Shrugging, Kirk handed the pipe to Sam, who rubbed off the fingerprints, then wiped the dark spots off his feet. There was blood on his knuckles too. He spat on the towel and scrubbed it off. Sam took the towel and added it to the bundle. Then together they walked from the shower. Neither looked back.

At the stairwell, where Leslie was on the point, Sam said, "Leslie, you'd best disappear. And Kirk, you'd best duck into your cell. They might get smart enough to question the block workers. . . . We're the only ones supposed to be around. I'm going to dump this stuff"—he indicated the bundle of clothes—"somewheres out of the block."

Kirk walked to his cell. Leaning tiredly against the wall, he stared at the floor, drained. From the bottom of his feet, something crawled up, up. Then he bent over the toilet and retched. Stringy strands of muddy black spewed from his nose and mouth. All that remained of the tunnel was gulped by a hungry toilet. All but the smashed body. He retched again.

[XXXV]

"Yeah," Hank told Kirk early the next morning, "he's alive, but just barely. Concussion, punctured lung, six busted ribs, nine fractures in one hand, seven in the other . . . should I go on?" He stared curiously at Kirk.

"Take me off display, Hank," said Kirk, fidgeting uncomfortably under Hank's gaze. "You know what the creep did."

"I know," Hank agreed, then paused a moment and added: "Why didn't you just kill him?"

"How often you been buried?"

Hank chewed a thumb. "That's a point, I suppose," he said as though he wanted to believe but could not. "You can be pretty sure

229

he won't rat, anyway," he added briskly. "They tried to pump him a little when he woke up last night, but he just stared at them. They already issued orders to lock him in protective custody when he springs the hospital."

"Just as well," Kirk said. "Chances are better than even that I would kill him next time . . . unless he killed me first. Just leaving him alone, I can't picture."

Hank chuckled wryly. "It ain't likely that guy would kill a grasshopper. When the bulls got done questioning him last night, Lowry taped a report. So after he left, I got into the cabinet where the tape was and played it back. Hippo was booted out of the army for being yellow, then he ran around setting houses on fire. And he escaped from Walla Walla, all right; but he didn't go out through a tunnel. He was working outside the walls on some minimum-security job. . . . He walked away . . . lit some houses on fire and turned himself in. . . ."

When later in the day he showed up at the fat old man's cell, he was invited inside with a manner that Kirk felt was grasping and greedy. Right off, he became uncomfortable.

"Here you go, Doc," he said, dropping the watches on the man's bunk. "Just thought I'd bring them back. Don't need them any more," then he turned to leave, and added, "Thanks."

"Son . . . wait . . . stay . . ."

The voice crawled down his throat and got stuck there. He could not bring himself to leave, so he turned and looked at the old man, then at the floor, for the forlorn and hungry eyes of Doc Gillis did something to him. He could not stand it . . . whatever it was.

"Son, would you like to keep one of those watches . . . ?"

"No, thanks, Doc."

"Son . . . ?"

"All right, Doc. Thanks a lot."

"Would you like to sit down and talk for a while?"

"Well . . . there're things I have to do. . . . Yeah, I'll stay for a few minutes. . . ."

Doc Gillis was a killer; a murderer five times. A doctor of medicine, a preserver of life, taker of the oath of Hippocrates, Doc Gillis had shot five men to death. Surely there was a reason . . . ? But if so, it was private, unsharable. Reasons, Doc didn't talk about; ni-

hilism, he did. And because he did, Doc Gillis had had 142 electro-
therapy shock treatments. On 142 different occasions Doc Gillis'
brain had been electrocuted. They had given it up as a bad show.
And so it was that Doc Gillis spent his life observing his keepers as
they should have been observing him, "a whale in a fishbowl," a
260-pound whale, all nihilism and loneliness.

And once again Kirk found himself in the main corridor, hurrying. In his ears rang the old man's parting lines:

> I am the spirit that ever denies!
> And rightly so; for all that's born on earth
> Merits destruction from its birth
> And better 'twere it had not seen the light.*

[XXXVI]

Perhaps two weeks later, perhaps two months—he was unsure, did
not think about it, did not care, for he had lost himself in a place
without time—he walked from his cell, going to lunch. He was not
hungry, but the noon whistle had blown, and it was something to
do.

Emerging from the first-floor stairwell he noticed Sgt. Carol, the
mustached guard who thought Warden Benson might have tits,
rush through the block door and race to the guard's office. Stopping at the doorway, he peered inside, then turned and sprinted
back toward the main corridor. As he passed an idle group of convicts near the door, he slowed down and yelled fiercely.

"Don't go near that office! Any of you! Or it'll be brain-busting
time!" Then he was through the doorway, racing up the corridor.

Curiosity was dead, but some perverse compulsion visited Kirk,
made him walk to the guard's office. And no wonder Carol was in a
dither.

For Dunn was asleep, and noisily involved in staying so. The sergeant had evidently received the word from a right-minded convict.

It had long been apparent that Dunn would never win a warm
spot in the guard's fraternity—if there was one; for guard and convict alike knew him as Big Stupe.

* Goethe's *Faust*.

231

So Kirk decided to wake him. He entered the office and swept Dunn's giant feet from the desktop. "Get up," he called, shaking the guard's shoulder.

Dunn snorted and snuffled, then opened his eyes and jumped to his feet, his hat falling off. "Huh? Huh?" he stammered, wide-eyed. "What the hell . . ."

"Act like you know where you're at," Kirk said, "and get me some cleanser. Carol's after you."

Dunn cast him an empty look. "Huh? Wait a minute . . ."

"Cleanser, Dunn, cleanser!" Kirk broke in, expecting Carol to reappear at any moment. *"Move!"*

The guard scratched his head and finally went to the supply cabinet, and fumbled inside.

Kirk heard the sound of running feet, then they stopped directly behind. There was a piteous groan.

Turning, Kirk saw Sgt. Carol and a lieutenant with a face like dusky marble. Both were breathing hard. And the sergeant was looking at the lieutenant with a pleading expression, as though he'd been told to turn in his uniform, he couldn't play any more.

Kirk gave each of the guards a pleasant smile. "Hello, Sarge," he said, filming the air with grease.

The sergeant's eyes flamed. *"You!"* he screeched, pointing an accusatory and trembling finger. "You woke him! I told you . . . told you not to move! You . . . you . . ." Whatever Kirk was, he choked on it and turned red.

Kirk, his mouth a huge O, lifted his hands in a "Who, me?" gesture, and went wide-eyed with stunned incomprehension. "Huh?" he said stupidly. "What'd I do, Sarge?"

Carol was too choked up to answer, but he kept sputtering and pointing his finger until the lieutenant finally told Kirk, "Come with us."

With a shrug, Kirk assumed a stoical expression and walked dejectedly from the office feeling a thousand miles from the brink of excitement, but millions of miles closer than he had been.

With the sergeant bouncing on one side and the lieutenant walking on the other, Kirk was escorted through the corridor to the administration building, then into a small, windowless office. He was ordered to be seated in the single chair before the desk that almost filled the room. With an expression of pain, he obeyed and watched

232

the lieutenant squeeze behind the desk and into a leather-covered chair. The sergeant remained beside Kirk, glaring down.

After a moment the lieutenant looked up at Carol, and said, "Get his ID card . . . then go pull his and Dunn's records."

Kirk pulled his identification card from a pocket and handed it to Carol, who snatched it and almost hopped out of the office.

The lieutenant, with eyes the color of seaweed, stared at Kirk, drumming on the desk with tobacco-stained fingers. "What'd you wake him for?" he said quietly.

"Wake who?" Kirk leaned forward, eyes curious.

Ignoring the question, the lieutenant continued to stare. "Where do you know Dunn from?" he finally asked.

"Where do I know him from?" What kind of a question is that? Sounds tricky. But he could make no sense of it. "From G block."

"You've never seen him before you came to the joint?"

"I don't understand," Kirk answered, truthfully enough.

"Do you know Dunn from outside?" The lieutenant was being patient.

Kirk understood now; he made himself frown as if with perplexion. "No. I never knew him before I came here," he said solemnly. "Why do you ask?"

"I'm asking the questions," said the lieutenant, half to himself, then stared some more. "Has Dunn ever taken money from you? Has he ever brought you anything inside the prison?"

"No, sir," Kirk said piously.

"Why'd you wake him, then?"

"I didn't."

"Sgt. Carol saw him asleep. You think the sergeant's lying?"

"No, sir. But maybe he's mistaken," said Kirk, trying to look very wise and understanding.

"What were you in the office for?"

"I needed some soap . . . some cleanser."

"Cleanser? What for?"

Kirk met the lieutenant's eyes. "What do I use cleanser for?" he said, screwing his face into thoughtful lines. "Well, sometimes I clean my sink and toilet with it. Once in a while, if I feel ambitious, I'll wash a wall. It works pretty good for nicotine stains—"

"All right," the lieutenant interrupted, holding up a palm. His stony face had settled into lines of boredom, lines that said he was tired of stupid convicts saying the same things, the same way, time after time, constantly straying from the line of questioning, offering trite and tiresome irrelevancies, making the life of a guard one to be borne with stoic and ever-lasting suffering; he didn't like his job or his wife or the warden or the captain or his religion. All this was written on the lines of his face. Then he spoke again.

"I'm going to check your record against Dunn's. I'm telling you now, if there's any indication you two've known each other in the past, you're in trouble."

"You won't find anything like that," Kirk assured him. "Like I said, I never knew the man before I came here, and he wasn't asleep. All I wanted was some soap and . . . well, here I am." With a nervous smile oozing from his face, he shrugged fatalistically.

All the fawning lit a secret smile behind the lieutenant's eyes. Sometimes, said the smile, the job could be rewarding. "Maybe this was just your day for good deeds," he said with a show of indifference. "You can leave now." He waited while Kirk rose from the chair, then leaned forward, his eyes alert. "One more thing to put in your pipe," he added quickly, "Dunn'll be getting a job change out of this . . . so get your narcotics dealing straight with him."

The game was over; Kirk was bored. "Come on," he sighed. "Your records will show I've never had anything to do with drugs. . . . I wouldn't know opium from chewing tobacco." He walked from the office.

Back at the block, he went to see Dunn and gave the nervous guard the cigaret he wanted. "Have they talked to you yet?" he asked.

Dunn used three matches before his trembling hands were able to fire the cigaret. When finally it was burning, he inhaled deeply and said with a rush, "No. What'd you tell them?" and coughed on the smoke.

"Just that I asked you for some cleanser; that you weren't asleep."

"It's true!" Dunn exclaimed, his eyes panicked. "It's true! You know it is!"

"Yeah. I wouldn't lie," Kirk lied.

"It ain't a lie! It ain't a lie!" Dunn grabbed a frantic handful of his limp hair.

"Breathe easy, Dunn," Kirk said, disgusted. "I know it isn't a lie," and pausing, added: "The lieutenant said he's giving you a job change."

"A job change," Dunn squeaked, his face disintegrating. He sucked on his cigaret until the paper fell apart, hung on his lip. "But I'm steady," he managed to say unsteadily. "Didn't you tell him I'm a steady worker?"

"You tell him, Dunn," said Kirk in quiet contempt. "But don't push it—you still have your job, they can't fire you on one man's word. And everybody knows how steady you are, Dunn. . . . If you were any steadier, you wouldn't move at all."

He lay on the bunk, full of anxiety and rage. For the incident with Dunn was over—much too soon and anticlimactically. Why hadn't they at least tried to beat the truth out of him? Surely they knew he'd been lying. He stared blankly at the wall. Something to do. . . . Something to do! Anything. Yank his hair out . . . better, someone else's. . . . Should he go find somebody to beat up, maybe break a nose or arm? Would it break his terrible ennui?

He snarled at the wall, cursed it until he ran out of breath.

Then he leaped from the bunk, snatched his towel from the rack, rushed out the door. He had to move . . . had to. Opening the shower door, he started to step inside, then stopped. He stared in at the too-familiar stained tiles, the window cracked and chipped, the two-dimensional stalactites of mineral crystals hanging under the shower nozzles. And as he stared a choking, desperation rose from the pit of his stomach, pushed his heart up into his throat, made his head pound. He was lost . . . lost on the other side of nowhere . . . with only his heartbeat to fill empty hours. . . .

Reality stepped up behind with a garrote.

Next he knew he was at Leslie's cell, wrenching wide the partly open door. Darting inside, he blindly snatched the convict who sat at the foot of the bunk talking to Leslie.

"Out!" he hissed into the man's frightened face. "Out! Come around here again, they'll bury you!" He slammed the convict's head into the wall, again and again and again.

"Kirk!" screamed Leslie, leaping off the bunk, punching at him. "Stop it! Please, God, stop it! You're killing him!"

Kirk stopped it when the convict was semiconscious, wet with blood. He let him crumple to the floor, then wheeled to Leslie and caught his flailing fists and yanked him from the cell. Kicking the door shut, he half-carried, half-towed Leslie's squirming body to the third-floor television room.

Sam and Gypsy were alone there, staring vacuously at a televised quiz program. Hearing Kirk, they turned.

With a hand clamped over Leslie's mouth, Kirk demanded of Sam, "Open the door!"

Sam stared for a moment, unmoving, blank-faced. Then suddenly, he chuckled deep in his throat and rose, and walked to the blanket room. Seconds later he pulled open the door. "You need any help or pointers," he said with a sardonic grin, "call me."

Ignoring him, Kirk lifted Leslie and threw him inside. He followed, and the door clicked shut behind. The room was dark, noisy with labored breathing.

"Take off your clothes," Kirk said into the gloom. For a fleeting instant he wondered what he meant.

Then his eyes began to use the faint light coming under the door, he saw Leslie standing defiantly in the middle of the room, and he knew what he meant . . . he knew. . . . A huge, fiery lust welled up into his throat, choked him, blinded him to all but Leslie, killed all thoughts but thoughts of Leslie . . . ah, Leslie . . . lewd, licentious, lascivious Leslie Lemman . . . Leslie. . . .

He yanked a fistful of blankets from a shelf and tossed them haphazardly over the floor, then stripped off his clothes.

At that moment he could not have said where he was, what he was doing, or why . . . only that he must do. . . . He was driven, compelled by some nameless thing. . . . He would not, could not question it. . . .

Naked, he saw Leslie staring at him, still dressed. Panting from suppressed fury, he snarled, "You take them off or I'm ripping them off. Or maybe you'd like to slap me again? How about it, queer, want to slap me?"

"Kirk," Leslie whispered softly, so softly he doubted his ears. "Kirk baby, don't . . ." Stepping closer, he held Kirk's heated face. "Don't do it, baby. . . . Tomorrow you'll hate me worse . . . and yourself, too. Don't hurt me any more, baby. . . . There's too many scars. . . . Tomorrow will be—"

Knocking the hands away, Kirk spun Leslie around, ripped open

236

his shirt, tore it from his shoulders. "I spit on tomorrow!" he hissed, and spat on the wall.

Leslie turned to look at him and, with a resigned shrug, undressed.

Kirk lay down on the blankets, wondering if it was fear or desire or love or lust or hate that surged in violent spurts through his fevered body, his frothing brain. But more than anything he wondered what was happening when Leslie lay beside him as naked as he. . . .

Then his fingers were entwined in Leslie's hair, his face buried in its softness, and his stretched body was kindled fiery by the warmth of Leslie.

Thought winged.

You don't know where you have been or where you are going or who you are or what. Even the now is shadowy and unreal, warped and surrealistic. You find yourself squeezing and clutching the only warm thing left in the world and you know that to let go is to lose it. And, too, you know that you cannot live alone with yourself another moment, not with your emptiness. You must begin to feel something; self-worth or self-contempt—it matters not—for anything is preferable to the apathy corroding your inside. You cling.

Then suddenly—how did it happen? You'll never be quite certain—you find yourself trying to devour the warmth beside you, move bothers you little, for it's warm and alive and good to cling to.

Next you find yourself kissing *his* eyes, *his* nose, *his* ears, first one, then the other; your tongue is a roving thing, and soon it's licking under *his* chin. And that is when you detect those stiff little hairs that not even a hairless queer can eliminate. Ah, but it's so quickly forgotten, for you next discover yourself with a *man's* lower lip caught between your teeth . . . odd. . . . After only a few moments of nibbling on *his* lip, you find that those stubby little bristles are gone . . . or maybe not, but to you they are gone. . . . It makes you wonder. . . .

And that is when you open your eyes and find yourself kissing *her,* your mouths glued wetly together, your tongues in friendly sport.

You are fiery. So is *she*. And suddenly *she* explodes. . . . You are a thing to be ravaged. . . . And ravage you she does. . . . *Her* mouth, that soft, delicious mouth, strays from yours . . . wanders here, there, and here and there.

This you want to last forever, think it can, but know it won't. You want to laugh, to weep. You tell *her* to stop, then change your mind. You wish it was over, pray it never ends, curse it to be done, beg it to begin anew. . . . It's ecstasy, then agony. You explode, disintegrate into sparks of white fire. Your fever is drained.

Was it ever like this? No, never; you are certain of it.

Her knowing mouth wanders again, loving and cruel, tender and maddening, a sybaritical lip-walk.

Suddenly your eyes open, and hovering above you is that mouth, *her* mouth, which has been everywhere, tasting of everything. And etched into that mouth is the start of a tremor, for it is wondering at your thoughts, fearful of your revulsion. Why? Unless it fears to have its lip chewed off or its tongue swallowed. . . . You try your best, and a little more . . . that is all you can do. And through it all you cling to *her* warmth while you lick and lave, slobber and nibble. You cling.

Some place in there you see *her* opening that mysterious plastic bottle. . . . *She's* oiling you. . . . Whatever for? So you won't tear hell out of *her* cunt, silly boy. . . . Nonsense, whoever heard of such a thing? Is this some cruel hoax? This was never necessary before. . . . Or was it? It's been so long. . . .

Next, you're on top of *her,* face to face, driving *her* up the mountain, into the clouds, higher. Meantime, while you're trying to eat *her* face, you cannot help but wonder what is pushing against your stomach.

But it flies from your mind as you rut in old scars. Scar abrading scar; twisted clinging to twisted.

Then it is over. But only for a moment. It will never be entirely over, not now; not now that you have found *her*. Ah, would that you were a poet . . . would that you could warm the world with *her* warmth. . . .

But what the hell is that ridge pressing into your belly?

Later . . . you'll concern yourself with it later. For right now your teeth are too busy nibbling, nibbling; your tongue is too busy lapping those water-cool blue eyes . . . the eyes that have for so long haunted you . . . the eyes that visit you when you sleep. . . .

Ah, yes, these are those eyes. . . . Your dreams have seen day's light in blanket room's gloom.

She rolls you to your back, settles gently onto you. And there *she* sits for a while, smiling into your smiling face. *She* falls forward and you try some more to eat *her* face while you grasp *her* hair with clinging fingers.

All this makes you wonder why you have spent the last thousand years painting the ceiling of your cell with women, fleshless and vague, naked but ethereal. You wonder at the last century—or was it four centuries or six?—that you have been jacking off, making your belly stiff with your futility. And always *she* had been so near, so inviting, and seemed to care so much. Ah, but that was yesterday. . . . Who among the blind regrets when he can see again?

Then *she's* a fiend, a dervish. Stop. *She'll* peel the skin off. Go. *She'll* break it. Stop, Don't. Never.

She moans and sinks *her* dagger-pointed nails into your shoulders, and falls, still moaning, *her* face buried in your neck. Blanketed with *her* warmth, you cling.

But what is this? Spots of cold on your chest . . . spots that a moment ago were liquid fire. Odd.

You push *her* gently up until *she's* sitting upon you, and in the dim light, you see several spots of wetness glistening in the middle of your chest; looking farther, your navel holding a puddle of . . . of what?

Ah, yes, that is when you truly know that it has all been a hoax, for your delicious *she* is a *he,* and dangling limply, oozing semen in your navel, is *his* dick.

You're staggered. What in the world have you been doing kissing a *man?* letting *him* lick and eat of you? kissing *him* some more? repeatedly shoving yourself into *his* perfumed, nonshitting ass?

Pondering that thing hanging there, you wonder if it makes you a bad fellow or a queer or a pervert . . . like the degenerate squatting atop you, abashed and flushed and embarrassed because *he* comes the way you do, because you saw *his* thing, that teensy whammer which is half again the size of your own.

"Son of a bitch!" you mutter in disgust. "You filthy, stinking queer!" you mutter in revulsion.

And he weeps.

And you lick away her tears.

And her tits . . . pathetic little things. . . . Perhaps if you lick

239

them long enough, they will grow. All you can do is try. You try. And try.

Then you are at it again, licking-kissing-rutting. And now you know where you are at, what you are doing. You are committing a gross, heinous offense against nature; you are performing illegal surgery on the scars twisting your insides. Around you there are bars and walls and righteous men to tell you of your unnatural actions.

Yes, you have moments of lucidity wherein you know that what you are doing is futile and immoral and contrary to what you held yourself to be and contrary to pulpit platitudes and contrary to man's laws and, worst by far, contrary to prison rule number D-1206, whereby no inmate shall commit or get others to commit any sexual or immoral act, nor shall he place himself in a compromising contrary to prison rule D-1207, whereby no inmate shall have in his possession . . . any . . . indecent material.

"Leslie, is this an immoral act?"

"Baby, is this indecent material?"

Ask the steel bars, and if they stand rigid and mute, ask the wall of gray stone, and if no answer is forthcoming, ask God.

For a price of 35 years a shudder, you enjoy a lot. And neither do you care who knows. In fact, you want to tell somebody, feel you must. It might be the most important message of your life. But considering it . . . how puerile! how degenerate! It's too ridiculous! Thinking of it makes you writhe with discomfort, you sink your teeth in her lip and twist. She cries. And you despise yourself, your cruelty.

PART FOUR

[XXXVII]

Looking back it was hard to believe. Somewhere behind, lost in time, he'd left a year of life. For weeks now the realization had been haunting him. It seemed that he should recall each past day with a feeling of horror, but was haunted because he felt nothing, only a heavy numbness. Though each second slammed in his chest and thundered through his skull, making it feel ripped and torn, once past, time dropped from memory as leaves from a calendar. What memories he did retain seemed a series of flash cards that flickered in his mind, surreal and grotesque, against a backdrop of abysmal emptiness.

Shortly following their coming together, he had moved with Leslie to a third-floor cell, a cell that soon took on a perfumed scent and a pink light, a cell Kirk never wanted to leave. Though it was necessary for them to emerge to eat, shower, and clean the second floor—their rehabilitative assignment—Kirk was never outside without feeling that the step ahead might be the one that plunged him into a bottomless pit. But slowly, slowly the day would fade and night fall, and he would be back again in the cell with Leslie, safe. Lust waned—which happens—but his need to be near Leslie waned not at all; seemed in fact to grow into a painful obsession, an obsession that made him clutch the little fruit's closeness with a madman's fervor. When imagining being away from Leslie, he became filled with an overwhelming dread, a frothing anxiety that tortured his mind, seized him with desperation and despair. He incessantly pushed aside such thoughts, fought to believe that what he had would always be.

Oft-times, with Leslie asleep and the night quiet, he would peer into the mirror, sneering at the image there, calling it degenerate, perverted, queer. That would cause him to laugh: whatever the label read, the cloak kept out the cold, and for moments of warmth no cost was too much. Having grown so intimate with boredom, he had in thought become a thorough hedon, and now with the step from thought to deed behind, he was content to wallow in sodomy's greasy sensuality and cared little what mess was made of tomorrow.

Within days after moving in with Leslie it was as if the prison population tripled, for every convict seemed to know that he had taken the plunge; some hid their mockery behind bland-faced masks; others, as Sam, wore their mockery in wide-open smirks, smirks that Kirk ached to smash pulpy—but where to start? There were so many. Still other convicts came around with back slaps and oily-sounding congratulations—Kirk wondered if he was expected to pass out cigars or something. But the most insidious of all were those convicts who sought to fill their empty hours with gossip and rumor; Kirk heard daily tales, much embellished, of whom Leslie was seen talking with and why, of how he wiggled his ass and for whom. He learned to listen with an attentive expression, deaf ears. But all this and much more was a price he would have paid five times over; for throughout the entire prison there were only blunt and rusty instruments wielded ineptly to turn yesterday's scars into raw and purulent wounds; there were no set of bars that smiled, no stones that could give back.

He clung.

One morning, Shorty, the tired black janitor from E block, showed up at their cell door and was invited inside. With a nervous grin and much foot shuffling, he handed to "Miss Leslie" a small white box, then said "By now, y'all," and left in a cloud of hopelessness.

Inside the box was a belt buckle worked from a solid rectangle of monel, painstakingly engraved around the edges with a design of vines and hearts; in the center was a strip of inlaid abalone, and in the center of that was an initial of jade, an initial *L*.

Kirk stared at it and felt inside his skull a fiery ache; Leslie stared at it and cried, softly, bitterly.

Time passed, quiet time, even peaceful, then Sam had stepped into their cell with a tight face and bad news. Kirk listened, felt each word smash into his skull, felt his happiness—the tenuous and fragile thing he had begun to call happiness—crumbling, falling upon him, smothering him.

Sam finally finished talking and left the cell with a rush and an errand: get Kirk a knife, a big knife.

Kirk then turned to Leslie, who turned away, his pallid face flooded with tears and guilt. Kirk asked a question, just one, and the second time he asked, Leslie sobbed the answer: Louis Farrell.

Louis Farrell, Leslie's anonymous-faced ex-friend, the convict whose head Kirk had flattened against the wall on that foggy but unforgotten day. Farrell, Sam had said, was rumored to have hired Kirk killed; the kill price, supposedly paid the Mexican Mafia, was 20 cartons of cigarets. . . .

He patted Leslie's hand, then walked from the cell and closed the door, while in his mind doors opened, dark things crawled out.

Sneaking into the guard's office, it took only a moment to scan the roster for *Farrell, Louis* and get his cell number.

And minutes later he was standing before Mexican Rudy's cell, a long double-edged knife down the back of his pants. Without preliminaries, he questioned the blank-faced Mexican, questioned about the contract, the price paid; he questioned and questioned, and was answered by a flat-eyed stare, silence. Yet back of the stare the answers glittered: Rudy knew, knew all of it.

Kirk finally drew the knife and offered a proposition: Rudy could keep the 20 cartons and get a fruit—without leaving his cell, *or* he could do his best to earn the kill price. . . .

Rudy pondered that for a while, and finally turned the choice into a white-toothed smile, a small, bashful boy's smile. "Put away the *filero*," he said with no trace of fear, "and tell me of the *chabala*. . . . Who . . . ?"

Kirk had indeed told him of the *chabala*—he lied and lied. . . . Rudy believed. . . .

Shortly, with Sam pointing for the guard, Kirk rushed, mindless and rabid, into Farrell's cell, knocked him to the bunk, bounded onto his chest and shoved the knife point hard under Farrell's ear. He snarled accusations, got blue-lipped denials; pressed the knife deeper, drew blood and the truth: Farrell had paid Rudy to kill him . . . had in fact gratuitously doubled the usual ten-carton fee. . . .

Kirk, smiling pleasantly then, offered up another proposition: die or . . .

He popped open his fly. . . . The ginger-colored stubble around Farrell's mouth caused him a tickling irritation, though not unbearably so. . . . He twisted the knife, pressed a little . . . not much . . .

And with eyes squeezed shut, mouth fallen open, Louis became Louise. That easy.

Rudy seemed happy, and happier still to share his good fortune with his *camaradas*. Louise seemed not so happy, walked oddly for days, but finally managed a limp smile . . . wrist. . . .

From afar Kirk watched what he had wrought, felt guilt and sorrow scream inside his head, wished he could erase what did not have to be or trade places or anything. . . . But it was done, and time went only one way . . . on and on and . . .

He tried to lose time and himself by hiding in the library, but soon learned that no one could escape the pompous, no-necked librarian, called Mother Toad, who seemed to hang in the air there, peering down with his round, red face. From table to table he waddled, ever ready—and very willing—to treat all ears to his stilted speeches that somehow managed to sound like soliloquies. It soon became apparent to anyone who could bear listening to him that Mother Toad knew everything, maybe a little more. He was only kept from spouting all he knew by half-hourly trips to his office for tea and tranquilizers.

After a while Kirk gave up the library, tried hiding beneath his blankets.

Someplace in there the routine was jarred when Hank appeared with a saxophone case full of whiskey and dope. Kirk pondered that, and finally decided he'd learn more listening.

So Hank explained. He was soon to appear before the parole board and wanted to clean his hand, get out of jailhouse hustles— part of the way out, anyway. He had a horse—a guard who packed most anything inside the prison, for a price, of course. Hank offered Kirk a piece of the action: 50 percent after costs and horse fare.

Now, money, though available, was not allowed. That meant it was worth more than its face value. Therefore, depending upon its availability at the time, it would be worth in cigarets—the exchange medium of prisons—25 to 100 percent more than its face. Hence, the horse might pack inside a half pint of whiskey and sell it to his convict connection for 5 dollars, while the connection in turn sells it for 20 dollars to another convict, who must buy the money for from 25 to 40 dollars' worth of cigarets. There was something unnecessarily complicated about the whole thing, Kirk felt, but money is money, and he needed it as much as any other convict.

So he accepted the saxophone case and with it an opportunity to become a jailhouse mogul. He should have been more excited.

After thinking about it for a while, he decided to find a fall guy. To sell dope you have to meet buyers—cobras are friendlier. So he went to see Rudy—20 cartons lasts a while, and he could always earn more—and offered him a ten percent to do the leg work.

Rudy frowned, said *"Ai!"* and wanted a better deal, but finally accepted the offer.

And shortly Kirk found his cash roll—mostly fives and tens—had become an uncomfortable bulge in his pants, a bulge that seemed to scream and jump around whenever a guard passed by. He approached Hank with the problem and was given a solution: a cut-down aluminum cigar tube.

"Just roll the money inside," Hank said with a smirk, then made a sucking noise and jammed a thumb into his fist. "And shove it in your ass."

Kirk eyed the phalluslike thing, then Hank. "Oh, no!" he blurted, taking a step back. Trying to be rational, he added: "Besides, if they shake me down and look in my asshole, they'll find it anyway."

"No," Hank said, shaking his head. "That's just one of their gimmicks to make a guy feel like a worm. Back a few years they crammed a finger in everybody's ass—now that's a no-no, so they just look. But they can't see nothing except a brown eye looking back. . . ."

So Kirk had carried the tube, along with a great reluctance, back to the cell, and without a word showed the thing to Leslie, and awaited what had to come. And it did. . . .

"Grease it up good, baby," said the little fruit with a catty grin.

Kirk cursed him, but followed instructions, for quite obviously Leslie knew all about the ins and outs of such things. It seemed a painful forever before the tube was shoved where it went but surely did not belong, and then he sighed. "Phew!"

"Phew!" Leslie mimicked, again and again and . . .

Kirk tried to snarl, red-faced.

At some time in there the guard Dunn was banished to a gun tower and replaced by another, named Brooks, who with eyes made beady, almost obscene, by thick glasses and with a furtive air about him, soon had all the convicts in G block nervous. Rumors, perhaps enhanced and lent credence by his looks, of the guard's strange sex hangups grew, became rife, until he seemed to trail a dark fog. It was said that Brooks read convicts' mail, pored over pictures of their wives and families, and jacked off. But though he was often seen prowling the floors, slipping into various cells, nobody claimed to have caught him whipping it—yet the rumors grew, leaving in Brooks' wake a host of eerie vibrations and edgy convicts.

Kirk cared little whether or not Brooks beat himself into a stupor, but he came to dread the days the seemingly omnipresent guard was on duty, for they meant eight eternal hours and an arm's length between him and Leslie. He despised the guard.

Then came a day when he entered the stairwell on his way to the cell—and Leslie—and he heard from overhead a faint scraping noise. Looking up, he saw hanging ominously off the second-floor rail a mop bucket.

Without a thought he dove backwards down the stairs, hit the wall and crumpled into a breathless heap. While lethargy turned to fury, he fought to gulp down some air. Then he was up and racing up the stairs, hands crossed protectively over his head. On the halfway landing, when nothing crashed down upon him, he stopped and ventured a glance toward the bucket.

It was being held there, balanced precariously on the rail, by a thin and angular black convict, who stared down with unseeing eyes. Beside him stood two more blacks, one big, the other monstrous, with biceps the size of a healthy man's thighs.

Kirk, angry, hurried to the second-floor landing, where a quick glance told him that the bucket was filled with water. He glared at the three of them and snarled: "What the fuck's the story?"

The convict with the bucket kept staring down silently. But the big-armed one, his boxlike hands hanging heavily, moved toward him, glowering.

"*Freeze*, Iron Man!" ordered the third, grabbing the big man's arm, pulling him back.

Kirk kept glaring but was more pleased than he let on. For Iron Man—a not inappropriate moniker—with his giant arms and baleful face of ebony, seemed a long way from home . . . 50 or 60 thousand years. . . .

With an inward shudder, Kirk turned to the other man and asked, not so angrily now, "What's happening?"

The convict stared back, dark eyes searching; then, still watching Kirk, said over his shoulder, "Tell him, LeRoy."

The convict holding the bucket, LeRoy, turned toward Kirk, looking far away. He was young, too young by a year or more to have graduated high school, with a growing boy's gangling body. While he stared, his heavy mouth worked at saying something, then abruptly his eyes spilled tears. He sobbed, "Dat *po*-lice!" and became incoherent.

Kirk, curious now, turned back to the other man with a questioning gesture. Releasing Iron Man's arm, the convict asked Kirk his name, then introduced himself. "Knight," he said, distantly sardonic, and went on:

"See, LeRoy walked in on that red-neck bull, Brooks. . . . The bastard was jacking to a picture of the kid's ma. . . . So the kid's just doing what he has to. . . ."

Kirk spent a moment pondering that. No matter what damage the bucket did—assuming it didn't entirely miss the guard—it would be slight compared to the retribution taken by custody until it was learned who was responsible or a culprit found—whichever came sooner. A hurt guard meant bad tempers in the bull pen. He explained all this to Knight, who already knew it, then finished with a suggestion that they together figure out a means less compromising, something that would rid the block of Brooks for all time.

When he was finished talking, Iron Man lowered darkly and Knight said blandly, "You still ain't said nothing."

Kirk grinned at that. "We all know the creep is some kind of freak," he said, "so custody has probably heard rumors. We ought to be able to build something around that."

Knight's mouth turned into a grimace. "What's with the 'we' shit?"

"Why shit?" Kirk wanted to know. "You think I go to town on weekends? He turns the key on me, too . . . and the creep has the whole block psyched. He ought to go, but your way won't do anything except lump his head and make him a hero. And nobody needs the kind of heat they'll put in the block till they find somebody to blame."

Knight stared at him for a silent moment, then, "You still ain't said nothing."

True enough, but he felt inward stirrings as he sensed himself tumbling headlong toward excitement. "Tell you what," he said finally. "If I can't come up with a better scheme in a couple days, I'll help you drop the bucket."

After an exchange of doubtful looks among the three, Knight turned back to Kirk. "He's white. . . ."

He caught the hanging words and tossed back: "He's khaki. . . . I'm blue. . . . That makes me a nigger and him Mr. Charlie."

Knight grinned a little, said they would hang tight a while and see if together they could figure something cinch.

And they did.

Two days later, shortly after Brooks' shift had begun, Knight, his shirt buttoned haphazardly and collar askew, framed himself in the office doorway, and began shuffling his feet and scratching his head while ol-darky-drawling: "Suh, dere be a fah . . . dere be a fah, suh. . . ."

The guard, finally understanding that something was amiss, though apparently not what, worked out of his chair and followed Knight, who was suddenly clumsy-footed, to the third floor, where a trash-can fire blazed.

Meantime, Kirk, with Leslie pointing, slipped into the office, picked open the desk lock, found the guard's lunch pail, and dumped into the thermos a quantity of white powder, then sprinkled the two sandwiches with the same powder. He was finished and out of the office within a minute.

Shortly, having triumphed over the trash-can fire, the guard returned to the office and sat there, thumbing through a girlie magazine, sipping a cup of coffee. Then another cup. And another. He ate a sandwich. And not much later he rose and stretched, then flopped back into his chair and crashed backwards to the floor.

Kirk and Knight stepped into the office then and glanced down at the sprawled guard, at his perspiration-beaded gray-white face. They grinned.

Brooks was not entirely unconscious, but close enough. For the powder Kirk had been so liberal with was from four crushed Mysoline tablets, a virtually tasteless epileptic medication that causes an extremely nauseous and vertiginous condition in anyone unaccustomed to it, a condition not unlike being simultaneously drunk and seasick. A half tablet will cause a normal person two days of total misery—and Brooks had swallowed perhaps four times that amount.

Moving quickly then, Leslie took the thermos to a sink and dumped the contents, while Kirk and Knight propped the guard in his chair and planted pornographic snapshots in his pockets and wallet. Finished, some whiskey was splashed on the guard's shirt front, then a few fingers poured into the thermos, which was replaced in the lunch pail.

They left Brooks making glug-glug noises.

Once found, the guard had been rushed to the hospital, where his stomach was pumped, both to relieve his very obvious distress and to analyze the contents. But with no success, for the guard kept on making noises and somehow, somewhere, the contents of his stomach vanished.

"Odd," Hank had commented with a puzzled look.

And since there was no gun tower or dark corner in which the administration could hide the talk of Brooks' snapshots or whiskey smell, the guard was cast from the embarrassed ranks—though it was probably several days before he realized it.

After that there grew between Kirk and Knight a friendliness that was deeper than skin, though not much. Prison is hard enough without sharing soul cankers.

He was awakened one morning by violent hammering on the door, and sat up, looking. Nobody there. He glanced down at the lower bunk, and saw his own tense curiosity reflected on Leslie's face. Still looking toward the door, he slipped from the bunk and into his pants. After a moment, when the knocking was not repeated, he was about to forget it, thinking it had been a stray passerby amusing himself; then the door was again hammered on and again there was no face at the window.

Who? What did they want? He was uncertain, but not sure he wanted to find out. . . .

He grabbed up the short-handled cell broom, then, crouching, went to the door, twisted the knob and kicked it open.

Nobody leaped inside. . . . Nobody there. . . .

Adrenaline coursing, he tensed to spring into the hall, there battle with the mysterious door-banger. Then a throaty laugh sounded, a familiar laugh.

And a guard poked his head around the corner. "A coupla goddamn queers," he said—Yancy said.

Kirk laughed and threw a punch into the guard's massive body, while back of him Leslie babbled, something about a big goon.

They'd made him the regular block bull, Yancy explained, then stood there looking at them, but mostly at Kirk, with a wry expression. He finally asked Leslie if Kirk had made a man out of him yet, then bent and lifted Kirk's pant leg. "Well," he said, "at least he ain't got you shaving your legs."

"Dry the fuck up," Kirk said, faintly embarrassed. "Leslie's a real girl—ask him . . . uh, her. . . . Besides, all we do is read to each other."

"Yeah, read," Yancy mocked. "You got tattoos on your pricks or what?"

Leslie rescued Kirk with: "Lay off, you goon! You know I don't have one of those things. . . . It was removed in an operation. . . ." He swished toward the guard.

And Yancy retreated, asking, ordering, then pleading with Kirk to call the man-eater off. Kirk said, "Huh?" and watched the big guard back to the door and there flap a hairy, limp-wristed hand. "Later, dearies," he squeaked, and leaped from the cell. Shutting the door, he put his lumpy face to the window and gave them the finger.

Two minutes later, the window curtained, they were in bed again, *a* bed, laughing, bouncing all around.

As time crept along an unusual and even eerie sight became familiar in Alhondiga's corridors: Warden Benson and his daughter, a timid girl, long-haired and soft-faced, in her early twenties.

She had at first followed her father around the prison as he thrust his smiling face into this group of convicts and that, asking questions, even answering them. Between them there seemed generated a vibrant but unsettling aura, as if Benson, his personality enhanced and reflected by female presence, exuded a wholeness that left the convicts with the bitter taste of their own alienation.

The girl, according to talk, was studying medicine, and as she became a more familiar sight—yet somehow always more feared than fearing—she ventured from her father's side to spend hours inside the hospital block, helping with the patients.

"A regular Florence Nightingale," said some with what passed for sardonic smirks. "I wonder what Benson would say if she married one?" said others with a sort of wistful sarcasm.

Though Benson was responsible for many procedural changes and individual kindnesses that left the convicts knowing their own names better, his daughter's presence seemed responsible for a more pervasive change, as if, loved and hated with otherworldly passions, passions too long denied, she had become an abstract testament to the futility and barrenness of the lives she walked among. Yet when she passed through, something like life breathed in the corridors.

Kirk, during the rare instances when he saw the girl, felt a maniacal hunger within, a hunger to tear the flesh from her bones; a hunger to possess and, with possession, devour; a hunger that plunged and pounded him into the seat of Leslie's being, that drove him to the other side of sanity—and finally exhaustion. This happened several times before Leslie stopped him in the middle of a bout and, with more anger than petulance, said that he wasn't plastic, he was only a boy, and if that was too heavy for Kirk to handle, then he ought to pack it in, find somebody who dug pain.

Kirk took a walk after that; he searched all around for escaped pieces of himself, but found none.

That night, with a strange and distasteful combination of contriteness and fear, he slipped onto Leslie's finger a ring he had accepted for a debt—a gold wedding band.

Leslie stared at it for a long moment, then burst into tears. "Baby," he sobbed, holding tight to Kirk, "don't let me go . . . not ever. . . ."

"Not ever," Kirk promised, his head filled with some nameless ache. "Not ever. . . ."

Time passed somehow. Then one day Hank came around with a grin on his face and surprises in every pocket. He'd been granted a parole, he said, laughing; and since that meant he was rehabilitated, he now had no use for some collected escape gear, neither did he have any use for a narcotics-smuggling guard. "So," he finished, "how would you like to inherit a horse?"

Kirk's immediate thought was to say yes, but other thoughts followed fast. The keistered tube now held close to a thousand dollars: what would he do with more when it would be hard to spend what he had in two years? And the prospect of being the jailhouse Mr. Big left him with no excitement. Still . . . money is money. . . . If a guard packs things in, maybe he'd pack something out . . . a convict or two. . . . "Who is he?" he wanted to know.

"Carol," said Hank. "Sgt. Carol."

Kirk declined the offer: horses are horses, mad bulls something else.

Hank grinned a little at that and, staring into the distance, faintly misty-eyed, said, "You might be the guy I meant to give this stuff to," and handed Kirk a small rectangular box and a large envelope. Then, ignoring Kirk's curiosity, went on, talking fast. "Look, I'll be springing the first week of April, next year—not tomorrow, but not too far away. After three jolts, I've figured out that guns weigh too much—but I got too many strikes in this ball game to think about catching up with the Joneses. Even so, once I get a taste of the glitter out there, I'll get stuck off in the middle of things again and either get blown away or be back counting days. . . . I'm fading forty—more joint time means the same as a bullet. So I'm leaving the country, not a week or a month after I get out, but the same day. I've been running that bloodsucker Carol for four years and I'll run him till I go, for the passage money. I've got some Merchant Marine connections that'll put me on a boat. I ain't sure where I'll wind up, but any place that won't extradite me will do for starters—stateless in Greenland sounds better than caged in Utopia, wherever the fuck that is. Anyway, I can't make it in that mad house out there—the whole fucking country is sicker than I know how to be." He paused to stare at Kirk. "Hang on to the fruit— she's the only thing between you and the gas chamber—but don't ever forget that cyanide ain't the only kind of poison. . . . And don't let her take all your madness. . . . It's your only sanity. . . . Think about what I said. . . ." His voice trailed off; he turned, walked away.

Kirk stared after him, thinking.

Back in the cell, with Leslie looking on, he opened the large envelope and found within an assortment of identification cards, all with his or Leslie's picture or description affixed, all forged. There were credit cards, draft cards, drivers' licenses, and lastly were two cards with their pictures, doctored prison mug shots, each proclaiming the bearer to be a prison guard. Leslie, a bull . . . ? A screw . . . ?

He turned his attention to the rectangular box and found inside the cotton-lined interior the parts, some blued, some shining, of a convict-machined single-shot silenced pistol.

The barrel—five inches long, threaded for two inches at one end and a quarter inch at the other, with a multitude of tiny holes drilled into the bore along the two-inch threaded length—was screwed into a milled breechblock, and an aluminum butt slid onto that, then locked in place with a small wing nut. Housed in the butt was a single-action trigger mechanism actuating a large hammer. A quarter-inch steel disk screwed onto the threaded two inches of the barrel. Next, an aluminum sleeve, drilled with holes like those in the end of the barrel, was held tight against the disk, and a second disk screwed to the end of the barrel to secure it. The silencer tube screwed to the first disk, and once filled with alternately bored sizes of aluminum mesh washers, a third disk screwed inside the tube to retain the washers. And the gun was complete.

In the bottom of the box, taped fast, was a row of ten .22-caliber magnum bullets standing like little lead-headed soldiers, awaiting orders as lead-headed soldiers do.

Kirk fumbled loose a bullet, thumbed back the hammer, and slid home the cartridge, which was held fast with a U-shaped clip hinged to the breech. He sat there hefting the ugly little tube-nosed gun. . . . He stared out the window while something inside his head opened an eye and looked around, trying to see. . . . If only there was a route whereby he stood no chance of being caught, locked away from Leslie. . . . If only he had the will to find one. . . .

253

Disassembled, the gun, along with the ID papers, was buried in the basement; not buried so deep was his fear. . . .

One day two psychologists and a psychiatrist appeared at the prison gate and, after much intradepartmental haggling, were admitted and assigned office space in G block.

Shortly, Kirk had found himself assigned to the caseload of a Dr. Steiner, a psychologist in his middle forties with wise gray eyes and hairy ears. Steiner had little to say but listened a lot, smoking a smelly little pipe.

One morning while plying his prison-learned trade, the doctor stuck his foot in front of Kirk's broom.

"Whalen," he said from someplace inside a cloud of smoke, "come in the office for a moment."

Kirk did, and waited while the doctor poked at the pipe dottle with a tortured paper clip, then leaned back in his squeaky chair and stared at him with his gray eyes. "You're scheduled to go before the parole board next month," he said.

Kirk grinned sourly. "That's just some more of the go-by-the-numbers shit. They don't want to see me any more than I want to see them."

Steiner held a match to the pipe bowl and sucked noisily. "Be that as it may," said a smoke cloud, "but I have to write your board report. Would you like to help me?"

"Would I what?"

"Like to help me make out your board report?"

Kirk eyed him with suspicion. "What if I recommend myself for an immediate parole?"

"What if you recommend yourself for an immediate parole?"

"Yeah."

Dr. Steiner stared at him with unwavering eyes; and Kirk tried to stare back but started to fidget, for the man's eyes seemed to eat inside him, seemed to see the things Kirk kept from the world and himself. So he dictated his board report, and Steiner wrote, pausing only to stare at him on occasion. And on those occasions Kirk usually altered the glowing self-praises of all his shining attributes. When the report was finished, he walked from the office cursing Steiner; cursing mind-benders and brain-pickers and hairy ears and smelly pipes; then cursed himself because he was what he was, and not so blind that he could not see.

* * *

There dawned a gray morning that promised nothing, and he was ordered to report to the parole board. The waiting room, in the administration building, was filled with convicts and their cigaret smoke and anxiety. They all sat there, waiting, their postures wooden, their brave faces looking as if molded of fragile glass. Before them was the last step in the judicial process; they were only a door from justice. . . .

Came Kirk's turn and he walked through a door into a room filled with an aura of monumental importance and four overweight men who wore blue suits with mysterious gold lapel pins. Each wore a different face but somehow managed, together, to look like quadruplets.

Kirk sat in the chair before the table they were behind, a table piled high with papers. The four men of importance stared at him, and he stared back. After a long moment one of them, a former chief of police, leaning forward as if to distinguish himself, said tiredly, "You're a punk."

Kirk supposed that he was expected to become choleric, yank out fistfuls of hair while screaming curses; but the vacuous-faced former cop spoke a language he could not hear. He answered with a stare.

Another one, jowled and crusty-scalped, a former minister, said listlessly, "What have you done for yourself since you've been here?"

"Time," Kirk said.

The former minister sipped some water and belched politely into his little pink hand.

A third man spoke, a wall-eyed former district attorney. "Well," he said, clearing his throat, "we have a report here stating some improvement on your part. . . ." He looked closely at a paper, then handed it down the table to the next man. "A doctor," he muttered, turning his attention to some other papers. A moment passed before he picked up several that were stapled together. "Hmm . . . says here you're a real problem maker. . . ." Sitting straighter, he handed this report to the next man also. "That was written by *Doctor* Trintz," he said. "What should we do with you?"

"Parole me."

The fourth man, puffing a huge meerschaum, a former F.B.I. agent, spoke up. "Who else are you going to kill?"

Kirk stared at him.

255

"Do you want to tell us anything?" asked the former policeman.

"No."

"Do you have anything to ask us?" asked the former district attorney.

"No."

"Are you taking a trade?" asked the former F.B.I. agent.

"No."

"Are you taking group counseling?" asked the former minister.

"No." But he was getting disgusted. "Would it help?"

"No."

He stood, turned to leave.

But the former minister, stern-faced, stopped him with an upraised palm. "Get some Jesus Christ in you, son!"

"Same to you," he said, and left.

He was denied any more parole consideration for five years.

He laughed: what did one year or five mean when tomorrow did not exist?

One midmorning Knight stepped into the cell and stood there, his face knotted with ebony ridges, fists clenched, nostrils flared, staring toward Kirk, through him. Finally he spoke:

"Iron Man bought hisself a white sissy from the *chicanos*. . . . Some white boys got hot. . . . One thing led to another till one of the trashy punks spit on me. . . . We was on the yard. . . . If I'd of raised a hand, we'd of got blowed all over . . . so I told the punk let's go somewheres and fight. . . . He says he ain't fighting—he's killing. . . . So just to stop a race riot I'm supposed to meet him in the chapel with a white dude and he's bringing somebody black. . . ." He paused, staring at the ceiling with his teeth bared, breathing hard. "I got me nine in on a murder," he continued, almost afire with the rage burning in his eyes, "and if they bust me giving that punk honkey a bloody nose, they'll try to gas me. . . . *Fuck it!*" he exploded, and looked at Kirk. "Will you take my corner while I fuck this punk in his scurvy red neck?"

Kirk nodded, then nodded again because he knew who Iron Man had bought, because he knew that Knight's coming duel was a turn of a wheel he had himself started spinning. . . .

Minutes before the noon whistle was due to shriek, he watched from across the corridor as the priest and the minister came from

256

their offices on either side of the chapel door and locked them, then walked through the hall together, smiling as if they really liked one another.

As they disappeared, two convicts approached. Only then did he realize who Knight was to fight: Zeke. It was surprising that the tattooed convict had the stomach for it, though it was reasonable to assume that Zeke, that breed of leader who chased the led, had been nominated avenger of his pack's "honor."

The convict beside Zeke, a light-skinned mulatto with Caucasian features and straightened hair, Kirk knew only as "He's a good spook."

As they neared, Zeke spotted Kirk and his eyes widened. "You with that nig?" he called excitedly.

Kirk said he was with Knight, and felt in his groin an ache that made him yearn to rip off Zeke's eagled scalp.

"Man!" Zeke exclaimed, almost jumping for joy. "That's a dumb fucking nigger, choosing you. Know what I mean? Man, I'm carving that nig in hunks his cannibal mama wouldn't eat. Know what I mean?" From his shirt he eased a ten-inch knife and flashed it proudly.

His companion remained silent, wearing a smile as frozen and artificial as the waves in his hair.

Knight appeared down the corridor then, so Zeke and second went inside the chapel. When Knight was close, Kirk told him about the knife, then led the way into the chapel arena and locked the door behind.

Zeke, knife in hand, stood before the altar, waiting. Knight stopped in the aisle to pull from his pants a 15-inch long pipe. Both ends were lightly taped while one end dangled a leather loop. This he wound over his thumb, across the back of his palm, and gripped the pipe securely in his fist. He had at least learned something from the police.

He moved toward Zeke. "How's it going to be, red-neck?"

Zeke looked from Knight's pipe to Kirk and back to the pipe. He took a small step backwards, then puffed up to mutter: "All of it, nigger. All of it."

Knight crouched, pipe held horizontally in both hands. "Come on and get it then, punk."

They feinted and they parried; they thrust and slashed and circled round and round. Zeke, fright-agile, retarded Knight's unhur-

257

ried stalking with throat-aimed thrusts, but on his face, naked and ugly, was the need for his pack—or a back door. Fear-spurred, he began to curse Knight with words sharper than his knife blade; he cursed and cursed.

And soon the words cut through Knight's defenses; he angered, moved in, flailing the pipe with careless ferocity.

Still Zeke taunted, unscathed.

Knight whistled the pipe toward Zeke's temple with too much anger, too much power. Zeke ducked, and as the pipe arced past, drove the knife upward, toward Knight's heart. Knight twisted aside.

But not enough. The knife pierced his shoulder, stuck there. While Zeke tugged to extract the blade, Knight could only watch, for it had stabbed into the shoulder of his weapon hand. So there he stood, looking on through eyes gone muddy and frozen in pain, as Zeke yanked on the knife.

Suddenly, unexpectedly, it came free, sliding like a bearing on a greased race, chased by a geyser of blood. Zeke staggered back, back, then tripped on the edge of the rug before the altar. Down he went, sprawling, knife squirting from his fist.

Knight moved, a blur of black and blue and red. Then he was over Zeke, the pipe now held in his good hand.

Zeke stared up at him, raised his head, opened his mouth to say something, but did not. Could not.

For the pipe smashed into his eagled skull.

Came the sound of an egg cracking. Zeke's skull slammed into the floor with such force that his legs flew up, up, and over, somersaulting him to his feet. Bloody-faced, he made a slow turn, staring blindly around the chapel. Then his eyes glazed and very slowly he toppled to the floor. And there he lay, sprawled, still.

Knight straddled him, his arm dripping blood, the blood commingling with that flowing from Zeke's head and mouth. He knelt, raised the pipe.

"Knight!"

Kirk started at the sound of his voice, at its unexpectedness, for he had had no intention of speaking: Zeke, dead, would be a mistake buried.

Knight, the pipe poised to crush Zeke's skull, turned toward him.

In silence they stared at one another; they stared past friendship and brotherhood and love of man, past rubbled cities, scorched earth and gutted villages and men, past human carrion and bleached bones; they stared past boundless time until finally they met in a primeval ooze: how had man survived men?

With hypnotic slowness Knight turned to look upon Zeke's battered skull. The pipe rolled from his hand. He labored to his feet, went toward the door.

Kirk lingered only to wipe fingerprints from the doorknob, then stepped into the alcove and shut the door behind. He and the other convict propped Knight against the wall and ripped loose his bloody sleeve, using it to press over his wound. Kirk then stripped off his own shirt and hurriedly buttoned Knight into it. Supporting him between them as best they could without drawing attention, they went through the corridor as quickly as Knight was able, passing several guards who woodenly guarded nothing in particular.

Arriving finally at the hospital door, Kirk sent an orderly to find Hank. Eons later, it seemed, he showed, then took one look and ran back inside the hospital to check the positions of guards and free personnel. Moments later he reappeared with a second orderly, and without a word they rushed Knight through the door.

Later the same day Hank came around with a frown. Zeke had been found by the priest, he said, and was now in the hospital with a busted skull; Knight's blood trail had also been found, and the entire joint would be shaken down till the wound was uncovered. "You think Knight'll crack about who sewed him up?" Hank finished, chewing a thumb.

Kirk doubted it: for Knight to admit anything would be to admit hitting Zeke.

"You want a fact of life?" Hank said. "One out of three spooks tells the man too much. Call it racist bullshit or my bias or examine it and call it the result of centuries of conditioning. . . . But, buddy, call it my ass if he cracks. . . ." He slapped a yellow capsule into Kirk's palm. "I told him I'd send something for the pain." He fished from his pocket a second capsule identical to the first and dropped it into Kirk's other hand. "The first one's Nembutal," he said, staring at Kirk with uneasy eyes, "and the other's cyanide. The decision's in your hands." He walked quickly back toward the hospital.

Kirk stared after him, his head reeling. In a flash everything was weighed. If Knight talked, Hank would lose his parole . . . serve another year or five or . . . Where was the choice . . . ?

259

He cursed Zeke for an asshole, Knight for being black, then remembered Farrell. . . .

He looked down at the twin capsules for a long moment before arriving at a decision: he would juggle them until there was no way to know one from the other. Easy. Dropped in the laps of the gods, fate would decide. . . .

Knight was propped up in bed, his shirt unable to conceal the bulge of his bandaged shoulder. Kirk asked him how he felt, and with a weak grin, Knight said, "Knee's shaky," then asked, "They find eagle face?"

Kirk nodded. "With a busted head. They're looking for you."

Knight's expression went from anger to fear to resignation. He shrugged. "Black and bad luck come with the same roll of the dice."

Kirk studied him for a moment, then tossed him a capsule, said, "Luck," and walked from the cell.

Back in his own cell, he stared into the toilet, at the capsule floating there; he saw Zeke lying before the altar like some sacrificial offering, bleeding from opened eyes and mouth, his eagle's feathers a sticky mess of red; he saw Farrell, shaven legs, plucked eyebrows, owned, sold and resold. . . . If regrets were bread, he could have fed the multitudes, then absorbed the waters of the seas. . . .

Twice he reached toward the floating capsule, twice something held his hand; then he punched the flush button, and the toilet swallowed the cyanide. . . .

Knight was found. He never talked—not even on death row.

Sam died.

He appeared at their door on a misty day early in November and asked Kirk to buy into a poker game he was running in the chapel; he needed the money to pay debts, bookmakers, dope dealers, and loan sharks. "Do me something, Kirk," he finished. "I'm drove to the nutsack. . . ."

Kirk looked at him, then away. Sam had come a long way, all down. Seeing him close, the elasticity gone from his face, the abysmal tiredness behind his eyes, Kirk could not help wondering if he were looking at his own face from a point only time away. Sam was too many whistles and sirens, too many head counts; he had become a piece of the prison machinery, a victim of the granite dinosaur; Sam was all these, and none of Sam. Sam was dead.

Kirk agreed to sit in the game if he could bring Leslie along; Sam did not argue. So they went together to the chapel, into the priest's bedroom behind the altar drapes, where five convicts were already seated around a blanket on the floor. Sam took one of the seats remaining, and Kirk the other, with Leslie behind, watching. Sam then counted out stacks of chips to the players; finished, he shuffled the cards, said, "Low—put your dough where you crow," and dealt.

The game turned into a quiet war that screamed with tension as Sam's desperation infected the others; the passing hours eroded smiles, left tempers showing through raw and ugly. Almost as if he had intentionally created the atmosphere, Sam began to laugh; and the more he laughed, the more the others bet, and lost; so along with the house cut, he raked in pot after pot, laughing.

And thus the afternoon crawled by; time numbed by choking clouds of tobacco smoke, too much coffee, too much tension, and Sam's laughter. Faces sweated and hands shook, bets were thrown down as gauntlets, and Sam laughed and won.

Kirk grinned to himself at the sound of Sam's laughter—it seemed a thousand years since he had heard it. He let the game's desperation wash past him, for he needed no money and saw no reason to lose any; so as his chips dribbled away in antes, he watched the players. Poker he did not enjoy, but watching the players was another game; little men roar and big men slaver, cowards fold or bet all, eyes glint with fleeting truths, winning nothing for their owners or losing everything. He watched a convict called Frisco Fats chew on a sweat-soaked cigar as he came apart at his suety seams; he watched a Filipino fruit called Suzie Wong eat off all his fingernails, then start on his knuckles; he watched a one-legged convict called Dippity Dan rub his erection as he lost his every cent; and he watched Sam laugh.

Emotion stroked emotion until the little room throbbed at orgasmic pitch, ready to explode, then one of the players rose, his sweat-filmed face dancing and twitching to some inner tune, his mouth taut, fists clenched. He glowered and checked out.

Others followed, grumbling, sullen. They would enter the priest's bathroom and emerge moments later to pay their losses with cash, putrid-smelling money faded yellowish in keistered rolls. Sam soon sat in a cloud of stink.

Finally, playing four-handed, Kirk said, "I've had it," and stood up.

Sam nodded. "Three-handed ain't going to get it," he told the two remaining players, Frisco Fats and a tall convict with an empty face, called Slim, both heavy losers. "Cash your chips in."

While they did, Sam handed a malodorous wad of bills to Kirk. "How about sticking some soap to these?"

Kirk took the bills into the bathroom, where he used soap and water to wash away most of the smell, then slapped each bill against the wall to dry. Finished, returned to the bedroom, he found the others whiling away the 40 minutes left until count time with a no-stake rummy game. So with nothing better to do, he began snooping through the closets. He found little but had not expected much. There were boxes of tracts depicting bloody hearts, torn palms, somebody gazing rapturously toward a gold-colored cloud while being roasted, and various other things, all gory, all with messages of *Peace* and *Love* written in sticky-candy prose.

"You son of a bitch!" sliced through the quiet.

Kirk spun, looking.

Slim, cards scattered before him, crouched to spring, glared across the blanket at Sam. *"You son of a bitch!"* he hissed again.

Sam's face tightened, he half-rose. "What's on your mind, punk?"

Slim, teeth-bared, said in a venomous whisper, "Cheating's on my mind, son of a bitch."

Sam leaped up and kicked his mouth shut. Slim tumbled backwards spraying blood and teeth, then bounded up and across the room. Somehow his hand became a flash of steel, and into Sam's lung he sunk a knife hilt-deep. Then again.

Kirk moved with the third knife thrust; both feet with him flying behind smashed into Slim's skull, slammed him to the floor, unconscious. He wheeled to Leslie. "You and Fats get the hell out of here! Tell Hank to get surgery ready. . . ."

Leslie said he wasn't going anywhere, not without his baby; and Frisco Fats leaned against a wall holding his heart.

Kirk went to Sam and knelt beside him. He was on his stomach, blood seeping from under him. He moved his head to look up at

Kirk, a curious grin on his blood-smeared mouth. "Hell of a deal," he whispered, grinning a little wider. "Hey, old buddy," he continued, weaker now, "do me something . . . one last thing. . . ."

Barely able to hear him, Kirk leaned his ear close to the red mouth. "Yeah, anything. . . . But don't talk crazy. . . . You'll be on your feet in two weeks."

"Yeah," Sam whispered from far away. "Yeah, two weeks. . . . Kirk, tell Gypsy I said . . . fuck his mother. . . ." Dark crimson blood gushed from his mouth, sprayed Kirk's face. He reared suddenly, then collapsed, eyes closed. Kirk was feeling for a pulse when Sam's eyes opened again and the smile returned to his mouth. He winked and, chuckling, died.

Frisco Fats then hurried from the room, ashen-faced, tucking away the money from the bathroom wall, while Kirk slapped Slim into groggy consciousness. "You killed him, scum-sucker," he snarled into the convict's bloody face, then stabbed the knife through his wrist tendons. "You're on your own."

Then he and Leslie ran from the bedroom, from the chapel of gray stone and spirits, from death.

In the cell he stared out the window, his thoughts as roiled and impenetrable as the swirling scud outside. "Sam's dead," he whispered, not wanting to believe it.

Leslie took his hand. "Baby . . ."

Kirk turned to him, saw the tears welling in his eyes. "Don't cry," he said quietly. "He went out laughing. . . . Wherever he'd been, he came back. . . . And he didn't care, not really. . . ."

Nodding, Leslie snuffled and blinked the tears from his eyes. "But why, baby . . . ? Why, when we were just playing for fun . . . ?"

Kirk shrugged. "Who knows . . . ? He'd lost heavy . . . he just came apart. . . . I thought about killing him, but what would that erase . . . ?"

"Baby," Leslie said, shaking his head, "I'm not talking about Slim. . . . I meant Sam. . . . Why'd he do it? Why'd he cheat when we were just playing for fun . . . ?"

It took a moment to trace the pieces that so lustingly led to culmination, a culmination that some omniscient eye could have foretold. And then he laughed with a bitterness so profound his eyes grew wet.

And so a year had passed.

There now seemed nothing warped or strange about his surroundings, for though he failed to understand all that he experienced, he had developed a sort of unthinking tolerance; and where understanding is lacking, tolerance will do, much as the hungry might call a rat a rabbit in order to live another day.

And because of this unthinking tolerance there had grown within him a virtual symbiosis with the prison. He, if asked, could not have stated that it happened on this day or that, for it was a cancerous thing that grew little by little, making him become an extension of the prison, the prison of him. To someone looking on from afar it might seem that man and stone had found rapport, yet who knows what hate smolders in the hearts of even the longtime wed? Prison, however, demands the face of rapport, for it is too rigid an organism to allow difference or dissent. Thus it is an organism doomed by evolution. But so was the dinosaur, and that took 10,000 years.

So Kirk wore the face of rapport, perhaps out of cowardice, perhaps out of some deep-seated will to survive, perhaps both. But any face worn long is difficult to remove, sometimes impossible, always painful.

On a morning during the second week in December, as he and Leslie walked from the block toward the prison canteen, he was not thinking about pain or anything—it was easier that way. But as he stepped from the block into the corridor, the thing that had grown inside him, the symbiotic something, backed him flat against the wall. Something was wrong. It was neither feeling nor intuition nor imagination. He *knew* something was wrong as he knew Leslie stood beside him, as he knew a heart beat in his chest.

The corridor was nearly deserted, ominously hushed; tension hung miasmically in the air, almost a scent.

Diagonally across the corridor, in front of A block, a group of black convicts were clustered around Iron Man, all still and silent.

And to the right, before E block, a group of white convicts stood equally as still, as silent.

Then the why was answered as a pallid, shaven-headed convict emerged from E block and stood with the others, staring toward the blacks.

"Zeke!" Leslie whispered hoarsely. "Zeke's back!"

Kirk felt himself nod. He understood now. The understanding crawled up his spine, quickened his pulse, made his nerves hum.

He watched and read the signals passed from eye to eye with the feeling that he could step into the middle of the corridor, catch the messages and tear them up. They were that palpable. And in the messages, he read promises, promises of death.

A convict passed, talking to himself, biting his fingers. Then came another swishing daintily, seemingly oblivious to anything but keeping his hips gyrating just so. Another passed who felt it, who knew, and his eyes were wide and frightened as he hurried, looking over both shoulders, probably certain he would never make it wherever he was headed. Then Shorty shuffled by, sneered by the blacks as an Uncle Tom, offering Kirk and Miss Leslie a mumbled greeting, a nervous smile. Another convict followed on his heels, whistling the tune of a midnight graveyard stroller, his head swiveling, trying to see everywhere at once.

And suddenly a jagged streak of light crackled through Kirk's skull.

"Shorty!" he screamed, electrifying the entire corridor. But too late, much too late. Forever afterward he would wonder what made him scream, but it would not matter, for he was too late by eons.

As he raced after Shorty, it was as if the universe abruptly shifted into a much higher gear. Time slowed, gravity became a quagmire sucking at his heels. From a point far in space he watched Zeke draw a huge knife, almost a sword, and plunge it with a sort of tired slowness through the center of Shorty's chest, out his back. The little black man settled slowly to his knees, then rolled to his side, came to rest on his back, the knife pushing back through, sticking from his thin chest, a conqueror's standard.

With Shorty down, time picked up.

The convicts with Zeke looked up from the body, saw Kirk, and as mice from a cat, darted into the block. Zeke lingered, gazing down at Shorty with a practiced indolence. Then he happened to notice Kirk, something twisted his face, widened his eyes, and he, too, sprinted into the block.

Still racing toward E block, bounding over Shorty's body, Kirk heard behind a growing roar, a guard's whistle, the fire engine sound of the riot gates closing. But then he was skidding into E block, scanning, searching for Zeke.

He spotted him racing up the stairs. He followed, almost flying, the steps passing underfoot three at a time, sometimes four, without thought, knowing only that Zeke must be caught, crushed.

He gained, his body seemingly urged on by some alien nervous system, going faster and faster.

On the fifth tier Zeke looked back, blowing hard, eyes frantic. Then he dashed down the tier, headed toward the back stairs.

Kirk, mere yards behind, still gained.

Just short of the end of the tier, Zeke snatched a hold of the guard rail, slammed to a stop. Leaping over him, Kirk crashed into the rail at the end of the tier, then spun and headed back. He saw the tattooed convict half off the tier, attempting to drop to the fourth tier.

Kirk dashed to him, raised a foot to smash his fingers.

And Zeke, a bright pink scar bisecting his tattooed forehead, looked up at him with a tremulous smile touching the corners of his mouth. Then his eyes glazed with panic, and before Kirk could mash the holding fingers, Zeke let go. And down he went in silent slow motion. His toes finally touched the concrete five stories below and he melted into it, becoming a rumpled splotch of pallid flesh, blue denim, and a widening, ever-widening pool of scarlet.

Kirk stared down at the heap for a long moment before he became aware of the head-filling clamor that shook the very building.

"Leslie!" he yelled, barely able to hear himself. "Oh, God, don't let anything happen to him," and then he was running again, dashing to the stairs and down.

At the E block door convicts ran, raced, sprinted, crashing past and over one another, fat ones with scared eyes heading into the block, thin ones with cruel eyes trying to get out. Kirk kicked and slugged a path to the door, screaming for Leslie, his voice swallowed in the cacophony.

Finally battling through to the corridor, where there was more fighting, less noise, he searched until his eyes lit upon a small cluster of convicts standing over Shorty. Pushing his way through several fights, he came at last to the gathered convicts and found Leslie kneeling beside the small black and red body. Shorty, holding Leslie's hand, was smiling weakly, blood bubbling from his mouth at every choppy breath, dribbling down the side of his gray-stubbled mouth. The knife in his chest moved less and less as he breathed more and more shallowly.

266

Kirk knelt beside Leslie and looked into Shorty's bleary, yellow-rimmed eyes. He and the little man spent only a moment gazing at one another, for that was all the time there was.

A tear dripped from Leslie's chin, hit Shorty's cheek, and rolled into his ear. "Shh . . . shh," the little man whispered. "Don't cry. . . . Shorty ain't gotta be sweeping . . . where he be going. . . . No more Tommin'. . . ." His voice trailed off. With fingers contorted, eyes popped wide, he sat straight up, the knife quivering in his chest. His mouth opened, gushed blood, and he crumpled back to the floor, dead. All the way dead.

Leslie choked. And Kirk yelled, bellowed at the concrete, squeezed Shorty's lifeless face. A dead man had died, but why? Why? Concrete echoes mocked him. Why?

A fight fell across his back, and he kicked to his feet, pulling Leslie with him. He backed to the wall of the corridor and stood there, looking, trying to understand.

The prison was in riot; the poison tree had borne fruit. Here, black fought white; there, a Mexican fought both. Over in the corner a gray-haired fag lay bleeding for his sins, mostly for his gray hair.

Farther down the corridor, the riot gates before B and C blocks had been jammed open with chairs and broken benches.

There were no guards to be seen.

Only convicts, here fighting, there dragging a young fruit into one of the blocks. He watched a gang of convicts, black and white together, laughing, as they clubbed a hunchback mulatto stool pigeon into a soggy mash.

Then suddenly at the riot gate between A and H blocks there appeared a squad of guards armed with gas-gun clubs, led by Capt. Bradley. They halted at the gate and the captain raised his club overhead, flailed the air, flushed, then stabbed the club toward the door in the gate. But none of the guards went near it. Not even himself.

The captain continued his pompous pantomime for some moments with no appreciable results except for increased jeering from the convicts. Then a guard came running up with a tear-gas cannister. At the gate, he pulled the pin and stuck it between the bars.

And a convict snatched it and gave it back, bouncing it off Bradley's flapping jaw. It dropped to the floor, billowing white smoke. The guards retreated. All but the captain, who glared and shook his club at the smoking thing. He coughed, and for a moment his face was obscured; next seen, he was running, a sort of ungainly and vulgar display of jiggling flesh. He soon caught up with the others.

The bittersweet gas boiled through the bars, spread the width of the corridor, and rolled relentlessly toward the end of the hall. Convicts who were able ran, shattering corridor windows as they went.

The hallway was almost clear of convicts when Rudy and two friends darted into the gas fog and snatched a fleeing man. They stabbed him with glistening steel, expressionless faces; they stabbed and stabbed. And when they were finished, Rudy led the others across the corridor, into G block. Back of them, with death throes over, the stabbed convict lay still, deep in his own blood, his eyes staring into nothing, mirroring his last fear, his fingers frozen grotesquely, as if he sought in death to defend the life he had too easily given up.

The gas kept advancing. Passing the broken windows, it thinned, as ghostlike soldiers seeking to flank the enemy. But the main body, only slightly diminished, roiled forward.

The guards reappeared carrying two-foot-long clubs. There were no convicts directly on the other side of the riot gate. Capt. Bradley led the charge, uncontested.

At least for a while . . . until they passed the B and G block doorways. Then they were set upon by an enveloping wave of screaming and cursing and armed convicts all pouring from the doors of the honor blocks. Over some heads were pillowcase hoods; in all hands were crude weapons, but cruel: knives and pipes, chair legs and soap-filled blackjacks, sink stoppers on leather thongs and splintery slats of lumber, and an occasional club abandoned by fleet-footed guards.

Stool pigeons and fruits—both young and old—were forgotten now. Instead, everybody whaled on everybody but mostly on the guards, who had circled into a tight knot, their clubs battering at anything that moved, sometimes nothing.

Capt. Bradley boldly broke from the protective circle and leaped onto a convict's back, trying to ride him to the ground. A lieutenant aimed a gas gun at the convict's face from point-blank range. He pulled the trigger. But the convict had already ducked. And the charge exploded full in Bradley's face.

The captain fell to his knees, then to his face, wailing all the way down. The lieutenant knelt to solace his captain, and got slammed across the neck with a two-by-four. He crumpled, lay flat beside the captain. Bradley continued to wail.

A convict wrenched loose Bradley's gas club and rolled him on his side, gently. And while softly patting the captain's head, he shot him between the eyes, destroying the bridge of his nose. The convict then rapped the gas gun across Bradley's skull, and when he lay still and silent, pushed the club into his mouth. Standing up, he stared at the captain for a long moment, then kicked his mouth closed around the club, and strolled off, swallowed by the maelstrom of noise and battle and tears.

And through it all Kirk watched and vaguely wondered that he felt nothing. Nothing. There was in his mind only the memory of the splotch that was Zeke, the corpse that was Shorty; and before his eyes there were surrealistic scenes of carnage, of blood; and there was the gas hanging in the air—the gas made to make men flee, but which seemed only to anger them unto tears of fury. Yet with all of it, there was nothing with the power to reach through his numbness. Watching the madness before him, he was left with the feeling of having seen it all before, of witnessing what even an insensate fool, once having breathed of prison air, would have known must come. And for the first time while seeing mindless destruction of bone and flesh, he felt separated from it, not one with it, even frightened by it. He might have been at a movie, watching a street brawl, for no reality could be so mad, so terrible. Nothing was real, nothing but the stink of gas and Leslie.

And so with Leslie held close, he pushed and shoved and kicked a path toward G block, toward their cell where it would be safe to awaken. Convicts, now snarling, now laughing hysterically, occasionally snatched at Leslie's clothes, and he would stop momentarily to kick at them until they dropped or turned loose. Just short of the block doorway a cluster of guards held a convict spread-eagled, while one, a firm grip on each of the convict's ears, bashed his already pulpy skull against the concrete. The guard doing the bashing looked up and spotted Kirk staring at him. He smiled, bashful and abashed, as if to say that he loathed such distasteful but necessary duty. Kirk spit on him and kept going.

Directly before G block, a convict, teary-eyed and smiling happily, moved toward him, a guard's club held high. He may have been as friendly as his smile or as angry as his tears; Kirk didn't ask, didn't care. He leaned sideways and stomped a heel into the convict's groin, then yanked the club from his hand, and continued on through the door, into the block.

Nothing was real. It was all staged by a race of madmen, for madmen. The blood; the battered bodies; the occasional teeth crunching underfoot; the unrestrained tears flowing from red eyes. None of it real. Nothing but Leslie, and to that reality he clung.

About to enter the stairwell alcove, he noticed a gang of red- and wet-eyed convicts buggering LeRoy, who lay naked and broken-faced on the concrete. His friend, Iron Man, was presently in the saddle.

Turning away, he looked toward the guard's office. Just inside the door, Yancy, red-eyed, tears streaming, his face battered and bloody, was sitting on Rudy's chest, his thick hairy fingers sunk deep into the Mexican's throat.

It took a while for the scene to focus, and then Kirk was looking on with tears that might have been real, with a rage that made his legs shake, his stomach ache. He watched Yancy's hands leave the frail brown neck and slap Rudy awake, then once again strangle him unconscious. He watched Rudy's face turn a livid purple, eyes bulged and bleeding at the corners; he watched him twitch and writhe and foam at the mouth.

Only after watching all this repeated four times could he bring himself to believe it. *"Get off him, you scummy motherfucker!"* he screamed, moving toward Yancy, the club poised to smash his skull. *"You scum-sucker! You . . ."* He choked on the words, on tears, on the blackness welling up inside of him.

Yancy looked up, his eyes blank and dazed. And as Kirk neared, he rose from Rudy's chest, hands by his sides. He glanced down at the purple-faced Mexican, then back at Kirk, and shrugged.

Kirk continued toward him. "Why you? Why you?" he repeated over and over. Unable to think, to understand, with tears of anger making his vision swim, he stalked the big guard.

Yancy stood still, not raising his hands, staring as if in shock, bleeding, nothing more.

Within clubbing distance, Kirk looked down at the Mexican, saw him twitch, then stared at Yancy. "You bastard!" he hissed, and raised the club higher. A long frozen moment passed. Kirk vaguely

270

wondered at the weight of the club as it dropped slowly to his side; he stared for another long moment at the guard before suddenly hurling it into his stomach.

Wheeling, he ran toward the stairs, wanting only to leave the madness behind.

Halfway upstairs he remembered Leslie. Leaping back down, he dashed into the corridor in time to see Warden Benson, alone and unarmed except for a white plastic megaphone, step through the riot gate, the maelstrom boiling before him.

Benson lifted the megaphone and spoke through it. "Please," said his electric voice that seemed to come from everywhere. "Please."

Quiet washed down the corridor until there was an eerie hush. Movement ceased as eyes searched the warden's wrinkled face. Fists unclenched, weapons clanged and clunked loudly in the silence.

The warden's head swiveled, this way and that, and it seemed as if he looked at each man in turn, taking on all the guilt and misery, all the grief and hate that hung pall-like in the gas-reeking corridor.

"Please," he repeated. "Please, would some of you stay behind to help carry the hurt to the hospital? And, please, would the rest of you go to your cells?"

They went. Some woodenly, as if saying they had fought a good fight and were ready again at any time; others went on tiptoes, hoping perhaps that it would dull others' memories of their parts; but they went, and in minutes the hall was cleared of those who could walk. Many could not. Three never would.

Kirk stayed behind with Leslie. He watched Benson's daughter walk timidly in among carnage. She stopped for a second to stare down at Capt. Bradley's mangled face, then walked on to kneel beside a bleeding convict.

Those guards who had not beat a strategic retreat fell to, mumbling praise and sympathy to their own, whispering the birth of tomorrow's legends, and a greater hate.

The gas was almost gone now, and Kirk, too far removed from any of it, could do nothing but slump against the wall, rubbing at the stiffness of his face, at the tightness inside his skull, and watch Leslie as he stooped beside this convict and that, smiling down upon one, helping lift another onto a stretcher.

And that was when two stretcher-bearing convicts walked slowly

271

toward the hospital, carrying between them a twisted and tangled mess, half body, half amorphous ooze, all bloody. Zeke. Zeke, alive and staring at him.

Kirk spun, pushed his face hard against the wall. "Oh, no," he whispered, feeling everything inside him ripping loose. "Oh, no . . . no . . . God . . . where am I . . . ?" and vomited a poisonous black.

It might have been a century later when Leslie shook him back into the present. Shuddering, fevered, he turned to look up and down the corridor. He watched a guard wipe at the trickling blood under his nose and stare at the red wetness on his hand, then raise his eyes to look across the hall at a convict, also bloody-faced, who stared back at him. They stared and stared, and finally both walked off in different directions, still blind.

Kirk made himself glance down the corridor where Shorty had lain, and saw all that remained: a splotch of darker red against the red concrete. It was thick and gummy, with someone's footprints having disturbed the crusty scab of coagulation, tracking the corridor in memory of the seventeen years the little man had shuffled through it. Footprints of blood fading into nothing . . . Shorty's story was writ.

[XXXIX]

"Come on, baby," said Leslie, tugging at Kirk's hair. "Let's go see what Hank wants."

"Go ahead," he muttered in distraction. "I'm tired."

"You can't be tired. You've been moping in that damn bed for two weeks."

"Not moping, thinking." He eased Leslie an arm's length away.

"Oh, goofy," Leslie said petulantly. "When you do it, it's thinking; when I do it, it's moping. How come?"

Kirk could not stop the grin, but winced inwardly at the pain it caused him. "Because you're a fruit. Fruits mope." He stretched. "What day is it?"

"Get dressed and I'll tell you."

"By that time it'll be useless information."

Leslie flapped a hand in frustration. "And you talk about me acting like a bitch."

Reluctantly Kirk dressed.

And a while later he and Leslie went to the first floor to see Hank, who awaited them with a shining-skinned mulatto called Coco, a fruit with a delicate, feminine face, slinky, green eyes, and small breasts—leftovers from the days of dresses and silicon treatments. Where Leslie was something of a shock, Coco was electrifying. Kirk could not help staring.

Smiling sweetly, Leslie kicked him in the leg, and Hank pulled a tobacco pouch from a pocket and handed it to Leslie.

"Happy New Year," he said. "Roll your own. But make it last, that's the end of it."

Leslie opened the pouch and poured a pinch of marijuana into his palm, then kissed Hank's cheek.

With blazing eyes, Coco incinerated them both two or three times.

And Hank, caught in the middle, glanced uneasily from Coco to Leslie, back to Coco, and finally, chewing a thumb, cast Kirk a silent plea.

Kirk grinned silently. After all, Hank could have spared himself Coco's green-eyed death ray by merely putting the pouch in Kirk's hand. He surely would not have been kissed. His eyebrows weren't plucked.

Hank finally resolved the crisis by putting an arm around Coco. "I just buzzed by," he said in a rush, "to ask you two to come with us to the Jocker's Ball."

Kirk had heard tales of this . . . this New Year's revel. He would pass the invitation. "Thanks, anyway," he said, shaking his head negatively.

"We'll be there," Leslie said.

"No, we won't be there," Kirk said tiredly.

"We'll be there, Hank," Leslie reaffirmed.

"We'll be in the cell if you want us for anything," Kirk said, and started for the stairs, dragging Leslie behind.

"*He'll* be in the cell," Leslie said firmly, pulling away. "How about you taking me, too, Hank?"

Coco sneered.

Hank fidgeted.

"All right," Kirk said, stifling a grin. "We'll be there."

Everybody smiled.

273

"Come bombed," Hank said in parting. "It's easier to take that way the first time around." Then he walked up the corridor, a hand patting at the back of Coco's neck, while the fruit's hip patted his thigh at each jiggling step.

Kirk could not help staring, not until Leslie assisted him with a foot to the shin.

Later, when they went toward F block, where the festivities were being held, they were both bombed. Kirk was not altogether certain where he was, and that was good, for too much lately he was beginning to understand where he was; and that understanding was driving him deeper and deeper into some dark mind place where lay promises of blissful lunacy. But now there was nothing dark in sight, only bright, electric life colors.

Nearing F block a grating, scratchy sound pounded its way into his skull, the sound of age-old records played at full volume on an ancient phonograph with a thumbtack needle. Battling through the raucous vibrations, they finally made their way to the door of the block and were able to recognize the tune: "My Funny Valentine," sounding as if rendered by brokenhearted foghorns.

Other than the sight of what might have been a million convicts, all bumping, shoving, jostling, rude, crude, and officiously polite, the first thing Kirk noticed was the scent of talcum powder and perfume and cologne. The smell stuck in his marijuana-numbed nose, felt thick enough to blow out.

Next he saw convicts—men allegedly—wearing skirts and halters and less. One flounced about in a grass skirt. Several wore wigs of thread and string. And they danced, cheek to cheek and other ways. Some were slobbering and kissing on one another. Many were drunk or otherwise high, and pretending to be sober in such a way that everybody would be certain they were not.

And off to the side several guards, wearing faces of revulsion and wagging their heads in righteous indignation, watched and watched and watched.

Dancing and laughing, capering and sniggering, mincing and giggling, the convicts seemed mirthless, cloaked with a shroud woven of pathos and Stygian grotesqueness.

Though numb—and not solely by marijuana—he stared at the

274

spectacle until he saw what he was seeing. And then he saw some more; he saw ahead a year or maybe two; he saw Leslie, skirted and wigged, they were dancing. . . . He believed it. . . .

He would escape. A carbine bullet would be cleaner. . . .

He turned to Leslie to tell him of his decision, and spotted Farrell some 50 feet distant dancing with Iron Man, who was falling-down drunk. Farrell, wearing rouge and a frozen smile, danced with the grace of a peg-legged ballerina. When finally the music stopped hammering at eardrums, and the mindless yammering of strident voices took its place, Farrell pushed away from Iron Man and absently looked around. Then his eyes found Kirk's and lingered for a long, searching moment. He glanced at Leslie, who was oblivious to almost everything, then looked down at his hands. Turning abruptly, he strode toward the rear of the block, out of sight.

Kirk stared after him, wondering if there was somewhere a clock that could be turned back . . . but, no . . . there never was. . . . He turned to Leslie.

"Let's get out of here."

"Can't take it, huh?" Leslie hooked a hand around his elbow, looked up into his eyes. "This is part of the facts of life."

Kirk shook his head. "Not life."

With his eyes probing, Leslie said thoughtfully, "Tell me really, do you hate me?"

"Talk sense."

"I am talking sense. Do you hate me?"

"Let's go back to the cell—I'll show you how much."

"You can fuck me and still hate me."

"Leslie, you've been smoking too much. I don't hate you, I just don't particularly enjoy watching these creeps."

"Baby, have you ever stopped to think about what I am? I'm a queer . . . and the things I do and like are queer . . . at least to you. . . . I like watching these creeps, as you call them. And I don't think they're creepy."

"I do. And I go to bed with you. . . . What does that make me?"

"Hard up."

"You say."

"I know. Baby, deep down you hate me. I know you do. I just figured it out."

"Dry up."

"I won't." He grabbed Kirk's face with both hands. "Say, 'Leslie, I love you.' "

"You're acting like a damn fool."

"Say it, you bastard."

"It."

Leslie twisted Kirk's ears and shook his head around. Tears welling in his eyes spilled over, ran down the sides of his nose. "Say it, you bastard! Say it!"

"What in the fuck got into little Miss Muffet?" Kirk asked of the ceiling as his head rattled around.

Leslie suddenly released him and stood there grinning sheepishly. "Don't say it then, but you're still a bastard."

Kirk glanced around, saw that nobody was particularly interested in them, and said, "What I meant before you went into your thing was let's run away."

Leslie stared at him with eyes gone wide. "What?"

"Let's get out of this garbage can."

"Serious?"

"Maybe for the first time in my life."

"When?"

"I don't know yet."

"How?"

"I don't know that, either."

"Did you just say that to shut me up? Are you going to leave me parked here?"

"Don't talk stupid."

"That's not so stupid when you hate me like you do. Anyway, I love you. . . . Let's go to the cell."

"That's what I've been saying. . . ."

"What? That you love me?"

"You've been blowing too much ha-ha."

"You haven't had enough. How about you blowing a joint and I will, too?" He wagged his tongue around.

"Let's go."

"That's what I've been saying."

"No, that's what I've been saying."

"Let's fight about it."

"In bed?"

"Yep."

They traded sniggers, then told Hank that they were leaving, and went toward the door, arm in arm.

Near the door Kirk watched from what seemed a vast distance as Farrell ghosted up beside them and plunged an ice pick into Leslie's heart.

Time froze, seconds melted past with the speed of a glacial floe.

Leslie, rooted to the spot, watched Farrell duck back into the crowd, then looked down at the wooden haft protruding from the center of his chest. He turned to Kirk with an apologetic smile as his legs became rubbery and he slumped toward the floor.

Unthinking, Kirk's head flew back and from his mouth bellowed a roar to shake the building. The block was instantly hushed. He dropped to his knees, caught Leslie before he could hit the floor. Then he was up, screaming for Hank, racing through a suddenly grown opening in the crowd.

Gravity sucked at his heels, a viscous syrup.

Yet somehow, and it seemed much later, he made it to the hospital. He kicked the door until it was thrown open, raced past a wide-eyed orderly to the second, then the third floor. Leslie, limp across his arms, was no weight at all. If only his heels would not drag so. Finally at the operating room, he kicked open the door, ran inside, laid Leslie on the green-covered table.

Then he was back in the hall, yelling. He screamed for a surgeon, a doctor, a medicine man. He begged God, Mary, and the Holy Ghost. He fell to his knees beseeching Allah, Yahweh, Mary Baker Eddy. He prayed to Abaddon, promised his soul; cried to the saints, offered love; implored Lucifer, swore fidelity; entreated the gods, pledged sacrificial blood.

Hank came running.

Back of him a doctor hurried.

Tearing his hair, clawing his face, Kirk dropped, lay prone on his face. "Leslie . . . Leslie," he whispered, "I love you," then gnawed at the skin on his arm, tearing it away, and could talk no more. He wept. Tears poured forth as water from a riven dike, welling up from the bottom of his being.

Morning came, a feeble gray light, and shortly afterwards the warden keyed open the isolation-cell door and stepped inside.

Kirk stared toward him, his vision swimming. "Get the fuck out of here!" he screamed at Benson, then once again ceded to the pain that was his master, a master of whom he could ask no questions, and wept, noiselessly, tearlessly, but completely.

The warden sat on the bunk beside Kirk and clasped his shoulder. "Your friend is alive."

Kirk was not listening but heard anyway, droning words that stumbled one over another, incoherent, meaningless.

"Leslie is alive," Benson said, and shook his shoulder.

His mind toyed with it. Then suddenly from far away a glaring, blinding thing blasted into his consciousness. With hammering pulse and muscles drawn taut, he leaped from the bunk and spun naked and feral to face the warden. Through bared teeth he hissed, "Are you lying?" and was ready to take a long time listening for the wrinkled-faced man's last wheezing breath.

Benson looked down at the floor, then back at him. "I do my best not to lie, Whalen," he said quietly. "Would you like to go with me to see Leslie?"

Kirk crumpled against the wall. Pleasure ripped through his skull, made his ears ring and his knees weak. And then he straightened up, bouncing around and yelling. "Let's go! Let's go!" and ran through the open door.

Smiling faintly, Benson stopped him and pointed to the isolation coveralls he had never thought to don. "How about putting them on?"

Kirk hopped into them, hoppped out the cell door pulling them on. And back of him the warden walked so slowly.

But ages later they made it across the corridor and into the hospital, taking more ages to climb to the second floor, where the patients were roomed.

Hank met them, a smile lighting his sharp face. Through blurred vision Kirk saw a halo around the weasel-like head and did not dispute it.

They arrived at long last before a door that the warden eased open, and the three of them silently entered.

Leslie lay on the bed in the corner of the small room, under an oxygen tent, unconscious. Through the rhythmically expanding and contracting plastic cover, tubes could be seen running into his arms and nostrils.

Beyond emotion, Kirk leaned against the wall and stared. He

was floating, weightless, in a place without time; the only noise anywhere was the ringing in his ears.

A while later Benson laid a hand on his arm and the present came back. Hank and the warden led him from the room.

And once out the door, he squeezed his eyes shut, rubbed at his temples. It would take some time to catch up with all that had happened.

The warden coughed. "Whalen, do you know who stabbed him?"

Without thinking Kirk nodded.

"Would you tell me who?"

Eyes averted, he cursed himself. By now he should know better than ever to answer a question before first considering the merit of all possible answers but the truth. Perhaps in another six months or a year it would be a conditioned reaction. Turning to Benson, he screwed on his face a look of mild curiosity. "How can I tell you, Warden? I don't know."

"But . . . didn't you . . . ?" The warden's baffled expression turned into a tired smile. "All right," he said simply. And after a long pause he went on: "I assume you know that you were taken to isolation because it was thought you knew who stabbed him."

Kirk shrugged; he had not thought about it.

"Well," Benson continued, slowly and thoughtfully, "what would happen to him—this fellow you don't know—if you were released from isolation?" His eyes probed for Kirk's reaction.

Staring vacantly at the floor, he thought about it. "Nothing," was his answer and the truth. Had Leslie died . . . who could say . . . ? But he had not, and reviewing everything from the beginning to the frail body on the hospital bed, he found injustice only in the fact that the ice pick had been driven through the wrong heart. Thinking of Farrell excited no anger in him, only curiosity, but of a detached sort, without emotion. Yesterday he might have called his curiosity pity, even guilt. But not today, for Farrell had had both the opportunity and the ice pick, and sought to kill one who had toyed with him, rather than the one who had made of him a toy. A poor choice.

The warden, suddenly with a wide smile, clapped his hands together and said, "Come on, Whalen, I'll walk back to isolation with you and leave orders for them to release you in the morning."

Back in isolation, Benson got the cell-door key from the guard

279

on duty and went with Kirk to his cell. Following him inside, they sat side by side on the bunk. After studying his hands for a while, Benson spoke.

"Four men have been killed since I've been here," he said quietly, distantly. "I guess that's not supposed to bother me since it's a lower rate than average." His chuckle was a bed of nails upon which the tender are maimed. "What's wrong with these places?"

"Got time for three million words?"

Benson wove his fingers together and studied them for a moment. "You know they spend more than two billion dollars a year running places like these? And you know what comes out of them?"

"Man-kissers."

The warden chuckled. "Yeah, them, too. But the man-kissers are about the most human we let go. If every fellow in here had a Leslie, we might be able to save maybe three-quarters of them. That'd be about three times the number that are able to save themselves despite what we do to them." His chuckle was sardonic. "The public hollers about the homosexuality in the prisons they build and they don't have the faintest idea of the murder and rape it spares them. On the other hand, of course, they have a pretty good idea of the robbers and murderers born in these places. But they go on building them . . . Why?"

" '. . . Ours not to reason . . .' et cetera," Kirk said with a bitter laugh. "But seriously, I don't know. And I don't think I like them enough to care."

"You don't care about them; they don't care about you. Where does it all end?"

"In ashes."

"Must it?"

"Doc, places like these are built—with the walls and all the rest of the dark mystery—so people can hide from themselves what they most fear about themselves." He grinned. "Duality is nothing I thought up, but it intrigues me whenever I let it. Sometimes I'm so damn nice, I think I'd make Albert Schweitzer feel like an evil old man. Other times I flatten people's skulls. And inside of everybody are the same things that're inside me—maybe not to quite the extremes. But if I can look in the mirror and see baby-rapers and saints, I can also see enough to know that crime wouldn't stop if they locked up every wrongdoer in the world, including the mousy little guys with three kids and money in the bank." He stared around the cell with unseeing eyes, then continued. "See, Doc, people don't think. Who's going to argue with that?" Not Benson, so Kirk went on. "But think or not, they have some sort of compulsion to dare the gods, to look to the stars, even without knowing the significance of what they're looking at or for. On the other hand, they don't—or won't—look down; they refuse to see what they're walking in or where. They'll shoot a man to the moon, then slog through blood and gore shooting others through the head. They'll make hearts of eternal plastic and plant them in bodies with plastic brains. And through all of it they'll preach and teach love of man and brotherhood—things that can't be taught—and meantime take the man out of man. . . ." He leaned against the wall, staring at the doctor. "And from a thousand miles in the sky, they'll laugh at things that aren't funny while a kid grows into a killer, and a killer into a man-kisser. . . ."

There was a long silence before Benson spoke.

"Whalen," he said slowly, "when do you go back to the board?"

Kirk filled the cell with a poisonous laugh. "Five years."

Placing a hand on his shoulder, Benson said, "Help me, Whalen. Help me, and I'll get you back to the board early."

Kirk gazed at him for a few moments, then snorted. "Now you sound nuttier than me. Maybe you want me to take the stand against somebody . . . ?"

Benson smiled. "Knock it off. If it sounded like I was trying to bribe you, I'm sorry. I'm not, but I probably would if I thought I could get away with it."

"Hell, Doc," Kirk said, laughing, "at least try. I bribe easy. What do you want help with?"

"Saving lives."

Staring at him, Kirk wanted to tell him that he sounded ridiculous, even puerile, yet within himself, as surely as his heartbeat, he felt the man's sincerity. "Doc," he said finally, "that makes three people I know with starry eyes. I just put you in a pot with a weasel-faced three-time loser and a teary-eyed fag. You like the company?"

"Would I be here if I didn't?"

"Would Bradley or Lowry?"

"Forget I asked. But you can never tell; if there are three, there might be more."

"Thousands born every day," Kirk conceded. "But what do you have five, ten, or fifteen years later when the dove is dead and the olive branch an ash?"

"Can't we hope that someday men won't tamper with humanness?"

"The bridge is out just ahead—you're going to stop this runaway train with hope?"

"You're half my age, and you've already given up."

Kirk answered with a shrug and a mirthless laugh.

"I've got the ear of a friendly congressman," Benson continued, looking closely at Kirk. "Don't repeat this or you might put my tit in a wringer, maybe the whole deal." Without awaiting Kirk's assurances, he went on. "Okay, I have a man in Congress who's drafting three bills I outlined. Chances are about 50 to one that they'll laugh them off the floor. But if I had a couple or four inmates who could talk to them, I might have a fighting chance to squeeze even one of them through. It might upset their complacency to learn that convicts don't mutter out of the sides of their mouths or walk on all fours. . . ."

"Not a chance, Doc," Kirk broke in. "They'd probably hate you for it. If you could prove white was black, you'd upset them till they got used to it; but if you showed them that white and black are joined by shades of gray, you'd insult them. Men become righteous by denying their dark sides . . . and if they didn't think they were right—a hundred percent right—how could they believe in their supreme importance? No, you'd have a rash of congressmen taking the long jump or something if you started meddling with their sanctified guidelines."

"It's not that bad," Benson said. "The way you would have it, nothing would ever get done. People would still live in caves."

"Doc, you've been leading a sheltered life. People do still live in caves—caves of the spirit, mental caves. The other kind they at least figured out how to get out of." He paused for a breath, not for long. "Look what they did to Galileo, Socrates, and everybody else who ever threatened to take off their blinders. Look what they do in the name of God and country, the Hitlers and McCarthys and all the twisted righteous men they're able to rally—including that strangest of all beasts, the common man. And when the periodic geniuses come along to explain laws of the universe, what happens? The righteous pervert the knowledge into atomic bombs and other

282

infernal machines, curse the tomorrows of a whole planet." He took another needed breath and looked at Benson. "No, Doc, don't bother telling me that goodness and wisdom will triumph, it's inconceivable. Look at me, Doc, look at me. I'm their reflection; magnified sometimes and distorted, but still their reflection. They're me; I'm them. And they've hidden me here. . . . I don't exist. . . . And now you want to tell me that wisdom and light is just around the corner."

"Some speech," Benson said with a grin. "But you're wrong. And if everybody was of your mind, another generation or two would see the end of men. There must be people willing to fight for everybody's tomorrows. Look at your generation; they're doers, fighters. . . ."

"Doc," Kirk broke in, "if you looked real close, you wouldn't say that. The majority, like always, are perverters of the leaders' idealism. They say that the old and established must go. They're probably right, but replaced with burned buildings what do you have . . . ?"

"Scratch a cynic, wound a romantic," said Benson, smiling faintly. "And you're too damn young to be bleeding all over. Bandage the wounds, Whalen, and do something with yourself, something for everybody."

Straight-faced, Kirk held his arms wide, silently blessing the multitudes. Benson chuckled, sounding as if he were being strangled.

"Okay, Doc," said Kirk, relenting, "what're the bills you mentioned?"

"Okay," Benson echoed, sitting straighter. "First, I want them to lift the ban on alcoholic beverages." He flapped a hand at Kirk's curled lip. "I'm not one of those who think alcoholism is a quote disease unquote." He paused for a moment, frowning. "You see, I have an idea that alkies can drink socially as long as they have a guardian angel, so to speak, on whom they may lean until they're able to walk alone, until they're able to straighten whatever emotional kink they may be burdened with. And if it can be shown that they're able to drink normally, it'll mean not only a saving of about a billion taxpayer dollars a year, but also a saving of lives and families—plus enabling the men themselves to be taxpayers and taking their families off relief." The doctor looked up at the ceiling.

Kirk looked down at the floor. "One thing you ain't, Doc: a warden."

Benson continued. "The second one would allow either furloughs or conjugal visits." Kirk laughed at that and when he ran down, Benson added, "with women."

"Doc, your prejudice is showing. Don't knock boys till you've tried them."

A dry chuckle, and Benson said, "There're other places that allow it, and 90 percent or more of the prisoners don't get around to trying boys."

"They'll laugh you off the floor. And if they don't, they'll grant it only for married convicts. So guys like me will still be saddling hairless boys."

"But we have to start somewhere. . . ."

"Or not at all. . . ."

Benson shrugged. "Anyway, the third one is to let fellows like yourself tell us what we're doing wrong. In other words, fellows who get out and want to help could become counselors and counselor aides. You see, the way we're going, we'll never get anywhere. You understand these men and their motivations better than I ever will. And if I can't empathetically equate, then all I *can* be is a warden. I don't want that. I want fellows who can rest a foot in the convicts' world and another in mine, and tell me how to steer this ship. We've been building these places blind for two centuries, and each time we hit an obstruction and sink, we build another blind ship with all the same built-in blunders, and try again."

"You know what would be quicker and a lot less painful for everybody?" Kirk asked. "Just let the garbage cans rot. You can't turn a rusted tin can into much else but another tin can that'll eventually rust. And these dumps are like tin cans: they can't become other than what they are: cesspools. And if they can't change, can't evolve, then they have to finally die. And they're well withered now, so just lay back and enjoy the fire, Doc."

"Is that what you would do if you were me—enjoy the fire?"

"I'm probably not as smart as you. Besides, I'm antisocial, a psychopath—and that's just for starters. I don't know any better than to complain and howl at the moon; it's my nature.

"Will you help me?"

"Yes."

In the wake of the riot the prison was left hushed and subdued, its orgasm over, resting for the next one. But somehow he saw light just ahead, elusive and flickering, but light. And though he was without Leslie now, he felt less an alien, less alone. A dark and frothing mind is loneliness; a quiet mind with light is solitude; solitude is good.

But on the sixth day after the beginning of the new year the light, ever flickering, faded, died.

"Tell me you're joking, Hank . . . please tell me you're joking . . ." Kirk said, almost whispering; the corridor whirling around his head gagged him with fear and disbelief.

"I tried to tell you before," Hank said, his voice a hammer smashing Kirk's skull. "He was too heavy for them. It was a matter of them getting crushed or dropping him. They dropped him."

With eyes squeezed shut, Kirk rubbed at the ache in his temples. "Hank, Hank, Hank," he mumbled, "go slow. They can't fire him. . . . He wouldn't quit. . . ."

"But he did," Hank broke in. "Look, his daughter was seeing too much of a guy working in the hospital. Lowry and the captain got word from some rat—nobody knows who—and they put a stake-out on the broad. They didn't catch her with her clothes off, but they beat on a locked door for ten minutes before she showed. . . . And she was closeted alone with a convict. What more do the guardians of purity and virtue need?" He laughed bitterly. "So they put it to him: either step down or the newspapers would hear of it. And his daughter helped a lot, too. Instead of clamming up, not admitting anything, in front of everybody she tells Benson to let the newspapers have it, it don't matter because she loves the guy, wants to marry him. Nice broad, but not too bright."

"But what could the newspapers have done with that besides get sued?"

"They could have just reported the facts, and one of the facts is that after Benson knew about the episode, he ordered the convict released from the hole and reinstated on the same job. It's just a step from there to exposing to the public all the little things he's been doing that the brainless idiots out there call 'coddling the prisoner.' And I suppose he stepped down because he'd made about three inches headway and didn't want it erased. I guess the doc is hoping somebody else'll gallop up on a white horse and pick up the banner."

Kirk, silent, turned away and walked numbly toward the block. The gallow's trap had sprung; he dropped, dropped. . . . When would he hit bottom . . . ? He dropped, dropped. . . .

"Kirk!" Hank called back of him. "Kirk, Leslie was awake for a while today. She said to tell you 'be good' and she'll be better quick. . . ."

Kirk heard nothing, kept walking.

It took him days to cover the prison grounds, sneaking where he was not allowed, mentally mapping every nook and cranny, trying to discover a way out or create one. Nothing else mattered, no other thoughts could live in his mind. He studied angles from this gun tower to that, from another gun tower to cover; he calculated roof slopes and blind spots and camouflage and niches in the wall. He asked discreet questions, picked brains, and walked and paced and studied some more. And drew a blank. Nothing.

Oh, he might get away with a hostage even though the towers were ordered to shoot regardless. He might get away if this or that stretch of ground could be covered without being seen. He might get away by tossing a Molotov cocktail into this or that gun tower. He might get away if only he had five or ten or fifteen reliable convicts to work with, but he did not and never would, for one prisoner in three had his soul leased to custody and it took only one word from any of their legions to put him in isolation for the winter, the next one, too.

Depression, with her gargoyle sister, despair, seized him, dragged him down, down.

And lurking there in his mind was Leslie . . . Leslie . . . that unrelenting and ineradicable vision of Leslie. . . . It brought him calm and anger, peace and near hysteria, serenity and nightmares. He would be out of the hospital in six or seven weeks. An interminally long time . . . but so few short days. . . . Leslie, at once his wings and his chains. . . .

He could not get Leslie out of his mind; he could not get himself out of Alhondiga.

But on the fourteenth morning after Leslie was stabbed nothing seemed to matter. Nothing.

He was showering when giggling but shy Tudi came to bathe, dolling. And he did, but not before Kirk, with Tudi before him, bent like a broken shotgun, was finished. Hairoil is good, vaseline is better, but soap will do in a tight spot. Dolling.

There was Annie followed by Ruth followed by Tudi again. Then Sally, then Lola, then Linda, then Frenchie. Came Sugar and Honey and Candie; and to prod time's hounds: April, Mae, June, and Summer. He spent himself on Pearl, Diamond, and Rubi. Then Ty and Kim and Toni and Vicki and Becky and Cherry and Wendy the witch. . . . Ah, yes, not to be forgotten were Charley, Big Jim, Rex, and Rocky; the name of this game being "Can-you-keep-a-secret?" Sure. Certainly. Yes, you *can* . . . but . . .

And "Roll 'em over" Gerty. She tried to she you. And she got his eye blackened. Repeatedly.

And Mary. Congenitally hairless Mary. Pleasant, amiable, plumply pretty—if you find boys pretty. At the head of his (her?) bed, glued fast to the wall: a huge crucifix. Bed chatter: the Lord's Prayer, and Hail Marys . . . CoNsTaNtLy . . . HaIl MaRy, FuLl Of GrAcEeSe. . . .

But with the twin brothers (sisters?) Heckle and Jeckle, Kirk met his match.

They liked him, they said. And they were kind of cute. For boys.

They would give him a carton of cigarets if they could nibble on his body. A couple of cute little things.

Two fruits at once? Why, he would have paid them. They were cute, Heckle and Jeckle.

He was invited to strip and did. And then was invited by Jeckle (or was it Heckle? It was difficult to be certain) to kneel face down beside the bed.

Hold it a minute! That didn't sound right, not at all. Fucking boys, that's one thing; but getting fucked . . . ? Oh, no, he wasn't ready for that. What did they think he was, queer or something?

Of course not, dear.

And so along with their bushels of smiling reassurance he complied, but kept a wary eye peering over his shoulder.

Heckle, or maybe the other one, crawled under the bed and gave him a tongue bath. Nice, but ordinary enough.

And Jeckle, or maybe Heckle, used his tongue, too. But for a prostate massage . . . ?

There is a lot to be said for it—quite a lot in fact—but when you're buggering boys, the step from a tongue to a whammer is only a matter of inches. . . .

So there he was, back playing with himself.

But only for a while; it gets tiresome, abysmally tiresome.

He searched for something new, and his search was rewarded by barbiturates, opiates, amphetamines, and other, even stranger and more exotic drugs. The prick, the little drop of blood, then watching while the rubber bulb beat back blood pressure, pumped the liquid into a vein. And the explosion, the brilliant red and white fire burning, searing through brain passages.

And for the first time in his life he came into tune with the universe.

Days floated by without pain, emotional travail. Life, as such, was good. He had found his niche. He needed nobody. All his world, all the world he wanted lived on the ceiling of his cell. He was content to watch, and he did, and slept.

But one day, after a quarter grain of morphine, Yancy stepped into his cell and for a while unbalanced the cosmos.

"The least you could do is hide the outfit and wash the blood off your arm," Yancy said quietly.

"Fuck your mother."

"Kirk . . . let me talk to you. . . ."

"Fuck your mother."

"Kid, what you need is a good ass-kicking."

"Or maybe a little strangulation. . . . Now why didn't you think of that before . . . ?"

"Kid . . ."

"Do one of three things, you hideous asshole: take me to the hole, kick my ass, or get the fuck out of here and go fuck your hair-lip mother."

"Kid . . . lighten up on me. . . . I'm just a dumb bull. . . ."

"To tell the truth."

"The Mex killed a guy. . . ."

"Why didn't you just kill him back?" Kirk snarled, breathing hard. "You know what you did to him, you gruesome bastard? He can't talk, he doesn't have a brain any more. And now they're going to make him breathe their gas." He sat up and waited until the blood found its way to his head, then stood and snatched up the cell broom. "Either get out of my cell or I'm shoving this down your ugly face."

Hands hanging, Yancy stood there and looked at Kirk, his eyes mirroring torment. "Let me talk to you, kid," he said quietly, unmoving.

Kirk slammed the broom to the floor and pushed past the guard, heading for the door.

But Yancy grabbed him, lifted him to the bunk like a bale of rags. He felt like that, too.

"Listen to me, kid," Yancy said, more than half pleading, "I ain't trying to say I'm a swell fella. I told you before I'm just a simple slob trying to get past this rotten bastard in one piece. All right, so maybe I ain't done too swell a job. But I hate Mexicans. . . . Yeah, I know it's crazy, but I still remember how the little bastards used to rub my face in horse shit when I was a kid; I never got big enough to forget it maybe." He looked down at the floor. "Look, I'd had a bad time. My head'd been mashed a couple times. Then I told those three to up their shivs and they came for me. I had a big shitter brush. . . . Two of them ran. . . . After that I don't remember too much. . . ."

"I'm doing ten years for less."

"But didn't you kill a guy . . . ?"

"That's not what I had in mind . . . and I didn't torture him."

"Kid, I'm sorry. I'm sorry. Does that make a difference?"

"You're too big and ugly to snivel. Get away from me, Yancy, and don't come around any more. Not ever."

"Kirk, clean yourself up. Leslie will be back soon. . . ."

"Check the newspapers for Sunday school positions. . . . They're always looking for assholes like you—I'm not."

"You're looking for something, kid. What is it?"

"I'm looking for you to get the fuck out of here."

"I like you, kid. . . . I'm sorry . . . sorry it came to this. . . ."

Kirk sat up, screaming. *"Get the fuck out of here, you bastard!"*

"Climb out of it, kid. Climb out before they shovel the dirt in."

Yancy walked from the cell, heavy of foot.

And after he had gone, Kirk pumped another quarter grain of morphine into his arm. "Yancy . . . Yancy," he whispered into the pillow, tearing at it with his teeth, "you dirty low-life bastard . . ." and passed out.

* * *

289

More days. More morphine. Only morphine, for nothing else could bring such blessed euphoria, such tingling to his skin. Life, as such, was good.

Then there came the afternoon when he dissolved two quarter grains, injected them in a vein, and lay back to take a slow-motion romp of his ceiling world, and a drawn, death-headlike face appeared. "Hi," it said, looking very gloomy and sad.

Ah, he thought with a sort of joyful foreboding, now the voices start. The face was magically transformed into a little pink hand that tugged at his hair. Hmmm . . . odd. . . . Then the hand went away and the face came back, blinking. Kirk blinked, too, several times, but could not rid his vision of the thin and spectral-like image of Leslie.

"Go 'way," he mumbled at it.

But it did not; instead, it smiled—a soft and tired smile—and said, "Baby, it's me."

Kirk covered his eyes. Something pulled at his fingers. He ventured to peek with one eye. And even numb he knew that spirits and apparitions don't lift fingers from your eyes. Yes, it looked a little like Leslie . . . even talked like him. . . . Eerie; very eerie indeed. Then it lifted him and poured coffee down his throat, steaming coffee that did not feel a bit hot. But most of it did not get down his throat, and for the mess he made, he was slapped. That hurt. Even numb, that hurt. And when he was slapped a second time, he began to wonder if maybe there was as much here as met the eye. . . .

He glanced furtively around the cell, making certain that nobody else was near, and asked tentatively, "Leslie . . . ?"

"Gawd!" exclaimed the specter.

And that did it, all the wretched world crashed back to reality, gloom. He cursed and cursed and cursed.

"What an absolutely lovely welcome," Leslie said, his thin face pouting. "At least you could kiss me or tell me how dreadful I look . . . or something."

Kirk thought about it, then began sniggering, couldn't stop.

Or not until Leslie threw a couple of cups of cold water on him.

Then he began feeling miserable and abject and confused. His mouth tasted as if he had eaten a mattress; his stomach was a pit of snakes; his brain a sty of stinking black muck. But finally he was able to form a coherent thought: Leslie is back, not looking well or even very much alive, but he is back. He held out his arms, and Leslie came to him, warm and real.

But the warmth and reality frightened him, chased away his chilled but secure world of fantasy. He cursed himself for holding out his arms, then cursed Leslie, and the world.

"Baby," said Leslie sometime later, "you look worse than me. Even your thing looks starved."

"It hasn't had any exercise." That made him bite his lip. "At least for a while. But I couldn't look worse than you—you look awful."

"You're sweet."

"But it's true. Don't let it get you down, though—I feel worse than you look."

"I'll bet," Leslie said, and after a thoughtful pause added with a rush, "Baby, do you want me back?" His lips curled in concern.

"Do you want me?"

"Why shouldn't I?"

Kirk closed his eyes, remained silent while his insides writhed with memories of where he had been.

"Oh, silly," Leslie said finally, with the tone of a mother cutting her baby's long, curly hair for the first time, "you know I don't listen to anything anybody says about you. And even if it was all true, if you like me best, who cares?" He did, obviously, but smiled bravely, if a little sadly. "Hey, look," he went on, as if trying to leave the subject behind, and pulled open his shirt, exposing a long, diagonal scar, lumpy and pink, across the middle of his chest. "Do you still like me a little . . . ?" His voice, heavy with concern, shaded with guilt, smothered Kirk.

"Leslie . . ." he said, almost choking, and exposed the needle tracks on his arms. "You still like me a little?"

"Are we okay again?"

"Are we?"

"Damn you," Leslie said, frowning, and touched his face. "You haven't even smiled at me or anything. Say something nice. . . ."

"I'm the guy who needs petting and three legs to stand on. If you start needing the same things as me, we're both going to have to go shopping." He grinned. "I'm still smashed."

"That was a lovely little speech," Leslie said, smiling now, beginning to look more as Kirk remembered him. Then he frowned. "Baby, are you going to keep on like this?"

"Like what?"

"Like sticking that stuff in your arms?"

"No . . . yes . . . I don't know. Don't pry. Get out of my face." Anger began to stir his sluggish heart.

"Okay," Leslie said, and rose from the bunk. He went to the locker and rummaged through it. "How long has it been since you've eaten?"

"This morning . . . yesterday. . . . Quit fucking with me."

"There's not even anything to eat in here," Leslie persisted.

Kirk sat up. Slowly. "Damn it, Leslie," he said petulantly, "don't start right off like that." He rubbed his temples and finally smiled. Deep within he felt a banked fire sputter to life. "Okay, I'm a creep. Yeah, I'm glad to see you; I like your scar; I like you; you've been haunting me; you look bad but God-awful good. Come here, Leslie, please come here. . . ."

Leslie did, soft, serene.

[XLI]

He sat on the edge of the bunk and stared into the darkness outside. The night grew old, and still he stared, making himself think, digging inside his skull with a shovel full of burrs and barbs.

He had been a little way up, but mostly down. Down so far that death seemed a lofty goal; up so far that sodomy smelled like life.

He had killed a man, a man smelling of putrefaction, of the gutter, of vomit and flophouses and foul red wine; a man whose face he had never seen, would never see; a man who had perhaps known love, probably hate; a wino, a derelict; a weak and feeble creature who died smelling of the grave and whining; but for all that, a man.

And perhaps he had killed his father, the almost-man who had been enough man to sire him; the scarred man who had scarred him inside and out; the poisoned man who had poisoned him with the lash of leather; the unheroic man who had demanded that his son "act like a man," and pissed his pants in fear; but for all that, a man.

And he tried to remember his mother, that hazy someone who

292

had given birth to him, but not life, and who had smothered him with lilac-talcumed arms; the mother who had looked pained while he was tortured and twisted, and who went on looking pained. He wished he could remember her face, but there was nothing in his memory but that smell.

And then to prison, where he had learned how childish was his childhood hate, and had learned a hate that had real teeth, death's teeth. And he had gladly thrown himself body and soul into the chill, carnivorous fires of the prison.

And then he had been dragged from the chill by lust for a fag, a big-butt boy who came on his navel and got little-girl embarrassed; a fruit, built like a man, but not, upon whom he must lean or die inside; a nut-nuzzling, pink-assed pervert who cared, that care growing fragile scabs over purulent wounds; a shaven-legged fairy who had pointed the way to other shaven-legged fairies. . . .

And when the grease had worn thin, or whatever it was that had pulled him up, he stumbled into the cobwebbed lair of Lady Death, the deadest death of them all: morphine.

Then Leslie again, bringing him back to a reality more maddening than any fantasy. And both wanting to and not, he found himself clinging again, clinging to Leslie, while all around a desolate quagmire sought to claim its own. With feelings of futility and uselessness, he wanted only to fall back, sink to oblivion, yet he fought up, up, and knew not why.

Once again the pungent scent of sodomy filled his nose. But there seemed a difference now. For as he stared toward the lights atop the distant night-black wall, he smelled death's harbinger. He smelled it, but death no longer held yesterday's allure.

He reached down and touched Leslie's sleeping face, gently traced his brow. From a dark corner a fear stepped out, ugly and full-grown: free of the muck sucking at his heels, he would be free of Leslie. Was it a freedom he wanted? Would the gray come back? overwhelm him? Had he the courage to battle demons alone?

Or would he lie in bed buggering the fag who had twice pulled him from the edge of the abyss? The fruit who fed his seed to the fish and disguised the fetid stink of death with pink lights and perfume and squeeze-bottle douches?

Leslie was the good in him, and his fetter to the devils; Leslie, a bent bar in the dark jail that kept secret the light deep within himself; around Leslie he could see the light, weak and feeble, but could reach toward it only so far, no further; Leslie, at once his salvation and his coffin.

And Leslie loved him. . . .

Kirk stared down at him, touched him. He wondered if the quiet ache in his chest was pity or compassion or a hunger for warmth or the stirrings of love. . . . Perhaps all of them. . . . Perhaps only love; Jean Valjean's love for Javert, Caesar's for Brutus. A love that would chain him to the heavy scent of sodomy until he turned to dust. . . .

Or until he could get out. . . .

But how . . . ?

The foolish attempt on the roof had failed.

The tunnel had caved in.

Benson was gone.

How then? How?

No way.

Or was there . . . ? He could work for a parole. He could take up a trade program, learn to fix dents in metal fenders in an age of plastic; take up group counseling, vent his spleen to a sergeant of the guards because the potatoes were too soggy or not soggy enough; he could cede entirely the will for moral initiative, however immoral, and become a Model Prisoner, the most twisted and dangerous beast of all; he could talk 15 minutes a year with his "counselor," and a little more often with Dr. Steiner; he could learn the social graces from Capt. Bradley and (now) Warden Lowry; he could learn virtue and righteousness from Sgt. Carol. But he would not, for a hangman's noose was too easy to make, and if nothing else, make one he would.

Somewhere there must be answers, a path through the mire he had encircled himself with. But were there answers to slay even a small devil? He had so many.

It began to grow light outside, but the gloom did not lift. He searched it for answers, for a glimpse of tomorrow, for the key to the lock that pent his sickness inside him, for the weapon that would kill the murderer-rapist-thief that skulked through his inner gloom.

Would the murk never leave him? It had become so terrible that even his vision was hazed, fogged—?

Fog!

"Leslie! Leslie!" His heart thumping in his ears, he grabbed a handful of Leslie's hair. "Leslie," he repeated as the little fruit stirred and worked open his eyes. "We're getting out of this death trap. . . . We're getting out!"

"What's happening, baby?" Leslie asked with a curious frown.

"Fog," he said, trying to control his trembling voice. "Fog. I can't see the wall."

"Oh, that." Leslie rubbed his eyes. "When it comes in," he said, almost indifferently, "they bring in extra guards and make them walk the wall. . . ."

Kirk thought about it for a fraction of a second, then: "Are you game?"

"Now."

"Does the fog get worse than this?"

"Later this month. . . . But usually in late March there're a couple days when it gets like dirty cotton candy."

Kirk bounced off the bunk, his teeth clenched around the ecstatic joy singing through him.

"He's yust a wittle baby," said Leslie in baby talk, and lay back, smiling.

Kirk finally sat down, tried to be practical. "How's your health? In all seriousness."

"I can do anything I've ever done, but I'm sort of wobbly on my feet."

"Start exercising, running around the yard. Don't kill yourself, but push hard, there's not much time."

Leslie didn't argue.

And Kirk went on, weaving plans, ironing out minor difficulties, ignoring impossibilities. He was going over the wall, whether he was alive or dead on the other side really did not matter; either way, it would be a good trade.

[XLII]

"Yeah, Hank, I'm serious," Kirk said, and added a wry smile. "I might even be dead serious."

Hank laughed. "I'm about ready to kiss you."

"Fuck around, and you'll get kissed back. I play that shit, too." He grinned. "Listen, I came around to ask you for a few things." He looked down at the floor. "You know, while Leslie was gone, I blew over 600 dollars . . . and now that Rudy's locked up, I don't feel up to trying to fill the gap. . . ."

Hank broke in. "How much you got left?"

"Six seventy."

Hank's eyebrows furrowed in thought. "Don't sweat it," he said finally. "I got enough for the three of us."

"But I need something else that's going to cost."

"What?"

"I want to go over near the tower they put Dunn in. I need to find out when he's on, days and hours."

Hank frowned. "Yeah, that'll cost. . . ." He brightened. "Doesn't matter. Carol'd sell his grandmother's hobnailed boots." He paused, and added slowly, "You know how dangerous it'll be to get that information . . . ? You wouldn't be the first guy that ran into a setup. . . ."

"I'll take my chances."

"When're you going to make the move?"

"Leslie says late March is best. . . . But I'll have all the necessary stuff in a few days. Won't cost but about a bill. That means once I get the information, I'll be ready to leave when it looks right."

Hank nodded. "I'll have it in a week at the most. That'll give you three, four weeks to sit."

"Where'll we meet?"

"Serious?"

"Hank, a guy like you is too good to let get away. . . . Besides, you have the money. . . ."

"What do you want, a kiss or something?"

"I'll give you 'something' outside."

"On the boat?"

"On the boat."

"You sound like a queer."

"You look like an ermine."

"A weasel."

"That was yesterday. Today, an ermine."

"You're a creep."

"That's my word. Let's talk about the boat."

"Let's."

They did.

* * *

Through the night he sat by the window probing the dark, waiting to end waiting, wondering why and what awaited. No fog came, nor did any answers come thundering in with a burst of white light, no kindly sage appeared; no answers anywhere.

During the day he left Leslie exercising and puzzled while he went in search of the devil slayers.

An errant quirk visited him, and next he stood at the door of the priest's office.

"Come in, son," said the priest from behind the desk where he sat writing something.

Kirk, his palms suddenly wet, peered in at him. He wanted to leave, but said, "Hello," and walked diffidently into the office and stared down at the bright red veins webbing the priest's nose. He tried to think of something to say.

"Just wandering around," he finally managed to mumble.

The priest smiled. "You're welcome to wander," he said, and his eyes took on a questioning cast. "I don't believe I've seen you before. Do you attend Mass?"

Kirk shook his head and wiped his hands on his pants.

The priest pulled open a desk drawer, taking from it a rosary of wooden beads and pot-metal links. He held it out to Kirk, saying tentatively, "Perhaps you'd like to start coming. . . ."

Shrugging, he accepted it, wondering what mysteries it would unlock. He glanced down at it lying in his hand, saw the cold, snakelike coils.

"Mmmm . . ." the priest muttered.

Kirk looked at him, sensed his discomfort, and became more uncomfortable.

Then the priest reached inside another drawer—how many did he have? One for every sin?—and pulled forth a fistful of tracts. "Perhaps these will help," he said, and extended them to the convict. "If you wish to come to Mass, please do." He glanced down at the papers before him, then back at Kirk, then back at the papers.

Kirk, tracts in hand, turned to leave.

"Son," called the priest as he reached the door, "are you of the faith?"

Kirk shook his head and the priest's face fell apart.

Outside the office Kirk found a trash can and dropped into it the tracts and rosary, then put his hand in his pocket. It felt cold.

He wandered to the Protestant minister's office and found nobody there, but the door was open, inviting. He stood on the threshold, bouncing on his toes, scanning the little cubicle for something . . . he had no idea what. Behind the desk was a bulletin board with several yellowed newspaper clippings. He walked to the desk and stared blankly at the clipping. It took a moment before he saw what he was looking at: a well-weathered newspaper picture of a man with a vast stomach and reversed collar, smiling benignly, proudly displaying a revolver. The caption beneath the picture read:

Prison Chaplain Joins Hunt For Escaped Convict

Tough prison chaplain, the Reverend David McDivott, packs a Smith and Wesson revolver in the massive manhunt for escaped burglar Joseph Leon, who went over the wall of Alhondiga State Prison last Monday. Says Reverend McDivott: "We try to instill certain traits in the men we handle, but some are nonamenable. Under no circumstances must such men be allowed to run loose among decent, God-fearing citizens."

Kirk thanked the reverend's god for giving him business elsewhere, and went to see the rabbi. The rabbi had a blond-haired, green-eyed clerk.

"You don't look Jewish," said the clerk, his green eyes squinched in suspicion.

And next he went to the Gavel Club, a club wherein a man might develop the self-confidence to stand before people and express himself, to communicate. Ah, communication, the final key. A fine idea, the Gavel Club.

He was met at the door by what might have been the fattest, most lubricious, lardaceous, and sycophantic convict he had ever chanced upon. The fat one invited him, in a tone at once imperious and humble, to "Please, won't you enter, please?"

Kirk did, and listened to a half dozen convict speeches that ranged from puerile to pseudo-intellectual. One, however, was quite interesting: a convict talking of the want-to-be-bureaucrats in blue; the convicts' usual advocacy of mom, apple pie, and law and order; a political awareness so shallow that even Mr. Welch would blush.

At length came time to award the "Best Speaker of the Day" trophy, a weekly event, and Kirk was jostled by the fat one.

298

"He was wonderful, wasn't he?"

"Who?" Kirk wanted to know.

"Why, Inmate Liggins, of course," wheezed the fat one, and looked at Kirk as if he wondered how anybody could be so dense but so nice, too, of course. "The last man to speak—that was Inmate Liggins. Positively brilliant, wasn't he?"

That was the one Kirk had tagged "pseudo." He glanced sideways at the fat one and shrugged noncommittally.

The fat one, not to be put off, leaned close, whispered conspiratorially. "Besides, it's Inmate Liggins' turn to win this week. So when it comes time, be sure to clap for him, won't you? Please?"

"No." Kirk moved his chair away.

The fat one "humphed" and began buzzing in somebody else's ear.

Came time to applaud, the loudness of which decided the best speaker, and Kirk clapped briefly for the convict who had spoken of star-spangled prisoners. He clapped alone.

"Pseudo" won the bronze-plated plastic cup. He stood on the slightly raised stage, bowing and smiling while his picture was taken for the prison newspaper, which was no newspaper at all, but always seemed to contain numerous pictures of happily smiling convicts beside happily smiling guards.

As Kirk was leaving, the fat one, talking to another convict, raised his voice loud enough by anyone in the room interested in what he had to say, and many who were not.

"Well," he said, hitching his ponderous belly without much success, "well, really, we don't want anybody in our club that isn't the highest class of inmate."

Back in his cell he stared out the window, searching for himself in the dark.

"All the information is on this," Hank said, handing Kirk a folded paper. He frowned, looking haggard, even anguished. "Kirk, if I don't see you again . . ."

"Dry up—you're starting to look like a weasel again. Besides, there might be a month left yet. . . ."

Hank tried to grin, almost made it. "Yeah," he mumbled, and turned twice to leave, turning back each time, flapping his mouth.

"You have any idea how ridiculous you look?"

"Yeah," Hank muttered, and turned away again, this time with resolution, and took a giant step. "Damn!" he exclaimed, stopping short, turning around. "I just remembered!" he blurted. "Zeke . . . Zeke wants to see you."

"What for?" He did not want to see Zeke, not at all.

Hank stared down at the floor. "Look," he said finally, and met Kirk's eyes, "go see him. I'll fix you up with a green shirt and a phoney worker's card."

Kirk thought it over. "Why didn't you do that when Leslie was in there?"

Hank grinned, a little abashedly. "You needed to have a long talk with the dead."

Kirk eyed him narrowly, sardonically. "The Great-Wise Weasel . . ."

Still grinning, Hank said, "Just because I look funny doesn't mean my secret self ain't profound," then, frowning, added: "Seriously though, you should talk to Zeke. In fact, call it an order."

"You're the doctor, I guess," Kirk said, uneasy. "But why?"

"Be at the door here—two o'clock sharp." Hank went quickly into the hospital.

Chewing his lip, Kirk stared after him. In his mind was a too-vivid picture of Zeke; the mangled body, the terrible eyes. He decided not to show up.

But at two o'clock he slipped on the green orderly smock and accepted the forged hospital pass from Hank. He was then led to the second floor, to a door. Hank said, "In there," pointing at the door, and walked away.

Kirk stood there for a moment, staring first at Hank's retreating back, then at the door. After two false starts, he pulled open the door and entered.

Inside, he stepped purposefully toward the bed in the corner, toward Zeke. Zeke—was it Zeke?

Kirk felt his feet grow heavy and vomit clog his throat; his head reeled. He reached a hand to the wall and leaned against it, unable to move, staring.

Zeke, lying on the bed, looked toward him, smiling. His hair had grown out long and black, decapitating the eagle across his forehead. His legs . . . legs encased in plaster casts, casts less than three feet long. . . . He might have been a four-legged spider . . . except that his arms were longer than his legs. . . .

300

"Come here, Kirk," Zeke said, and put aside a tattered paperback book he had been reading.

Kirk kept leaning against the wall, unable to leave it, trying to choke down the taste of vomit. Across his mind flickered fragments of isolated events, events he had influenced, events leading to . . . to a four-legged spider. . . . It was no help to close his eyes, for still he could see a Stygian montage of perversion and death and hollow eyes, accusing eyes, all scenes flowing against a background of gummy crimson. And with his eyes open he saw before him the culmination of his contributions . . . what remained of his contributions. . . . For the death in his wake he could rationalize, finally ignore. . . . Dead is out of sight, under the ground, a clean tombstone. . . . But how to ignore this destroyed thing that lay before him, alive . . . ?

"Come here, Kirk," Zeke repeated. "I can't talk to you way over there."

Kirk tried, one step and then another, and finally made it to a chair beside Zeke's bed. He dropped into it, eyes downcast, staring blindly, his head filled with ringing noises, grotesque imagery.

"Kirk," Zeke said quietly, "don't let it get to you. . . . I don't." He paused for a moment, then went on, speaking with painful slowness, as if searching for each word. "I had to see you. You probably already know it, but I'm going to the row for killing Shorty. I guess you have a pretty good idea why I did it . . . why it was him. . . . I'm only just now realizing why. . . ." His voice trailed off for a moment. "You might not want to believe this," he continued, "but they won't down me till I get Knight commuted. After that I'll try to save myself. . . . Not because I'm real scared of dying, but because I feel like I was just born. . . ."

Forcing himself, Kirk looked up, saw the quiet smile, the candid eyes; then he was staring at the floor again, his skull aching, tumultuous.

"You see," Zeke went on, "in a funny sort of way you did more for me than my whore mother and wino father. . . . You gave me life. Sounds weird, don't it? But now, even with these sawed-off legs, I want to learn about this life thing. All the years I've been breathing, I've been blind and scared. . . . Now I'm learning to see, to be unafraid. . . . It hurts . . . it hurts more to see and be unafraid than it does to be blind and scared. . . . It hurts to live.

. . . But I've got an idea that without the pain there's no life. I think that's what it's all about and I don't think that I'd trade the legs I got for the ones I had if it meant I'd always be blind and scared. They'd have found it out it was me that killed Shorty even if I hadn't gone off the tier. But they'd have gassed me after I got done pissing all over myself. I think if it comes to it that I can go good now. . . . I can breathe their gas and know they're as blind and scared as I was, and not hate them for it. Anyway, whatever happens . . . Look."

Kirk did, and saw the pile of books that Zeke pointed to beside his bed.

"Why didn't somebody tell me . . . ?" Zeke said, his voice remote. "I thought I was the only one scared. . . . I made a face to cover my fear . . . and it covered my eyes, too. . . ." He picked up one of the books and opened it at a marker, then read: " 'Which of us has known his brother? Which of us has looked into his father's heart? Which of us has not remained forever prison-pent? Which of us is not forever a stranger and alone?' * " He closed the book, stared at it. "We're all aliens," he went on. "And fear-masks blind us. . . . If somebody'd told me . . . if I'd known . . . maybe I wouldn't have this goddamn bird on my forehead; maybe I wouldn't have spent a thousand years in joint subconsciously trying to get myself killed while being scared to die, scared of everything. . . ."

Kirk, bewildered, numb, looked at Zeke. His vision danced, his throat constricted. Zeke, struggling from a cocoon of ugliness as a crippled-winged freak to be ostracized and ridiculed by the blindness and fear he sought to transcend.

Zeke smiled. "Kirk," he said quietly, "don't hurt for me. I'm a little funny to look at, but the doc says I'll be able to walk—even without knees—after another six or eight operations. He says he'll take this goddamn bird off my head, too. . . . Sure would hate to have the thing in a box with me forever. . . . Anyway, don't let it eat on you, that's not why I wanted to see you. I just wanted to tell you that whatever I am now is more than I was . . . even with being shorter." He grinned, an easy grin. "In a weird kind of way," he said thoughtfully, "you're a little like God. You made the pieces, and Hank and the doc put them back together. So don't be sorry.

* Thomas Wolfe's *Look Homeward, Angel*.

. . . If you want to be anything, be glad . . . glad that the Zeke you scared died of fright and another with sawed-off legs took his place; be glad that the new Zeke is part kike, nigger, and greaser . . . and can't ever forget it. . . ."

Kirk stared at him, looking close, and had the feeling he could see behind Zeke's eyes; and what he saw was what he sought: consciousness, a will to see tomorrow.

"Zeke," he said suddenly, unnerved and even frightened by what he could see, "do you have money for a lawyer?"

"Money?" said Zeke with a quizzical grin. "If that's what it's going to take, my lungs are going to get full of the shit."

Kirk walked to the toilet. And minutes later, returned and dropped the aluminum tube into Zeke's hand.

He popped it open, looked inside. "No," he said, holding it out to Kirk. "I can't take it."

"You can. It's yours. And use it . . . that's an order from God." He hurried to the door and out.

"You went in there a pissy-pants brat," Hank said, eyeing him narrowly. "You went in there 15 years before me. . . . I hope to God you came out as smart as me. . . ."

"Maybe. . . . You gave him the books, didn't you?"

Hank nodded. "And about a hundred thousand windy speeches."

"He heard. . . ."

"Yeah, he heard. . . . I should've listened closer myself."

"Hank . . . I gave him the tube, the money . . . all but enough to keep us eating till we see you. . . ."

"I've got enough—more than enough. I'll give him what we won't need."

Kirk held out his hand. "I don't want to see you any more . . . not in here."

Hank grinned. "Good idea." They shook hands. "On the boat?"

"On the boat."

They parted.

[XLIII]

"Baby, why're you acting so funny lately?"

"Funny?" Kirk asked.

Leslie frowned. "I don't know . . . quiet, I guess."

Kirk smiled. "Just thinking."

"About us?"

"Sometimes."

Leslie was silent for a long moment, then: "Baby, you're growing away from me. . . ."

"I think you have it backwards."

Leslie thought about it. "Kirk," he said softly, "are we finished out there . . . ?"

Kirk spun the ring on Leslie's finger, remained silent.

"Thank you," said Leslie after a long minute. "Thank you . . . but you're allowed to change your mind, Kirk. . . ."

"Sleep now—you need the rest."

"Love me?"

"Let's."

"Okay, but I didn't mean that. Do you love me?"

"Yes."

"Baby . . ."

"Shh. You're my baby now. Into bed."

Leslie slipped under the blankets, smiling. "I like being your baby."

He sat on the bunk, looking out the window, waiting for the fog, occasionally staring down at Leslie's sleeping face. But mostly he thought.

And slowly, cloaked by the surrounding darkness, a light began to shine through, something hazy and nebulous found roots deep within him, began to grow.

Perhaps he would find the answers he sought in the questions he asked; perhaps wisdom, maybe peace, lay on the other side of continual questioning.

And his devils, the dark things lurking within him, would always be there, must be there, for with their death would come a dying of the urge to question, to strive; and, too, it would mean that he must forfeit all chance of fulfillment, must remain forever bound in the vacuum of a collective consciousness. It came to him then that the freedom he had so long, so ineptly pursued lay in constant strife, in tension, in the fight between demon and reason, between cannot and aspiration. So to be more than a reacting thing he must remain divided within himself, for between the poles of duality lay his hold on humanity, on uniqueness, on sameness, on freedom.

And beginning to understand all this, he began to understand his difference; looking back, now with eyes unblurred, he saw the little plastic people, saw, too, where they were taking themselves as they stumbled past with eyes closed to all but the mundane, heading mindlessly toward a glitter-brightened nowhere; seeing them now, he understood that his sickness was a hunger, a grasping for humanness—though with more intensity than direction, but still of a dual nature, not plastic, able to grow, without the will-lessness of the stoic, the cynic.

Slowly, then, the light within glowed brighter, shone on the dark things lurking in the corners; he looked at them without fear now. He saw. The devils within were guilt—not guilt of his yesterdays, not blood guilt; guilt much darker, much heavier; a heritage, something etched into his being by a leather lash, something his father had been lent by other men, by man. How to bear the dark weight of a hundred thousand centuries . . . ? He did not know, but the choice between trying and a Procrustean bed was no choice at all.

He would try, he could do no more.

He was ready.

But March grew old, and still the fog he awaited did not settle over the prison. First would come a heavy ground fog that left the wall lights bright and glaring; then a fog to cover the lights but not the ground. So he waited.

Days passed.

And still he waited, bracing his faltering patience.

More days.

And then it was there, thick, heavy.

"Leslie. Leslie, wake up," he said, and when he wakened, added, "it's here."

Leslie rolled from the bunk and dressed.

Meantime, Kirk ripped open the hand-sewn stitches along the side of his mattress and dumped out tools, the ID papers, the gun, rope, and more. He quickly inflated several plastic bags and fashioned them into dummies.

Finished, he stepped to the window, where Leslie had already removed the fake putty and three panes of glass, letting in the cold, damp night. He held a screw jack between the steel panes and began working it tight with a crescent wrench. Back of him Leslie lay flat on the floor, a mirror held under the door, watching for the guard.

With the jack snug, the steel panes creaked in tortured protest. He forced the wrench tight, tighter. Came a nerve-rending crack, and the first pane snapped loose.

"All right?" he asked over his shoulder.

"Nobody's on the floor."

Kirk worked quickly, deftly, gliding through motions so long mentally rehearsed. Then a second crack, and the second pane was out.

"You ready?"

Without a word Leslie rose and stood beside him, watching, waiting while he dropped a doubled rope secured by a heavy steel hook out the window. A quick caress, a slow smile, and Leslie was out the window, fading into the black below. A moment later the rope jerked.

Kirk threw several soft-wrapped bundles out the window, then slid out himself, and down.

Beside Leslie on the wet grass, he breathed of the redolent night, and smiled to himself. It had been a long time. He pulled one end of the hanging rope until it dropped with a muffled shush to the ground. Leslie began coiling it.

Kirk, meantime, opened one of the packages and pulled out four pieces of hooked steel, each wrapped in heavy cloth, then began binding them together with adhesive tape until he held a grappling hook. He attached the rope to it, separately securing each of the four hooks.

He loaded the gun, pushed it into his waistband.

"Set?" he whispered.

Shivering, Leslie smiled and nodded.

They talked in silence to the end of the block, turned left, and kept on toward the wall. Back of them G block faded, disappeared; before them F block looked large, then they were past it, then past E block. And on they went toward the invisible wall, toward gun tower three, Dunn's tower.

Kirk was calm; Leslie smiled a lot.

And the fog was thick and wet and cold. Ahead and above, a fuzzy luminescence grew. A little farther and the wall was there before them, craggy and forbidding. At the bottom, able to see nothing but a spot of light hanging high and to the left, over the invisible gun tower, they squatted.

Eyes closed, Kirk concentrated on listening. But the night was quiet, no sounds broke its stillness. No sounds. Still he listened.

And then he heard it: footsteps, muffled and far away, nearing; closer and closer, finally overhead. Some scuffling noises, and footsteps again, retreating now. Kirk began counting, counted until the footsteps sounded again. He pulled Leslie close and whispered.

"A little less than two minutes. . . . Don't take your time."

He rose, grappling hook in hand, listening to the footfalls.

They inched closer. Inch by inch, it seemed. Then they were overhead, probably an arm's length from Dunn's gun tower, and they stopped. Stillness. Moments later came a blowing noise—the guard warming his hands or shivering. Then footsteps again; slow, dragging footsteps, fading, fading, gone.

Kirk grinned to himself, and hurled the hook into the overhead murk. There was a muffled sound as it landed on the other side of the wall. He pulled the rope back. The hook caught.

"Go," he whispered, but Leslie was already going. He watched his feet kick into the dark, and counted to ten, but too fast, so he counted five higher, faster. The rope went still. He gripped it, and climbed.

Near the top a heavy, gray shadow formed into the shape of a gun tower. The hook hung from the top railing on the wall, four feet below the tower windows, ten feet away. It was closer to the tower than he had meant, but as long as Dunn was Big Stupe, far enough.

Once atop the wall, he saw Leslie lying prone, facing the tower. Kirk slipped under the rail, lay flat on the walkway, and pulled up the rope. Then, wrapping the line once around the railing, he dropped both ends off the side, the outside. He squeezed Leslie's ankle—they were ready.

Leslie scooted back to the rope, wrinkled his nose, and dropped off the edge.

Kirk waited for a moment. There was plenty of time. He looked back toward the prison blocks, backwards at the tortured and the torturing, the dying and the dead; faces passed in imagery, some mocking, some hating, most fearing, but all two-dimensional, empty of threat, of promise, of tomorrows. He tried to penetrate the gloom blanketing the prison but could not. For there was nothing but gray, nothing there but gray. Nothing.

With a curious feeling of sadness he turned back to the rope. It was slack now, Leslie was down, outside. He slid his legs over the side, felt the granite tear at his pants. As he started to slide down, he glanced to the side at the reflectionless black windows of the tower and saw Dunn. His face pressed to the window, the guard gawked in vacuous surprise.

"*Run!*" Kirk yelled, shattering the night's hush, and dropped down the rope.

The night exploded. A machine gun chattered. A carbine barked, then another. To the right, down the perimeter road, a motor roared to life; headlights flashed on, caught Leslie crouched, dazzled Kirk.

"*Run! you damn fool! Stay along the wall!*" Kirk yelled, and shoved Leslie aside, out of the headlight beams, against the wall. With screeching tires the car leaped forward, toward them. Kirk snatched at the gun, pointed, fired.

Came a poof and a headlight shattered, blinked out. He bounced off a fender and ran, Leslie before him, the wall beside them protection from the machine gun.

Suddenly the machine gun quieted. Then the mercury-vapor searchlight atop the gun-tower roof touched them with its ghostly finger. Carbines cracked, again and again.

Kirk crashed to the ground, wondered why, tried to get up. A leg was numb.

More shots, and Leslie stopped abruptly, spun around. "Kirk!" he screamed, and came running back.

Kirk pushed to his knees, saw a bullet plow the muddy earth six inches ahead. "Run! I'm all right!"

Leslie froze, looked from Kirk to the searchlight, back to Kirk. Gunfire hammered at the night.

Then Kirk was up, feeling no pain, dashing with a limp toward Leslie. "Run! For God's sake, you dumb fag, run!"

Leslie looked at him for another long moment, then turned and raced toward darkness. Suddenly, as if snatched from behind, he dove through the air, sprawled, somersaulted, came finally to his hands and knees. No farther.

Kirk cursed, ran lopsidedly toward him. His leg was beginning to

308

burn. A bullet ticked his side. He cursed some more, kept running.

And coming to Leslie, he swooped an arm under his, wrenching him to his feet. Together they ran beyond range of the light, and on into the night. They ran.

Back of them a horn ripped through the dark, a siren shrieked, whistles screamed. A machine gun joined in, yammering its dirge. Dunn was on the job, filling the night with noise . . . steadily . . . steadily. . . .

[XLIV]

"Leave me, baby. . . . I can't go any further. . . ."

"Shut up, keep going."

Leslie sagged. "Baby . . ."

"Listen, in just a little while it'll be light. . . . By now the whole goddamn area is surrounded. . . . If we stop and the fog lifts, we're finished. . . ." But he stopped anyway and sat Leslie down, for it was obvious he could not go much farther. Kirk pulled open his shirt and dropped a plastic-wrapped bundle to the ground, then began tearing his T-shirt into strips.

Leslie lay back on the weedy earth, his face pain-twisted. Reaching a couple of fingers behind his lower lip, he fished out a tape-covered razor blade half, and handed it to Kirk.

Taking it, Kirk peeled off the tape, then knelt beside Leslie's bloody leg and cut away his pants. Low on the shin, almost to the ankle, was the shredded exit hole of a .30-caliber bullet. When the blood was wiped away, along with gritty fragments of bone, the flesh around the hole looked faintly blue. He stared at the wound, sickened, weighted with defeat.

"Baby . . . how bad . . . ?" Leslie asked, tears squeezing from tight-shut eyes.

"Not too," Kirk lied, and quickly bound the wound with strips of T-shirt. The entry hole, high on the calf, bled little so he left it alone. He then wrapped his own leg wound on the outside of his pants. He had been hit high in the thigh, the bullet apparently missing anything too important in its straight-through path. Unlike Leslie, whose wound said he had been shot by a guard on the wall, he had obviously been shot by somebody on the ground—whoever had been in the waiting car. Carol, he was sure; too bad he had only a single-shot gun. . . . A second flesh wound on his side showed the gray of his hipbone. He was stiff and getting stiffer, but could go on. Leslie could not. He forced himself to think calmly.

After several minutes he ripped open the plastic-wrapped bundle. "Change of plans," he said, half to himself, and spread a map on the ground. He studied it. A red X marked their rendezvous point with Hank . . . a rendezvous two weeks away. . . . It had been planned that they stay afoot for several days, avoid towns and people . . . but they now needed a car, a doctor. . . .

"Leslie," he said, his mind made up, "we're going to the highway."

Leslie opened his eyes and pulled himself to a seated position, wincing. "Don't be a damn fool. That's eight or ten miles away, in a different direction—back toward the joint. And even if I got that far, how do I get across the river?"

Kirk stood and spent a moment loosening his stiffening leg. He then reached down to pull Leslie up, onto his back.

"No," said Leslie, lying flat on the ground. "You're being stupid." His voice was flat and harsh; his eyes, too. "It turned sour, that's all. Now get the hell out of here."

Kirk knelt, grabbed a fistful of his hair and yanked him to a seated position. "If you argue any more, you won't be at all pretty," he said quietly, in deadly earnest.

"Please?" Leslie's face became pleading, full of helplessness and hopelessness and anguish. "Please, baby . . . don't be a dummy. Send me a postcard. . . . I'll come see you when I can. . . ."

"Hang on." Kirk lifted him to his back, then turned south and began plodding over the weed-covered, muddy earth, passing scrubby manzanita, now a stunted pine, now a twisted oak.

He estimated that they were five miles west and a little north of the prison. The river they must cross to get to the highway was about four miles south. There would be a perimeter of emergency guard posts strung around the area in a radius of eight to ten miles from the prison. Guards would be posted on any nearby bridges. There would be, were now, squads of guards out searching, probably having already found their trail. But until the fog lifted they were relatively safe, for it was a certainty they would all know by now that he had a gun. If he could make it to the river . . . trees, undergrowth. . . .

If not . . . ?

He stopped for a moment to check the gun, the load, the mechanism, then plodded on.

It was light, the sun two hours high behind the covering fog, when he topped a slight rise. Twenty yards farther, the ground sloping, and he was in the open, below the fog. A half mile distant he saw trees, green against the gray. The brush around, thicker now, sprouted with the tender green of early spring, occasionally full and lush. It was quiet except for a light ground breeze that rustled through the grasses, and here a lark's raucous song, there a small creature skittering away. He went on, one leg leaden, the other rubbery.

Halfway to the trees, just as he dared to hope, a shot cracked the morning quiet, then another.

Twin echoes thundered.

Kirk spun around, staggered, fell to a knee.

Four hundred yards behind were three . . . four . . . five guards, carrying carbines, running. One stopped, lifted his weapon, fired. The bullet winged past, or maybe into the ground.

Kirk didn't ponder it; he pushed to his feet and ran, heavily, clumsily, much too slowly. His legs turned to dead things, dead things that hurt, yet did not. He staggered, tumbled. They sprawled.

Rolling quickly to his feet, he pulled Leslie up, then over behind a clump of manzanita. "Keep on toward the river," he said, breathing hard. "Stay low, behind cover."

Face twisted with pain and indecision, Leslie looked at him, then toward the trees, then back at the running guards. "Baby—"

"*Go!*" Kirk spat, and pushed him away. Leslie turned toward the river; three hops on his good leg, a pause, three hops, he went toward the river.

Kirk pulled the gun from his waistband and unscrewed the disk holding in the mesh washers that filled the silencer tube. The washers went into his pocket.

Poking his head above the brush he watched the guards come closer. Three hundred and 50 yards, 325. He pointed the gun toward the sky and squeezed the trigger. It sounded like a petulant cap pistol. He shook out the shell, inserted another, fired again.

Three hundred yards out of range the guards abruptly stopped, crouched, and, fanning out, disappeared behind the brush.

Kirk took time to grin, then ran, bent low to the ground. Catching up with Leslie, he took his arm around his neck, put an arm around his waist, and kept running, half dragging, half carrying him. He cursed with every gulp of air, every heartbeat, but kept running, Leslie growing heavier and heavier and heavier.

They made it to the trees.

Kirk lay Leslie on the ground and crashed through the brush, looking, searching.

He found a spot where the dirt was soft under some heavy brush and dragged Leslie to it.

"Baby . . ."

"Dig!" he hissed, then went searching again, this time for loose brush. He looked toward the river. It was wide and shallow, rushing from mountain snows to the sea, freezing, white-capped water.

And the guards came on, slowly, warily, crouched. But on and on. Four hundred yards. Three hundred. Closer.

He found Leslie clawing at the damp and sticky earth. He dropped the gathered bundle of loose brush and joined in the digging.

Short minutes later he said, "Get in."

"What . . . what about you . . . ?"

He grinned, and ran a muddy finger down Leslie's nose. He scratched at the dried blood under his lip, the lip he had chewed raw. "Today," he said, "is my day to act like a mother quail."

"Baby . . ." Leslie chewed on his lip some more, made it bleed more. His eyes were haggard, pinched with pain and grief.

"It's the only way, Leslie."

His mouth trembling into a smile, eyes filling with tears, Leslie nodded. "Say it again, baby. . . . Say my name like that again."

"Leslie . . . Leslie . . . Leslie. . . ." They held one another for a brief moment. "In," said Kirk, almost whispering, then pushed away and opened the plastic bag. He dumped several bars of chocolate into the pit, then directed Leslie to lay flat in it, his head against the roots of the bushy shrubbery. He buried him, leaving only a small area to breathe through. Working fast, he covered the fresh turned dirt with rocks and twigs and leaves.

Finished, he stood back and studied it. A wild creature would find it, nothing else. "Come out tonight if you can't stand it, but don't stray. I'll be back in three days . . . less if I can make it." He started to turn toward the river, and stopped. "Leslie, it's just starting. . . . It'll be good. . . . I love you. . . ."

Came a muffled sob. "Kirk . . . thank you . . . thank you. Go now; please go."

He did, backwards, using a leafy branch to erase his tracks. And once at the water's edge, he stepped in and sprinted and splashed downriver. But not far. For as he rounded a bend he saw a bridge less than a quarter of a mile ahead. And on the bridge a splash of red and khaki moved—a guard. He turned back upriver, still in the water, still running. He passed Leslie's position, kept on for another hundred yards.

He then stopped and walked backwards out of the water, leaving tracks to the undergrowth. He peered through the brush and finally spotted two guards, then a third and fourth, approaching Leslie's hideaway. He fired the gun.

A moment later the guards crouched lower and turned, then scattered for cover. They were about 110 yards distant.

He fired another bullet and ran to the river, leaving another set of tracks.

Then he was in the water, splashing. It was cold, an unbelievable cold; the current fast and strong; the bottom rocky and treacherous. The frigid water numbed him, his knees, his thighs, higher, finally to his chest. He faced upcurrent, fought forward and sideways, went sideways and backwards. Slowly, very slowly the water became shallower; the far bank, overhung with heavy leafy brush, neared; 25 yards, then 23, 20.

Suddenly, from the bank he fled, something lashed out, slammed him sideways. He went under. From far away he heard a shot, the shot's echo; then his chest was seized by icy fingers. The current swept him backwards. He saw the sky through rippling water, then surfaced, gulping air. Something tugged at the plastic bag tucked down the front of his pants; then came the sound of another shot. He went under again, rolled over, dove toward the bottom. An arm did not work. He gave himself up to the current. His ears pinged and his heart hammered, but he stayed under. Rocks glided by. Pain in his chest, growing worse. He stayed under. The current carried him fast, yet slow, so slow. Hollow explosions behind, the sound of water-muffled shots, far away, getting farther.

313

He had to breathe. Had to. He rolled over, kicked toward the surface. His face broke through, another gulp of air, under again. He began kicking for the far bank. He surfaced twice to breathe as the water became shallow, shallower. And then his stomach was scraping the rocky bottom, his back breaking the surface. He found his feet and bounding up, splashed a yard, two, and dove into the undergrowth. He lay there, floundered, gasping, his body a riot of aches. He found the bullet wound in his shoulder: it had entered high in the left shoulder cap; and after feeling around for a moment he found the exit hole, shredded, bleeding steadily, in his lower right chest. The slug had traveled the width of his frame. Poking and probing, he could feel nothing broken, and the hot line under his chest muscles probably meant that the slug had not torn into his rib cage. He put it out of his mind.

He rose to his knees and turned to peer through the brush, across the river. He had been swept about 180 yards downriver. Some 90 yards upriver, near Leslie's position, still coming, were three guards, walking slowly, scanning the river, carbines poised. Kirk grinned. Two of the guards he recognized: Dunn, sniggering nervously, the sound carrying across the river; the other was Sgt. Carol, who was also obviously nervous—but not sniggering—perhaps he was thinking of ten little bullets, wondering whose name might be on them . . . or perhaps he was only wondering why it was so difficult to hit a moving target during a foggy night after waiting for that target all those many nights. . . .

But Kirk didn't care, for they were clear. Not entirely, but with a little assistance from fate, or even its neutrality, their chances were good. He cupped his face in his hands and knelt there with a sort of numb joy. They were clear. . . . They'd made it. . . .

A sudden gunshot thundered across the river, then another. A guard was firing toward the water, aiming at a leafless tree limb that bobbed and spun in the current. A second guard joined in, blasting away at the dancing thing. The third guard entered the fun. And moments later the other two crashed out of the undergrowth. Bullets from five rifles banged into the limb, knocking it this way and that, and back again.

Kirk grinned at the sight of them, at the sound of their nervous laughter drifting across the river, at the yammer of their weapons, which seemed a mournful lament that they must spit their death

314

into something already dead. Or maybe not, for the limb seemed to mock them, slowly now to take on ounces of lead, now dancing on to spin in an eddy, then bobbing and weaving a little farther, taking on more lead, pirouetting.

He was chuckling when it happened, when the day darkened and the earth split asunder.

Back of the guards, the bushes parted. Leslie hopped through, bounded onto Carol's back, clawing at his throat. The sergeant went to his knees, Leslie on top, screaming.

Dunn, carbine poised toward the river, froze, then dropped his gun and raised his hands.

The others rushed to Carol's aid.

And in seconds Leslie was spread-eagled; seconds more and he was handcuffed and shackled.

Kirk stared, dazed, bewildered, his head filled with a hollow roar. "You stupid fag," he whispered. "I'm here. . . . I'm all right. . . . Oh, God . . . it didn't happen. . . ."

[XLV]

The day was getting old and colder. He had lost a lot of blood. His body would not work as it should. He could barely lift his feet. But he went on, now two shuffling paces forward, now on his face. He had to go on; he had to rest. He went on. Behind him there was nothing. Nothing. He told himself that over and over; but viscous strands of warm memory kept urging him to stop, turn back. Fighting his body and memory's chains, he went on.

He looked ahead, staggered ahead. In two weeks he must meet Hank. He must. But now he must rest . . . had to. . . . Check the map . . . find his position. . . . Yes, check the map, he could rest . . . only for a moment.

He staggered to a bush and fell and crawled under it. He pulled the map, now soggy, from the bullet-holed plastic bag, and searched it for the red mark. It was covered with red marks . . . dancing spots . . . everything was covered with dancing red spots. . . . His shaking fingers tore apart the water-softened map. He was cold . . . too cold. Forcing himself to sit up, he began pulling off his clothes. With only one usable hand, it took a long time, but then it was done, and he struggled into the civilian clothes—stolen from the prison dry cleaners—which had been in the plastic bag. They were damp, but drier than what he had been wearing. He groped inside the bag again and found the identification papers; they were moist and wrinkled, but mostly still usable—usable if he could ever move again.

The hole in his side was still bleeding; he used the discarded shirt to bind the wound. If he had matches, dry ones, he could burn the hole closed, even wait until dark and build a small body-thawing fire. If . . .

He looked down at the plastic bag, at the other clothes still inside it . . . clothes which would never again be worn . . . black slacks . . . fuzzy green sweater . . . clothes meant for Leslie . . . Leslie. . . .

He was about to rise, to go on, when there came the sound of trampled brush. Then again, closer.

He looked through his cover of greenery, scanning. He had come too far. He would not go back. He hefted the gun, put in a shell. Then slowly, quietly, he fished the mesh washers from his discarded pants and dropped them one by one down the muzzle of the silencer. He was weak, his vision danced, but he could aim the gun, pull the trigger. And he would, for there was no going back. . . .

But Leslie . . . Leslie . . .

No, not even for Leslie . . . not for yesterday. . . . He would remember. . . . He could never forget . . . not the stirrings of love, nor the tortured hate and death from which it sprang. . . . But he would not go back. He breathed slowly, calmly, his mind made up. He cocked the gun.

The brush crackled. Heavy footfalls, no attempt at stealth. Closer. Directly toward him. Closer. A splash of red moving through the bushes . . . the guard on the bridge. . . . How had he forgotten him? He had obviously been seen leaving the water. . . .

Twenty yards away, still coming. A bit of flesh. A little more. Then a head, a guard's head. A guard clad in a scarlet parka. A guard with a slung carbine. A guard named Yancy. . . .

Kirk clamped his teeth in the wrist of his numbed arm and sighted the gun with the other. His vision danced.

He must do it . . . must. . . . He was not going back. He steadied his trembling fingers, kept the gun pointed at Yancy, at the center of his face. It was cocked.

316

He was not going back.
Leslie . . . Leslie . . .
No, no going back to yesterday . . .
Leslie . . .

EPILOGUE

An insect chirruped and was answered by another. Something skittered over the ground, hurrying home. A soft wind rustled the grasses and hummed through nearby trees. In the distance a frog croaked, and another bellowed back.

He stopped for a moment to look up at the moonless sky, at the many stars winking and blinking there. The night was chill, but he was warm. He smiled, and walked on.

Ahead, headlights shone, silhouetting some men standing around. When he was near, he found that they were staring down at the ground, at something lying there. Stepping between them, he looked down, too, then knelt. And long moments later he turned to stare up at the others.

"How?" he asked, shivering now. "In God's name, how?"

The men shuffled their feet, looked away. One finally spoke.

"We were lifting him into the jeep. . . . He came up with a razor blade. . . . I don't know where it came from. . . . He just had it. . . . I don't know. . . ." He turned away, head down. "I've never seen so much blood. . . . Why his throat . . . ? Why . . . ?" He trembled. "Dear God . . . what've I done . . . ?"

One of the others patted his shoulder. "It ain't your fault, Sergeant . . ." He turned to look at the group, then at the newcomer. "He got the other one, too . . . crossing the river. . . . Got him right through the head. . . . Seen it myself. . . . You'll see, he'll wash up somewheres. . . ."

"That's enough, Dunn."

"But it's true! You did, Sarge! I seen it. And along with that hunch of yours, you'll make lieutenant, Sarge. . . ."

"*Shut up, Dunn!*"

"But . . . sir . . ." He looked around at the others. "He done it all himself . . . almost single-handed. . . . He's a good man, the Sarge."

"Yes," whispered the man who knelt beside the body. "Yes, he's a good man." He stood up. "Let's get him into the jeep. It's cold here . . . cold . . ."

"Don't know why you're looking like that," Dunn told him. "They was just a couple queers. . . . Look at that ring . . . a goddamn wedding ring on his finger. . . . Musta smashed it on with a rock . . . won't come off. . . ."

"Yes . . . a couple of queers . . . real queer. . . ." He shivered again, unable to stop.

Shouldering Dunn aside, the sergeant took hold of the other man's arm. "Come on, Yancy, you're freezing. Let's get you a jacket. . . . There's a couple extra in the jeep. . . ."

Yancy shook off the sergeant's grip. "Thanks . . . thanks, Sarge, you're a good man. . . ."

Dunn nodded wisely, then patted his pockets. "Hey, anybody got a cigaret? Musta left mine somewheres."